BOOKS BY JEFFREY POSTON

ACTION/ADVENTURE THRILLERS

American Terrorist: Where is the Girl?
Contagion: American Terrorist 2
Escalate! American Terrorist 3
American Terrorist Trilogy

The Joshua Experiment (Call Sign: Raven Book 1)
The End of Everything (Call Sign: Raven Book 2)
The Queen (Call Sign: Raven Book 3)

JASON PEARES HISTORICAL WESTERNS

Courage (Book 1)
Legacy of an Outlaw (Book 2)
Warriors (Book 3)
Manhunter (Book 4)

JEFFREY POSTON

WHERE IS THE GIRL?

AMERICAN TERRORIST

"Whoever fights monsters should see to it that in the process he does not become a monster."
–Friedrich Nietzsche

CHAPTER 1

1204 MST, TUESDAY

ALBUQUERQUE, NM

CARL JOHNSON SMILED AT HIS interviewer because she didn't know yet that she was a hostage.

Anita Chapman said, "Mr. Johnson, can you share with our audience how you became the one whom the FBI is calling the American Terrorist?"

Not *an* American terrorist.

The American Terrorist.

When he hinted to the reporter in a phone call that he was ready to discuss his side of his violent—and now highly publicized—conflict with the US government, she jumped at the opportunity to make history. Very few reporters actually got face time with a terrorist of his magnitude while they were actually at war.

"Ms. Chapman, the world doesn't care about how I became who I am. What the world really wants to know is what I intend to do next, and I'm going to answer that question in a moment."

When Chapman and her crew entered the abandoned downtown jewelry store, Carl required that the two canvas director's chairs they brought in be positioned facing each other. He was very precise about them being ten feet apart, with the cameras stationed behind and to the side of their shoulders. The reporter was still smarting from losing that small battle for control over the interview setting. Normally, Anita

Chapman wasn't a woman to be trifled with. If one wanted access to her global audience of hundreds of millions, one had to follow her rules.

It wasn't international exposure that Carl Johnson wanted, though. He was concerned only with an audience of one. He knew her father would be watching.

Anita Chapman was widely renowned as the most relevant news reporter of the current times, but Carl knew she wanted the interview as much as he did. His research told him she already had all the top credentials. She'd won multiple George Polk Awards for television reporting and George Foster Peabody Awards. She'd been granted an International Emmy, as well as multiple honorary doctorates from numerous journalism schools. She'd won the Walter Cronkite Award for Excellence and was on Forbes Magazine's list of the top one hundred most powerful women in the world.

Her interview with Carl Johnson would cement her reputation as not only the most relevant TV news reporter *now* but *in all of history*. She'd be bigger than Anderson Cooper. Bigger than Barbara Walters. Bigger than even Oprah or Walter Cronkite.

The empty jewelry store was merely a large room of maybe twenty feet wide by forty feet long. Situated one block south of Central Avenue in Downtown Albuquerque, the store was a victim of the recent recession and a testimony of unsuccessful attempts to revitalize the downtown area.

All the shelves, decor, counters, and display cases had been removed long ago. The floor covering was gone also, though Carl suspected from the faded coloring under his feet that the last flooring design might have been an Art-Deco-stained concrete. In fact, the only furnishings in the room were what Chapman's television crew had brought in—two lightweight folding chairs facing each other, two cameras on sturdy tripods, six portable diffuse lights bracketing Carl and Chapman, portable curtain racks with beige fabric that served as an attractive but featureless backdrop behind the chairs, and the computer and cabling equipment to remotely operate the cameras and broadcast the interview.

Chapman and Carl each wore a virtually invisible wireless microphone clipped to their jackets, and they were each illuminated by three lights. One light faced each of them from their front left, just out of view of the camera. This was for primary illumination, according to the guy who set up all the equipment. Another was the fill light, which lit up the backdrop and filled in the shadows caused by the primary light.

On Chapman, the third light was mounted in front of her and high above. The equipment guy called that one the hair light and said it was intended to add depth and prevent someone from appearing flat or two-dimensional. Since Carl was bald, the hair light for him was mounted in front of him near floor level to prevent a shiny reflection off his head.

Chapman wore a skirt and blazer, and she kept her legs crossed since they were facing each other. In fact, Carl had planned the positions of the chairs for precisely that purpose.

"So first things first," Carl said.

A faint glimmer of irritation flickered briefly across Chapman's face, and she opened her mouth as if to regain control of the interview.

Carl held up his hand and shook his head. "There is really only one rule for this interview," he said, pulling a small remote control from the left pocket of his windbreaker.

He pointed the device at two thin-panel TVs mounted to the wall at his right and out of view of the cameras. Those were the only two items in the room that did not belong to the camera crew. He pressed the PWR button, and one of the panels flicked on after a brief warm-up. On the screen was the media feed that the entire world was watching. It showed a split-screen view of the interview. On the left half of the screen was the near-frontal view of Anita Chapman from the camera behind Carl's left shoulder, and on the right half of the screen was the view of Carl from the camera behind Chapman's right shoulder.

Carl slid the remote button to AUX 1, pressed the ON button again, and the other TV came on. On that screen was a man, a teen boy, two young children, and a baby. All except the baby were bound and gagged. The baby was asleep on the father's lap.

Anita Chapman gasped.

Carl said, "So the rule is this—and I truly hope your producers are paying attention—if this live feed is interrupted for any reason whatso-ever, then my people will kill your family."

He gave Chapman a few seconds to digest his message. At his hand signal, the cameraman commanded his remote-controlled computer to pan the camera parked behind Carl. The view of Anita Chapman left the split-screen and was replaced by the TV that showed the bound family. He signaled the cameraman to pan the camera back to Chapman.

The entire world would now be sitting on the edge of their seats, glued to their televisions or internet feeds, waiting to see if or when he would kill again. He'd given the world an opening hook, and now, millions of viewers were waiting to see and hear the story of intrigue that he was about to tell.

He knew the police and local FBI SWAT teams would be mobilizing outside for a hostage rescue attempt as soon as they tracked her cell phone. That's why he had not confiscated her cell. The HRT—Hostage Rescue Team—would hold as long as the threat against Chapman's family was viable, but they'd make their move as soon as they were certain that he would kill Chapman.

It was part of his plan. Carl wanted her father to feel the effects of that particular terror event more than anyone else.

"So, let's continue with the interview. While you take a few moments to gather your faculties, I'll answer your previous question. You see, it was actually the US government that made me who I am. Of course, I understand that tomorrow, everyone from the president down to local authorities will deny this and will put their spin machines in motion. Tomorrow, though, the world will already know at least my version of the truth.

"As little as a month ago, I was just a regular guy—an ordinary, tax-paying citizen. Then, however unintentionally, the US government forged me into this terrorist that you see before you."

"Why are you doing this?" Anita finally found her voice, but her question barely came out as a trembling whisper. "What do you want from me?"

Carl paused before answering. He inhaled the faint scent of her expensive European perfume. It had a pleasant aroma and maybe included a musky wood scent like the rare sandalwood from Africa. Or was that wood grown in India? Whatever.

"I don't want anything from *you*, Ms. Chapman. I want something from your father. He took someone from me, so I'm going to do the same to him." Carl glared into the camera because he knew the man was watching. "And the *whole world* is going to see it happen."

CHAPTER 2

1302 EST, FRIDAY — ONE MONTH AGO
ARLINGTON HEIGHTS, VA — UNDISCLOSED OPERATIONS HOUSE

ALMOST BEFORE THE DRIVER STOPPED the car, Aaron McGrath exited the rear seat. He flung the door closed without acknowledging the driver and made the front door of the operations house his immediate destination. He'd run ops out of dozens of such houses across the country, so he already knew what he'd find inside. There would be three or four bedrooms upstairs, along with a couple of bathrooms, and the brain center of the current terror event operation would occupy the downstairs living and dining rooms.

By habit from over four decades of covert intelligence work, McGrath studied his surroundings as he followed the walkway from the street to the front door, careful not to appear too curious. He saw no threats on the residential cul-de-sac. Still, his heart raced as he approached the front door. This particular terror event was no ordinary kidnapping.

McGrath reached into his front right pants pocket and pulled out his Department of Defense identification card. He never carried a wallet, so he didn't have to waste time fumbling to find the card. He only carried two other cards in his pocket—his driver's license and a debit card, but never any cash—so the maneuver was fast.

He waved the DOD card in front of a scanner mounted on the wall beside the door, and the device scanned the embedded chip. Instantly, he heard a brief buzz as the lock disengaged. He entered and faced a serious-looking uniformed guard with a Micro-Uzi pointed at his mid-section. The guard was a big Black man, maybe six-foot-five and 250 pounds, and his biceps stretched the fabric of his shirt tight. Sticking to procedure, McGrath let the door close behind him and turned to another wall-mounted scanner. He pressed his right palm on the fingerprint reader, looked into a retinal scanner, and uttered his personal ten-digit security code for voice recognition.

The scanner beeped, and a green LED flashed once.

"Thank you, Director McGrath," the security guard said.

McGrath nodded and hurried up the hall. He turned left into the living room and froze in the doorway. On the wall monitors in front of him, he saw the destruction that remained of the kidnap site as well as photos of the kidnapper and the girl who was taken.

"Sitrep," he said loudly.

Agent Nancy Palmer, his deputy for this terror event, turned to face him. She stood immediately behind the four analysts who sat at computer workstations in front of the wall monitors. She was orchestrating the analysts' data searches and coordinating the activities of other federal agencies—DHS, FBI, CIA—on her encrypted cell.

Palmer tapped an analyst on the shoulder. "Put up the video on the left monitor."

Almost instantly, McGrath saw the back of the limo from the dash-cam of the following police cruiser. A flash of light streaked into view from the right, and the front end of the limo smashed into the pavement with a huge explosion. The back end lifted off the road a few feet, then crashed back down.

Another missile streaked into view, and the lead escort cruiser lifted skyward on a pillar of fire. It flipped end-over-end before crashing down and exploding. Then suddenly, the camera view twisted and spun crazily as a third unseen missile blasted the trailing police cruiser into the air. The camera came to rest upside down facing the halted limo.

As Agent Palmer stepped over beside him, he said, "They used a low-yield RPG just powerful enough to stop the armored car."

She nodded at the monitor.

"They clearly wanted the passenger cabin undamaged, but there's no way the officers in the escorts could have survived."

A large, black SUV drove into view and pulled alongside the limo. It stopped slightly across the adjacent lane, and two upside-down figures in black tactical gear got out. One man carried a black circular device. It was about the diameter of a dinner plate and maybe six inches thick. He held it against the limo's rear passenger window for a few seconds.

Agent Palmer said, "I'm guessing it's a high-speed diamond-tipped drill."

McGrath nodded and watched as the second man attached something to the center of the black plate, then both men stepped away from the limo a moment later, pulling the black plate with them. Smoke issued from the small hole in the window.

"They gassed them."

As soon as he uttered those words, the door on the opposite side of the limo opened, and a man and woman in black suits stumbled out with their handguns up. Gagging and coughing, they pulled a teenager out with them. The two tactical aggressors made quick work of the suits, shooting both in the head. Then they dragged the girl over to the SUV. A man inside shoved the door open, and for a brief moment, he faced the dashcam.

The video froze, and the man's face filled half the center monitor. His vital information filled the other half.

"Alfonso Reyes," McGrath said as he scanned the info. "How does a mid-level Mexican drug lord pull off this kind of snatch-and-grab in the middle of DC?"

He glanced at the third monitor. It showed a high school photo of the smiling face of the sixteen-year-old girl who had been kidnapped.

She was Melissa Mallory, America's darling daughter. He had to get her back.

Agent Palmer seemed to read his mind. "You're too close to this, Aaron. Let me run this op."

"I take orders from one person, and that's the president. You also take orders from one person, and that's me." He paused. "Am I clear?"

The young agent hesitated for a moment. She was a slender woman with a lithe, muscular physique. Her narrow face was framed by short blonde hair. She wore a hint of a sneer, like she had expected him to react that way, and she gazed at him through sky blue eyes. "Of course."

Palmer stepped back over to the analysts, but McGrath could tell from her body language that she wasn't satisfied with his response. She was a tactical genius, though no longer a field agent. She was hard to read, but he got the feeling she considered him a dinosaur. He was old-school, and she represented the new, modern, elite agent. She wasn't shy about expressing her opinions during ops.

The problem was that she was extremely good at covert work, and she was rarely wrong. Still, this wasn't the first time he'd bumped heads with her, and he knew it wouldn't be the last. But there was no one he'd rather have as his second, especially on an op as important as this one. Unfortunately, that meant he had to tolerate her confrontations.

McGrath was very aware of how Palmer viewed him. He was sixty-three years old but looked perhaps a decade younger. At six-foot-one, he was slender and fit, with salt-and-pepper hair that made him appear both wise and serious at the same time. He wore a neatly trimmed mustache and beard, which accentuated the hard features of his thin, angular face. With his piercing steel-gray eyes, he looked like a man who had "been there and done that."

He wore fashionable, titanium, wire-framed, bifocal glasses because, no matter how fit he looked, he could no longer clearly see the data on the wall monitors or read an electronic pad in his hands without glasses, and there was no way he was going to let a doctor cut into his eyes with any kind of correctional laser beams.

Though the president had picked him to set up and run the domestic counterterror agency because of his vast experience, he knew he was getting long in the tooth. Palmer could see it too. While he wasn't ready to retire just yet, he had recently begun to consider life after government service.

Still, the Terror Event Response agency—or TER—had a perfect performance record under his command during its brief one-year existence. Over a dozen domestic terror plots had been foiled by the highly mobile task force. If he was going to transition out, he wanted to go out at his peak, just like a pro athlete.

Administratively, McGrath reported directly to the president of the United States. Functionally, when a terror event was in play, McGrath basically answered to no one until the event was satisfactorily terminated.

A triumphant shout brought him out of his reverie. "I got a hit!"

He didn't know the analyst's name. He was a chubby, Black kid with a big 1970s Afro and a round, nonathletic body. As McGrath stepped over to the analyst's station, the young man's thick fingers flew over his keyboard.

The air in the room was stale with the scent of stress and belches, and the room was hot and stuffy from the cooling fans of multiple desktop computers, monitors, and data equipment. It was the middle of winter, so the air conditioning for the house wouldn't be turned on because the rest of the house would be uncomfortably cold for off-duty personnel. That was the only drawback of using civilian houses as op-centers. Since the operations house had just been activated that morning, the portable room air conditioner needed to counter the heat produced by the electronics was still en route.

Aaron McGrath looked at the center wall monitor. It was the only monitor on which the picture had just changed. Now he stood looking at a flashing blip on a street map of…

What the hell?

"Albuquerque?" he asked.

The analyst took a swig of his Red Bull and set the can dangerously close to his keyboard. McGrath waited patiently for the young man to continue. What was it about computer geeks and Red Bull, anyway?

"Is that a mistake?" McGrath said, pointing at the monitor.

"No, sir. The target is in Albuquerque, New Mexico. Our facial recognition algorithm just picked him up on a traffic cam. I've notified the local field office of the FBI."

McGrath glanced at a wall monitor again. "How the hell did our guy get from DC to Albuquerque in under four hours?"

Agent Palmer was standing behind the two far analysts. "Private plane?" she asked.

The big-Afro analyst shook his head. "He'd have had to sneak out from a private airfield since all the local transport hubs around DC were locked down tight within five minutes of the snatch—Ronald Reagan, all the regional airports, air force bases, as well as train stations, bus terminals, even rental car outlets. Everything was locked down."

"Unless our target anticipated our response and brought in his own support crew—logistics, transportation, fuel, supplies—so he could maintain operational security."

Palmer put two other analysts on the task of researching logistics to find a financial connection to the cartel.

McGrath turned to the big-Afro kid again. "What's your name, analyst?"

"I'm Jimmy, sir." He swiveled in his seat and held his hand up for a fist bump.

McGrath ignored the gesture. "What kind of plane would Reyes need to get to Albuquerque in under four hours, and what airports can accommodate that aircraft?"

"Well, sir, it would have to be something like a Citation X or a Gulfstream 650. Those could make the fast trip. It's what? Sixteen or seventeen hundred miles as the crow flies from here to Albuquerque? It wouldn't take more than two and a half hours for the flight at seven hundred miles an hour, plus maybe half an hour for him and his people to actually get to the airport with the hostage, then get a plane that was already prepped into the air, plus a few minutes on the ground in Albuquerque—"

"So find a private airport within a half-hour driving distance of the kidnapping site during rush hour traffic this morning. Won't be too many of those with a runway that has a rated takeoff length of five to six thousand feet."

"Naw, three thousand feet will do it, Boss. The runway rating means a plane has to get to full takeoff speed and then be able to abort without running out of runway. If they don't plan on aborting—and these guys weren't—they can take off on a far shorter runway. They'd really only need three thousand feet to take off fully fueled with six to eight passengers."

Palmer turned toward McGrath. She had one arm wrapped across her belly like it was supporting the elbow of the other. Her fingers played across her chin thoughtfully. "Aaron, they grabbed her on the George Washington Memorial Parkway just a few minutes north of Reagan

International. There are a lot of off-ramps in that area and a lot of ways to get lost in plain sight among all the residential neighborhoods, shopping areas, and industrial complexes up there. If they changed vehicles, they could've even sneaked her back across the Potomac. And there are quite a few private airports within, say, twenty miles of DC."

McGrath nodded and turned to Jimmy again. "Let's assume he took off after the lockdown. How could he do it?"

Jimmy worked his keyboard for a moment. "Well, he certainly couldn't take off from a major airport. But if someone wants a flight from a small airport to *not* be found, there are plenty of ways to hide or temporarily disable electronic traces of a takeoff—local radar signals and comm traffic and transponders—with the right amount of money." He held up a beefy hand and rubbed his thumb against his fingers.

McGrath removed his glasses and examined them for nonexistent smudges. "Nancy, continue tracing the logistics here in Virginia. Jimmy, your priority is finding that plane in Albuquerque. It has to be parked at the international airport."

"Or Santa Fe," Jimmy added after consulting his computer screen. "They can handle a Gulfstream jet up there." His fingers flew over his keyboard. "Or Los Lunas. They have a suitable airport within a half-hour driving distance to Albuquerque." After a moment, he added, "Looks like there's also an old airport on the west side of Albuquerque called Double Eagle that's closed down. With some advance planning and logistics, they could have landed there too."

Agent Palmer said, "If he's got logistics teams in the US, either here or in Albuquerque, then they've got local accomplices assisting them either as volunteers or under duress, with housing, fuel providers maybe, radar jamming, or communications equipment, so we need to find them."

"Agreed," McGrath said. He tapped the analyst sitting next to Jimmy on the shoulder. "Tell me about the Albuquerque sighting."

The analyst was a big bald kid with a blond beard that reached to his lap. McGrath could tell if the fellow stood up and reached overhead, he'd easily touch the ceiling. His fingers tapped on his keyboard with a steady thrum.

"The traffic cam facing east from the interchange of I-40 and I-25 made a 62 percent identity match. He's driving an open-top Jeep

Wrangler, an older 1980s model. It's not a high-def camera, so a 62 percent match is as good as we're going to get. We got lucky."

"Put his image up on the center screen next to Reyes's photo."

Reyes's biographical data vanished and was replaced by a black-and-white photo of the man in Albuquerque. The photo was grainy from being enlarged from a distant camera shot, but McGrath had no doubt it was the same man. The still frame of Alfonso Reyes from the kidnap site showed the man wearing a mustache and goatee, but the Albuquerque photo showed he was clean-shaven.

"Why would he think shaving would throw us off?" McGrath paced the floor behind the analysts for a moment. "Do we have any other recent photos of him?"

A window opened on the center monitor, and McGrath watched pages from Reyes's charity website open. He saw photos of Reyes in various types of clothing, from expensive casual to formal. In some, he was clean-shaven, and in others, he had facial hair. In every picture, he wore designer glasses.

McGrath muttered to Palmer, "That's him." He paused. "Why in hell would he stop in Albuquerque, though, especially after pulling off the biggest kidnapping in the history of the United States? In a Citation or a Gulfstream jet, he could have been out of the country by now. He *should have been* out of the country."

Palmer tapped the bald analyst on the shoulder. "What kind of surveillance assets do we have in Albuquerque?"

"Ma'am, it's New Mexico, not New York, and they're pretty low on the terror threat list. There are only a couple dozen traffic cameras on the city network with live feeds. Our standard Homeland hack can access the usual live cameras inside banks and airports and hotels large enough to host major conventions—those kinds of locations."

He worked his keyboard, then pointed at the center wall monitor. "Got him! He just pulled into the Hyatt underground parking structure. Picked him up on the parking garage surveillance camera."

McGrath narrowed his eyes. "All right, people, we may have caught a break here. Looks like our guy got careless."

"Hmm," the analyst said. "The license plate of the car he's driving is not a rental car. It's most likely stolen."

Palmer added, "He knew we'd be watching airports and car rental outlets. Maybe he stashed Melissa in the house, where he commandeered the car. Maybe his plan is just to make a quick trade for cash. If he has the owner there too—and he most likely killed that poor soul—then the car wouldn't be reported stolen."

"You are *not* going to believe this," the bald analyst said. He pulled up some more data and pointed McGrath's attention to the center wall monitor again. "That's actually *his car!* He's had a safe house right there in Albuquerque for almost twenty-five years! He's using an alias we haven't seen before, though. His house and car are titled in the name of Carl Johnson."

On the center monitor, everyone stared at the now-familiar face on the drug lord's New Mexico driver's license—brown skin, no hair, pleasant disarming smile, and slightly graying mustache and goatee. Five-foot-nine and 170 pounds. Blood type B-positive. Their target was a good-looking man.

McGrath nodded to himself. "Okay, get our team in the air. Inform the local FBI of a potential hostage situation and have their SWAT teams mobilize heavy assets. Tell them they can expect resistance. And make sure they know they're on the clock." He paused. "Maybe he's meeting a customer for the trade."

Palmer leaned over the bald analyst's shoulder and examined the maps on his desktop monitor. "If he gets out of there, we'll lose him. There aren't any live networked traffic cams within half a mile."

"Understood," McGrath said. "Everyone, drop what you're doing and concentrate on Albuquerque. Let's see if we can get some eyes inside the hotel and find out who he's meeting. Get me some live feeds of all elevator and hallway cameras inside the hotel." He clapped his hands sharply. "Let's go, people! If we lose him this time, Melissa is as good as dead."

A sharp pang of dread gripped his gut, and he rolled his head back and forth to release his tension. With his new job, he hadn't been able to see Melissa much over the past year, and now he regretted that. McGrath refocused on the center wall monitor and tried to examine the motivations behind the smiling photos of the charismatic drug lord.

Why Melissa Mallory? And why Albuquerque?

"When we find the target, I want him immobilized immediately. Have the FBI sedate him on-site. I don't want him bribing a disgruntled cop with a million dollars. No one speaks with him except our people."

Agent Palmer pointed at the far-right wall monitor, where her analyst had put up an FBI bio. "Special Agent Lenore Cummings. You called her in to interview with us earlier this year when she was an applicant to the Secret Service."

McGrath scanned the agent's no-nonsense photo—dark blazer, light blue blouse with the collar open, oval face, minimal makeup, serious brown eyes, and blonde hair pulled severely back.

"She was impressive," McGrath said.

Palmer added, "Strategic and tactical skills off the charts. She'll make a fine addition to the TER agency."

She said it like the decision was hers. Like hiring Cummings was a foregone conclusion.

McGrath said, "Assign her local command of the op and get her special agent in charge on a secure video link. She takes control of the target. No one else."

Palmer nodded, then looked away for a moment as though concentrating on something else.

"Aaron, I have Pete Klipser on comm channel four."

"On speaker."

Palmer retrieved her cell from her hip holster and pressed a pad, then stuck the device back on her hip. She nodded at McGrath.

"Pete, your target is in Albuquerque. Take our plane at Andrews Air Force Base and get there ASAP."

A subdued, gravelly voice floated from the desk phone speaker. "My rules of engagement?"

McGrath glanced over at Nancy Palmer, who had trained the former Special Forces soldier in the subtle art of *domestic* covert wet work. He had excelled, becoming the TER agency's go-to field operator. In his short career since being recruited from the army, his exploits rivaled the accomplishments of Agent Palmer. As usual, he didn't ask irrelevant questions and always got straight to business.

McGrath said, "He's a Tier-One suspect. Full rendition protocol is authorized. If Melissa is not at the foothills house, interrogate Reyes on-site. Employ any means to discover her—"

"Negative," Palmer interrupted. "Reyes is Tier Three, Aaron. We need him alive."

McGrath glared at Palmer for a moment, then she said, "Stand by, Pete." She touched her Bluetooth earpiece to put the channel on hold.

"Aaron, you know how Pete can be. If he loses control of the interrogation or pushes too hard, we lose the only lead we have to Melissa's location. Let's bring him back here for experimental interrogation, where we control all the variables."

McGrath tried to find fault in her argument, but her assessment was flawless, as usual, unlike his own emotional state of mind. He nodded, and Palmer touched her earpiece again.

McGrath said, "Palmer is correct, Pete. Reyes is Tier Three. Nonlethal action only."

"And if we get in a firefight with his people?"

"Use of deadly force is not authorized. If you can't take him alive without a firefight, let him go, and we'll find another way to track him."

"Understood."

The analyst named Jimmy called out, "I got him on another camera!" He worked his keyboard. "And we've got a human asset in the lobby. It's an off-duty FBI field agent in plain clothes." He paused and scratched the back of his neck under his massive Afro. "Okay, now this is weird."

McGrath said, "Don't keep me in suspense."

The analyst swiveled in his chair. "Uh, well, sir. It looks like he just stopped in for coffee."

CHAPTER 3

CARL JOHNSON CLIMBED OUT OF his open-top Jeep Wrangler and pushed the door closed. Twice. It still didn't stay closed, so he gave it a hard hip check, adding another dent under the door handle. It stayed closed.

"Piece o' shit," he murmured affectionately.

The 1980s-era Wrangler was his dream car, and he'd finally bought one last year after procrastinating for nearly twenty years. The old car represented freedom and dreams come true. He always smiled when he saw the car, even though little things here and there were starting to break down with increasing frequency. It was dirty, but not the honorable off-trail dirty. It was pickled with dried raindrops and residue from high-desert dust storms and air pollution. He hadn't washed the damn thing since he bought it.

He loved that car and his personal motto that it represented: "And don't forget… Life is good!"

He'd borrowed that motto almost twenty years ago from a friend who was a salesman. The guy could sell cars in a recession. At the time, his friend was the "Life is good!" guy, and everyone knew it. He had that slogan on his stationery, on his license plate (LYFSGUD), and on his voice mail recording.

"Hey, this is Joseph. Leave a message. And don't forget… Life is good!"

At first, Carl used to say it because it sounded positive and affirming, and he'd been going through marital problems with his second wife. He said it to other people, but he really only said it to convince himself that life could get better.

Two years later, he realized if you keep saying something like that over and over again, day after day, year after year, until it became something more than just a cool slogan or motto, then eventually you actually started to believe it. It evolves into a fundamental part of your life and your belief system. Also, Carl found that there were a lot of people who needed to hear it too. So, he included his motto in the signature line of his cell phone text messages, his emails, and on his voice mail.

Now, Carl was the "Life is good!" guy. He even had the motto printed around the circular edge of his spare tire's cover, which was bolted to the rear gate of the Jeep. Everyone following him on the road could read it: "And don't forget... Life is good!"

He removed his gloves and thick thermal skullcap, dumping them on the driver's seat. He pulled a thin head glove from the left pocket of his well-worn, brown bomber jacket, fitted it on his hairless dome, and smoothed out the ripples.

He made his way over to the elevator and pressed the button to go up. He waited a couple of minutes. Then a bell dinged, the "up" button light went out, and the elevator door slid open to the right. He stepped into the box, did a 180, and examined the panel to the right of the sliding doors. There were only three buttons—P1 for the level where he'd parked, P2, plus one more labeled L for the lobby.

Carl pressed L, the light came on, and the door started to close. He pressed the button a couple more times, mostly out of habit, just like he did at crosswalk signs. That was just in case the elevator light was lying to him, and the elevator wasn't really going to the lobby, even though he knew there were no levels between P1 and the lobby. Crazy.

The front wall of the elevator, the sliding door, and the ceiling were all reflective brushed steel with a subdued gray color. The back, left, and right walls were highly polished wood. There were posters on the left and right walls of the elevator. The one on the left advertised a new shop in the mall section of the lobby. The shop sold authentic southwestern art and jewelry—turquoise, silver, copper, and Native American wall art—no doubt for out-of-state conference attendees looking for high-quality souvenirs but lacking the time to find the same merchandise in Old Town or Santa Fe for half the price.

The other poster to Carl's right showed a stunningly beautiful plate of food. The color poster was so vibrant, he figured it could make a tourist get hungry on the spot and go immediately in search of the new restaurant.

A bell dinged, and the elevator slowed to a stop. The L light went out as the door slid open to the left. He stepped out into a wide hallway. Directly in front of him was the lobby bar, but it was closed at that early hour. To his left, the long wide hallway led to the elevators that serviced the south tower of the Hyatt Hotel complex.

Between his elevator and the south tower elevators were several offices that catered to business travelers staying at the hotel—a copy shop, a popular shipping outlet, a dry-cleaning drop-off, and a rental car outlet. There were also a couple more tourist shops—jewelry, art, and other knickknacks. Two stores were vacant, but the front display windows were tastefully papered so the vacancies weren't glaring to hotel residents.

To Carl's right, the lobby opened up to its full splendor. It wasn't as extravagant as he'd seen in conference centers in larger cities, but for Albuquerque, it was a top-tier hotel lobby. The space measured perhaps fifty feet by fifty feet, and it had a step-down section in the center with couches and chairs for lounging, along with two long desks with power outlets and internet access for computer work. All the furniture was arrayed spaciously around a seven-foot-high clay vase. Water gurgled from its top, slid down the exterior, and disappeared into a rock-covered grating in the floor.

Arranged around the upper edge of the lounging area were more chairs and small tables for one-on-one meetings. It was, in fact, in this area that Carl was to meet his eleven o'clock client, who had pushed back the meeting just fifteen minutes ago. Now he had an hour to kill.

Normally, he rescheduled clients who were late to meetings. He made them wait a few days. His cash-flow returns for commercial income properties were typically a hundred thousand a year, sometimes more, so he had the leverage of a valuable product that clients wanted.

The woman he was due to meet today had been referred to him by another investor in his network. She allegedly had access to several partners with significant cash reserves. She wasn't looking for small one- or two-million-dollar assets. She was shopping in the ten- to twenty-million price range, so that level of interest earned her an additional hour of Carl's time.

The direct route from the elevator to Starbucks in the northeast corner of the lobby was blocked by a janitor working on a stain in the carpet, so Carl took the scenic route to the coffee shop. He proceeded around the lobby, past the bar and the restrooms, the check-in counter and the valet entrance, the ATM, and two competing art stores—one of which was the new art shop advertised on the poster in the elevator. Then he stepped through the open door of the coffee shop.

The cream and sugar station was along the wall on his left, and the pickup counter was just inside the door on his right. The order counter was just beyond that, featuring a glass case full of pastries, chilled water, and juices one could order if one wasn't in the mood for coffee. Beyond that glass case, the order line stretched almost to the other entry door from the street on the opposite side of the coffee shop.

Carl walked across the shop and took his place at the end of the ordering line. When he got to the counter, he ordered a "tall house with room"—Starbucks lingo for the store's house-brewed blend in a *tall* cup, the smallest size available, and "with room" meaning a half-inch or so left at the top of the cup so he could add cream.

He got his coffee fairly quickly because the two servers had a well-rehearsed procedure. The first charged his debit card while the second, who had just delivered her customer's fancy order—some kind of frou-frou "venti half-caf ninety-degree breve" something or other—grabbed a cup and filled it with the house brew. She slid it into a cardboard sleeve and placed it on the counter in front of Carl, just as the first cashier finished ringing him up.

He thanked both servers, and they both told him to have a wonderful day. He made his way to the cream and sugar station, where he waited behind two women in business suits as they dressed up their coffees. One of the women wore a two-piece, dark gray pantsuit, and the other wore a dark blue skirt suit. Both had small airplane carry-on bags on tiny wheels by their sides with the pull handles fully extended. He wondered if that was just a business fashion statement or if they actually had laptops and presentation materials stuffed into the small rolling cases.

They reminded him of his time as an Air Force engineering contractor, but that was back in the days when real men and women carried their stuff in briefcases without wheels and toted their laptops in over-the-shoulder satchels.

At fifty-three, though, that life was far behind him. He'd left the corporate world almost ten years back, gotten his real estate license, and opened up his one-man shop. Then he got bored with selling houses and moved into commercial brokerage, selling income properties.

As the women departed, Carl did the "man thing." Almost by subconscious habit, he examined them both with a quick glance down their physiques and back up.

He stepped up to the creamer station and set about dressing up his brew. He carefully pried the plastic top from the cup, then grabbed three yellow packets of fake sugar. He pinned their edges together and shook the group with a couple flicks of his wrist to get all the sugar away from the top edge that he planned to tear off. He ripped the tops off all three packets, dumped the contents into his coffee, then reached for one of the stainless steel jugs of half-and-half cream and filled the coffee cup almost to the rim.

He grabbed a thin wooden stirring stick, and on a whim, as he stirred, he decided to steal another glance at the two departing businesswomen to his left as they passed through the doorway into the Hyatt lobby. He just wanted to see how they walked. That was when he noticed the man in beige slacks and a black windbreaker eyeballing him from the lobby doorway. The man's bearing and short-cropped haircut screamed, "Cop!"

Carl held the man's gaze for a moment, then glanced to his right and behind him to see what the man was looking at, but there was no one else near him at the moment. The man had been clearly concentrating on him. He turned back to the cop, but the guy had turned away.

Carl pressed the lid of his coffee cup back on and took a sample sip before departing the cream station. He inhaled the bitter fragrance as he swallowed and decided his coffee was softened and sweetened perfectly.

He took another long sip, gently slurping in enough air to cool the liquid so it wouldn't burn his mouth.

Smiling to himself, he walked through the doorway and headed back into the hotel lobby. He glanced to his right and saw the cop window-shopping at the jewelry store—the new one from the elevator poster. Carl sat down in the lounging area and listened to the quiet trickle of the fountain while he checked his email on his smartphone and caught up on the latest tech blogs. After ten minutes, he started getting drowsy and decided to take a walk outside.

He stood and walked back through the coffee shop, making his way to the street exit that opened onto the corner of Third Street and Marquette. Knowing it was chilly outside, he stopped and put his coffee cup on an empty table near the door and pulled his head glove from his right coat pocket. He fit it on properly, then retrieved his cup. His right hand holding the coffee would be plenty warm enough, but he parked his left hand in his jacket pocket and used his butt to back his way through the glass door.

As soon as he turned around, cops in black tactical gear jumped him.

CHAPTER 4

1120 MST, FRIDAY
ALBUQUERQUE, NM

T HE FIRST TIME FOR ANY difficult experience is always the hardest. Carl's first terrifying experience with the police had happened four years ago and effectively prepped him for his current experience.

Pop quiz: How many White cops does it take to beat the crap out of an unarmed Black man?

It was a question he and his friends discussed every now and again. All of his Black friends—every single one of them—had been taken to the ground by White cops at some time in their lives. It didn't matter who they were, where they were from, how highly educated, how rich or poor, how properly they spoke, or how nicely they dressed. It had happened to them all.

He'd always wondered why the vast majority—over 90 percent—of Albuquerque cops were White, when White folk made up only 43 percent of the city's population. He'd researched it four years ago. Minorities on the police force were severely underrepresented. There had to be some kind of strategy behind that statistic, though the police chief back then was quoted as saying that minorities couldn't pass the entrance exam.

Yeah, right. It's not like you need to be a rocket scientist or something.

So, if someone had asked Carl the "how many" question four years ago, he would have given the answer as *two*. Back then, he had gotten bored with living in a five-bedroom house in the foothills all by himself. He rented out his house and found a loft downtown just a block south of Central on the corner of Fourth and Gold. One particular Saturday, the mayor had shrubs planted on all the downtown streets to make the deteriorating area look more inviting for shoppers. On Sunday, Carl had gone downstairs to water the shrubs planted in huge pots on the sidewalk in front of his loft. In the middle of that event, he'd glanced up to see two cops walking toward him with their right hands on their guns and their concentration focused fully on him. They'd jacked him up good.

"Up against the wall! Hands high and wide. Feet spread. You know the position!"

Up to that point in his life, he, in fact, did *not* know the position. He had survived forty-nine years with zero police encounters. But he'd done what his father had told him and his siblings repeatedly while growing up. When you get stopped by cops, just say, "Yes, sir," "No, sir," or "I don't know, sir."

Don't give them a reason.

He hadn't given those particular cops a reason, but they'd jacked him up anyway. He had just gone downstairs to water the plants and didn't take his ID with him. All he had was a water bucket and his door keys because the exterior door to his loft was always locked. The downtown cops didn't believe he really lived there, though, and they were ready to haul him to jail. The cops didn't even know there were lofts on top of the stores until he gave them his keys and told them to go up and check. They'd done so after cuffing him to a lamp post.

It had been a Sunday afternoon, so while there was minimal street traffic, there were plenty of folks window-shopping, perhaps while waiting for their movies to start at the cinema two blocks away. The stores near his loft were open, so word about what was happening to Carl had spread quickly. A few workers came to their front windows or stepped out their doors and stared at him standing handcuffed with his back to the lamp post. They all knew him. They knew he lived upstairs. They'd spoken to him daily or waved to him through the windows whenever he walked by. Now, he could see by the expressions on their faces that they were wondering what crime had been committed by this man they'd previously thought was such a nice guy and a successful local businessman.

The experience had been totally and utterly humiliating.

The cops came down a couple minutes later and released him. One said they had responded to a silent alarm, then they left. Carl had been seething inside, and there were a lot of things he'd wanted to say. He'd wanted to ask the cop what the fuck a silent alarm had to do with him, but instead, he'd just said, "Yes, sir." He then watched the cops walk away toward the jewelry store.

They'd walked right by a young White couple who had been standing under the awning of the bar right next door to the jewelry store with the silent alarm. They'd been standing there the whole time, but the cops didn't give the young couple a second glance.

They'd simply started asking questions of a man who was actually carrying stuff out of the jewelry store the entire time the cops had been jacking up Carl. There were no hands on the guns, no handcuffs, no harsh language, and no asking for ID. Carl later discovered the man was the owner of the jewelry store and was moving his merchandise to another store. He didn't know he had tripped the alarm. After the cops left, the store owner—who had watched Carl get jacked up along with all the other store workers on the block—had walked up the street and apologized to Carl for "the misunderstanding."

It had occurred to Carl that the cops hadn't even confirmed there was actually a crime taking place. They simply thought he had committed a crime. They'd *assumed* it was him.

The next day, Carl had packed up all his belongings and moved out of downtown. He took a hotel room while he moved the tenants out of his big foothills house so he could move back in there.

If he was going to be completely fair and honest to Albuquerque's cops, Carl had to admit that most of the homeless guys and panhandlers that hung out downtown were minorities. Brown Native Americans or Hispanics or Blacks accounted for the overwhelming majority of complaints for disorderly conduct and other minor crimes. In all likelihood, even if one or both of the cops had *not* been White, the same thing would have happened to him.

At the time, actually being a victim of the police and racial profiling, Carl didn't want to hear about any rational explanations for what had happened. Actual crime statistics meant nothing to him. Instead, it had made him feel somehow vindicated, being able to blame the whole event on racial injustice. It was easier to place blame on the cops. It invoked a sense of historical righteousness and empathy, and it certainly made for a better story to tell his Black friends.

You'll never guess what the White cops did to me downtown.

But that had been four years ago. Today, the "how many" question had an entirely different answer because the sea of anxious faces that had magically appeared in front of him spanned the entire spectrum from white to dark brown. There was even an Asian face in the group.

So, the current question was: How many not-necessarily-White cops does it take to beat the crap out of an unarmed Black man?

Answer: All of them. Every last goddamn one of them.

They came out of nowhere. One second, the sidewalk was empty of all life—not a living soul or a single car on the street. The next, the sidewalk was filled with men in black. All were fully decked out in black tactical gear and Kevlar vests with the big, white capital letters SWAT over the left breast. They all wore black helmets with face shields, and they all had shotguns and automatic rifles.

He froze, stunned, with his coffee cup inches away from his lips. He'd been just about to take another sip. The steam wafted up through the tiny hole right in front of his face.

"Well, fuck me sideways," was all Carl could think to say.

Then suddenly, everyone was shouting at him, all converging on him. The cacophony of voices behind all the face shields sounded like a muffled cheering section at a sporting event. Every man seemed to be shouting something different.

"Freeze!"

"Hands!"

"Get on the ground!"

"Drop it!"

"Up against the wall!"

"Show me your hands!"

On the street in front of him, behind all the screaming SWAT cops now rushing toward him, three big black SUVs raced from the west on the one-way street in front of the Hyatt and slammed to a stop just shy of the corner. Just like in the movies, two tactical agents rode on the runners on both sides of each vehicle, one hand gripping a railing on top of each SUV and the other gripping an assault rifle. They all jumped off their vehicles in unison before the SUV had even come to a complete stop, and they all headed straight for Carl, rifle stocks jammed against their shoulders and barrels aimed at Carl. Their Kevlar vests had big white capital letters saying "FBI" stenciled on the front. Then, all the doors of the vehicles opened at once, and even more FBI men in black jumped out.

And a woman.

Carl heard more vehicles screech to a stop to his right, and another stampede of combat boots thundered across the sidewalk toward him. He stole a glance to his right and saw a dozen FBI combat troops weaving around the big brass statues of family figures—walking parents and kids on skateboards. Some of the troops took cover behind the artistic structures and aimed at him, while others proceeded toward him, staying out of the lines of fire of the squatting troops.

As a result of the confusing calls for action, Carl didn't move a muscle. Not only did he not know what to do, but he also didn't want to pull his hand out and get shot by some nervous rookie SWAT cop on his first takedown. He could see some of the rifle muzzles wavering in front of his face, and he knew this was the first time up at bat for some of these kids. They were nervous.

Carl just stood frozen in mid-stride. Then, in a weird alignment of cosmic events, there was a sudden, brief moment of complete silence. Maybe, Carl thought, they all had to catch their breath before they began shouting again. He heard the coffee shop door hiss closed automatically behind him.

It occurred to Carl that he was strangely calm in the face of all the hardware pointed at him.

The first takedown is always the hardest. The second, not so much.

He remembered the man that looked like a cop who had been eyeballing him from the lobby doorway of the coffee shop. He slowly pivoted his upper body to the left and spied the man in the beige pants and black windbreaker, ushering the last of the coffee shop employees and customers into the lobby, out of harm's way.

He faced back forward again. The first time you get jacked up, you're paralyzed with fear. The cops know this. They approach you and start shouting at you, trying to overwhelm you with sheer volume and surprise, and it works.

Shock and awe.

It's human nature to retreat from shouting and loud, violent words. When those violent words are focused at you—especially by men in uniform, especially with guns pointed at you—human nature automatically forces you to assume a posture of submission. You wonder what the hell is going on or what you've done. You're scared shitless. You answer all their questions.

Yes, sir. No, sir. I don't know, sir.

Only later, after they release you and the fear fades, do you experience the emotional aftermath of humiliation, shame, and helplessness. Then you start to feel the anger. After that, you feel frustrated because you have no target for the anger.

The second time it happens, however, you jump back in time and pick up emotionally right where you left off the first time, even if it happened years ago. You skip the fear. You just go straight to the anger, contempt, and frustration you tried unsuccessfully to get over from the last time. But those emotions have simmered over the months or the years, residing just beneath your consciousness, an echo of a memory that never quite faded.

That's what Carl felt as the initial shock of his new encounter faded. He figured a psychiatrist would say he was still suffering from post-traumatic stress, but he didn't care. He knew these cops were going to take him down hard. Cops didn't bring SWAT and the FBI tactical guys to a party with this many guns if they were going to let you go. Like, "Oh, sorry, Mr. Johnson, we thought you were robbing a coffee shop this time. Our mistake. You're free to go now."

These cops were going to bust his ass hard, and he knew it. The reason didn't matter. No amount of cooperation was going to change that.

So, after the initial two seconds of shock, his wildly thumping heart calmed, and he dredged up all those raw emotions that had been simmering inside him for four years.

"Fuck you," he said to the nearest cop. He waved his coffee cup at the crowd with his index finger pointing at them. "Fuck all of you."

Then he took a long slurping sip of coffee.

Carl watched the woman cop follow the FBI assault troops from the SUVs. She side-stepped her way through the crowd of weapons.

"Make a hole," she commanded.

Then she stopped five feet from Carl. She had tied-back blonde hair, brown eyes, and a serious look on her face that suggested she could kick his ass with her pinkie finger if she wanted to. She wore denim pants, white and blue running shoes, and a gray pullover sweater under an open, dark blue windbreaker with "FBI" in yellow letters over the left breast. She wore a badge clipped to her belt and an empty holster on her right hip. She gripped her service weapon in both hands, its barrel pointed roughly at Carl's feet.

She was the boss of all this mess, Carl figured, because she wore no Kevlar vest or other combat gear, and she had brought only a handgun to the party.

"I want you to slowly pull your left hand out of your pocket," she said.

He locked gazes with the woman cop and decided not to comply immediately. He gave her a derisive, cocky smile.

"Fuck you," Carl said. Then he took a long sip of coffee. "Just don't shoot me." He slowly pulled his hand out of his pocket.

They shot him.

CHAPTER 5

1122 MST, FRIDAY
ALBUQUERQUE, NM

FIRE RIPPED THROUGH HIS BODY as four SWAT cops zapped him with stun guns from eight feet away. The world tilted to the right, and a portion of the sidewalk rotated up and slammed against the left side of his body. He lay there sizzling and could actually see his arms and legs twitching and flailing as the four cops continued to juice him for a few more seconds.

When they finally stopped, a detached part of his brain registered men moving near the edge of the roof of the convention center diagonally across the street. Two of the men held long rifles, and their partners held high-powered binoculars.

He had a couple of unpaid parking tickets, but snipers?

What the fuck?

The female cop squatted in front of him and said, "Not so cocky now, are you?" Then she said, "Hit him again."

In his peripheral view, he saw three of the cops reach to their belts and start replacing cartridges in their black stun guns. One of the cops had a yellow and black gun that didn't need recharging. Carl recognized it as one of the new multi-shot Taser guns that could hit three separate targets in rapid succession.

Or one target more than once.

Electrical fire ripped through his body again, and he screamed in pain. When that cop was done with him, Carl saw the woman pull a syringe from her blazer pocket and felt a prick as she plunged the needle into the right side of his neck. An unpleasant sensation of heat spread into his neck and chest.

His eyes focused on the lid of the coffee cup that lay on its side near his face. The lid hadn't popped off when he dropped the cup, and a trickle of brown liquid gurgled slowly out of the sipping hole. He saw the engraved words on the lid that read, "Caution Contents Hot." A huge boot nudged the cup aside. Another boot stepped on the cup, and coffee splashed all over the concrete.

The cops near him began to disburse, but the woman cop kept her position, squatting near his head. She was obviously watching and waiting for the drug to take effect, and Carl felt it taking over his body gradually but quickly. The woman's left hand fiddled with the expended syringe. The sleeve of her right arm had hitched up a bit, exposing a simple digital wristwatch. The face of her watch was pointed downward, right at Carl's eyes. He noticed it was twenty-two minutes after eleven. He was going to miss his noon appointment.

He felt himself fading into blackness. A cop rolled him onto his belly and roughly restrained his wrists with plastic zip cuffs. Then two cops grabbed him under his armpits and dragged him across the sidewalk toward a black box van. He tried to regain his feet and at least walk with some tiny bit of dignity, but his body wouldn't respond.

Should have kept my hand in my pocket a while longer. Could have at least finished my coffee.

He passed out halfway to the van.

CHAPTER 6

1530 EST, FRIDAY
ARLINGTON HEIGHTS, VA

O N THE CENTER MONITOR, AARON McGrath watched the video conference feed that originated in the conference room of Guillermo Figueroa, the SAC, or special agent in charge, of the Albuquerque FBI field office. The high-definition camera was aimed from the middle of the top edge of the wall monitor at the end of the conference table, and the FBI agents that sat with Figueroa looked like they were gazing at something just below the bottom of McGrath's monitor. He knew he appeared the same to the FBI people.

At McGrath's instructions, Special Agent Cummings was one of only three individuals in the room. While the two male officers were dressed in typical dark suits, Cummings was dressed in jeans and a pullover gray sweater. She'd been pulled in on her day off. Her FBI windbreaker was draped over the back of her chair. Her blonde hair was tied back but wasn't braided. Intense brown eyes gave her narrow face a serious look.

Cummings was an elite federal agent, and that was why he'd considered recruiting her into the Terror Event Response agency. She displayed extremely high competency in the physical police skills—marksmanship, fitness, and special weapons and tactics—but she also brought a measured and deliberate approach to her investigative research. While big-city agents often competed to be the first to solve a crime or catch the *unsub*, or unknown subject, Cummings took a more Zen-like approach to her cases. As a result, Cummings had amassed an impressive list of successful case results and commendations.

Figueroa sat at the head of the conference table, and his tactical commander, Special Agent Ed Murphy, sat to his right. Special Agent Lenore Cummings sat to the left of the SAC. Murphy and Cummings had their chairs swiveled so they could look at the wall monitor.

"Agent Figueroa," McGrath said, not using the man's full, formal title. "The information has been relayed to you that the suspect you have in custody is a Tier-Three terror suspect of interest to the Department of Homeland Security, correct?"

Figueroa nodded.

"His associates have the resources to mount a rescue, should his location be disclosed, so you should consider your building a target of imminent assault. Implement immediate protective measures to defend the building."

Figueroa narrowed his eyes, then glanced at his tactical commander. He gave him a brief nod, and the man left the room. McGrath knew the building would be emptied of all but essential personnel and then sealed, with heavily armed, combat-trained security personnel stationed at every entrance at street level and on the roof. They'd call in local law enforcement to establish a defensive perimeter around the building, along with sniper support. Nearby buildings and industrial complexes would be evacuated to minimize collateral damage should a firefight take place.

Figueroa said, "May I know the nature of the terror event?"

"A high-profile child has been taken. The man you have in custody is our only information source regarding her whereabouts at the moment." McGrath nodded and shifted his attention to the only other occupant in the room. "Special Agent Cummings, you have responsibility for the suspect until my people arrive. You answer only to me and to my retrieval team when they arrive. Is that clear?"

Cummings nodded.

"The suspect is in isolation?"

"Yes, Mr. Director, and he is sedated. He'll be out for no less than three more hours."

"Keep heavily armed security officers outside his cell, with orders to answer only to you. You will personally see to it that absolutely no one is allowed inside his cell until my team arrives."

Figueroa sat forward and balanced both his elbows on the conference table. He was short and compact, his upper body thick and muscular. His hairline had receded so far that he was nearly bald. His round face featured heavily lidded eyes, a broad nose, and full lips, and his skin held a deep brown hue. The man held his fingertips in a steeple formation, and McGrath sensed his curiosity.

"Agent Figueroa, this is as much as I can tell you at the moment."

The man nodded. "You'll have our full cooperation."

"Agent Cummings, you have an encrypted cell phone?"

She nodded.

"You have a SCIF in the building?" He pronounced it "skiff."

Again, she nodded.

A SCIF was a Sensitive Compartmented Information Facility, a specially shielded communication room used to discuss classified information. Typically, it was a room within a room, wrapped in copper mesh to prevent any signals from being intercepted from the outside. The double walls were filled with vibration-absorbing foam to prevent the transmission of voices. White-noise generators added another layer of protection, and the SCIF had no windows that could be interrogated by lasers to sense vibrations from voices or transmissions like electrical signals from computer keystrokes. Even the electrical conduit pipes had high-tech isolation filters to prevent interception by any laser-based or mechanical eavesdropping devices.

"See to the prisoner, then call me from the SCIF to receive an additional briefing and further instructions."

McGrath terminated the conference call and turned his attention to Nancy Palmer. During the video call, she had stepped outside the field of view of the camera. Some of the time, she'd been giving instructions and queries to the analysts. Now, she was doing that athlete thing, rolling her neck from side to side and stretching muscles like she was getting ready for a workout. She noticed him watching her and stepped close to him. He pointed at the monitor showing all the heavily armed men that captured the terrorist.

"Christ, Nancy, we instructed them to use nonlethal force only." He shook his head as he watched the replay of the takedown. "One mistake, and our only lead would be dead."

"This can't be our guy, Aaron. There's no way that takedown should have been that easy."

The point of view of the video feed was one of the sniper units on the convention center roof diagonally across the intersection.

"He's our guy. I'll bet my salary on that. He's the exact same height, weight, eye color, skin color, and age."

Palmer shook her head, and a short flock of her blonde, close-cut hair dropped over her right eye. She stood nearly as tall as he, and she wore a perfectly tailored, two-piece black suit over a black turtleneck.

"He's such a minor player on the world stage. We don't have recent intel on the guy yet, outside of his website, but in all of the photographs, he is wearing glasses. The man we have in custody is not, and he's not wearing contacts either."

McGrath raised an eyebrow, and Palmer preempted the question forming in his mind.

"I asked Cummings to check him." Palmer shrugged. "That detail bothered me." She head-nodded toward the wall monitors.

The photo collage of Alfonso Reyes, along with the image from the Albuquerque traffic camera, had been moved to the left monitor. The frames Reyes wore at the kidnap site were dark and square. As Palmer pointed out, in all the images except for the traffic camera, Reyes was wearing stylish frames of various shapes and colors.

"Except for that detail," he said, "this guy is an exact match from everything we know about him. Not a close resemblance, but an *exact match*. And he's been under our noses the whole time."

"Agreed," Palmer said. "Maybe he had Lasik surgery and just wears stylish, nonprescription frames to confuse people. But this guy saw our off-duty FBI agent and didn't react. Hell, anybody with half a brain would have made that guy, yet Reyes took no action."

"Yeah." McGrath slid his hands into his pockets and looked at the images again. "That FBI agent should be dead, either by Reyes or by his bodyguards, which we have yet to find. In fact, Reyes should have fled the scene immediately."

Palmer nodded. "He never would have allowed himself to be seen in public in the first place, not after snatching Melissa." She paused a moment. "They've searched the Hyatt towers completely, top to bottom, floor by floor, room by room. There's no evidence of anyone meeting with him, and there's no sign of any of his bodyguards."

"Well, we have him now," McGrath said. "So we'll proceed under the assumption that he's our guy unless we find out otherwise."

Palmer said, "I'm only suggesting that we keep an open mind until we're certain."

"I'm certain." He gestured with his shoulder toward the analysts seated in front of them. "How is the search going?"

She deliberately showed a hint of frustration with a forced exhale and a subtle shake of her head, then used her right index finger to push the lock of hair away from her eye. "Jimmy, anything on the plane?" she asked.

The big Afro wobbled as the analyst shook his head. "I've got nothing here in Virginia yet."

Next to him, the bald kid said, "And I can't find any plane that made an unscheduled flight into *any* airport in or near Albuquerque."

McGrath said, "Then check scheduled flights. This kidnapping was well-planned and well organized. Maybe they sedated her and stuck her in a box or a coffin. Hell, maybe he flew to Albuquerque and let himself get caught as a distraction while the girl was taken out of the country by some other means."

Palmer nodded. "We assumed they moved Melissa from the scene in the SUV, but they could have used a helicopter to get her outside our lockdown. Check all buildings, parks, and parking lots near the kidnap site that are large enough to land a helicopter."

"And check legitimate limousine carriers for missing or overdue limos," McGrath added. "Also check cargo trucks, mail trucks, and moving companies to see if any have reported any missing vehicles. Double your radius of search and double-check everything."

The icy fingers of panic were starting to twist his gut. They were six hours into the search for the girl, and the only hope they had of finding her was forcing a terror suspect nearly two thousand miles away to tell the truth.

CHAPTER 7

1745 MST, FRIDAY
ALBUQUERQUE, NM

S LOWLY, CARL FELT HIMSELF RISING from the drug-induced slumber into consciousness. As the fog in his brain cleared, his face and head felt itchy, like spider webs were stuck to his skin. He tried to bring his hands up to rub away the cobwebs. That's when he discovered his hands were shackled behind his back. The chains rattled when he moved his arms. He wiggled his feet and found they were similarly shackled to the chair.

The hell?

He took a deep breath and raised his head from the table with great difficulty. He regretted the move immediately, for a wave of nausea made his stomach contract in dry heaves. A hot sweat broke out on his face and torso, and his mouth felt dry like cotton. His breath tasted like stale coffee, and he was suddenly so hungry his stomach started growling.

Carl laid his forehead back on the table. Then he remembered the female cop had injected him with something. He was feeling the after-effects of her drug.

He sat still and calmed his breathing even as an electronic buzz accompanied the door opening to his left. He lifted his head off the table. It was the female boss cop, except now she was dressed in a dark two-piece pantsuit over a light blue blouse. Her dark blonde hair was still tied back. He could tell she wasn't a regular street cop. Maybe she was a detective or a lieutenant or something.

The door closed behind her, and she stood there for a moment, looking down at him with her hands on her hips. Her blazer was unbuttoned, and as Carl glanced down and up her frame, he got the feeling that she was fit, though she was perhaps five years past her prime and maybe fifteen or twenty pounds heavier than her ideal weight. She was a desk jockey. Still, she was attractive and had what he considered a really nice chest. Larger than average.

By the time he raised his gaze back to her face, he found a dark, almost hate-filled look in her brown eyes. He swallowed with great difficulty and spoke, but his voice rasped through his dry throat.

"What the hell is going on?"

She stepped up and sat on the table just to his left. The table was one of those old appliances that he'd seen way back in his early military days. It was fitting for a jail cell. It was a dark gray metal thing with square, hollow legs that were wide where they met the tabletop and narrow at the floor. The tabletop was overlaid with decades-old, scratched, and beat-up Formica that was white fifty years ago when the government bought it.

The cop just sat there silently. If she was trying to intimidate him, she was doing a damn good job. Carl took a deep breath and looked forward. He didn't give her the satisfaction of looking up at her. When she tapped her knuckles on the table to get his attention, he turned his head and focused his gaze to his left, eyes level with her breasts. He could see that she wore some kind of thick, under-wire bra, which he could certainly understand, being that she worked with a bunch of testosterone-filled, macho cops. A thick-stitched bra like hers wouldn't give men anything to fantasize about.

When she spoke, her voice was deep and husky, though still feminine. From her tone, he had no doubt that she was accustomed to getting her way and having her questions answered. From his military days, he recognized the commanding presence in her voice. She didn't bother to introduce herself.

"Where is the girl?" she said.

He kept his gaze locked on her breasts, the only defiance a chained man could show. "What girl?"

She leaned down with her left hand on the table until her head was in his personal space. Carl turned away and faced the concrete wall in front of him again.

"Look, we can do this the easy way or the hard way," she said.

He grunted at her. "You mean the *harder* way?" He wiggled his wrist and foot chains.

"This is your last chance to cooperate, Mr. Reyes."

Carl looked her in the eye. Her face was barely six inches from his. "Do I look like a fucking *Reyes*, you racist—"

She struck fast. One moment she was sitting on the table leaning sideways. The next, Carl saw a flash of motion and felt an explosion of pain under his armpit as she jacked her right knee hard into his ribs. He felt the tight grip of her hand on the left side of his head as she slammed his face onto the table. The right side of his head throbbed in pain as she held him there.

He gasped. "Bitch!"

"Where is she?" she whispered. "Give me a location, a contact name, something."

He felt her fiddle behind his ear, and suddenly, that nerve bundle erupted in pain. He screamed and squirmed, but he couldn't escape the pain. If he'd been in a wrestling contest, he could have surrendered by pounding a palm on the mat. All he could do was stomp his chained feet on the floor, but she got the message and let up the pressure.

He hadn't realized he'd closed his eyes, but when he opened them, he could hardly see through the tears of pain. He blinked, and his breath hissed through clenched teeth. A new wave of nausea swept over him as he tried to find his voice.

He heard a ping and saw the female cop retrieve her cell phone from her left pants pocket. She checked the screen, then replaced the device in her pocket.

She said, "You can either tell me, or you can tell my friends from Homeland. They're not as friendly as I am."

Carl nodded, and she let him up. He raised his head and glared at her. Cops can't beat the shit out of prisoners. No way was he going to let her get away with that. He'd hold out until someone of authority arrived, then he'd get his attorney and sue the crap out of the city and ruin this woman's career.

"I'm waiting," she said.

"You must be from Arizona, where all the cops think brown people are Mexican, aren't you?"

Without shifting her seated position on the table, she kicked him again. She rammed her knee into the same exact point of impact as the first kick.

He howled in pain, then nodded. "You want to know who has her?"

"Well?"

He gave her a line from one of his favorite TV shows. "Ima."

"Ima who?"

"I'm a gonna kick your—"

Blam!

He saw another flash of motion as she raised her left palm off the table. He heard the crack of bone on bone as her elbow hit his forehead. His head snapped back, and he fell forward onto the table, almost out cold.

He was dazed by her blow and let his head fall so that he faced away from her. He didn't want to give her a reason to keep beating on him, so he just played possum until someone else arrived.

He heard her mumble, "I've seen that show too, asshole."

What the fuck is going on? Cops don't beat prisoners! They can't.

He kept his eyes closed even while the door buzzed open.

CHAPTER 8

1752 MST, FRIDAY
ALBUQUERQUE, NM

H E WAS SAVED. ONCE HE raised the specter of having been beaten by this cop, he'd be isolated from her, and other cops would investigate his claim.

Heavy footsteps entered the room. He thought the footfalls sounded more like combat boots rather than street shoes of other detectives in suits. The door closed again with a metallic echo in the empty room. Carl was just about to raise his head when something about the voice of the new arrival sent chills down his spine. The man had a deep voice that was smoky and gravelly. He sounded like a cross between Vin Diesel and Jack Bauer, and he spoke in an almost hushed whisper.

"What are you doing in here, Agent?"

The female cop answered, "He's my prisoner, Agent Klipser."

"Your instructions were clear. No one was to be allowed in here."

"And no one has been."

"*You* have."

The female cop remained silent.

Agent Klipser's hard-edged voice paused for a moment, then said, "Did he wake up? Did he say anything?"

"No."

What the hell? She lied!

Carl realized the female cop was afraid of this new man, and suddenly so was he. His fantasy of appealing to someone who might protect him from the raging cop had morphed into the nightmare of a man who was even worse than she was.

The tone of the man's voice changed, and Carl got the feeling he was addressing someone else.

"Check him. Make sure he stays out for the next six hours for the trip back to Virginia." The man paused. "And you, Special…Agent… Cummings." The way he emphasized each word of her name gave Carl a mental picture of a big bully poking her in the chest with each word.

Special, poke, Agent, poke, Cummings, poke.

"Get us an APC with a full police and SWAT escort to the airport, and police chopper coverage. I'll give you the route once we're on the road."

Armored personnel carrier? What the fuck?

Cummings said, "Yes, sir."

The door buzzed open, and heels clicked on the concrete floor as someone—presumably Cummings—left. One of the newcomers moved closer behind him, and something hard landed on the table near his face.

The man to Carl's right said, "She is a complication."

The one with the gravelly voice, now known to Carl as Agent Klipser, said, "Operational security is Director McGrath's call. He still wants to recruit her."

"Mm-hmm," the other voice said. "Well, if they hit us, they'll hit us hard. Probably on the interstate, a known route to the airport from here."

Klipser replied, "I want everyone to think we're going to the airport, but we're not going anywhere near there. I've arranged for the Air Force to send a chopper to take us down to Holloman Air Force Base. I'll send our jet down there ahead of us, and we'll fly out of there to Virginia. I want to keep everyone guessing."

Carl opened his left eye, the one nearest the table since he was facing to his right. Unless the newcomers leaned down to the level of Carl's face, neither would know that his eye was open. He spied the case as a pair of hands opened it, and one of the hands removed a syringe with clear fluid in it. The syringe disappeared from his view, and the clear needle cap bounced on the table.

He remembered the intense pain from the first injection, and he pretended he was waking up to cover his gasp when he felt the agent roughly jab the long needle deep into his neck. Then the heat spread from his neck and into his chest again.

Then darkness enveloped him.

CHAPTER 9

TIME: UNKNOWN; DAY: UNKNOWN
LOCATION: UNKNOWN

CARL FLOATED SLOWLY TO FULL consciousness and found himself completely immobilized. In the full-length mirror before him, he saw that he was standing, strapped to a panel against a wall, except his orientation *felt* wrong. His brain's internal gyroscope told him he was lying on his back as if gravity was pressing against the front of his body, but the mirror against the wall six feet in front of him told him that he was, in fact, standing up.

He closed his eyes and took a deep breath. He heard voices nearby, but he couldn't distinguish what they were saying. He felt uncomfortable, and his jaw hurt. He tried to work the kink out of his jaw, but he couldn't move it. He couldn't swallow, either, which was extremely disconcerting because his throat was so dry it hurt. In fact, he couldn't move his mouth at all, he realized suddenly, because there was something stuck in it.

He opened his eyes again and realized he was, in fact, lying horizontally, and the mirror was mounted on the ceiling above him. At first, he studied the reflection of his own face. There was some kind of clear rubbery disk locking his mouth wide open. He explored the device with his tongue. It was smooth and had a hole in the center, maybe half an inch in diameter. He tried to wrestle the disk out with his tongue, but it was lodged tight. He tried to bite through the material, but the rubbery material flexed just enough to prevent him from breaking his teeth on it.

Then he focused on his body. He was naked, and there were

dozens—no, hundreds—of long and extremely thin acupuncture-like needles protruding from his body. The needles were stuck into his flesh from the top of his skull to the tip of his extremities and everywhere in between. The tip of each needle was connected to some kind of hair-thin, insulated filament wire. The filaments were loosely strapped into several bundles, and the half a dozen bundles extended up toward the ceiling, then across and down to a small metal box on a table that he could only barely see at the extreme edge of his peripheral vision. A man in a white smock was working at a laptop connected to the box.

At first, Carl thought he was undergoing some kind of surgery, and he had regained consciousness in the middle of the procedure. He tried calling out to the man who looked like a doctor, but only unintelligible grunts came from his throat because his mouth was locked open.

The doctor turned and studied Carl with emotionless eyes. He touched a Bluetooth device on his left ear and said, "The terrorist is awake."

Terrorist? What the hell?

Carl protested and tried to speak. If the doctor would only take the plug out of his mouth, he could find out what they wanted and answer their questions.

The doctor listened for a moment, then said, "Very well." He looked down at Carl. "This is going to hurt a bit. You see these leads." He pointed at the bundles of filament wires. "They will allow me to direct microvolts of electricity along any nerve path of your body that I choose. Let's begin with your right arm."

Carl saw the doctor retrieve a small tablet from his table and begin tapping on the surface. Suddenly, a jolt of electricity flashed from his shoulder to the fingertips of his right hand. The instantaneous pain was excruciating, and his arm felt like it was being microwaved, burned from the inside. He screamed, but only for a moment because the pain disappeared as quickly as it had begun.

Carl lay gasping, panting partly through his nose and partly through the hole in his mouthpiece. He watched in the ceiling mirror as his chest heaved with each breath. It was then that he noticed how many straps held his body to the table. Each leg had a leather strap at the ankle, at the shin, above and below the knee, and at the upper thigh.

His pelvis was strapped tightly to the table, as was his abdomen, but his ribs were not, and he realized that was so he could breathe. Each arm had straps at the wrist, above and below the elbow, and at the shoulder. There were foam pads under each elbow, no doubt to prevent injury.

His head lay in some kind of padded cradle, and his forehead was firmly strapped in. He also had two straps crossing his upper torso: one extended from his right armpit to his left shoulder, and the other extended from his left armpit to his right shoulder. The result was that his body was locked to the table and was completely immovable.

He had just watched his right arm tense and jitter violently under the jolt of an electric current. If he wasn't so thoroughly strapped down, he would either break a bone, pull a muscle, or tear a tendon or ligament from the strain.

"Okay, now you're going to feel this from your left shoulder, down your left leg, and down to your ankle, but only on the surface skin, not inside as you just experienced."

Carl interpreted that comment to mean the pain would not be as intense, but he was wrong. The skin of the left side of his body suddenly felt like it was on fire, as if someone was holding a red-hot iron against the whole left side of his body. He watched in the mirror as his body twitched and jerked, but the tight straps held him firmly.

First, he tried to bury the left side of his body deeper into the bed's foam pad. Then he tried to arch his back and jerk his body to dislodge the needles, but the straps prevented that. He couldn't escape, couldn't make any sudden moves, and couldn't dislodge any of the needles by scraping them against the leather straps.

All he could do was scream.

For a moment, the pain disappeared, then it moved to the right side of his face. He felt the involuntary fluttering contractions of his cheek muscles and felt a screaming pain rip through his ear. The pain was so intense, he swore he actually *heard* a ringing in his ear. It was an unbearable cacophony of sounds screeching inside his skull.

Then he saw a flash of red as the sight in his right eye dimmed to nothing, and he was filled with panic that the doctor was taking his eyesight. He begged and pleaded with unintelligible grunts, then screamed as the pain became too intense to bear.

Don't take my eyes! Oh God, please don't take my eyes!

It was too late. When the pain subsided, his right eye was blind. All he could perceive was a red splotch, an after-image of a burned-out retina. Then he started to cry, a great sobbing that racked his entire body.

He heard the doctor say, "I think he's ready."

The man paused and then said, "I know. This is a new record. Didn't even take one minute. He's not so tough strapped to the table."

A few seconds later, Carl heard steps approaching the table. They were heavy, clunky steps like the ones he'd heard in the FBI cell. His un-affected eye darted to the left as a man came into view. The man looked about mid-thirties, with military-cut black hair and a scruffy five-o'clock shadow, the kind that women would find sexy. He had a razor-sharp nose that made his black eyes look even more sinister. He was dressed in all black, at least the part of his upper body that Carl could see. He was a slender yet muscular man, and his turtleneck sweater flexed as his muscles worked. His collar covered his neck up to his chin.

The doctor handed the man a metal tool, which he inserted into the center of the plug in Carl's mouth. He grabbed Carl's chin and yanked downward, then easily levered the plug out. Carl worked his jaw open and closed a few times, then worked it left to right to relieve the muscle pain. Then he coughed and tried to swallow a few times. The doctor held a small plastic squirt bottle over his face with a narrow L-shaped straw. He squeezed the bottle, and a brief stream of water entered Carl's mouth. He swallowed gratefully.

When the newcomer spoke, Carl recognized his gravelly voice immediately. The man was Agent Klipser, one of the men who had re-trieved him from the female cop. His voice was deep and husky with a rumbling texture.

"Mr. Reyes, where is the girl?" he said. His words came out like a harsh whisper.

"What girl?" Carl said weakly. Tears flowed from his eyes. "I don't know anything about any girl." He gulped again, wishing for more water, then said, "My name is Johnson. Carl Johnson. Not Reyes."

Klipser nodded at the doctor, and a sudden flash of pain ignited Carl's spine. His screams echoed around the small room, as his voice was no longer muffled by the plug in his jaw. He screamed and screamed until he could no longer produce sound. He just lay there with his mouth wide open. His body jerked with an intense pain like nothing he had ever experienced. He felt like someone was cutting his back open and plucking his vertebrae out one at a time.

Suddenly, the pain disappeared, and he gasped for air, sobbing like a child. "Why are you doing this? I don't know anyone named Reyes. I don't know any girl."

Klipser said, "Well, when your memory improves, I'll come back." To the doctor, he said, "Hit him where it really hurts."

The doctor tapped on the pad, and before Carl could plead further, his groin ignited in pain.

CHAPTER 10

TIME: UNKNOWN; DAY: UNKNOWN
LOCATION: UNKNOWN

CARL WOKE UP IN A tiny, dimly lit, concrete cell smaller than his walk-in closet at home. It was maybe five feet square. The first thing he felt was a savage pain in his shoulder joints, and for a moment, he thought the doctor was still shocking him. Then he realized he was kneeling, hanging over to his left. His hands were cuffed behind his back, and the cuffs attached him to the concrete wall in some manner he couldn't see. The result was that his arms were wrenched painfully back and upward while his upper body leaned forward. His butt couldn't quite rest on his heels nor the floor, and almost his entire body weight was supported by his hyper-extended shoulder joints.

He tried to get upright on his knees and screamed from the pain of the effort. The tops of his feet felt like someone had used coarse sandpaper to grate all the skin off. For a moment, he sat gasping from the effort of trying to ease the pain in his shoulders, and that's when he noticed the stink of urine, vomit, and feces. He saw that he was actually squatting in it—his own waste—and so his stomach heaved, adding more waste to the floor.

Then he remembered the electroshock torture, and the memory brought back a very real echo of the pain in his spine and his groin. His body still hurt all over. As he looked around the room, he realized he could see out of both eyes. The throbbing pain that lingered in his right eye felt more like a mild headache compared to his other aches and pains.

Before he could get himself upright on his knees, the steel door opened, and two men dressed in black stood framed in the darkness beyond the doorway. Carl's prison cell was suddenly lit by an extremely bright halogen spotlight in the ceiling. He could feel its heat on his skin and saw his dark shadow on the floor. But the hallway beyond the door was dark, and he couldn't make out any of the men's features until one stepped into the tiny cell.

The man held what looked like a narrow fire hose with a chrome nozzle. He yanked back on a square lever and hit Carl point-blank in the face with a hard stream of cold water. Carl screamed, and when he did, he took a mouthful of water. The water slammed down his throat and up his nose, and he choked and gasped as the hard stream of water scoured the rest of his body.

He tried to clamp his legs together to protect his privates, but the man had expert aim. The water hit him so hard, he felt like he'd been kicked in the groin. He threw up again, which earned him another blast in the face. He took the torrent of water in his eyes, nose, and mouth, and even on his throat, leaving him with the feeling he'd been punched in his Adam's apple.

The man aimed the flow of water around Carl's feet, effectively clearing the floor around him. After he shut off the water and stepped back, the second man stepped forward. He held a one-gallon tank that looked like something you'd spray roaches with. Carl found this mental analogy disgusting. He was the roach.

The guard pressed a button on the nozzle and sprayed an antiseptic liquid over Carl's body for a few seconds. The liquid stung, especially on his feet and in his eyes, but he found the pain insignificant compared to the torture. It was merely a nuisance pain, a troublesome mosquito, depositing an itchy stinger that couldn't be scratched.

Both men retreated into the hallway, put down their appliances, and came back in. One grabbed Carl in a choke hold while the other detached whatever was holding him to the wall. When the restraint came loose, Carl simply collapsed, and the two men dragged him out of the cell and down the hall. With his wrists still cuffed behind his back, the two men hauled him by his armpits. Now he knew why the tops of his feet hurt. The hallway floor was rough and grainy concrete. As the men pulled him down the hall, the tops of his feet dragged across the floor, further agitating the raw, burning wounds.

They put him on the table again and strapped his legs down. Then they uncuffed him and strapped his arms and torso down. He didn't fight them. He couldn't fight them. His body was too weak and too sore. All he could do was plead with them to listen to him—that there had been some kind of mistake, that he wasn't the man they thought he was. His pleas fell on deaf ears, though. These were hard men, probably soldiers, and they were emotionless. He could tell they'd done this many times, and his pain and agony meant nothing to them.

After they left the room, the doctor came in, still dressed in his white smock. Or maybe he was wearing a different white smock. Carl pleaded with him too, but the man was equally emotionless. He grabbed Carl's jaw and pressed his fingers and thumb into the soft flesh and nerve bundles under the jawbone. When Carl opened his mouth to scream, the doctor forced the soft plastic disk into his mouth again. The skin at the corners of his mouth split from dryness. Then the antiseptic residue caused the split skin to burn. It stung and itched, just like other parts of his body, but now the individual occurrences of pain were starting to compound into something more than a nuisance. And he couldn't massage the bruises or wounds. He couldn't lick his lips for a temporary respite. All he could do was suffer through the discomfort.

Carl refocused on the doctor as the man grabbed what looked like a green plant-watering jug and began pouring water into his open mouth. The doctor kept pouring even after his mouth was full, and water was running down his cheeks and neck. He put the jug down on the floor and stood over Carl, watching.

Carl breathed slowly through his nose, and his eyes went wide as the doctor calmly pinched his nostrils. He tried to plead again, releasing tiny bubbles of air with the effort. Then the doctor punched him in the belly and stepped back. Water from Carl's mouth sprayed upward, and when his reflex made him try to suck in air, some of the water went into his lungs. And then he started drowning.

The need to cough and breathe at the same time was excruciating, but he couldn't fight the reflex. He simply lay there choking, watching the doctor watch him. Finally, he managed to swallow the water that remained in his mouth, even as he kept choking. After a few more seconds, he was able to regain some composure. The doctor stepped forward and used the metal piece to remove the disk from his mouth.

"Please! You don't have to do this. I'll tell you whatever you want to know."

The doctor tapped his earpiece and said, "He's ready for you." He paused. "Yeah, for real this time."

Familiar boot steps entered the room a minute later, and Mr. Gravelly Voice stood over Carl. "I understand this is going to take some time, Mr. Reyes. Opponents of harsh interrogation techniques argue that a suspect will say anything under duress just to stop the pain. You see, right now, you still have hope. You're still thinking you can manufacture some believable story that will stall us. Something we will have to actually go out into the world to verify."

Klipser nodded at the doctor, then continued, "But we're willing to go through this time-consuming process with you for as long as it takes. Or—" he shrugged. "You can just tell me what I want to know." The man paused. "Where is she?"

"Okay, okay." Carl paused for a moment, still breathing heavily. "Okay, I killed her."

Klipser smiled. "I can see in your eyes that you're lying."

He nodded at the doctor again, and the man levered the plug back into his mouth. This time, he produced a thick plastic tube that fit precisely through the hole in the disk and stuffed it down Carl's throat. He fought and struggled and screamed. Then he gagged as the tube blocked his air passage. He couldn't breathe. He felt it actually moving down into his throat.

The doctor reached for his water jug again and began pouring water into a funnel on the upper end of the tube. The water flowed straight into Carl's lungs, except this time, he couldn't cough it up. He felt his chest muscles constricting, tightening, fluttering, and his heart was thumping wildly as he panicked. He was suffocating for real this time, and he knew it. He was dying.

After a moment, the doctor pulled the tube from his throat, but Carl had no energy to breathe. His eyesight dimmed to a distant tunnel before he died.

Almost.

Klipser jabbed him hard just under the sternum, and a fountain of water exploded from his mouth. The doctor quickly rotated the bed so that Carl faced the floor, and the rest of the water drained from his lungs. Then, he began a painful hacking cough as his body strained to get air. He retched again and again.

That was when he noticed the drain hole in a depression in the floor. It had no cover plate that could get clogged with debris from the torture victims. The bastards had thought of everything.

They had the torture thing down to an exact science and probably had the goddamn table designed or modified specifically for the purpose for which it was now being used. The engineer in Carl recognized that they had bearings at the head and foot of the table so the table could rotate along its long axis. He figured the device had a spring-loaded locking pin that was easy to pull out with one hand, so the doctor could effortlessly rotate the table with the other hand.

The doctor hauled the bed faceup, and Klipser looked down at him again. "We can do this all day."

Carl said, "She's alive. I promise. I'll give her back." He started sobbing again. "Just let me go, and I'll give her back."

Klipser said, "I'd rather you tell me where she is before I release you."

He gave a head-nod to the doctor, who then found a prominent vein in Carl's right arm and stuck a needle in it. Then he taped the catheter in place. He reached out of Carl's sight and brought back a metal rack with several hooks on it. Clear bags with liquids of various hues hung from the hooks, and clear plastic tubing draped from the bottom of each bag. The doctor fiddled with the tubes, and Carl got the impression he was connecting them all to the catheter he just stuck in his arm.

At first, he just felt a mild warmth spreading throughout his body. He'd heard that the heart was such a powerful biological pump that it could circulate blood to anywhere in the body in less than thirty seconds. Carl felt the warm tingle of the chemicals flowing through his body.

Suddenly, the warmth turned into a painful icy feeling. Then, a few seconds later, his entire body erupted with a searing fire, as though every vein and artery burned. The pain was everywhere at once. It filled his head, his chest and arms, his legs and feet, his back and neck, and there was absolutely nothing he could do about it except scream.

CHAPTER 11

TIME: UNKNOWN; DAY: UNKNOWN
LOCATION: UNKNOWN

T HE NEXT TIME CARL AWOKE in his cell, he felt different.

The first time is always the hardest.

He'd forgotten what famous person tossed that bit of wisdom out into the world a hundred years ago. Maybe it applied to a first kiss, or a first job interview, or a first sporting competition, but whoever thought up that little saying had never been tortured, Carl thought. The first time had been hard, but the second time had been far worse.

It seemed as if Klipser and the doctor were pacing themselves. Maybe that strategy was, in itself, a psychological component of the torture. Maybe they figured if Carl concluded that each successive interrogation was going to be worse than the previous torture, then he'd cooperate sooner.

The first time he woke up in his cell, he'd still had the feeling that this whole affair was a big misunderstanding—a case of mistaken identity—and that he could explain his way out if given the opportunity to prove who he was, or rather, who he was *not*. Now he knew there was no hope of rescue or salvation.

After the first torture session, he had quickly realized that his eyesight was not gone. The result of that particular torture—electroshock to the eyes—was temporary. He recalled his sheer panic in believing he had lost an eye. The discovery that he could still see had given him a small amount of hope, but now he had the distinct feeling that Klipser and the doctor had planned that outcome.

The pain from the second torture session lingered. His body had been fried on the *inside* by whatever chemicals the doctor had injected him with, and he was still aching as his body absorbed or broke down the chemicals. His throat was raw from screaming. He felt a fatigue deep inside every muscle of his body.

The government agents were convinced he was someone named Reyes, but they would not explain why they thought so. He knew instinctively that they would not stop torturing him until he told them what they wanted to know, but he had no information to give them.

They just kept asking him about a girl, but they wouldn't tell him who she was. Maybe if he knew her identity, he could give them some kind of meaningful answer. Maybe it was someone he'd seen before. Maybe she was the daughter of one of his clients. Maybe she was the daughter of some politician who had attended one of the many charity events he typically spent time volunteering.

He groaned loudly as he tried to take his weight off his stressed shoulders. He was again chained to the wall with his wrists hiked way up behind his back. His knees were sore from extended contact with the concrete floor. The tops of his feet still throbbed.

He examined the floor of his cell. It was clean this time because he hadn't taken any food or water since his capture. Still, he noticed the drain in the center of the tiny cell. Like the torture room, this drain had no grated cover. The floor of his cell was smooth, no doubt for easy cleaning, while the hallway that tore up the tops of his feet was rough concrete.

He got his balance on his knees, but he was weak and wobbly. He started to lean forward but screamed in pain as the strain on his shoulders ignited again. He tried to settle back with his butt on his heels, but his wrists were chained up too high. He tried to fight his way to his feet. He was halfway up when the two guards opened the door.

They were watching him, he realized, on some kind of closed-circuit camera, and they showed up always right after he awoke. The guard with the hose hit Carl in the groin straight away, and he fell almost to the floor, screaming as his arms were yanked back by the chain. The guard was oblivious to his pain and kept hosing him down with the hard stream of water. He gagged and choked as water was forced up his nose and into his mouth again.

The second guard sprayed him with disinfectant, and they dragged him down the hall and into his private torture chamber. Then they strapped him to the table, and the doctor went to work on him again.

The next time he awoke in his cell, he entertained a small number of positive thoughts. He realized the doctor had actually fed him intravenously during the chemical torture. He figured they were also slipping antibiotics and vitamins into the chemical concoction they used to fry his insides. It certainly wouldn't do to have a prisoner die of starvation in the middle of his interrogation, certainly not when they apparently needed him alive so badly.

As he fought his way to his knees, he actually chuckled. At least he was getting enough water to drink. He probably swallowed half the water they poured down his throat on the table, even as he choked on the rest. By his count, Klipser and the doctor had suffocated him by water four separate times in between the chemical and electroshock tortures, and he was pretty sure his heart and lungs had completely stopped functioning two of those times.

They actually killed him twice. Both times, he awoke to find the doctor resuscitating him with emergency medical equipment, and it was that specific fear that kept breaking him. *It was one thing*, he thought, *to know you were going to get tortured* almost *to death, but it was quite another thing to know they were going to push you over the edge and really let you die.* The true panic came from not knowing if they were going to bring you back the next time.

Even though they watered him and fed him intravenously, he was still extremely hungry, and his stomach growled fiercely as he noticed the brown food packet on the floor just inside the door. It was an MRE— Meal, Ready-to-Eat—in military parlance. It was an individual, self-contained field ration pack that contained plenty of nutritious calories. He'd seen them, but he'd never eaten one. He'd had plenty of C-rations, or combat rations, back in his military days thirty years ago, when pre-packaged military meals in cans tasted like shit. Then someone had invented the MRE, which was cheaper and easier to mass-produce, and reportedly a hell of a lot tastier.

The MRE packet was just outside his reach. Maybe they had measured the lengths of his legs and put the package that length away plus one additional inch.

Fucking jerks.

At that moment, he realized the guards had not come to get him, even though he'd been awake for over a minute. He gazed up at the tiny dark camera lens stuck in the concrete wall over the door opening.

As he got to his feet, he realized how depleted his body was. His legs quivered. His belly cramped painfully. So he just stood there waiting for the guards, eyeballing the dinner packet. After a few more minutes, it was clear that his captors were trying another method of torture on him. The MRE was nothing more than psychological torture. He knew that, but he wanted it anyway. He needed it.

Even if he could reach it, they probably would come and beat the crap out of him again before he got the packet open.

They're fucking with me, but what the hell.

Trying for the food would keep his mind off the residual pain from the torture that was still pulsing through his body. It would keep his mind off his next interrogation.

He stretched out his foot, but the MRE was just beyond his reach. He couldn't turn sideways either to get a little extra distance. He stared at the packet, but willpower alone did nothing to move it closer to him. Then he imagined himself using "the Force" to move the packet, but the Jedi mind trick didn't work either.

He stared at the packet and fantasized about its unknown contents. Maybe it held Mom's scrumptious meatloaf, mashed potatoes, and gravy. Maybe there was a cheeseburger in there. Then his eyes watered, and he found himself sobbing quietly, uncontrollably.

Fuck!

Forget the torture. Hell, he'd tell them anything they wanted to hear just for a bite of the contents in that packet.

With his wrists hiked up behind his back, he tried a little gymnastics. He leaned his head down, and with great difficulty, he got his cuffed wrists under his butt. Then he kicked his feet up and actually hung upside down by his wrists for a few seconds before he was painfully able to get first one foot through his arms, then the other. Finally, he stood facing the wall with his wrists now cuffed in front, and he easily stepped toward the door and reached the MRE packet with his right foot. He scooted it closer, then gripped it between his toes and raised it up high enough to grab it with a hand.

He knew that once they saw what he'd done on their camera, they'd come running. So he got the edge of the packet between his teeth, ripped it open, and hurriedly squeezed the cold, squishy contents into his mouth. It was spaghetti and meat sauce.

He had just swallowed the last bit when he heard boots in the hallway. Klipser stepped forward quickly. Carl didn't even have time to assume any kind of defensive position—not that it would have made a difference. The agent moved to Carl's side and struck hard and fast, jabbing him hard in the gut with a knife-edge hand strike.

Carl folded instantly and vomited his food all over the floor. Then he went to his knees, gasping for breath with his cuffed wrists hanging up over his head. For a brief moment, he entertained another positive thought—a small victory over the evil government agent. He threw up most of the food in his stomach, but not all of it.

Then he saw the doctor step through the door with a syringe, and he knew he'd fallen right into their trap, just like they wanted. The doctor jabbed him in the thigh and squeezed the plunger. Then he and Klipser left.

Motherfuckers!

The effects of the drug—nausea and diarrhea—were nearly instantaneous. Within minutes, he threw up everything remaining in his stomach and voided his intestines until there was absolutely nothing left inside him. There was no way to fight the chemicals.

Even after his body was completely empty, he continued to retch with dry heaves, and his bowels continued to work until he was so completely drained of energy that he couldn't even sit upright. He fell over sideways in his own filth and had no choice but to lie there and wallow in it.

And that, he finally realized, was the true essence of the torture. He'd been given a tiny measure of hope only to have it violently snatched away.

He felt the emotions of depression and self-pity wash over him, but he couldn't stop them. He began to sob again, and his body quivered.

He felt anger too. If he had the tools and the skills, he'd find a way to escape and hunt down Klipser, all his minions, and the doctor. Then he'd find their boss, the unseen man named Director McGrath, and that woman cop too.

But he had no tools, no skills, and no way to escape. All he could do was lay there in his own mess and acknowledge how truly helpless he was at the hands of these agents.

Suddenly, he froze. He stopped sobbing and sat upright. It was then he realized he had one way to escape, and they wouldn't be able to stop him. He still had hope.

CHAPTER 12

P ECULIAR QUESTIONS OCCUPIED MOST OF Carl Johnson's
waking moments. What kind of human would torture another
human? What kind of man would design instruments of torture,
from the primitive tools of the Middle Ages—designed to rip away
pieces of the body or stretch it until limbs tore off—to the high-tech
computer-controlled torture he had repeatedly endured? What kind of
human would use such tools to inflict pain on another?

Where did the US government find such men? Did they volunteer
for it, or was it required training for CIA agents, or Homeland agents,
or whoever those people were? How did they learn the processes and
techniques of torture? How did they learn the human body's threshold of
pain? On whom did they practice?

Who designed and developed the computerized torture equipment?
What kind of doctor consulted on such an evil device? Where did the
government find computer programmers to design and test the software,
knowing what the device would be used for?

What kind of person actually studied and refined the torture methodologies so they could be made to inflict pain even more efficiently and
more severely? Who taught the torturers the psychology of the effects of
such barbarism on their victims?

The short-term effects of torture psychology seemed, at least to Carl,
to be well understood. The goal was a fast and efficient path to the truth

if, in fact, torture actually resulted in the truth, but what about the long-term psychological effects of torture? Did the government also have a rehabilitation program for its agents who fell victim to enemy torture? How much pain could a normal man without intensive military training take before he broke or went insane?

Carl now understood the psychology of torture, both of the victim and of the torturer, but not because he'd been schooled in the science. He understood because he had witnessed firsthand the mental and emotional processes that he and Agent Klipser had morphed through.

He guessed he'd been captive three weeks, maybe four. For sure, he'd been tortured long enough for the government agents to know that he didn't possess the information they sought, and he wasn't the man they thought he was.

They *should have known* he wasn't the one, but they didn't. Agent Klipser was firmly convinced that Carl *was* the one. Despite having no logical reason to believe that conclusion, the man *knew* Carl was still holding out. The agent was determined to break him and get him to reveal the desired information. Because of his firm conviction, Klipser seemed incapable of realizing his victim was already broken. Carl knew the possibility that he was not Reyes was not even being considered, so Klipser had become even more brutal in his efforts to break him.

Part of the torture of being shackled to the wall with his wrists behind his back was that he was forced to try to sleep on his knees, which was extremely painful. As a result, he was severely sleep-deprived, no doubt a result planned by Klipser.

Twenty years ago, he could have knelt on his knees on concrete all day long. Now, at age fifty-three, his knees were on fire. He kept falling over sideways, yanking his shoulders back. Neither could he squat on his haunches or sit his butt on the concrete.

After a few days, he'd found a perfectly balanced *standing* position, and he found that he could actually sleep on his feet. With his heels about two feet away from the wall and three feet apart, toes pointed outward at about forty-five degrees, he found he could lean forward against the chain just far enough so he was a tad off vertical. That way, he could lock his knees so he wouldn't collapse when he nodded off, and there was minimal strain on his shoulders from the cable that bound his hands behind him.

As soon as Klipser and his crew realized Carl was sleeping on his feet, they positioned a huge concert speaker right inside his open door and turned it up to what had to be full volume. Heavy metal and rap. Screeching guitar solos from a 1980s rock concert followed the booming bass and shouting gangster lyrics from 1990s urban music.

Carl was old-school Air Force, though. When he enlisted back in the mid-1970s, all the young techs always got pulled onto the emergency exercise teams to practice wartime deployments. They never got deployed, but they spent many days sitting around on the flight line, waiting for the troop transport aircraft to fly them somewhere.

Carl, along with all the other bored deployment radio techs, became very adept at sleeping while sitting against the hangar walls, with the screaming engines of the C-5 *Galaxy* and C-141 *Starlifter* cargo jets taxiing by, not even a hundred feet from where they slept.

So Carl tuned out the loud music and continued to sleep lightly on his feet. He was able to rest just enough to allow his tortured body to recover somewhat between sessions. He got enough sleep to stay sane.

Sometimes, the bright halogen light in his cell was on for extended periods of time, and sometimes it was off. They fed him real meals from MRE packets at unpredictable times each day, though each time, he assumed they'd come in later to inject him and force him to regurgitate the food. Sometimes they did, and sometimes they didn't. It was all part of their torture.

The questions were always the same. It was always about a girl. Today when they asked him, he had been connected to the electroshock computer.

"Who are you talking about? Tell me, please. Maybe I've seen her. Maybe I know her."

Wrong answer. The doctor set fire to the nerves of his lower spine.

"Wait! Okay, okay. She's dead."

Wrong answer. More pain. Upper spine this time.

"No, please! I took her to Albuquerque." That's easy, right? That's where they arrested him. "She's on an abandoned farm in the South Valley."

Then the agent asked him the address. He made one up, but a quick map search on Klipser's laptop indicated there was no such place.

More pain. Left hip.

"South America."

More pain.

"Mexico."

What part?

"El Paso."

"El Paso is in Texas, Mr. Reyes," the agent said.

More pain.

Over time, Carl knew for sure the doctor had actually killed him—several times by drowning and at least once by focusing the current from the electroshock computer to make his heart and lungs cease functioning. He remembered that experience with particular clarity. His brain registered that his heart and lungs had actually stopped, and he was aware of the scary approach of the darkness of suffocation. Each time, his eyesight faded to a dim tunnel of light, then the light faded almost to nothing. The doctor resuscitated him, pulling him back from the brink.

Over the days of torture, Carl found himself silently begging for the pain so he would know he was still alive and that the doctor wasn't really going to let him die. He finally accepted the reality that the agents would never release him—never stop torturing him—until they found the girl. That resolution was completely outside of Carl's control.

He'd read somewhere that the FBI said if a kidnapped child wasn't found within seventy-two hours, the child most likely would never be found alive. Still, they kept at him like there was some chance she was alive. They must have figured his people—Reyes's people—had kept her alive for some other reason.

He had known all along that there was only one path of escape, but he didn't have the courage to attempt it. Now he was ready.

Clarity of purpose is an amazing equalizer.

Carl realized he wasn't as helpless as he'd previously thought. He also discovered the torture was an intense, full-body workout. For two or three hours at a time, sometimes several times each day, every muscle in his body was straining hard against the straps on the table.

Now that he had a purpose and a means to escape, he realized that while his mind had grown weak and pathetic as he fought depression, his body had grown hard and lean. He'd dropped at least ten pounds of body fat. He was amazed at how much stronger he felt. Still, he knew he had strength for only one escape attempt.

CHAPTER 13

TIME: UNKNOWN; DAY: UNKNOWN
LOCATION: UNKNOWN

THE EVER-PRESENT MUSIC WENT SILENT, and he listened to the guards approach his doorway. Since awakening, he'd been concentrating on stretching his muscles without moving to loosen up a bit. Now that the guards were coming for him, he worked his neck, rolling his chin to his chest, then rotating his ears to his shoulders, back and forth. One time, when he looked down at his body, he could see muscle definition in his abs, hip flexors, and thighs.

As usual, one of the guards hosed him down with a hard blast of cold water. This time, though, Carl jerked his body sideways and used his thigh to protect his groin. Every time the sadistic bastard tried to hit him where it hurt, he'd twist his body a bit and foil the man's aim.

He kept his head dipped down so the man couldn't force water in his eyes, up his nose, or down his throat. The guard kept at him, but finally, the man admitted defeat and shut off the hose. Carl closed his eyes as the second guard sprayed him down with the antiseptic solution.

He didn't struggle as the guards unshackled him from the wall. With his wrists still cuffed behind his back, they led him out of the cell, one man holding firmly to each of his arms. He tried to walk normally as they manhandled him down the hallway.

As he walked, he studied the details about the hallway. It was concrete, but it definitely looked residential rather than a subterranean chamber of an industrial building or medical complex.

The ceiling was low, and if his hands hadn't been cuffed, he could have reached up and touched it. He'd had a brief glimpse of the base of a stairway immediately outside his cell to the left, but he saw nothing beyond that. As a real estate agent, he'd seen lots of basements, and most looked a lot like this one—windowless, low, and cramped.

The hallway was maybe ten feet long. Then he turned to the left and passed through a standard-sized, unfinished doorway into the torture room. The room measured about fifteen feet square and had the same bare concrete walls as his cell and the hallway. The walls were laced with standard metal conduit a foot off the floor, with metal power receptacles spaced every few feet. The receptacles were outdoor types with spring-loaded, weather-proof covers, no doubt for when the torture room got hosed down. There were no windows.

The only furnishings in the room were the military-grade metal table and the torture table. The metal table held the doctor's electroshock computer gadget. An open cabinet mounted to the wall above the table displayed a variety of medical supplies and clear bags of the chemicals used in Carl's catheter. As he entered the room, he saw a deep, white plastic utility sink mounted on the wall to his right, where the doctor could get water for the drowning sessions.

Carl knew he wasn't the first man to be a resident of the facility and occupy the torture table, and he wouldn't be the last. The torture table was a heavy-duty metal device on a gleaming square post frame. A thick, sturdy, circular cradle was attached to the head of the bed, and another at the foot allowed the bed to be rotated upside-down lengthwise so water or other bodily fluids could drain into the depression under the table. Carl stepped over to the bed and noticed the thick plastic mattress pad was somewhat molded to the shape of his body.

The air in the room felt warm and extra dry. It was at least ten degrees warmer than his cell, a condition that his naked body appreciated. His cell was warm enough to survive without succumbing to illness, but it was not warm enough to be comfortable. Now he was able to relax a bit and release some of his tension, which seemed odd considering he knew he was going to be tortured again.

Along with the scent of antiseptic cleaner, he thought he could detect the faint smell of evergreen trees. The idea popped into his mind that the house was in the woods, or the mountains, where no one could hear him scream.

The guards hesitated behind him, and it occurred to Carl that they always had to drag him in and lift him onto the table. He helped them out of a predicament they were clearly unprepared for—getting a fully conscious man situated on the torture table. He turned and sat on the mattress, then pivoted on his butt and swung his legs up. He *let* the guards strap his legs down. He waited as they uncuffed his wrists and lay back as they strapped the rest of his body to the table. He didn't resist, and the guards traded glances of uncertainty at his cooperation.

"I hope you're proud of yourselves," he said.

He looked at each of the young men as they strapped his head into the cradle, and he was satisfied to see neither would meet his gaze. He could tell they were hardened soldiers. They were no doubt well-trained in the art of depersonalizing their torture victims—real or perceived terrorists—who were resistant or hateful until the end. Now he could see the uncertainty on their faces, the crack in their armor, but he knew neither man would ever act on that uncertainty.

As he waited for the doctor and Klipser to arrive, he studied the ceiling. To the left of the mirror was an air vent to deliver fresh air to the room. To the right of the mirror was the return vent for not-fresh air. He could hear the rush of air entering through the left vent, and he could feel the warmth flowing over his body.

As he waited, he wondered how his torturers were feeling. Surely, they must be suffering some degree of frustration, unable to extract the needed information they thought he held. Maybe they were as depressed as he had been. That thought made him chuckle out loud, and his two guards paused in the doorway and looked back at him.

Carl now realized the human body could survive extreme pain. *He* could survive extreme pain. On the other hand, he recognized it was not the pain itself, but the *fear of pain*, that left people malleable and susceptible to control and intimidation. He'd had so much of it for so long, he knew he would continue to survive it, no matter what they did to him.

The government agents still controlled his body, his environment, and his situation, but they no longer controlled his mind or his will. He had *hope*. They could no longer take that away. It felt amazingly powerful to have control of one tiny aspect of his situation. All he had to do was survive this last session.

Agent Klipser and the doctor walked in, and though Carl's head was restrained, in his peripheral vision, he saw both men pause as they looked at him. He saw their gazes dart toward each other, and as they moved into his field of view, he glared at them. He was certain that for the first time, they both saw contempt in his eyes instead of fear.

Klipser regarded him with equal contempt as he moved around the foot of the bed, but the doctor walked around the head of the table, and Carl eyeballed him the entire way. The doctor wouldn't meet his gaze, and Carl felt an immense satisfaction at the man's discomfort.

"Fuckers."

Klipser opened a laptop, and when the screen lit up after a couple seconds, he tapped some keys. Then he tilted the display in Carl's direction. On the screen were three faces that were now very familiar to Carl.

"Tell me everything you know about these men. I want their names, aliases, home addresses, bank accounts, family members, and other known associates."

Carl snorted. "How the fuck am I supposed to know someone else's bank accounts, you stupid mu'fucker?"

Klipser and the doctor looked at each other. The doctor narrowed his eyes. This was something he hadn't given them before—attitude. It felt good too. It made Carl feel powerful, even while he was helpless.

The three men on the laptop screen looked like hoodlums to Carl. They looked like drug runners he had seen growing up in his hometown of Compton, except these were Mexicans, not Blacks. In some of the surveillance photos, they wore khakis or chinos and untucked shirts of muted colors, like beige and cream and soft pastel mauve. They wore hats, earrings, and so many thick gold chains that each one of them looked like he might fall over at any moment if he leaned too far off-center.

In some of the photos, the men wore ridiculously expensive full-length tan cashmere or black leather coats. In the close-up photos, they looked cocky, like they were at the top of the hoodlum food chain, like they knew nobody would dare mess with them.

"I don't know those assholes," Carl said. "So quit flappin' your shit-hole at me, and let's get on with this."

"Where's the girl, Mr. Reyes?"

Carl laughed. "She's dead, bitch! You've wasted all this time tortur-ing the wrong guy when you should have been out looking for her." He paused as he glared at Agent Klipser. "Besides, do I look like a fucking *Reyes*, you White-trash, racist piece of shit?"

Agent Klipser remained silent.

Carl continued to rant, "You fucking pussies. I'm a patriot and a decorated Air Force officer. I've been entrusted with military secrets less than a hundred people on the planet know about. Even the president and Congress aren't briefed on the kinds of projects I've worked on."

Klipser seemed nonplussed. "Where is the girl?"

"Fuck you," Carl said. He'd had enough of their nonsense. He needed to get through the torture session so he could make his escape. "I don't know anything about that fucking girl."

Klipser, calm as ever, said, "I'm prepared to get much more aggres-sive with our questioning."

"More aggressive? Bring it on, you prick. I think you're running out of torture techniques, dickhead. I don't know where your fucking girl is. So quit yappin' at me and bring the pain."

They brought the pain.

Three hours later, the doctor removed all the electrical leads from his body. The guards reentered the room and unstrapped his leather re-straints. They started to drag his depleted body off the table, but they backed off suddenly when they realized he was still conscious.

He took a deep breath and rolled onto his side. He groaned and piv-oted on his butt to sit up under his own power. He paused on the edge of the table with his feet resting on the floor and his palms parked on each side of his butt to keep from wobbling too much.

He glanced over at Klipser and sneered at him. He wanted to shout and cuss at him, but his throat was too raw from screaming. He could tell the man was clearly displeased with the doctor's lack of progress. Or maybe the agent was pissed because Carl didn't succumb completely to their torture. He twisted and tossed a cocky grin behind him at the stunned doctor.

"Is that all you got, Doc?" he said hoarsely. To Klipser, he said, "You ain't shit, bitch. We can do this all day, every day, but I still don't know where that fucking girl is."

He turned away and slid off the torture bed, then pretended to stumble and lose his balance. He ended up on his hands and knees on the concrete floor, and both guards stepped forward to grab an arm. That's when he attacked.

CHAPTER 14

1706 EST, DAY 11

ARLINGTON HEIGHTS, VA, OPERATIONS HOUSE

AGENT NANCY PALMER PACED BACK and forth across the operations room. As she walked, she rolled her shoulders forward six times, then backward six, taking a slow deep breath with each roll. She did a variety of standing stretches, mostly in-place moves to relieve tension.

She paused and looked over the shoulders of the two analysts on duty. They were entrenched in the research tasks she'd given them earlier, but that wasn't why she didn't interrupt their work. She needed time to think, and she often did her best thinking on her feet. While stretching, a corner of her brain continued to pull at irritating fragments of evidence about the terrorist, trying to make sense of them.

Her shift began at four o'clock in the afternoon. She and McGrath each had twelve-hour shifts that overlapped slightly at start and finish, and she'd been on duty for a little over an hour.

It was day number eleven for Alfonso Reyes, and Pete Klipser hadn't broken him yet. That in itself was incredible. No terror suspect had ever endured the new regimen of interrogation procedures for more than three days. Most were babbling after less than a day of interrogation, giving up the requested information and even revealing secrets not asked for.

There had been several times when they thought Reyes had broken. Many of the sessions had left him a sobbing, whimpering shadow of a man, and he had pleaded for mercy every time except the current session. He screamed and hollered and cursed, but he didn't beg, and he didn't cooperate. All he gave Pete was attitude. That anomaly gave Palmer pause, and she was still trying to process that. It was as though the man had somehow discovered a well of inner strength.

Aaron McGrath was under increasing pressure from the president about their lack of progress. The whole purpose of the TER agency was to break down the will of a terrorist and get fast results by any means necessary, to save lives and prevent attacks on the American homeland. Yet, they were in the eleventh day of the terror event, and the suspect was still resisting, refusing to give them the vital information they needed to find Melissa Mallory.

Agent Palmer knew Aaron was the wrong choice to lead the investigation because he was too close to the victim. She knew firsthand the kind of inner turmoil and stress that was eating at his gut. Still, there was no way he was going to willingly relinquish command of the TER team, and the president most certainly was not going to remove him. That meant Palmer couldn't reveal the new suspicions about the terrorist that had been teasing her brain for the last hour.

She stopped in the middle of the room, unaware that she'd begun pacing again. Knees locked, she leaned over, placed her palms flat on the carpeted floor, and held that stretch for almost a minute. The carpet was a deep tan color with a tough knit texture. It looked expensive, unlike the cheap pile carpet in her own apartment.

Still leaning over, she massaged her hamstrings for a few seconds. The black fabric of her cotton-wool suit was tight against her body, but it flexed easily and allowed her to move freely.

Slowly, she raised upright with her chin tucked against her chest until she was standing straight. Then she rolled her head again and returned her attention to the terrorist.

She'd heard of extreme cases where foreign agents were programmed under hypnosis and other subconscious conditioning. In fact, they were so well-conditioned that they actually believed the lies and misinformation they would likely give up under harsh interrogation. She suspected that those agents were prepped for possible capture by being subjected to the same kind of intense interrogation techniques they were likely to face if captured. The idea was that realistic torture training would help them to be even more believable as they divulged misinformation under duress.

Alfonso Reyes was no espionage agent, though. He was a mid-level cartel drug lord. He was a bully who had risen in the ranks by threatening and terrorizing lesser employees or others affiliated with his drug trade. He succeeded in business because he could instill fear. His hold on others came from his small army of thugs, not from any skills or training he possessed.

There was absolutely nothing in any dossier on the man that suggested he'd had any kind of advanced covert ops training. So it was unfathomable that an untrained and unconditioned drug lord could survive eleven days on the table. To make matters even more unbelievable, Reyes wasn't even giving up misinformation. He was giving up *no* information.

Under torture, the man had given no coherent deception that would be expected of a trained operator. His babble had bounced from one extreme to the other. First, he said he didn't know the girl. Then, he claimed she was dead. Later, he proclaimed that he wanted a ransom, but the amount he wanted varied from a few hundred thousand to a few million, depending on what phase of interrogation he was in. Finally, he said he'd release her if the torture stopped. And all that was in the same interrogation session! In later sessions, he seemed not to remember what he had claimed or how much ransom he wanted in the previous sessions.

And he's done that repeatedly for eleven days!

Pete Klipser couldn't have survived eleven days of that kind of interrogation. Hell, she didn't think even she could endure what Reyes had been subjected to. There was no denying the obvious conclusion. The man was either extremely well-conditioned, or they had the wrong man.

An hour ago, the thought first entered her mind that maybe Johnson/Reyes might be some kind of deep-cover operator—American or otherwise. If that was the case, then any record of his true background and identity would be buried so deep, not even the TER could access it.

Over the last few days, the TER team had had many debates over whether or not this man—who called himself Carl Johnson—was, in fact, Alfonso Reyes using an alias. The consensus came back unanimous every time. There were simply too many known physical traits that were too similar to be a coincidence—height, weight, eye color, genetic baldness, body style, skin color, etc.

Just to be certain they weren't overlooking important facts or forming biased opinions, McGrath had commissioned the CIA to perform an independent assessment of all the data they had on their prisoner. Their conclusion was exactly the same.

The man they held in custody was Alfonso Reyes.

Palmer went back over to her management console and pulled up the terrorist's main file folder. The FBI had matched the suspect's fingerprints and DNA with an American man known as Carl Johnson, but a covert alias would be expected to withstand that level of scrutiny. Unfortunately, no such data existed for the Mexican national known to be a cartel drug lord, though Palmer suspected high-level interference within the Mexican government was effectively road-blocking the complete sharing of law enforcement records.

Alfonso Reyes flaunted his wealth on the international stage and was perceived as a globe-trotting playboy and philanthropist. In his media interviews, he spoke perfect English, like the man they had in custody, and he had no accent or ethnic dialect. That Carl Johnson's file indicated he was African American—actually half-Black and half-White—and not Hispanic was irrelevant.

She continued to parse the file, still looking for details she might have missed before. She sought anything that supported her theory that the man in custody was not Alfonso Reyes. She believed it, but she couldn't prove it. Even as that thought tumbled through her brain, she turned her attention back to the window on her monitor showing the interrogation in progress.

Agent Palmer tapped her keyboard and routed the audio of the ongoing session to her wireless comm unit. Finally, she found the proof, and even though she was looking for it, it still hit her like a punch in the gut. She gasped at the words she heard in her ear.

"You fucking pussies," the suspect said. "I'm a patriot and a decorated Air Force officer. I've been entrusted with military secrets less than a hundred people on the planet know about. Even the president and Congress aren't briefed on the kinds of projects I've worked on."

Palmer stood up so suddenly, her chair tipped over backward. In her peripheral view, she saw the two analysts, Lisa and Jimmy, rotate in their chairs.

She turned to face them. "Christ, we *do* have the wrong man!"

CHAPTER 15

1728 EST, DAY 11
LOCATION: UNKNOWN

ARL ROLLED OFF THE TABLE and pretended to stumble on wobbly legs. He fell to his hands and knees. The guard on his right had his left leg slightly forward, so when he bent from the waist, his extended leg bore most of his weight. Carl, balanced on his right hand, slammed his left palm into the guard's knee joint. He aimed *through* the man's knee. The man's leg bent unnaturally backward, and Carl heard the joint pop. That sound was followed by the man's scream of agony as he hopped away on his right foot.

At the same time, Carl kicked backward in a one-legged mule kick. It was a poorly aimed strike because it had been many years since he'd taken any kind of martial arts training. He just hoped to hit some part— *any part*—of the other guard, or his attempt at escape would be short-lived.

His heel caught the man on the inside of his hip. A couple inches to the left, and that guard also would have been down for the count. The man stepped back at the weak attack, giving Carl enough time to get to his feet and roll across the torture table. It was still damp from his perspiration and from voiding his bladder under torture.

He rolled off the other side and grabbed the surprised doctor by the lapels of his white smock. The man may have been an agency man, but he was not combat trained. Carl kneed him in the groin and slammed his face into the corner of the torture device's metal distribution box.

The first impact burst the doctor's right eye in a squirt of clear liquid. Carl pulled his screaming head up and rammed it down a second time, caving in his right temple. He died instantly, but even as Carl let him fall, he was aware that Agent Klipser was lunging toward him from the left end of the torture table. Carl grabbed the first object he could find—a stylus from the doctor's handheld pad—and charged at Klipser. He was intent only on stabbing the stylus into the agent's eye.

Agent Klipser carried a sidearm in a holster on his belt, and Carl saw the man smoothly reaching for the weapon. That was Carl's plan.

Suicide by cop.

A fiery pain ripped through Carl's body, and he hit the floor hard. He realized he was not dead, not free. Agent Klipser had not shot him. The guard that Carl had merely pushed aside with his back kick had tased him.

He quickly discovered two facts. First, the pain from the Taser was short-lived, and it wasn't even a fraction as painful as the electroshock torture he'd endured for the past few weeks. Second, his body was paralyzed only momentarily. It was as though all the weeks of electroshock torture had built up a resistance in him or had desensitized his body to the pain.

He lost the stylus, but he jumped back up and went for Klipser again. Or rather, he tried to. He was yanked off his feet and spun around in midair, only to be slammed face-first across the torture table. The guard twisted his right arm painfully up behind his back, but at this point, Carl stopped resisting. He just lay there as the man put him in the shackles again.

There was no point in struggling. He had made his attempt at freedom, and he had failed. That plan was over, and he knew the guards would never give him another opportunity. The torture would continue.

The guard manhandled him back to his cell and chained him to the wall. Then the guard left, and Carl started laughing and cursing at the camera. The guard had forgotten to turn on the blasting music.

Carl had made them nervous. He'd made them angry. In his attempt at escape, he'd given them something they hadn't planned on—an injured mate and a dead doctor. The guard was angry, and Carl had a feeling Klipser was too.

Rage and anger simmered inside Carl. He found himself glaring at the little fish-eye camera lens mounted above the door. He found himself talking to it.

"You better fucking kill me, Agent Klipser," he said. "Because if I ever get out of here, I'll spend every dime I have to hunt you down. There's nowhere on the planet you can hide. And you can tell that fuckhead McGrath the same thing. I'll find him too." Carl paused, then added, "And everybody that works for him."

CHAPTER 16

1731 EST, DAY 11
LOCATION: UNKNOWN

A S AARON MCGRATH WALKED INTO the operations room, he concentrated on keeping his game face on so no one would sense the conflicts roiling inside him. He'd been asleep less than half an hour when Palmer made the "All hands on deck!" call after the disastrous event at the interrogation house. Before his nap, the president had chewed his ass good. Upon entering the operations room, he quickly learned he had a dead doctor and a wounded operator, both taken down by an untrained fifty-three-year-old civilian.

"Fucking incredible," he murmured to himself. He immediately regretted that small outburst because Palmer heard him, and she'd known him long enough to know how uncharacteristic such an outburst was for him.

The two off-duty analysts came trudging downstairs a few seconds later. Both had stopped in the kitchen first and entered the op center with a cold turkey sandwich in one hand and a can of Red Bull in the other.

McGrath got straight to the point. "What's our status over there, Pete?"

Palmer spoke first. "We now believe with certainty that the man in custody is not Alfonso Reyes. He is who he says he is, an American named Carl Johnson. We also believe that he is a body double who was put in play to divert our resources from the initial search for Melissa."

McGrath growled under his breath, then said, "It was a very successful diversion."

Palmer said, "Reyes would have known his double would be interrogated, though he probably would not have known about the harsh regimen reserved for top-tier terrorists. Not that it would have made any difference to Reyes. He still would have used the man as a deception."

McGrath glanced at Klipser's image on the left monitor. The agent clearly was not happy that he'd been unable to break the terrorist, and now they had a probable explanation why. The only way a man could possibly survive such a harsh interrogation was to truly believe what he was saying was the truth. The only way that would be possible was if the man had no knowledge of the kidnapping and, therefore, had no information to give them.

McGrath raised his titanium specs and massaged the bridge of his nose. "I hope you have more than just supposition that appears to make all the puzzle pieces fit." He looked at Palmer again. "I'm still not convinced, and I cannot take this to the president without hard evidence and a plan of action."

Palmer nodded. "Carl Johnson made a curious statement. He said he'd held security clearances so high that not even a hundred people on the planet were cleared for, not even the president and Congress."

Klipser's rough voice drifted from the management console speaker. "I heard that too. What does that mean?"

Palmer addressed the monitor. "It means that Carl Johnson used insider lingo that people outside of an extremely limited circle in the intelligence community would not know. Pete, if *you* don't know the lingo, there's no way a foreign terrorist would.

"Lisa, pull up the inventory of Johnson's military documents on the center monitor."

McGrath nodded as he realized where his second-in-command was headed. Still, he was unwilling to fully sign onto her radical new theory.

He stepped in front of the analyst stations and examined the inventory list. Like many former military members, Carl Johnson had stashed his important military documents for safekeeping in a plastic baggie on the floor of the fridge under the vegetable drawers. In the event of a fire, the refrigerator would likely survive an inferno because those appliances were built to provide maximum insulation.

He examined the image of the front of Johnson's olive green military identification card. The card stated that he was a member of the Air Force Reserve, though McGrath knew he would be a member of the Ready Reserve, not the Active Reserve, since he had taken the early-out when the military downsized after the first Gulf War. His ID card showed his rank as captain and his pay grade as O-3. His social security number was on the front also, and on the image of the back of the card was his date of birth and other descriptive information, as well as his blood type and his classification as Category III under the Geneva Convention.

There was also Johnson's all-important original DD-214 sheet—his statement of Honorable Discharge—and an additional copy of that document. His birth certificate had been in the baggie also, along with his military immunization records and his passport. There was also a copy of his annuity payment schedule, indicating he was due a payment every October for thirty-two years.

Palmer stepped up next to him and said, "It wasn't so much that he claimed to have high security clearances, Aaron. It was how he stated the fact."

McGrath nodded. "Pete, a normal citizen, foreign or domestic, might know about highly classified programs, but they would likely describe such a program in generic terms, like "Above Top Secret" or "Eyes Only." Only a person who is or was in that high-clearance community would know that programs exist known only to a handful of people."

Palmer added, "An outsider certainly would not know that we have extremely sensitive programs requiring a higher clearance than the president and Congress."

On the monitor, Klipser shook his head. "That's pretty thin. You're saying the only true difference between Johnson and Reyes is that Johnson knows intel lingo that Reyes *probably* would not know." He paused. "Thin."

McGrath looked at Palmer, and she gave him a tented-eyebrow look as if to say that was the best she had. He wasn't totally convinced, but he'd be a fool not to give her analysis full consideration.

He said, "Not so thin when you consider he's been on the table eleven days. If he had information to give us, he would have given it up by now. I think we can all agree on that point."

He looked at both his team members, and they both nodded.

Klipser said, "If he's a double, then we have to stop asking him about a girl he knows nothing about. We need to ask him new questions. Despite his ambivalence, I can still break him."

Palmer rolled her head, and McGrath heard her neck cartilage crack.

She said, "We've still found no actual relationship or financial connection between the two men."

From the monitor, Klipser said, "So, we're now officially operating under the assumption that the man in custody here is a double named Johnson?"

McGrath said, "It seems that way."

Klipser shifted his focus so that his attention was on Jimmy, the analyst. He said, "You there with the big hair, transfer everything we have on Johnson so I can see it on my laptop."

Jimmy made the transfer.

McGrath added, "And show us what Pete's looking at on the right monitor."

A dozen small windows popped up on the monitor. Some came to the foreground and overlapped others as Klipser manipulated the material.

McGrath felt a rare moment of self-doubt and muttered to Palmer. "Nancy, how did we miss this for eleven whole days?"

"We thought we had Alfonso Reyes, so we didn't dig deep enough into Carl Johnson. There was no reason to."

"No," Klipser said. "We didn't *think* we had him. We *knew*. We went over the data a dozen times, and we all agreed with 100 percent certainty that we had Alfonso Reyes." He highlighted a particular window and expanded it to fill the entire monitor.

"What do you see, Pete?" McGrath said.

"Johnson has a thirty-year-old son named Mark." Klipser peered from the monitor and said, "Let's release Johnson and watch his son. Put out the word that Mark Johnson has agreed to testify to the FBI."

"You're suggesting we use his son as bait?" Palmer looked at the monitor. "An innocent civilian?"

Klipser said, "We don't know that his son is innocent."

Nancy shook her head. "There's zero evidence to even suggest his son is involved." She looked at McGrath. "Aaron, if we're wrong about this…"

McGrath said, "I'm willing to take that risk, and I'll answer for it if we're wrong."

"He won't sacrifice his son," Klipser said. "I guarantee you that. No father would. He'll give us Reyes."

CHAPTER 17

TIME: UNKNOWN; DAY: 12
LOCATION: UNKNOWN

C ARL AWOKE TO THE SOUND of assault boots long before the guards opened the door of his cell. He'd slept lightly—standing up, feet spread and knees locked, leaning forward just enough to keep his body from collapsing. Both guards entered with Tasers at the ready. They'd learned a lesson from their previous complacency. A black sack was placed over his head, and he heard plastic zip cuffs affixed to his wrists before he was unshackled from the cable holding him to the wall.

So this is how it ends, with a bag over my head while they drag me naked out somewhere to kill me and dump my body.

He wasn't at all surprised when they led him to the left instead of to the right toward the torture room. They went a few steps and then proceeded up the stairs. All he could think about was that the torture was over. He achieved his objective, though not the way he'd planned.

They didn't want him alive as a witness. He beat them, but now that he knew they were no longer going to torture him, he suddenly wanted to live. He wanted to see his son. He wanted to go back to his uncomplicated life.

They stopped at the top of the stairs, and he heard one of them open a door. The sound of it opening was very faint, like it hung on well-oiled hinges and maybe had rubber padding around the edges to keep it silent. It was just one more way a prisoner like himself was kept completely unaware of his surroundings.

Now the guards paused in their upward march, and Carl's rational brain told him that all three of them couldn't fit through the doorway side by side. One of his guards went through first, pulling him by the left arm, while the other guard pushed on his right arm. Both men stayed physically connected to him, obviously prepared to counter any move he might make to attack or escape.

They marched him through a room, and his bare feet felt rough indoor-outdoor style carpet underfoot. Then they maneuvered him through another door, where once again, he felt concrete beneath his bare feet. This time, he knew he was above ground and outside the main structure because the concrete was ice-cold. Maybe he was in a garage or a carport or something. The air was frigid also, and his muscles immediately tensed as he began to shiver. He smelled pine again. The air was heavy with the scent and felt thick and moist.

The guards manhandled him into some kind of utility vehicle or cargo van. He sensed it was the rear door they forced him through, and they dumped him on the cold metal floor. The ribs of the floor dug into his side, and the icy cold metal quickly numbed his skin.

As he lay on his side, he felt the vehicle dip as each guard climbed in, and he heard the squeak of old springs as the weight of the guards caused the van to shift. Someone shut the rear door, and someone else climbed into the front of the van and started the engine. No one spoke.

Carl's impression that the van was old was confirmed as it bounced and rattled along a rutted road on struts that were in serious need of replacement. The vehicle squeaked and groaned with every dip, and he had the impression that the rugged road was an unpaved trail winding its way through a forest.

Finally, they bounced onto a paved road, and they drove for another half an hour. Carl listened to the high-pitch hum of worn tires on asphalt. He leveraged himself up to a sitting position, though it was difficult to stay balanced with his hands behind his back. So he spread his legs out in a V and leaned forward to stay upright against the van's jerky movements.

He didn't know where they were taking him, nor did he care. He was certain they'd want to make killing him look like an accident. They couldn't just shoot him or cut his throat because that would leave a murder trail that would lead to an investigation.

Gradually, Carl became aware of other traffic sounds. They were in a city somewhere on a busy street. The muted sound of heavy traffic penetrated the interior of the vehicle. He heard car engines, bus engines, the hammer-heavy rattle of diesel truck engines, and the blaring horns of impatient drivers. The van stopped and started several times, presumably at stop signs and traffic lights.

He felt and heard one of the men beside him stand up. Then he heard the unexpected sound of one of the back doors opening, even though the van was still moving. The vehicle made a sudden lurch to the left, and Carl rocked the opposite way with the momentum. Then the van decelerated sharply. Just before Carl fell back against the motion, he felt the rugged tread of a large assault boot against his back. Then the big boot shoved, literally launching him out of the slow-moving vehicle.

He had no time to prepare for a tuck and roll, especially with his hands cuffed behind his back. He hit the asphalt hard on his butt, wrists, and left shoulder with a bone-jarring bounce, then tumbled ass over elbows.

He could see nothing through the black sack, but he heard the screech of tires on the road right beside him as cars swerved to miss him. He heard the blaring horns of panicked drivers right next to him. He waited for the impact—for one of those squealing and sliding cars or trucks to roll right over him.

Finally, his world went silent, and he rolled awkwardly onto his butt and just sat there. He smelled the asphalt and felt the heat of engines of cars that had panic-stopped within inches of him.

A smoothly purring engine nearby went silent, and a car door opened and closed. He heard the ticking of a cooling engine right beside him, and he knew he could have reached out and touched the front bumper of the car if his hands weren't restrained. Footsteps clinked on the pavement—a woman in heels.

"Oh my God!" she said. "Are you all right?"

Stupid question. *You find a naked man, hooded and cuffed, skinned raw from road rash, and you ask him if he's all right? Seriously?*

"Maybe you could take this sack off my head?"

Another door opened and closed. It sounded like someone else was getting out of the same car, and he heard a young girl's voice. "Don't touch him, Mom! Maybe he's a criminal or something."

Carl grunted through his hood. "Silly wabbit."

The sound of heavy footfalls approached.

"I got this," a man's deep voice said. Strong, warm hands grabbed Carl's shoulders and helped him to his feet. Then the man worked at untying the sack on his head.

"Brah," the deep voice said. "I done tol' you about wearing seat belts. Now look at you, all skinned up and shit."

Carl had to chuckle at that. Finally, the black sack came off his head, and he blinked in the sudden brightness. The man who had helped him up was a lumberjack-looking guy in jeans and a red plaid shirt. He was tall, maybe six-foot-five, with a flaming red beard and long unkempt hair bursting out from under his baseball cap. He had a barrel chest and an equally massive gut. Over the man's right shoulder, Carl saw a big cement truck parked in the middle of the street. The driver's door was wide open, and the engine was still running. The big mixer drum behind the cab spun slowly.

Squinting, Carl studied his surroundings. He stood in the middle of an intersection. Three cars sat near him pointed in haphazard directions. Long black skid marks ended under the tires of two of the nearest cars. One was a very old sedan that probably didn't have antilock brakes, hence the skid marks. The other was a new two-seater that had executed a nice sideways slide to avoid running him over. Either that, or the driver had panicked and lost control. Several other cars had swerved to avoid those cars.

There were mid-sized buildings all around, all between five and ten stories high. Most were glass and steel, obviously the result of relatively new infill construction in a growing suburban city that could only expand upward. It was early morning, and Carl had disrupted rush hour traffic. Cars and buses and taxis were stalled everywhere. The sidewalks were wide, and neatly trimmed young trees maybe eight feet high stood every few yards in circular cutouts in the concrete. There was no median in the center of the street.

As Carl examined the faces of the drivers and pedestrians gawking at him, he noticed everyone was bundled up in overcoats. It was then he realized how cold he felt. He started to shiver again, and his feet felt like he was standing on ice. Then he began to feel the first stabbings of pain on his elbows and butt, the parts of his body that had borne the brunt of the impact with the road.

It occurred to him that he should feel embarrassed at his nakedness. Everyone kept their distance from him, like they were afraid of him. Maybe they all thought he was a criminal, like the teen girl from the BMW behind him. Why else would a man be trussed and tossed from a moving vehicle?

He glanced back and saw the teen holding up her cell phone, like she was putting him on YouTube or Facebook. His first thought as he glared at the girl was that he'd better hurry up and call Mark before his son saw his naked butt on the internet.

He heard whispers from the gawkers, but no one except the trucker was bold enough to actually help him. He couldn't blame them. Before his arrest, if a naked man had been dumped from a van in front of his car, he wouldn't have stopped. He would have just called 911 and kept driving.

At the very least, Carl figured he ought to be feeling anger or thinking vengeful thoughts. In reality, though, he was simply relieved to be alive. He'd been certain the government agents were taking him somewhere to kill him. Along with his relief, he was confused. Why had they let him go? The only answer that made sense was that they finally realized he wasn't the man they thought he was and letting him go couldn't hurt them.

The trucker pulled a knife from his pocket and extended the blade. Then he stepped behind Carl and sliced open the plastic wrist cuffs. As Carl massaged his wrists, he noticed a building with a big white sign with a huge red plus symbol on it, accompanied by "Emergency" in red letters. Closer to the street sat a similar sign marked "Emergency Room" in red letters, scribed inside a large white plus sign.

Carl felt a belly laugh erupt from deep within. The fuckers had dumped him right in front of the entrance to a hospital emergency room!

Thoughtful bastards.

He nodded at the trucker. "Thanks, friend." Then he limped his naked butt up the long driveway toward the entrance of the emergency room.

"Seat belts next time, brah," the man said. "And maybe some clothes too!"

CHAPTER 18

0913 EST, WEDNESDAY
ARLINGTON HEIGHTS, VA

MELISSA HAD BEEN MISSING FOR twelve days, Aaron McGrath thought. Eleven of those days had been wasted scrutinizing the background of the wrong man. They'd been duped. The drug lord, Alfonso Reyes, had handed him a classic misdirection, and he fell for it. How the hell had the drug lord found such a perfect look-alike who hadn't been surgically altered? The odds against that were so astronomical as to not even get considered.

Carl Johnson wasn't a supremely conditioned operator. He was simply the wrong man, though it remained to be seen whether he was innocent or involved. The man had withstood eleven days of interrogation, eleven days of pure hell, but only because he didn't have any information to give them. McGrath knew that now. How Carl Johnson could have kept hold of his sanity after what they'd put him through, McGrath was sure he'd never know.

Aaron McGrath stood by the living room window, looking out at the tidy grass lawn of the operations house. The neighborhood was well-lit by the low morning sun that tried to burn through high, thin clouds. The streetlamp near the curb in front of the house next door was still on.

The operations house looked exactly like all the other houses on the cul-de-sac. He scanned the street left and right, more from habit than for any practical reason. Most everyone had already headed out to work.

Houses with more than two cars, maybe with teenage kids who needed a car, had their extra vehicles parked on the street.

It was somewhat ironic to him that his own house was located a mere ten miles northwest of the operations house. He lived in McLean, so he could actually go home for a quick meal and be back on duty in a little over an hour if he weren't on such a high-priority terror event. McLean was an enclave of million-dollar homes, typical of what director-level government employees could afford. Because of his intel background, McGrath had accumulated far greater financial resources outside the government, but he had maintained a modest level of living commensurate with his salary so he wouldn't attract unnecessary attention.

He considered the coincidence of his current location. In the year since he'd organized the TER agency, he'd set up five TER teams in operations houses across the country, though he'd never had an operation this close to the Capitol.

The current terror event was very perplexing. It was a high-profile snatch-and-grab rather than an actual attack. It was an intricately planned kidnapping—far beyond the capabilities of what one would expect of a Mexican drug cartel leader. McGrath wondered how a mid-level drug cartel bully had garnered the financial and intel resources to plan and execute such a daring operation on US soil.

Of course, McGrath himself had helped Alfonso Reyes escape by pulling all his resources away from DC and concentrating on Albuquerque to deal with the man he now knew was Carl Johnson. If the president ever needed a fall guy when the event went south—and it seemed increasingly likely that they were going to lose the girl—Aaron McGrath knew he had just served up his own ass on a big presidential platter.

His decisions had allowed Alfonso Reyes to flee the country with his captive. Now his TER team had the nearly insurmountable task of trying to recover the girl. But first, they had to find her, and in eleven days, she could have been moved anywhere in the world. The manner in which he had bungled the operation frustrated him deeply, but a deep breath was all the reaction he allowed himself in case any of his team members were watching.

In his peripheral view, he saw Nancy Palmer enter the living room operations center to resume her shift. She stood in the doorway watching him for a moment, and he thought she was going to walk over and make him justify his decision to use Johnson's son as bait again. Or maybe she was going to point out, in her subtle way, how badly he had managed the investigation. Instead, she did something even more disturbing. She ignored him. She sat at the management workstation and began her review of the latest shift updates.

He had tried to go back to sleep after the deadly event at the interrogation center last evening, but rest eluded him. He kept replaying the video in his mind, watching Johnson attack his men over and over again. Then he watched the man's tirade in his cell.

How the hell did he learn Pete's name? Or mine, for that matter?

About midnight, it was clear that he wasn't going back to sleep, so he finished out Palmer's night shift and told her to report in at 0930.

Like most operators in the intel business, Aaron McGrath had come up through the ranks in the CIA, and his four-decade career in clandestine operations had culminated in his appointment by the president to run the Terror Event Response agency. There was no time for training, cultivating, or mentoring agents, though. The agency had to hit the ground running with fully trained operators and experienced analysts.

He culled his analysts from the very best candidates of the FBI, the NSA, and the CIA. Most of his operators came from covert departments within the CIA—units that specialized in wet-work activities where discrete killing or assassination was necessary. Nancy Palmer and Pete Klipser, however, came straight from the military Special Forces. Nancy came from the first Navy SEAL training class that included women warriors, and Pete came from an army elite Delta unit.

Palmer came on board first in a command capacity. Pete Klipser, on the other hand, was one of the most effective and deadly operators who had ever served under his command. The agent was a relentless killing machine and a superb tactical commander when he had terrorists in his sights. He was a perfect operator for the new covert counterterrorist agency for which the rules of engagement were virtually nonexistent.

"Aaron?" Palmer said.

McGrath turned away from the window.

He nodded, and she said, "Johnson went into the emergency room a few minutes ago. As soon as he's logged in by hospital staff, assuming he uses his real name, the FBI is going to move on him again because he's still red-flagged as a Tier-Three terror threat. For this to work, we need him to be off that list."

"Agreed."

When he said nothing further, Palmer stepped closer to him and said quietly, "I'm having second thoughts about this plan."

"The president has given me broad latitude to deal with terror threats however I see fit. Are you on board with the plan?"

"I know the evidence says this guy is hip-deep in this mess, but this event just doesn't fit his profile. I've been over his records forward and backward, and I just can't make it fit. I think it's a mistake using his son like this."

He nodded. "The president is insulated from our activities and can claim no knowledge. But I can't think of a better plan right now, and we have no other leads on Melissa's whereabouts. If there's a chance that Johnson can lead us to Reyes or his people, we have to take it."

The TER analysts had snagged the computerized employment records of every job Johnson had held in the last twenty years, along with federal records regarding his various security clearance investigations. McGrath mentally reviewed all the new information about the man.

Johnson joined the US Air Force in 1976 at the age of eighteen. Because of his high scores on the military placement exams, he was placed in the electronics field. He was always rated proficient or higher by his supervisors and advanced rapidly in rank and responsibility, receiving all the regular commendations for good conduct and time in service.

According to his career counselors, Johnson said that when he watched the first Space Shuttle launch in 1981, he decided on the spot that the Space Shuttle program was his ticket to achieve his childhood dream. He confessed that, like most young boys, he had always wanted to become an astronaut.

He applied for and was accepted into the officer training program. He earned his college degree in laser engineering, then took an assignment to Kirtland Air Force Base in Albuquerque, New Mexico, where he continued to do the kind of research and development required to get into the Space Shuttle program as a mission specialist. He was methodically checking off all the boxes needed to achieve his goal.

Up until 1990, Johnson was a model officer with a stellar career trajectory, but his application to the space program was declined after he failed his physical. More precisely, he never actually took the physical. Johnson related to his commanding officer at the time that the doctor had closed his file folder and laughed at him as soon as he walked into his office, saying he couldn't get into the space program because he wore glasses. Corrective eye surgery was not yet an authorized medical procedure.

A year later, Johnson mustered out of the military after nearly eighteen years, when the Air Force began offering cash separation incentives after the first Gulf War. Apparently, his entire motivation to stay in the Air Force evaporated when he became ineligible for the Space Shuttle program.

Throughout his military career, Johnson got married, had a son, got divorced, got married again a few years later, and got divorced again. After the Air Force, he took a series of high-tech engineering and project management jobs with government contractors, each garnering more responsibility and pay than the one before, but he never stayed with a job for more than a year, sometimes less.

A common theme in his evaluations was that, though he was a brilliant problem solver and project manager, he never really played well with others. His personnel evaluations indicated that he was a loner, not a team player—unless it was his team—and he became labeled as having a defiant attitude. Still, he was too valuable to terminate. He contributed to his employers' bottom lines in big ways, so the companies he worked for kept him on.

Finally, in 2006, his last employer annotated his records upon his voluntary resignation, stating that he professed to have had enough of the bureaucratic bullshit. He walked away from two hundred grand a year with all the perks and a pending promotion to operations director of a major defense company. He moved back to Albuquerque and got his real estate license, making a meager income as a commission-only self-employed worker.

Carl Johnson was the real deal. The only question in McGrath's mind now was how this man had become involved with a drug cartel leader who happened to pull off the biggest celebrity kidnapping in US history. So far, the government had been able to keep the kidnapping secret. If the world ever found out, it would be bigger than the Lindbergh baby and bigger than Patty Hearst.

McGrath repeated his earlier declaration. "We have no other viable options at this point." He took a deep breath and let it out slowly. Because he was aware that the two analysts seated in front of him were trying to listen without appearing to do so, he spoke loud enough for them to hear. "We'll proceed on the assumption that Reyes recruited him as a deception and has some hold on him that we've yet to discover. We'll keep his son under surveillance and see who he makes contact with. We've already put out the word through FBI channels and on the underground intel network to all relevant government informants, especially in Mexico and Albuquerque, that Mark Johnson is going to voluntarily surrender to the FBI in two days and give up evidence on Reyes's cartel."

An analyst's station pinged. "Look who popped up on Facebook a few minutes ago!"

The young man tapped some keys, and a side view of Carl Johnson's naked body filled the center monitor. The picture quality was poor and shaky, obviously from someone holding a medium-quality cell phone. Johnson was facing away from the camera, and a big-bearded man had just used a knife to cut his plastic cuffs. Then Johnson glared at the camera, and McGrath had the distinct impression the man was looking right at him. He didn't look like a defeated man who just endured eleven days of severe interrogation.

McGrath's encrypted cell buzzed in his pocket. He pulled the device out, and when he saw who was calling, he pivoted to leave the room. He touched his Bluetooth earpiece to activate the call.

"Yes, Madam President." He had just passed through the living room archway into the hall when Palmer called him back.

"Aaron, you need to see this!"

When he turned back, he saw why the president was calling. On a wall monitor was an email to the White House specifying ransom terms for an unidentified American girl.

Jimmy, the big-Afro analyst, said, "The Defense Department's voice analysis algorithms show Mr. Johnson just made a cryptic phone call too, right before we received this email. He called an associate in Albuquerque whose phones we're monitoring."

McGrath growled aloud. "So he really *is* behind all this."

CHAPTER 19

0922 EST, WEDNESDAY
ARLINGTON HEIGHTS, VA

AFTER A FEW MINUTES OF wandering a couple hallways and not seeing a single doctor or nurse, Carl simply walked into a treatment room. The dull throb of pain after his initial contact with the street suddenly flared into a full-blown, fiery ache that seemed to envelop his entire body. He was aware of the pain, but he stashed it away in that dark corner of his mind, where he had recently learned to put Klipser's torture. He felt the pain, but he endured it while his mind considered other things.

Carl closed the door behind him. The treatment room held only a standard padded exam room gurney and a swivel chair where the examining nurse or the PA would sit. There was no pillow on the gurney.

He turned, opened the supply cabinet near the sink, and scanned the shelves. There were lots of creams and supplies like bandages and gauze wraps. He grabbed a handful of the supplies and dumped it all on the counter beside the sink. He ripped open the paper packages, then set about cleaning the dirt and pebbles from his scrapes. He spread antibiotic cream over all his scrapes, mostly on his knees, both elbows, and wrists.

He wrapped bandage gauze over his multitude of scrapes and taped everything in place. He didn't bother to tidy up or put his supplies back. Instead, he just stood in the middle of the room and tried to figure out what the hell he was going to do next.

That's when he saw a white smock hanging on a hook on the back of the closed door. It looked just like the one his torture doctor wore. He hesitated for a moment, then shook off the ridiculous fear that almost made him reject the covering. He shrugged his way into the garment.

He looked through the drawers and cabinets again for some kind of pain killer, but he found nothing. He chuckled at the thought. After what Agent Klipser and his doctor had done to him, it wasn't like he couldn't bear a little road-rash pain all goddamn day.

He thought about the doctor for a moment. Then it hit him. He had actually killed a man, and he did it with intent. The thought that he was actually a killer filled Carl with a mixture of emotions. He only attacked the doctor because he wanted to grab something from the table to use as a weapon to go after Klipser. He wanted the agent to kill him, but if Carl had been weaponless, Klipser would have just kicked his butt and put him back on the table.

At the moment when Carl grabbed the doctor, though, he'd felt a sudden eruption of rage. So, instead of merely pushing the man out of the way, Carl pulled him forward and slammed his face against the table. He had not realized the electroshock control box with all the wires was in the way, but he felt elated when the man's face struck the metal box. He felt an almost orgasmic pleasure when he saw the man's eyeball burst. So he slammed the doctor's head down a second time.

Suddenly, the door opened, and a woman in blue scrubs took two steps into the room, clearly not expecting to find him there. She stopped with a gasp as she noticed him. A twenty-something young man holding an injured left arm across his belly hesitated in the doorway.

The attendant glanced up and down Carl's naked frame under the open smock and seemed to instantly understand he did not belong in the room. Or maybe she just knew he had not been processed in through the normal reception area, as all patients should be.

"Wait right here," she said. "I'll get you a doctor."

Carl knew immediately she wasn't going to call a doctor because his taped scrapes didn't require that skill set. She was calling security, and he wasn't yet prepared to deal with that kind of confrontation. He wanted to think through what his next move ought to be.

He buttoned the smock but hesitated in front of the mirror again. He wondered what day it was. He stepped closer to the mirror and was surprised at how gaunt he appeared. He'd lost a lot of weight, true, but he'd lost something else too.

As a salesman, he made it a point of always walking around with a smile on his face because one never knew who might reciprocate with a greeting or a smile of their own and become a client. But now, he saw an emptiness in his eyes, and he found himself wondering if he'd ever be able to smile again, now that he knew the true nature of what humans were capable of.

How do you smile again after being tortured or after killing a man?

His reflection wore several days' worth of graying whiskers on his face and neck. He rubbed the razor stubble on the back of his head also, though the top of his dome was still smooth and hair-free.

Carl turned his head slightly and studied his reflection. He noticed his ear hair and shook his head. *Can't get shit to grow on top of my head, but it's practically bursting out of my ears and nose!*

All in all, he was an unkempt shocking sight to look upon. He reflected on how short his captivity must have been. If he'd been tortured for several weeks as it seemed, he would have had more than an inch of hair on his jaw instead of the scruffy growth he saw. As he rubbed the razor stubble on his jaw, he figured it might have been only a week, maybe ten days, max.

He shook off the thoughts with a shudder and left the room. He instinctively headed back toward the empty hallways that he'd traversed near the emergency room. Along the way, he started feeling anger mixed in with the pain of his road rash.

They dumped me out of a moving vehicle! What the hell were they thinking? He could have been run over, or he could have cracked his skull open on a curb. Even being dumped at the emergency room wouldn't have helped that outcome.

Evil bastards.

His anger quickly turned to thoughts of revenge. He wanted to find them and…what? Maybe he could try to get all *Rambo* on their asses. Find their headquarters and hose it down with a minigun or a couple RPGs or something. Unfortunately, he didn't have the knowledge or the tools or the skills to get revenge on the likes of those government bullies.

The agents were in the business of forcing their will upon other people, and he knew he wasn't their first target. He wouldn't be their last either, and there wasn't a goddamn thing he or anyone like him could ever do about it.

He was simply a victim, and somehow, he'd have to figure out how to live with that new reality. He was a victim of a secret part of the government composed of covert agents that did whatever the hell they wanted, and they didn't care whose life they fucked up in pursuit of their mission.

The rational part of Carl's brain accepted that what had happened to him wasn't personal. The government wanted something from him, and they either got it or they didn't, then they released him. It was over. All he could do was accept his ass-whipping like a man, tuck his tail between his legs, and go home. Somehow try to get on with life and pretend the last few days never happened.

Then he realized he was two thousand miles from home, with no way to get himself cleaned up and presentable. He had no money, no debit card, no cell phone, no identification, and…no clothes. He thought of various possible courses of action. He could call his best friend, Randal, and have him wire some money to a nearby bank or Western Union, but that wouldn't solve his ID problem.

There was no way he could get on a plane, train, bus, or even rent a car without an ID or a credit card. Agent Klipser and company no doubt had his driver's license and primary credit card, but maybe Randal could go over to his house and find his hidden spare key, then FedEx one of his spare credit cards along with his military ID card. Of course, that plan would take at least a day, and he had nowhere to stay.

Plan B was to hitchhike across the country with a trucker. First, he had to get out of the building and take his chances out on the streets. If hospital security or local police found him without clothes and ID, they'd haul him to the nearest precinct building to investigate his identity. Then, when they ran his prints and the FBI came calling, the shit would really hit the fan. He'd be back in federal custody all over again.

So he opted to avoid the police and the FBI as long as he could. They'd probably catch up with him anyway, but maybe he could get back to Albuquerque before that happened and get his attorney to square things away with the feds. In his current situation, he didn't see how fleeing would get him in any more trouble than he was in already.

Barefoot in his white smock, Carl wandered out the same emergency room door he'd entered less than an hour ago. His only detour had been to find a phone in an out-of-the-way, unoccupied office. He called Randal's home phone, his office phone, and his cell phone, but his friend didn't pick up. He hung up right before his calls to each of Randal's phones went to voice mail. He couldn't remember any time in twenty-five years that Randal didn't pick up at least one of his lines. He began to sense a nagging feeling of paranoia, like the nightmare wasn't over, so he quickly left that office.

Twenty seconds down the hall, it occurred to him that his son also had a spare key to his house. If he wasn't working, he could get over there within an hour and grab his ID and credit card, then get them sent off for overnight delivery. He'd have to find somewhere to stay for at least one night. There had to be a homeless shelter and a soup kitchen somewhere nearby, right?

So he called Mark.

CHAPTER 20

"I'LL BE DAMNED," MCGRATH SAID as he read the simple instructions of the ransom note on the center monitor.

I have a certain American girl.
For her safe return
Pay $250M
Account number to follow
–AR

"I had almost convinced myself that he was an innocent victim in all this." He read the note with a certain amount of relief that he was right about Johnson after all.

Palmer agreed. "This is extremely troubling to me, Aaron. I still can't wrap my brain around the fact that he held out on the table without breaking." She shook her head as if unwilling to accept the obvious conclusions. "It just doesn't seem humanly possible. It *shouldn't* be humanly possible."

McGrath shook his head. "In order for a subject's nervous system to avoid short-circuiting under such extreme conditions, there must be some kind of inherent, or trained, or mastered ability to control one's autonomic nervous system arousal to counteract fear and pain messages by reframing the brain's commands. We've seen reports that a high-level yogi is able to do this, as well as extremely well-conditioned members of the Israeli Defense Forces trained in Krav Maga."

"I agree," Palmer said. "But the new interrogation regimen was developed specifically to prevent these kinds of professionals from concealing the truth during an extended interrogation. There aren't half a dozen yogis in the world who possess that kind of mental discipline, and Johnson most certainly hasn't been trained by the Israelis. The human brain simply cannot maintain organized, cognitive awareness when the body is subject to these methodologies, and I just don't see Johnson having any kind of inherent ability to block or resist the new regimen."

"Yes, but he *did* break," McGrath said. "We saw that. He broke multiple times, or at least we thought he did. Maybe he was just faking." He took a deep breath. "We're going to have to reevaluate this new interrogation regimen after this event is concluded."

"I don't know, Aaron. We've had a 100 percent success rate to date."

"Until Carl Johnson came along…or Alfonso Reyes. Whoever the hell this man is. What was it that enabled him to survive?" He paused. "And he didn't just survive. He played us. He really played us good." McGrath sighed deeply. "How the hell can a person *fake* breaking down multiple times under that kind of duress?"

"And the first thing he does when we release him is elude hospital security and police. He placed some cryptic hang-up calls to his friend and then just disappeared." Palmer stood with her hands on her hips and nodded at the center monitor. "And now this."

"Have the local FBI bring in his friend, Randal Cunningham, for questioning," McGrath said. He took off his glasses and wiped his lenses with a handkerchief he pulled from his back pocket.

"Nancy, could his son have been in on this the whole time too?"

"This can't all be coincidental." Palmer looked McGrath in the eye. "But even though I've seen it with my own eyes, I still can't believe it. My gut tells me this man couldn't be involved in all this, but…"

"But what?"

"I saw an anomaly in his last interrogation." She walked toward the manager's workstation and worked the keyboard.

The data populated monitor three and showed two electronic graphs.

One graph was the squiggly lines from a standard lie detector test, and the other was Johnson's brain wave pattern.

"This latest chart from yesterday shows a distinct deviation from all of his previous charts." She pointed to several spikes on both graphs. "These peaks indicate deception. All his previous charts indicated that he'd been telling the truth."

"And yesterday, he tried to get Klipser to kill him."

"That was my initial assessment too. But what if it really *was* an escape attempt instead? What if he'd had enough? Or…"

"No, no, no," McGrath said, shaking his head. "You're suggesting that he withstood eleven days of harsh interrogation and that getting us to release him *today* was part of his plan?"

"All I know is that he underwent a drastic change yesterday. He suddenly displayed…I don't know…strength. He became belligerent. I've never seen anything like this before."

McGrath grimaced. "No one has seen anything like this or anyone like him. He really caught us with our proverbial pants down." He looked at the ransom text on the monitor again and muttered. "What is he, some kind of goddamn superhero?"

"He's not Superman."

"Are we overlooking some deep black-ops, enhanced-soldier program? Something that would give him the ability to resist this kind of interrogation?"

Palmer shook her head. "We're briefed into all the most classified development programs. There are no enhanced-soldier programs on the black books. That's all just science fiction."

McGrath barely mumbled his conclusion. "Then, as impossible as it sounds, we have a previously undiscovered civilian with inherent mental strength and possibly an operator skill set."

"I can't see it, Aaron."

"Well, he laughed off eleven days of pure hell. And he manipulated two lie detection systems. If he's half as resourceful as he seems to be, he'll find a way to backtrack to the interrogation center. Get everyone there prepared to evacuate and relocate. If he decides to go on a rampage, or if he calls in some heavies, that will definitely complicate our operation."

"I'll upgrade security at all our TER facilities in case he gets new intel or grabs a hostage," Palmer said with a nod.

"You mean *another* hostage." McGrath paused. "I can't believe I got this so wrong. We just put out the information about his son only an hour ago. He must have talked to someone else before he called his son." He clapped his hands together hard. "Dammit! Reyes or Johnson, it doesn't matter. We had him in custody, and I let him go!"

Palmer turned to address the analyst with the big Afro. "Has anyone else in his network received a call within the last hour?"

Jimmy's thick fingers flew over his keyboard. "He only called Randal Cunningham on his cell, his home phone, and his work phone, but there was no conversation."

"What is the likelihood that the calls were some kind of call-back signal?"

The analyst nodded. "The likelihood is high, but I'm monitoring the hospital for incoming calls from Johnson's circle of contacts, and I see nothing."

"What if Cunningham used someone else's phone or an untraceable burner?"

The young man shook his head. "Either of those options would still show the geographic point of origin as Albuquerque, and there have been no calls to the hospital from that location. Even if Cunningham called someone else in another state or country, who then called the hospital, I'd still see the incoming call, even if I couldn't trace it quickly enough."

"What about the extension he called his son from? Any other outbound calls from that phone or the one he called Cunningham from?"

"Nothing, ma'am. He spoke to his son for a couple of minutes, but the transcript shows no keywords or any kind of coded language."

"Hmm," Palmer spoke softly, as if talking to herself. "So perhaps his hang-ups were prearranged coded instructions for this Cunningham fellow to take a specific action, dictated by the order in which the phones were called. It wasn't a call-back code, but maybe it was a call-*forward* code."

"And within minutes, we get the ransom email." McGrath added, "That's pretty sophisticated for a civilian. You still think he's *not* an operator?"

Nancy Palmer shrugged. "Well, he'll either find a way back to Albuquerque to his son, or he'll meet him somewhere."

"Or he'll send people to evac him." McGrath paused, then said, "Update Pete and put a full surveillance package in play on Carl Johnson's son. I want to know everything that young man does from this moment forward. I want his phone tapped and his position tracked at all times by his cell GPS chip or by cell tower triangulation. We need to know everyone who makes contact with him." McGrath put his hands on his hips. "From this moment forward, Mark Johnson is our top priority."

CHAPTER 21

ALFONSO REYES FILLED TWO WINE glasses one-third full with a rich, smooth, Argentine Merlot. He swirled the rose-colored liquid in both goblets as he carried them back to the couch, where the journalist waited. She stood as he approached.

Marie Benoit was her name. She was French by citizenship and African by ethnicity. She'd been educated in the United Kingdom and had a British accent, which seduced his senses and increased his desire for her. She was lithe and tall and was conservatively dressed in a tan skirt and jacket. The light color of her clothing contrasted sharply with her ebony skin.

Marie took the glass, and her dark brown eyes seemed to pierce straight into his soul, or so he imagined. Then she appraised the wine glass.

"Are these diamond wine glasses?" she asked.

"Indeed they are. You're familiar with these, then?"

She nodded. "Last year in Mumbai, I interviewed a Saudi prince, and he served wine in a pair of similar glasses. I love the embedded diamond in the stem." She held the glass up a little higher as she studied the near-perfect rock that glittered in the stem just below the goblet. "I'm told these glasses can go for upward of five thousand US dollars each."

"They are a bit pricey," Reyes said. He'd wanted to impress her with his knowledge and his expensive collection, but it was clear she was not easily impressed. "The vessel is made from borosilicate, a type of glass known for its high resistance to thermal shock. So the glass maintains the wine's properties at normal levels while the glass is held in warm hands. The point-one-five-carat diamond is of G color and VVS1 purity. It and the borosilicate are fused at 1200 degrees Celsius, so the goblet is very durable."

Marie nodded and sipped, as did Reyes. She sat down, but he didn't try to sit next to her. That would have been too obvious, and he could tell that her shields were up. No doubt many men had tried to seduce this woman, and he would try also. He was patient, though, and he respected her personal space. He sat on the second leather sofa a few feet away, and for a moment, they both gazed into the fireplace.

It was a ten-foot-long appliance that only reached two feet off the floor. It featured an exotic gas log that stretched the full length of the chamber, giving the illusion of a continuous, ten-foot-long flame. Above the low fireplace was an expansive window wall that allowed them to gaze out onto the naturally landscaped courtyard of his estate.

She said, "We were discussing possible dates for an in-depth interview regarding your new children's hospital for cancer research. I think the European fundraising connection is particularly interesting. Ideally, my camera crew and I would want to accompany you on your tour through Switzerland and Germany."

"As you probably know, I'm chartering a private jet for the trip next week. You're welcome to accompany me on the flight and conduct the interview then, but I'm afraid my time will be very limited on the ground over there."

"Fine," Marie said. "Will Mrs. Reyes be available for an interview also?"

Reyes gazed at the journalist over the rim of his glass. "She'll be doing some prep work for some other local fundraising activities I'll conduct here and throughout South America on my return." He shrugged. "And quite frankly, someone has to make sure my stepdaughter goes to school."

After six years, he still couldn't bring himself to think of that little runt as his daughter, and he didn't want his wife within ten miles of Marie Benoit. His mind wandered a bit at the prospect of having Marie to himself on a ten-hour flight over the Atlantic. He was about to continue the discussion when his cell chimed. He looked at the device and saw it was Ricardo Guzman, his bodyguard and personal assistant. The man would never interrupt him unless it was urgent, so Reyes took the call.

"*Si?*" he said. He listened for a few seconds, then said, "Mark Johnson? Who is this man?" He listened again. "He's going to the FBI? What information could he possibly have about my business operations?"

He looked at Marie as Guzman spoke and smiled an apology at her. "Prep the plane and have our people do a background check on him and his family, and set up an interview. I want to talk to him personally."

Reyes disconnected the call and stood. "I'm sorry, Ms. Benoit, but business calls." He set his wine glass on the slate coffee table. "Check with your staff and let me know if you'd like to travel with me to Europe. Meanwhile, I have an exciting business opportunity to check out in Albuquerque."

CHAPTER 22

1025 MST, FRIDAY

ALBUQUERQUE, NM

CARL JOHNSON PREPARED TO LEAVE the cab of the eighteen-wheeler at the westbound off-ramp of I-40 at Juan Tabo Boulevard, near the east end of Albuquerque. The driver, Stan Harbor, was a genuinely nice guy. He shared his food and water—he was health-conscious and only ate healthy fast food on the road—and even gave Carl a full set of much too large clothes and boots to replace his white lab coat.

He'd given Harbor a sad story about being mugged and stripped, then said he had walked naked four miles in the frigid cold after midnight to get to the hospital emergency room. He showed his bandages as proof of his misfortune. An added touch that was partly true was that he didn't want to go to the police for fear they'd simply lock him up overnight because he had no ID. Harbor bought the whole song and dance. It was, after all, almost the truth.

The only fault Carl could find in the man was his incessant enjoyment of country-western music. He had the satellite radio on every minute of the day and night, even when he slept.

When Carl called his son from the hospital, Mark was on break at work, so he couldn't get online to wire money by Western Union. He wouldn't be able to get to the house to FedEx his ID and credit card for a few more hours. So, they talked for a couple of minutes, and Carl glossed over what had happened to him and where he'd been for almost two weeks. After hanging up, Carl got out of the building as quickly as possible.

He'd made his way west to the nearest interstate on-ramp and hung out at the truck stop until Stan came along and offered him a ride. As luck would have it, Stan was bound for Cali—"The *California* Cali," the man had said with a laugh. "Not the *drug capital of South America* Cali, Colombia"—and his route eventually hit I-40, which went right through Albuquerque.

Sitting on a road-rash butt for thirty hours—plus two additional six-hour sleep stops for Stan—was tough, but Carl sucked it up. He hadn't thought to carry a change of bandages and more salve cream for his wounds. As the wounds started to dry out and scab over, sometimes the slightest movement caused the newly formed scabs to crack painfully.

Carl waved one last time, then slammed the door and hopped down from the runner in his ill-fitting clothes. When the light turned green, the big truck thundered straight across the intersection and back onto the westbound on-ramp.

He made his way a few blocks north to his local bank branch, where he almost couldn't get money from his account without ID. He didn't blame the teller. With clothes that fit like big potato sacks and two weeks of razor stubble growing all over his jaw and neck, he looked like a vagrant, not a professional real estate agent with thousands of dollars in his account. Fortunately, the branch manager knew him—the bank prided itself on personal service—and she authorized his withdrawal.

He hopped a westbound bus, then caught a southbound connection and ended up at the huge Walmart superstore on Eubank Boulevard just south of the interstate. There, he bought a new set of clothes and shoes. He also picked up a light jacket and a thin head glove as the mid-November temperature in the high desert was unseasonably cool. He bought a disposable razor and shaved in the restroom.

Properly dressed and cleaned up, Carl trashed Stan's clothes and left the restroom. He walked north to Lomas, where he caught the westbound bus to Wyoming Blvd, then caught a northbound connection to his son's apartment complex three miles north. As he sat on the northbound bus, he reflected on how long he'd lived in Albuquerque—over twenty-five years. He'd tried to leave a few times to pursue other opportunities, but the call of home always pulled him back. This time, he thought, coming back home felt very different.

On the westward journey with Stan Harbor, he decided that he was not going to pursue legal action against the city police and the FBI. What was the point anyway? Neither law enforcement agency was going to admit any fault in the mistaken identity.

"Yeah, we're really sorry we gave you to some secret government agents who kidnapped you and beat the shit out of you and tortured you, but hey, we thought you were a terrorist. It was all really just a big misunderstanding, so no hard feelings, okay?"

He knew the city and federal governments could throw a hundred attorneys into combat against the one low-budget attorney he could afford. They'd keep paying their attorneys to stall the process with lots of trivial motions until Carl ran out of money and gave up. That's the way the federal, state, and local governments conducted legal business, and they didn't like to lose.

In truth, Carl just wanted to put the whole terrible nightmare of the ordeal behind him. He still couldn't believe he'd only been in custody for eleven days. Without a doubt, his captivity had been the longest eleven days of his life.

He sat in the section of forward-facing seats on the right side of the bus and wondered how he could ever get back to living a normal life after what he'd been through. He felt the same mix of anger and rage that had simmered inside him for nearly a year in the aftermath of his first assault by those downtown cops four years ago, except this time, it felt a hundred times more intense.

Carl felt someone touching his shoulder, and he spun around so fast, he nearly fell out of his seat.

The elderly woman seated behind him flinched at his sudden movement, then said, "Are you all right, young man?"

"What do you mean am I all right?"

"You were shaking and mumbling. I thought—"

"You thought what?" Carl said. "You thought maybe you were going to help me? You have no idea—" He stopped suddenly as he realized he was shouting at the woman, and everyone on the bus had gone silent.

They all stared at him.

"Just mind your own goddamn business," he said.

None of these people had the slightest idea how to help him. They were scurrying about their silly little meaningless lives, having inane conversations or arguments about pointless things, running stupid errands, or working at dead-end jobs. They had no clue how horrible their government was or what the government would allow their legions of covert soldiers to do to them on a whim in the name of national security.

Over the past four years, Carl had finally been able to let go of his anger after the downtown cops jacked him up, though it had taken many months. At least, he thought he'd let go. After his defiant reaction to the FBI during his takedown at Starbucks, he was sure he'd never truly gotten over that experience. Maybe a shrink would say his defiance was some kind of defensive adaptation.

"I wonder what a fucking shrink would say about me now."

The elder woman behind him gasped. He had vocalized his thoughts and hadn't even realized it. If he didn't have control over his thoughts and feelings, much less over what came out of his mouth, how could he go back to work?

In sales, one had to be upbeat and positive all the time. *"Always on,"* as they say in the business. He had to smile and mean it. If he couldn't do sales, how would he earn a living? What kind of job could he get?

Then he had a crazy thought. Even if he had a shrink to help him, who would believe his story? Besides, how would talking about it change anything or help him? It hadn't helped him in two marriages, and he sure couldn't see the benefit of counseling about his new trauma.

What he needed was to beat up somebody to work out his anger and frustration. Maybe if he ever had the opportunity to catch that woman cop or that government agent in a dark alley somewhere...

Carl laughed aloud, and the guy in the seat two up and across the aisle looked back at him.

He glared at the young man. *What the fuck are you looking at?*

The man looked away quickly.

Yeah, he was tough with a scared fat guy on a bus, but against Agent Klipser... Hell, ten of him couldn't beat up that trained agent. That was one scary government man, and the mere thought of seeing him again made Carl shiver involuntarily.

Sometimes you get the bear, and sometimes the bear gets you.

He forgot what smart person originally said that. He'd seen it on an old episode of Star Trek. The one with Picard, not Kirk.

Life wasn't fair all the time, Carl thought. Sometimes, you got your ass kicked, and there's nothing you can do about it. Sometimes, getting on with your life was the only real option.

Carl felt a tremendous need to see his son. Ever since Mark was a baby, they'd never gone a single week without talking by phone. Before his arrest, they still texted several times a week. So, instead of commiserating with a best friend, Carl felt an almost overwhelming desire to get a long, loving hug from his son, then sit around and eat popcorn and watch action flicks or goofy comedies all day.

Carl felt his eyes water, so he just closed them and enjoyed the pleasant warmth of the emotions and memories that flowed through him. Even though he and Mark's mother divorced shortly after he was born, Carl had made a conscious effort to stay in his son's life. In fact, he couldn't imagine *not* being in his son's life—couldn't imagine *not* talking to him every week or seeing him at every opportunity. When Mark was growing up, Carl flew him out to visit every Christmas and every summer.

When Mark relocated to New Mexico to live with him, their relationship continued to evolve, and they grew closer. Then, one day, Carl found his son perusing the classifieds, looking for his own apartment. Instead of getting angry, though, he made probably the single best decision of his life. He smiled at the memory.

"Don't worry about it, Son," he'd said. "You need your own place, so let's go furniture shopping."

He was convinced that showing support at what had to have been a very stressful time for his son actually made Carl the coolest dad in the galaxy. He never took that gift for granted because he knew what it was like to *not* have his father in his life.

The bus pulled to a stop right in front of Mark's apartment complex. The huge complex held a dozen three-story buildings, each with maybe thirty units. A brown iron security fence surrounded the entire complex at the very edge of the property where the sidewalk separated the property from the street, so Carl had to backtrack south thirty feet to enter the apartment grounds at a break in the fence at the entry driveway. Then he turned back north toward Mark's building and saw his son standing outside the foyer.

Mark was leaning against the glass wall beside the turquoise door, waiting for him. He had his cell phone in his hand and looked like he was busy texting someone. Or maybe he was playing on Facebook or something. Carl actually approached within a dozen feet of his son before the young man looked up from his slider cell phone.

Mark smiled for a moment, until a look of shock and confusion swept across his face. Carl figured his gaunt appearance must have surprised Mark. The young man pushed off from the wall and pocketed his cell. He walked quickly toward Carl, and the smile appeared again. They were just about to embrace when the gunfire began.

CHAPTER 23

1215 MST, FRIDAY
ALBUQUERQUE, NM

ALFONSO REYES RODE IN THE front passenger seat of the blacked-out SUV, and Ricardo Guzman peered out the driver's side window of the bench seat behind Reyes. The driver cruised the big black truck slowly southbound on Wyoming Boulevard next to the median. He flowed with traffic, careful not to draw attention by speeding.

"There he is," Guzman said, holding up a black-and-white printout. "That's Mark Johnson standing by the door."

"Good," Reyes said. "Let's pull in here and grab him. See what he knows."

The driver pulled into the left turn lane but had to wait a long time for a gap in oncoming traffic.

"Wait! Don't pull in there!" Guzman slapped his palm against the back of the driver's seat as if reinforcing the urgency of his warning. "It's a trap. I see *Federales* everywhere in there. I see two on the roof of the adjacent building, and four are shadowing that man walking toward Mark."

Reyes craned his neck around to assess the situation. He, too, could see combat-ready men in black sneaking across the parking lot, staying hidden behind cars.

"FBI," he growled. "Who is that man they're stalking?"

"I can't see his face from this angle, but he's definitely on an intercept vector with our target. Should we abort?"

Reyes thought for the briefest of moments, then shook his head. "I can't imagine that he has any information harmful to my operation, but with everyone looking for the girl, I can't take any chances and risk the ransom payment. We'll kill them both."

Before Reyes had even completed the command, Guzman had crossed to the passenger side of the SUV and had his window powered down as the driver pulled a U-turn and sped north in front of Mark Johnson and the unknown man.

Reyes powered his window down also, and both men stuck their automatic rifles out. They started firing even as a dozen FBI agents converged on the two men.

CHAPTER 24

1215 MST, FRIDAY
ALBUQUERQUE, NM

S UDDENLY, CARL FOUND HIMSELF SURROUNDED by shouting FBI agents…again. They were all dressed in black tactical gear. Agents appeared from around the back of the building and the front. They stormed from the sides. They even came from behind parked cars. It was all too familiar to Carl, but not to Mark. His son stopped in mid-stride with a panicked look on his face.

The front door right next to where Mark had been standing flew open. Carl's stomach jumped into his throat as he recognized Agent Klipser and the female FBI cop. They held Tasers instead of guns.

At the same instant, he heard the loud clattering sound of automatic rifle fire coming from the street. Just as suddenly as the FBI assault had begun, all the cops had flung themselves to the ground. Carl and Mark were left standing alone in the center of the ambush. Mark's gaze frantically touched Carl's as if seeking a rational explanation for what was happening. His arms still reached out to Carl, for they'd been mere seconds from embracing.

Carl felt only one instinct, and that was to throw himself on top of his son to shield him from danger, but before his brain could translate that thought into a physical action, bullets whizzed by his head, tugged at his jacket collar, and slammed into Mark's body. Blood splattered as Mark was literally lifted from his feet and slammed against the brick wall behind him. The bullets that missed Mark, and the ones that passed through his son's body, blasted brick shrapnel into the air along with glass shards from the apartment windows and the entry door.

Carl stood frozen with shock. In a slow-motion dream-gaze, he noticed the assault cops clamoring to their feet, dropping their Tasers and pulling handguns. They were stayed by Klipser and the woman cop. There was too much traffic. Too many innocent civilians were in the line of fire, they said.

In the sudden absence of gunfire, Carl heard the overpowered engine of an SUV racing away, and his gaze followed that sound. He stared at the black truck. The rear passenger side window was sliding up, but the man in the front seat was still peering out his window, staring right at Carl.

It was *him*. He was gazing right at the real kidnapper the FBI had mistaken him for.

CHAPTER 25

C ENTRAL AVENUE IS ONE OF the few streets that spans the entire east and west ends of Albuquerque. It was a sizable street with three lanes on each side for most of its length, and the lanes of each direction were separated by a wide median with street signs and streetlamps.

Carl sat at the north-facing window of the hole-in-the-wall burger joint on the west end of Central Avenue and watched his target. He was a big Hispanic guy with a bald head and tattoos covering his neck, shoulders, and arms. The man wore only a white wife-beater tank despite the cold, and he strutted across the street like he owned it—like he was daring drivers to hit him.

Carl wasn't really interested in the big man. He was interested in the man the fellow worked for. Still, he had to smile at the guy's gall. Carl had been to countries during his military career where drivers didn't give a shit about pedestrians. They'd just as soon drive over a human obstacle and then spit on the dumbass for the inconvenience of getting blood on their car.

He scanned the street east and west, looking for the ever-present FBI surveillance team. Until yesterday, they had been shadowing him for the past two weeks and six days. Technically, the FBI no longer had a reason to follow him since he was now officially dead. If he saw any FBI agents, then he would know his strategy to disappear had failed. That would effectively end his first amateur mission, his first foray into the shadows that comprised the US government's world of domestic covert ops.

Twenty-one.

That was the exact number of days since he'd last spoken with his son. Previously, the longest time without contact with Mark was eleven days, when he'd been in government custody getting interrogated. Before that, barely two days would pass without a phone call or a text with his son. Now it was twenty-one days…and counting.

This time, it was permanent. It was the beginning of forever.

The Thanksgiving holiday had come and gone the previous week. Carl found it almost humorous how folks found weird ways to measure the passage of time. Sometimes, it was the approach of birthdays or holidays, and sometimes, it was the changing of seasons, or the weeks or months between events, or sales, or other milestones. For Carl, it had become much more personal.

He'd stood there while his son was murdered within arm's reach. Reyes held a rapid-fire Uzi—Carl had seen enough action movies to recognize that weapon—but he had stopped shooting as soon as he saw Carl. He seemed as surprised to see Carl as Carl was to see him. That was the only reason Carl still lived.

In his mind, he replayed the scene for the hundredth time. Bullets had destroyed the front facade of Mark's apartment building, shattering glass and metal and stucco all around his son. He saw his son's body hit many times, both in reality and in the unending replay of his mind. Over and over again, he watched those bullets slam Mark against the wall. Blood splattered everywhere, and he sagged to the ground, a blood halo widening under his shoulders.

Carl had stood there through the whole gun battle, even though the cops had all smartly hit the ground. Mark was the only casualty, but Carl had trouble understanding how he had not been hit too.

He replayed the final sight again. The SUV accelerated away as he and Reyes stared at each other. His torture suddenly made complete sense. The days of custody and all the questions now held meaning.

Carl had gazed upon the man the US government was looking for— the man who had kidnapped *the girl*. It was also unnerving because the man in the SUV did not merely *resemble* Carl, and he was not *similar* to Carl. Reyes looked *exactly* like Carl.

Agent Klipser reacted first, touching his left ear and shouting into the air. Then he retrieved a belt radio and shouted into that device too. There were sirens everywhere as cop cars and unmarked FBI SUVs suddenly screamed onto Wyoming Boulevard from the side streets in pursuit of the gunmen.

A big FBI truck peeled around the corner of Mark's building and skidded to a stop a dozen feet from Carl. The agents ran right by him, close enough that he could hear their breathing as they raced to catch the *real* bad guy. They passed so close, he could smell their adrenaline-fueled underarm odor and minty chewing gum breath. He could smell the FBI woman's hair shampoo. They all climbed into the SUV, and it raced away from the murder scene with a roar of its engine and the squeal of rubber on asphalt.

A horn blaring outside the burger joint suddenly brought Carl back to the here and now. The tough guy he'd been watching threw up the middle finger at whoever was laying on their horn, but he didn't even turn around to see who it was.

His target got up onto the far sidewalk, then walked across the parking lot of a large grocery store. The man disappeared around the back of the store. Carl had been told to look for that man, for he would lead him to another individual.

Carl got up from his table and tossed the remainder of his cheeseburger and fries into the trash receptacle, then placed the red plastic tray in a basket next to the trash can. He headed out the side door and stopped at the curb, looking for a break in traffic so he could cross the street to follow his target.

This was the important first step of his plan. He needed money—a lot more than he had available. He had withdrawn all the money in his personal and business checking accounts, including the holding accounts for income tax and state sales tax. He didn't need those accounts anymore because he wasn't going to file any more taxes—ever. Why even bother? What he was planning to do was ten times more illegal than cheating on taxes. Still, he only had a tad less than ten grand to work with. He needed more. Much more.

Initially, he thought about taking a few months to make a fitness comeback. Maybe he'd join a karate studio or a street-fighting gym in case he ran into guys like Agent Klipser during the next phase of his operation. Then, he realized that while he might learn a few kick-ass moves, he'd never accomplish his mission with physical confrontations with people. He was fifty-three years old. He wasn't going to win any fistfights against men half his age, certainly not against highly trained FBI agents or covert operators.

If he was going to achieve his goal, he'd do so with brainpower and detailed planning. If he needed to go toe-to-toe with the likes of Klipser, he'd have to hire someone to do that for him, and that person was going to be very expensive.

The feds had military-grade weapons, armored SUVs, encrypted comm gear, sophisticated computers, and surveillance equipment, and maybe even access to military satellites and domestic drones. To match wits with the US government on that level, Carl would need that kind of gear also, as well as people to operate the equipment. Money could buy probably anything he needed, except maybe satellites and drones.

He knew his own limitations. He was an excellent executive planner and high-level thinker, but when it came down to the nuts and bolts of actually running an operation, he preferred to have someone else in that role. He needed to hire a detail-oriented person to run his ops.

He also needed to learn several things very quickly, things that cops and the feds were trained to do from the very beginning of their careers. He needed to learn how to avoid directly answering questions and how to parse out necessary information on a need-to-know basis. He needed to learn how to lie convincingly and instantly, without thinking, without hesitation, and without tell-tale eye movements.

He had to learn police procedures and FBI operations protocols so he could anticipate their tactical responses and stay one or two steps ahead of them. He also needed a refresher course on shooting handguns and maybe even some automatic weapons, though he demoted that task as a lower priority. He wouldn't win a shootout with cops or the feds, either. It was best to leave all the macho-man bullshit to professionals who were good at that stuff. Without a doubt, he needed to hire mercenaries.

He also had to learn how to change his appearance, how to disappear and fade into crowds, how to steal transportation, how to get fake IDs and passports, and how and where to acquire weapons, technology, and high-tech explosives. He had to actually find the mercenaries before he could hire them. Most important, he had to do all that discretely. One slipup, one word to the wrong person who might turn out to be a federal informant or an undercover cop, and he'd be under FBI investigation again and likely not even know it.

Money came first, for without money, none of the rest of his to-do list was possible, and that was why he was following the young man in the white tank top.

On a Friday night in the little-big city of Albuquerque, Carl was officially homeless. Even better, he was officially dead, and that was essential for the next part of his plan. He now walked around town with a wad of bills in his pocket and the rest of what remained of his withdrawal in a money belt strapped around his waist. He hadn't bothered to close his real estate business. He no longer cared about any of that. His creditors would find out fairly soon anyway as soon as their electronic bills bounced off his now-empty checking account. That chapter of his life was over, whether or not he brought formal closure to it.

Over the last couple of weeks, he'd spent considerable time trying to figure out why the feds had arrested him in the first place. If the kidnapper was so damned elusive, how was it that someone just happened to see him—Carl—and call in the cavalry? That kind of accidental coincidence only happened in the movies. The only conclusion Carl could come up with was that the feds had come across his face on some facial recognition computer program and thought he was *the other guy*.

As a result of that conclusion, he had changed his appearance. A quick stop at Walmart yielded some dark wrap-around glasses, which he had removed when the sun went down. Next door at Sally's Beauty Supplies, he found some face cream that went on dry. He bought two shades of cream—one that went on very light so he'd look White, and one that had a dark tint that would make him look several shades darker than his normal skin color.

At a wig supply store across town on south Broadway, he'd purchased two wigs. One was dreadlocks for his brown-man disguise, and the other was a short, simple brown hairstyle for his White-man disguise.

The latter was a woman's wig, but the plain style would look just as generic on a guy.

It was in his Caribbean disguise, with dreadlocks and darkened skin, that he followed his target across Central Avenue. He found a break in the eastbound bumper-to-bumper traffic and stopped on the median next to a sign that was prevalent at almost every intersection from downtown all the way out to Coors Boulevard, prohibiting cruising.

Carl knew for a fact that the signs did little to discourage the decades-old weekend practice. Cruising was what the young folks in the South Valley did on the weekend. They drove slowly up and down Central Avenue, *cruising*—looking for whoever they could see and whoever could see them.

Carl found his break in traffic, then jogged across to the sidewalk. Then he crossed the same parking lot his target had crossed moments ago. He darted behind the grocery store, where he saw a group of young men talking. He guessed they were about to conduct some not-quite-legal business. The parking lot was well-lit, but the delivery docks behind the store where the young men stood were only sparsely lit by weak lamps. There were too few lamps, and those that functioned offered only small pools of light.

The group of five men stood huddled together in the dark space between two dim pools of light. They all turned toward him as he approached. The tough guy in the wife-beater T-shirt split off from the group and took two steps forward. If the man's resistance to the near-freezing cold was any indication, he was a hell of a lot tougher than Carl, who wore a T-shirt under a pullover sweater under his jacket.

"You lost, Homes?" Tough Guy said.

Carl looked past the man and at the other four for a long moment until it was clear he was intentionally ignoring the challenger. Three of the other men glanced at each other, then they collectively looked at the fourth. It was clear to Carl that this fourth man was the alpha dog of the group, so that's who he centered his attention on.

The slender young man stood about five-eight and weighed maybe a buck-fifty. In the dim light, Carl could see the fellow wore dark pants, maybe Dickies or chinos, dark shoes, and a heavy, red plaid shirt over a dark undershirt. Black hair peeked out from under a skull cap, and the young man had dark eyes.

The slender man nodded at him and stepped forward. "You come up here to do some business, brah? How much money you got?"

Carl smiled. "Two thousand," he lied.

The man raised his eyebrows in surprise. "I tell you what. Why don't you let me hold that for you? I wouldn't want anything bad to happen to you. This neighborhood is kinda hard on tourists, you know?"

Carl shook his head calmly. "I'm no tourist."

"If you don't give me your money, Esteban might kick your ass."

The leader stuck out his hand and waggled his fingers for the money. The big man, Esteban, stood just over the six-foot mark and probably weighed over 250 pounds. He was thick in the chest and gut.

"That's not how we play the game, my friend. I'm not going to give you my money because he *might* kick my ass. If he's going to take my money, he actually has to do some ass-kicking first." Carl shrugged. "Of course, then you'll be missing out on ten times that much."

CHAPTER 26

1849 MST, FRIDAY
ALBUQUERQUE, NM

ALPHA DOG'S EYEBROWS RAISED A notch, and he shrugged. "Okay," he said. "You have my attention."

"I know three businessmen who each have about two hundred grand available in cash. We have your boys babysit the family while you and I go to the bank tomorrow with these men for a cash withdrawal."

"And how were you able to quantify each man's liquidity?"

Carl was taken aback by the young man's word choice, and he felt a shiver of fear flash up his spine. He'd figured these guys for simple gangbangers, but now he sensed there was something more devious to this particular young fellow. He suddenly felt he might be out of his element against a man who was obviously educated in the arena of illegal finance.

Skeptically, he said, "They're investors, and I used to be their real estate agent. Whenever they made offers on income property, I made them submit a statement of cash on hand to show their purchasing power."

The young man nodded. "So you propose that we just waltz into three banks tomorrow and walk out with two hundred grand each time?" Carl narrowed his eyes and nodded, but the man shook his head. "You're new at this, aren't you?"

Answer like a cop would. "What makes you think so?"

"My friend, that is most definitely *not* how that game is played unless you want to be a house guest of the FBI."

The young man gave the big guy a head-nod and said something to him in rapid-fire Spanish. Carl watched as the big guy moved over to the edge of the building, where he could keep an eye out for police.

The young man said, "Let's step into my office over here." He took Carl by the arm and guided him across the alley, out of earshot of the others. They stayed in the shadows between the pools of light.

Carl said, "It sounds like you may be familiar with this particular game."

The young man nodded. "I have…um, family members in the trade." He paused and looked Carl up and down. "You look like a Jamaican island boy, but you don't sound like one."

"It's a disguise."

"No shit, homey. So, how exactly did you happen to be in this neighborhood?"

"I stopped at the MMA gym over on Isleta."

"I know the place. And you told them you needed some money, and they just gave you my name?"

He said it innocently enough, but Carl knew it was a test. "There were some guys standing around outside. I told them I needed someone who could help me collect some money from some folks."

"Mm-hmm," the young man said with a nod. "You a cop?"

Carl shook his head. "The guy that told me where to find you struck me as the kind of man who could smell a cop from a mile away. But he gave me a code phrase. He said to say your mama wears combat boots."

"Remind me to kick his ass later. But, in fact, my mother was in the army back in the day, so she did wear combat boots, literally."

Standing close to him, Carl figured the man was maybe half his age. His dark eyes held a mischievous glint, but he looked keenly intelligent. There was something else Carl saw in the man's eyes, and he liked it. He saw a little bit of recklessness and excitement, like he was familiar with the adventure of illegal finance and open to embracing the activity.

"Well," the man said. "Point number one: Taking hostages and extorting money are federal offenses, and the FBI takes those activities very seriously. Point number two: Banks have cameras and security procedures to prevent what you're suggesting. So, if a couple of—shall we say—men of color such as ourselves try to walk out of those banks with a briefcase full of greenbacks, we'll get our pictures taken, and we'll be marked as highly suspicious."

The young man took a deep breath and shrugged. "At best, we'll succeed once. Worst case, the first bank will be instantly suspicious. After all, nobody carries money out of banks like that anymore. They'll likely delay our departure while they check the federal database to see if we're legit, whereupon we'll be busted before we leave." He shrugged. "My uncle worked in the creative finance sector in Mexico for several years."

"Are you suggesting we hire him?"

The young man sighed. "Unfortunately, he's no longer available. He was retired preemptively and with prejudice."

Knocked off. Killed. Assassinated. Same thing that will happen to me if I'm caught. Same thing that happened to Mark. "What do you recommend?"

"I recommend setting up several offshore accounts in countries that don't have extradition agreements or shared information protocols with the US. You provide me with the address of each investor's family and his schedule. Then we send two guys that look honest and hardworking to visit the first family, and we send a scary-looking guy to visit the related investor.

"Our man gives each of your businessmen a smartphone with a picture of our other guys hanging with his wife and kids. Then he gives each businessman an account number, and he goes online to make the wire transfer. Rinse and repeat two more times. You and I are never connected with the crime or seen in public.

"Of course, I can't use these guys." He nodded over his shoulder at his crew of four. "They live here in the *Burque*, and two of them have police records longer than my dick." The young man held out his hands in mock surrender. "That's pretty damn long too, by the way."

"If you say so."

"I can use some guys I know who just came up from Mexico looking for work. Job gets done, and the guys go back home. This thing goes south, they can't be traced back to us. Once each transfer is made, I get an electronic notification. Then, I transfer the money out of the initial account and distribute it among our untraceable international accounts. I'll need a laptop, of course, with a prepaid wireless USB dongle and a prepaid disposable phone, all of which will also be untraceable. There'll also be fees to grease the wheels, as they say. Probably around the 20 percent mark, if that's okay."

"Where the hell did you learn all this stuff?"

"Like I said, it's a family trade." The man smiled and shrugged. "We kinda pass the knowledge along as a family tradition."

As a project manager, Carl had evaluated a lot of defense contract proposals to determine if his company was getting its money's worth. He'd learned over the years to quickly determine which parts of a proposal made sense, which parts seemed padded, and which parts were negotiable.

He looked at his new business partner and nodded. "I agree to everything except two points. For the time being, I control the passwords to all the accounts. We'll meet in person to do the actual transfer of funds, and you can have 10 percent of this first phase. If we pull this off without a hitch, we'll discuss 20 percent for phase two."

The young man nodded. "Very well. We'll see how the first phase goes. And by the way, my name is…Garcia."

Garcia was the most generic Hispanic name Carl could think of, so he matched him. "I'm Smith."

They shook hands, but Carl could see skepticism on the young man's face. He either doubted the mission, or Carl, though he couldn't tell which. The guy was in it for the quick buck. There was no trust or loyalty beyond the potential payday, and Carl was comfortable with that. He didn't want the kid getting comfortable or careless. In fact, he planned to use the kid for his first phase, then move on and maybe find another assistant for the next phase. He wanted to stay mobile—keep his team small and disposable.

"Mr. Smith, when would you like phase one to occur?"

"First thing Monday morning." He pulled a wad of cash from his right pocket. "Here's two thousand so you can get your disposable equipment." He handed the man the cash. "And your guy didn't even have to kick my ass."

Garcia smiled. "I've always believed that negotiation is a more powerful tool than force."

Carl reached into his left jacket pocket and pulled out two of his four prepaid smartphones—"burners," as the internet called them. He'd known he'd need them to make untraceable phone calls. He gave a black one and a silver one to Garcia.

"Use the silver phone only to call me, and for no other calls. Use the black one for the rest of your business. My number is preprogrammed into the silver phone as speed dial number one. When we're done with the first phase, destroy them both and the laptop, and we'll get another set. And by destroy, I mean smash and burn them beyond the point that anything can be salvaged, especially the chips and the hard drive."

They agreed to meet at nine o'clock on Monday morning at his favorite downtown coffee shop. The young man turned to rejoin his guys.

"Mr. Garcia," Carl called softly. "There's just one more minor detail."

Garcia stopped and turned. "And that is?"

"There are people who are going to be very interested in this operation as we progress, and these people make the FBI look like pussies. You get careless and fuck this up, there'll be nowhere on earth they won't find you." He paused. "And trust me when I say that you won't like it when they do."

CHAPTER 27

2352 MST, FRIDAY
ALBUQUERQUE, NM

CARL JOHNSON SAT ON THE ratty couch in the dark living room of the low-budget hotel not even a mile from his meeting with the young Mr. Garcia. It was close to midnight, but sleep would not come. It had nothing to do with the constant squabbling coming from the room next to his. The woman over there had lit into her man at eight o'clock about not having a job, for smoking too much, for getting high, and for cheating. She hadn't let up since.

He ignored her fussing and contemplated what he'd planned and accomplished in the past thirty hours, and what he was about to do in the next seventy-two hours. He'd broken several laws by setting his house on fire, though the internet said the investigators would call it a fireplace accident until they discovered the body. Then they'd call it suicide when they discovered all the booze and pills.

All bets were off if they discovered the body was not Carl Johnson. Then McGrath and his minions would get involved.

Monday, he'd start breaking federal laws by extorting money from his former investors and electronically transferring that money out of the country. But when people started dying from his version of justice, there would be no turning back and no surrendering. There was no doubt in his mind. There was no wavering in his commitment. They killed his son, so they had to pay with their lives.

Carl thought about Friedrich Nietzsche's most famous quote that most folks are familiar with: "That which does not destroy me only makes me stronger."

He found it interesting how he had used it over the years. All the life challenges he'd faced that he thought required the use of such a statement now seemed so trivial compared to what he'd experienced in the last thirty days.

Then he considered that most people were not familiar with another lesser-known Nietzsche quote: "When you look into an abyss, the abyss also looks back at you."

Alone in the darkness of his motel room, Carl was standing at the metaphorical precipice, gazing into the abyss. He was one step shy of literally jumping in there. It was a place where normal people never wanted or needed to go.

He wasn't afraid of what he saw in the abyss. In fact, he wanted to go there. He *needed* to.

The FBI woman was in there. Agent Klipser was in there. A shadow figure called Director McGrath was in there too. They were all staring back at him from just beyond the threshold, as if they were right on the other side of the event horizon of a black hole. The difference between himself and them was that they lived and breathed in the abyss. They were comfortable in there, lying, bullying, and killing innocent people.

Carl had been willing to get past everything McGrath and his people had done to him when he'd had Mark to return home to. Without Mark, though, he could never be whole or normal again. Justice and personal closure lay in the abyss.

Carl took a deep breath and looked to his left, toward the unseen wall in the darkness. The woman over there was throwing things now. Apparently, she was missing her husband, and her projectiles were thumping into the shared wall.

The inescapable fact that hurt Carl the most was that he himself shared the blame for Mark's death. It was his own defiance of Agent Klipser and his attempt to get the man to kill him. If he hadn't rebelled or become obstinate and confrontational, he'd still be in custody, and Mark would still be alive.

Carl began pacing again in the darkness. It was all because some rich politician's daughter got kidnapped. She was probably dead by now.

After all, she'd been missing for well over a month. Who the hell was she, and why did Mark have to pay for her life with his own?

Carl stopped pacing and shook his head. Logic told him the two events were unrelated. His son had not died for that girl, nor was she responsible for his death. A bad man named Reyes had killed his son, and another bad man, a senior government agent, had engineered the trap that led Reyes to commit the murder.

One man operated outside the law, and the other operated above the law.

Carl returned to pacing in front of the bed. He had just returned from flying Mark's body home to his mother just before the Thanksgiving holiday. It was a hell of a thing to put any mother through.

When he returned, his closest friends had all called him and left voice messages and text messages, begging him to call, begging him not to spend the holidays alone. He knew they meant well, but he ignored them all. They would never understand that the last thing in the world he wanted was to be around people, families, and kids.

For the last thirty days, he had been completely alone. It was a hard transition, suddenly losing an adult child who was his only true life companion.

He wondered if he really could find the government agent named McGrath. Then he wondered how he could even remain undiscovered, at least until the moment when he had his hands wrapped around the man's throat.

He'd taken the first step, though. The world now thought he was dead.

It had been easy to stage his disappearance, but he knew the ruse wouldn't last long. He just needed a couple of days to implement his plan. McGrath and his crew would certainly know he was still alive as soon as he hit his first target. Then they'd be out gunning for him.

Carl felt good about his plan. He'd done everything correctly so far. At least, he had no indication he'd made any mistakes yet.

Earlier the same day, before he met with young Garcia, Carl had emptied all his checking accounts and made a round-trip four-month reservation to Maui, scheduled to depart the next day. Then, he bought half a dozen bottles of whiskey from the nearest package store and a twenty-four-count bottle of over-the-counter sleeping meds from a convenience store. He wanted to create the impression of a depressed man trying to run away from his sorrow, a man trying to drink away his pain, a man who maybe hadn't slept in several days.

At home, he had spread all the bottles and the pills around the couch and stacked several armfuls of firewood on the right side of the fireplace. He then added a pile of kindling and newspaper carelessly close to the wood and spilled the box of long matches on the floor in front of the fireplace. Several landed amidst the wood, kindling, and paper. It was something an intoxicated man might do. Then he had used one match to light the logs in the fireplace. He left the glass doors and the safety screen open.

When the fire was burning fiercely, he had written his suicide note, roughly scribbled and intentionally misspelled, partly printed and partly written in cursive, and taped it to the outside of the front door.

I can't life without Mark

He had splashed whiskey on the note, more evidence that it had been written by a suicidal man who was already drunk.

Before leaving the house, he turned the plastic bottle of lighter fluid on its side, and with the snap cap open, he stepped on the container. The action splashed a path of flammable liquid that instantly spread flames outside the fireplace.

Hopefully, a cursory investigation by the fire inspector would conclude he'd gotten drunk and drugged, then let the fire get out of control. That would be easy to believe with all the alcohol and sleeping pills scattered around the room. He died in the conflagration. Slam dunk, case closed.

It helped that the FBI had completely trashed his house during his captivity. Every exterior door had been forced open during their raid, and every French door had the glass shattered. Every cabinet, drawer, and closet had had its contents emptied. The fuckers even left the fridge and freezer open, and the whole house stank of rotten food. He didn't bother cleaning up. It fit his scenario of depression.

Finding a body had been the hardest part. It had cost him almost a quarter of his ten grand to bribe a student at the medical investigator's facility at the UNM School of Medicine to provide him with a corpse that wouldn't be missed for a week or more. How the young man covered up the missing body was not Carl's concern. The young man needed cash for whatever reason and was willing to do the deed. The risk of discovery and the burden of punishment was on the student.

Carl was pretty fit, but trying to manhandle a 150-pound stiff body out of the back of his second car, a Jeep Cherokee, from the garage up to the second level was a serious challenge. Midway through the process, he'd broken into a sweat, but he finally dropped the nude corpse in front of the fireplace. Instead of trying to dress the body in his clothes, he simply wrapped one of his bathrobes around it. He left his car keys and driver's license on the kitchen granite counter so the investigator could easily find those in the rubble.

Then, after the fire was burning well outside the fireplace, he walked away from everything he knew—friends, family, neighbors, car, house, business—everything. Even his beloved topless Jeep Wrangler that was probably still parked at the Hyatt, if it hadn't been confiscated by the FBI.

From his experience claiming Mark's body for burial, Carl knew the medical investigator might do an autopsy on the dead body. At that point, he or she would likely discover the body had already been dead before it was burned. Then the doctor would likely discover the body was not the same ethnicity as Carl. Maybe then, he or she would do a toxicology test, and that test would show the body had no sleeping pill drugs or alcohol in it unless, of course, that corpse had also died by a similar suicide.

On the other hand, Carl figured the odds were equally good in a case like his. With no suspicion about the cause of the fire, the MI would just refrigerate the body and call Carl's next of kin. Since Carl's son was dead, his estranged father in California—whom he hadn't seen in nearly twenty years—would get the call.

The normal report of findings after a death might only take two weeks, but if a toxicology test was done, the test report could take up to six months to complete. Initiating that course of action would arouse

McGrath's suspicion, and his people would learn about the deception much sooner than Carl intended.

Either way, Carl figured he'd be presumed dead for at least enough time to launch his mission plan. He'd at least get the first couple of phases of his operation underway. He'd be able to hit his first target, the FBI woman cop. She knew McGrath and Klipser personally, and she no doubt knew how to find them. But first, he had to figure out how to make her talk.

It occurred to Carl that if and when he found Reyes, no one was going to throw him a party and thank him for ridding the world of a kidnapper, or hit man, or whatever the hell that man was. He'd have to answer for that murder as well. He wasn't fooling himself into thinking he was some kind of noble vigilante with a great cause like in a movie. When he declared war on the US government, and when people started dying, they'd come after him. He would hit the FBI's most wanted list for sure.

The only way to survive was to stay ahead of them. Keep moving. Always moving. He found it peculiar that he felt no fear. Someone had to make the shadow government agents pay. For Mark. For countless other victims McGrath and his ilk considered acceptable collateral damage.

Someone had to make them pay.

"If not me, then who?"

He smiled in the darkness as a new thought occurred to him. When he stepped into the abyss in two days, he was voluntarily going to become the terrorist and kidnapper they accused him of being. By subjecting him to extensive torture, McGrath and Klipser had unwittingly given Carl the inner strength and the lack of fear to cross over into the world in which they operated. By killing his son, they had also provided him with motivation. They couldn't hurt him or scare him anymore.

He turned to retrace his path in front of the bed for the hundredth time. Then he froze in mid-step as an absolutely crazy thought occurred to him.

"Who is the girl?" he said aloud. "Where is the girl? What if I can find her first?"

CHAPTER 28

1426 MST, MONDAY
ALBUQUERQUE, NM

B Y EARLY MONDAY AFTERNOON, CARL had accumulated a little over two and a half million dollars. Two-point-six million, to be exact. Minus 10 percent for the young Mr. Garcia.

"Not bad for four hours work," Garcia said. The young man was clearly well-schooled in the art of financial coercion.

Each of the two-member team of his three-man army had been given a cheap disposable smartphone with a camera, and Garcia had synced those phones to an online email account. One of the guys filmed the visit to the family of the target investor, and the other guy did the actual forceful entry. He carried a tire iron behind his back just in case they encountered a door chain or a storm door, but they had not needed it.

This was America, after all. The investors' family members did exactly what Carl would have done at his own house a month ago, before he knew what people were truly capable of. He would have simply opened the door when someone knocked, especially in his relatively exclusive part of town. He probably wouldn't have even checked the peephole.

As Garcia predicted, in Albuquerque, if you see a couple of honest-looking Hispanic men with shy smiles who looked like hardworking, skilled tradesmen, you opened up to see what kind of services they could provide and how much they might charge you—if you needed whatever they were offering. You certainly wouldn't expect them to shove a tire iron in your face, force their way into your house, and take you hostage, but that was exactly what happened to the investors who were home or to their families if the investors were not home.

Three of the targeted investors were work-from-home types, and the other two had regular day jobs. The latter took a little longer to coordinate because Mr. Garcia had to make sure the investor was actually available to discuss financial business at the moment his family was visited. Otherwise, they'd find themselves in an unacceptable extended hostage situation.

There was plenty of shouting, harsh language, and pushing and shoving as Garcia's two men initiated each brief home takeover. One of the wives had started screaming hysterically, but a quick punch to the belly dropped her to the floor and quieted her. That was the only physical violence necessary that day.

Each home invasion was recorded on video and uploaded as an attachment to a draft email, which was never actually sent to anyone. According to Garcia, a draft email that was not transmitted could not be intercepted since there were no electronic trails from a sender or a recipient for the all-seeing electronic eyes of the US government to trace. Yet, the video could still be viewed online.

The third man, also with a smartphone, simply visited the investor at work, showed him the video, and explained quietly what would happen if he didn't transfer a certain amount of money into Carl's account immediately.

No other convincing was necessary. The targets were not spies or hoodlums or corporate celebrities with hostage contingency plans. They were ordinary businessmen caught unawares. They simply did what they were told to protect their families. They had no recourse, but they still received a threat. Tell anyone about the event, and men would return to visit their family again in a week or a month or a year, except the next visit would involve no requests for money and would be much more violent.

After the wire transfers had been completed, Mr. Garcia deleted the videos and the draft email account. He had shown each member of the three-man army how to destroy the cell phones, removing and crushing the SIM cards, breaking apart the phones, and distributing the batteries and other parts in various trash bins behind grocery stores around the city. As motivation for the men to leave the country quickly, a double fee would be paid to them upon their return to Mexico, but only within ten hours. If they dallied, they forfeited their entire fee.

Carl didn't know how Garcia got the men up from Mexico or back there, and he didn't care. All he cared about was that there was no direct link to him. Eventually, the FBI and McGrath's agency would get involved when it became clear what Carl's true objective was. In fact, he was counting on that, but he planned to stay ahead of them until it was too late to stop him.

The mission was everything.

Still in his disguise of dreadlocks and dark skin, Carl sat in one of his favorite downtown coffee shops with Garcia. From their table at the second-floor balcony rail, they could see everyone who entered the chic establishment. They sipped coffee.

None of the investors had tried to be a hero. The three investors targeted in phase one simply got on their phones or computers and made the transaction happen, transferring two hundred grand each. Before noon, Carl had the first six hundred thousand dollars in his new business account. Phase one was complete.

Before the digital ink was dry, Garcia had transferred the money out of that account and into sixteen different accounts by what he called a blind transfer. Carl assumed that meant you could see that it left, but you couldn't see where it went.

Phase two of the operation was equally easy. Two construction companies, both run by associates Carl had done business with, were large enough to be able to transfer a million dollars each without difficulty, but not so large the decision-maker had to approach others in the company to get it done.

One owner ran a one-man operation where he subcontracted all his work to skilled tradesmen. The cash in his account was actually advance payments from construction contracts for work he had yet to perform. In his previous life, Carl had even considered the man a friend, and he knew his former friend would probably go bankrupt from the event. Unfortunately for him, Carl no longer cared about his wellbeing.

Do whatever it takes to accomplish the mission. Find McGrath and make him pay.

The other company was run by a two-man partnership, and both men had easily agreed it was better to give up the money than for one of them to lose a family member.

Garcia said, "Phases one and two all in the same morning. You don't mess around, do you, Mr. Smith?"

Carl said, "Fortunately, this time, there was no need for a demonstration of my commitment." He glanced at Garcia. "But there will come a time when a demonstration will be needed. For the next phase, we will need men willing to do that."

"Only men?"

Carl looked at Garcia and shrugged.

"I only ask because some of the, uh, talent I have access to might be female. Mercenaries come in all pedigrees, and we rarely put requirements on physical characteristics of the package."

Carl nodded. "People," he said. "We will need *people* willing and able to apply the necessary degree of persuasion to achieve my objectives." He let the meaning of his words hang between them.

Garcia nodded his understanding and said, "I assume that includes…" He lowered his voice to a whisper. "Killing?"

"You okay with that?"

Garcia nodded. "And I assume you are going to need my services for the next phase."

"Correct," Carl said. "But as my pops used to say, 'When the shit hits the fan, it's time to get out of the fan business.' You're going to need an emergency exit strategy for the next phase." He told the young man what he wanted him to do. "You have a family?"

He nodded. "Wife and new baby."

Carl said, "You're fixin' to be in the fan business, Mr. Garcia, so if I ever call you and say anything about getting out of the fan business, drop everything and grab your family and use the exit strategy. You may have a day or an hour or as little as five minutes to get out. You never know. Forget about me. Forget about everything." He paused. "This part is important. Sooner or later, the government will find me. When I go down, you don't want to be caught in the cross fire. Use your money and get out of the country. No heroics and no loyalties other than to your family, got it?"

Garcia nodded. "I've never encountered a client in this business that actually cared about the wellbeing of his partners." The young man paused, seemingly trying to figure Carl out.

"Let's get something straight, Mr. Garcia. Nothing interferes with my mission."

"I understand," Garcia said. "The mission is important."

"The mission is everything."

"So," the young man said. "You have a legal team available in case the FBI gets to you or me before you call?"

"I don't know the name of the agency that will come for us, but it won't be the FBI, and no legal team on the planet will be able to help you or me. If you get taken by these people, cooperate. Give them whatever they want. If you don't, they will hurt you and your family."

Garcia did not object or make any comment, so Carl leaned back in his seat and contemplated his next phase.

"So, for phase three, I need a professional who can get us fake IDs and passports so I can travel freely in my two disguises without government computers flagging me. And you'll need passports and new IDs for your family to leave the country if it ever comes to that. And we'll need some legitimate bank accounts with credit cards."

"I know some people who can hook us up with that kind of talent."

Carl was curious about how that process would happen and what the risk of the documentation surviving federal scrutiny was.

"So what do you do, have people use their address to apply for new documents, or do they create fake lease agreements and use those to get false IDs from the Motor Vehicle Department?"

Garcia smiled. "A lot of small-timers who want to get caught do it like that. You can really only do that a few times, though. Sooner or later, someone at the MVD is going to recognize you if you go in more than a couple times to get new docs, even if you use different offices. Some manager or supervisor might recognize your name on a summary sheet or something."

Carl nodded. He was familiar with the Motor Vehicle Department's process for registering cars and applying for new driver's licenses. Last time he went in, they had changed the process and no longer let you walk out with your license. Instead, they started subcontracting that function out to secure identification fabrication companies. Turned out, criminals were breaking into the MVD offices, stealing the license-making equipment, and using them to do exactly what Carl was planning on doing—creating new identity cards.

Garcia continued, "The only way to do it correctly and quickly, without risk of detection, is from the inside." He shrugged. "These men and women get ten bucks an hour to do that kind of work. We'll pay them a flat fee of two thousand to do each one of our requests. That way, we'll know it'll be done right. When they take our money, they become accomplices, and they don't want to get caught any more than we do. So they do it the right way, and they do it carefully."

Carl nodded, satisfied. "Okay, then for phase four, I'm going to need some mercenaries. I'm not talking about some backcountry, yahoo militia guys that grew up pretending the commies are coming. I'll need real shooters—ex-Special Forces with real combat experience and a bunch of kills under their belts. Guys and gals who can go hand-to-hand with the feds and covert ops agents, and who can handle themselves well in a firefight or any other crisis. And make sure at least one of them is a well-qualified, long-distance sniper because I guarantee you, the feds will bring their own snipers to the party."

He recalled seeing SWAT snipers at the roofline of the convention center during his takedown at Starbucks.

"I want our sniper to be able to hit their snipers from farther away than theirs can reach. And we'll need top-tier, military-quality weapons for the mercs, and some specific medical supplies."

He dictated a shopping list to Garcia.

"Sounds like you're going to war."

"I am." Carl nodded. "The feds don't do anything half-assed. They play to win, and so will I."

Garcia shrugged. "Finances I can handle. Fake IDs I can handle. But weaponry and explosives, especially on the scale of what you're looking for, are way out of my league. I know people I can talk to, but a transaction on this scale, or even a series of small transactions for this kind of equipment, can easily get flagged. The FBI and the Mexican equivalent—the Federal Ministerial Police, which everyone calls the

Federales, have a lot of informants. It's going to be hard to keep this quiet."

Carl had anticipated that. "Find the mercenaries first and give them the list. They will know how and where to acquire the equipment on the downlow."

The young man paused. "Don't take this the wrong way, Mr. Smith, but a lot of people think they can outsmart the FBI."

Carl shook his head. "The FBI isn't a person to be outsmarted. It's a system. I know that better than anyone now. For every gullible dumbass who tries to outsmart the FBI, there are a hundred criminal psychologists and detectives and forensics specialists and special agents with advanced degrees and technology and training and years of experience, and they're ready to kick some ass.

"The FBI exists to apprehend people who try to do what I'm going to do. And once they get mobilized, there'll be no stopping them and no outsmarting them because the US government will give them unlimited resources. And they won't quit until they win. They'll outlast us, out-spend us, and out-resource us, but my objective is not to win a shooting war against the FBI. They're merely a stepping-stone to other people in another agency."

Garcia nodded. "May I know your objective?"

"I want the people who killed my son. When I find them, I'll be needing all that hardware and the mercenaries to use it." Carl felt a surge of strength. The process of thinking through his agenda and actually put-ting his mission into words filled him with a sense of resolve.

"And the medical supplies?" Garcia glanced at his shopping list. "Some of these are controlled substances and won't be cheap or easy to acquire."

"I learned some things about questioning people from professional interrogators. I'll be needing those medical items to convince some folks to tell me the truth."

"Well, Mr. Smith," Garcia said, raising his coffee cup in a toast. "Here's to the fan business."

Carl clinked his coffee cup against Garcia's. The war had officially begun.

"There's one more thing I want you to do."

CHAPTER 29

0815 MST, FRIDAY
ALBUQUERQUE, NM

FOUR DAYS LATER, CARL MET Garcia at the same downtown coffee shop. Carl had arrived an hour early to see if he could detect any potential surveillance. Even if the FBI had discovered he'd set fire to his house to cover his escape, he figured there was no way the feds could have any tangible evidence linking his extortion activities or anything else in his plan to the blaze. Worst case, they'd have put out an APB on him and would rely on the police to locate him. That was why he was always in disguise.

Just in case, Carl had chosen that particular coffee shop for his meetings for a reason. It was expensive, and law enforcement personnel typically didn't eat there. He thought undercover cops or FBI agents would stick out like a sore thumb.

On the other hand, a dark-skinned man in dreadlocks stood out too, so today, he was in his White-man disguise, wearing the nondescript brown wig with the light skin cream. He wore a button-down shirt, slacks, and a gray cable cardigan sweater.

He sat at the same table as before, sipped coffee, and scanned the room, but no one seemed to be giving him even casual attention. He liked this particular disguise because he looked totally ordinary, just another clean-cut White guy in a preppy coffee shop. Then he wondered if he could really pick out a professional FBI surveillance team. Those guys and gals went to school to learn how *not* to be seen.

A shiver of doubt gripped his gut again, but it was too late to reassess. He was in the shit. Now that he had begun to implement his plan, he'd committed several federal offenses, including taking hostages, extorting funds, and illegal international money transfers.

If young Mr. Garcia was successful, then Carl would also be guilty of the purchase and import of illegal firearms, hiring mercenaries, and possession of controlled medical substances, if there were such crimes. In a couple days, he'd be guilty of far more serious crimes as well. No, he was too far into the abyss to even think about going back.

Garcia walked in the front double-glass door right at nine o'clock. At Carl's request, the young man was also nicely groomed and was dressed conservatively in a button-down shirt, slacks, and a nice jacket. He looked up at Carl but didn't recognize him. He turned up the corner of his mouth a bit as though displeased to find someone occupying their scheduled meeting table. His gaze kept searching, then he joined the line to get his coffee.

Carl kept scanning the faces in the shop, looking for anyone who might be covertly watching Garcia. No one seemed the least bit interested in him, and no one entered the coffee shop right after him. He got his coffee and dressed it up at the cream station, then headed up the curved staircase. At the top, his gaze passed over Carl again, and this time, Carl gave him a head-nod.

Garcia smiled. "Nice look," he said, sitting down. He patted a canvas satchel by his left hip. "All the docs for our operations and our emergency exit plan are in here."

Carl shook his head. "*Your* emergency exit plan. I have no need for such a plan." Carl knew any kind of long-term escape and evasion was not in the cards for him.

Garcia nodded. "I have two envelopes, each with $100,000 in cash and a credit card with a $50,000 spending limit drawn on a legitimate bank in Texas. Each has a California driver's license and a passport validated with a verifiable history of international travel. By the way, one license and passport has your picture in dreadlocks, as you requested, and your name is Kyle Fortune. Your White-boy disguise is for Kerry Fortina."

Carl looked at the kid sideways. "You had to go and call me a White boy, didn't you?"

Garcia chuckled. "I rarely get the opportunity to diss a brotha without getting in a fight."

"Mexicans," Carl said with a shake of his head. "Always gotta be deviants."

They shared a chuckle and clicked coffee cups in a mock toast.

"You've got docs for your wife and child also?"

Garcia nodded, and Carl pulled out a key fob from his jacket pocket. On the ring was a single key, but the key fob had a red button and a green button accompanied by four tiny inline white buttons.

He handed the fob to Garcia. "West of here on Central, there's a small mini storage called Store and Go. No gates, no cameras, no on-site manager. This is the key to unit eighteen. I have the only other key. It's one of those cut-proof and pick-proof super locks. Keep your docs close to you, but when our merchandise arrives, store it in that little garage unit." Carl continued, "I also bought a motion detector. As soon as the storage door goes up, the alarm circuit automatically dials this cell." He pulled another pay-as-you-go device from his left pants pocket. "If this thing rings and the number is all ones, then someone is stealing our stuff. Get over there with your boys and shoot whoever is there, but if it's the feds, just get out of the fan business. Go grab your wife and kid and drive away. Don't look back."

Garcia nodded, and Carl told him how to arm and disarm the alarm.

Carl ticked off the next agenda item of his mental plan. Nothing was written down, so there was no hard evidence yet of any plot, plan, or conspiracy. He knew the FBI excelled in finding the tiniest pieces of information and using their vast analytical capability to connect the dots and uncover conspiracies. So the entire plan, all the details, resided only in Carl's brain.

"Of the mercs you found, does one possess the intel pedigree I listed?" Carl asked.

"Pops found a guy," Garcia stopped when Carl tented his eyebrows. "I didn't tell you my pops worked with his brother until Uncle got retired? Well, Pops retired also, but of his own volition."

Carl revised his assessment of the young Hispanic man seated across from him. He had the physical presence—the mannerisms, the posture, the streetwise gestures—of a young man who got his education in the hood, either in America or in Mexico. He spoke proper English, though he lacked the finesse of college-educated, twenty-somethings who went on to take corporate jobs that required proper speaking and mainstream behavior.

He reminded Carl of many youths from inner-city Los Angeles who discovered at some point in their adult lives that if you wanted to succeed in the world, then you had to learn to think and speak and behave like the mainstream population.

He thought of sports superstars and rappers who became very successful and were able to manage the transition across cultural lines. Often, they had a mentor assist them in their transition, yet those young Black men always seemed to be able to keep some measure of their ethnic individuality with them as they traveled through their mainstream careers.

Young Garcia seemed to be the Hispanic version of the urban youth Carl was familiar with. There was a great age difference between them, perhaps twenty-five years, and Carl had the impression that Garcia considered him to be a mentor.

Carl had learned his proper speaking and behavior over a career of more than thirty years that included formal college education, training as an Air Force officer and a gentleman, and work in the corporate world. In addition, his mixed parents had raised him on a steady diet of watching science shows and science fiction movies, reading at the library, speaking proper English in the house, and not being allowed to hang out in the streets.

After fifty-plus years, it was easy to take his formal education and verbal etiquette for granted. It was easy to forget a young minority might like to emulate an older minority's polished speech and manners.

Volition. Good word choice, he decided. "Okay, you were saying?"

"Pops used a retired CIA analyst a few times. Well, he didn't actually retire. He was dismissed for a drug problem."

"You'd think the CIA would try to rehab a skilled asset like that."

Garcia chuckled. "Apparently, Henry Erickson was beyond rehabilitation. He used company assets to run a shakedown racket on some drug smugglers. Except one of his targets was an informant who ratted him out. Pops says he's a bit eccentric when he doesn't get his fix, but he's an absolute whiz with a computer, and he knows the intel business inside and out. And he knows how the FBI works."

"He can do everything I specified?"

"Pops swears by him."

"He can get into the FBI's computer system and other government systems?"

Garcia nodded. "We'll need passwords, depending on how deep into the system you need to go and what kind of information you want."

Carl nodded. "I figured as much." He'd foreseen that obstacle and incorporated it into his plan. "If he gets unruly, give him enough of what he needs to keep him sane. But I need him lucid and fully functional for at least a week. And we're going to need three safe houses. Create a holding company to lease one, then create a subsidiary of that holding company to lease another. Make the relationship hard to find, but not too hard. When the FBI finds it, I want them to think they've got me."

"Head fake?"

Head fake—when a player moves the head in one direction to cover a body movement in another direction. "Precisely. Lease the third place under a fictitious name completely unrelated to the other two because that'll be our base of operations. We'll also need half a dozen cars, all of them SUVs or minivans with darkly tinted windows. Old and disposable. Make sure they're all properly registered and insured. I don't want anyone getting pulled over by the cops for expired license plates. And make sure all our people have defect-free IDs.

"Get the first house set up first thing in the morning. Make it a vacant house way down in the South Valley—maybe somewhere south of Rio Bravo and Coors—with the utilities still on and an owner who will take cash. Get Erickson moved in and set up with whatever computer equipment he'll need. Make sure there's furniture and plenty of food, so no one will have to go out or order delivery. I want to keep our public profile to an absolute minimum."

Then Carl told Garcia what Erickson's first assignment would be.

Garcia nodded. "It's going to be a busy weekend."

"You have no idea."

CHAPTER 30

1744 MST, SUNDAY
ALBUQUERQUE, NM

C ARL SHED HIS WHITE-MAN DISGUISE and looked like his normal self when he went into the bedroom of the rented house. He was clean-shaven on both his head and his face, and he wore stylish glasses with thick, dark plastic frames just like he'd seen Reyes wearing four weeks ago.

The ex-CIA hacker Henry Erickson had pulled up quite a bit of information on Alfonso Reyes. There were a huge number of men named Reyes, both in Mexico and New Mexico, but there was only one that looked like Carl.

Erickson found a lot of public data from the internet, as well as low-level classified data from CIA and FBI networks that didn't need a lot of serious hacking to obtain. Information regarding the man's connection to Carl Johnson or a kidnapped girl was conspicuously missing. Curiosity teased Carl.

Who was the girl? Where was the girl?

The windows of the rental house were covered with blackout curtains, and a similar curtain hung in the archway that separated the living room from the hallway that led to the two bedrooms. When he opened the bedroom door, no light from the rest of the one-thousand-square-foot house invaded the tiny room that served as a prison cell for the FBI agent and his wife.

Their heads were covered with black cloth, so they had no idea who was visiting them. Carl turned on the light and just stood there for a few seconds. He knew firsthand the fear that was eating at their insides. The light was a low-wattage bulb on the ceiling. Special Agent Heinmann and his wife were zip-cuffed with their hands behind their backs, and their ankles were duct-taped.

Carl knelt next to them and pulled away the piece of blackout curtain wrapped loosely around each prisoner's head. They sat awkwardly in the center of the room, where they had been deposited. Gray duct tape covered their mouths. The internet said Reyes was fluent in English, so Carl gave them his best proper pronunciation.

"Special Agent Heinmann, my name is Alfonso Reyes. No doubt you know who I am, so you must also know what I'm capable of, yes?"

The man nodded.

Carl poked his glasses farther up onto the bridge of his nose. He did that because he wanted the FBI man to notice he was wearing them. He hadn't worn glasses for nearly ten years after having laser surgery, but having glasses on his face was a familiar feeling, and it wasn't hard to fall back into the habit of pushing them up.

He figured field agents were trained to notice that kind of detail, especially when they were being held captive. The tiny details would be helpful later when the FBI mobilized to begin the manhunt for the man who kidnapped an agent. The only question in Carl's mind was whether or not Heinmann would notice the lenses of his glasses were nonprescription.

When you look at a person's face through their prescription glasses, often their cheeks don't line up with the rest of their face above or below the lenses, depending on how strong their prescription is. The prisoners' room wasn't well-lit, so Carl was betting that particular detail might slip through the cracks.

"Good. Your two children are in the room across the hall. Twin girls. How lovely."

Garcia had reported that the family had been extraordinarily easy to capture. Two mercenaries Carl had yet to meet had simply picked the lock on the side door that allowed them entry into the garage. That door was not visible from the street, so they simply walked into the house through the garage. Like most folks, the Heinmanns no doubt figured if the roll-down garage door was closed, then their house was secure. It probably was secure from 99 percent of the population.

The mercs waited in the living room and ambushed the family when they returned from their Sunday afternoon activity. Then they were piled into a cargo van that backed up in front of the garage door of their North Valley home, and thirty minutes later, they were roughly pushed into the temporary house.

Mrs. Heinmann's eyes teared up when Carl mentioned her daughters, and she tried to protest, but the tape on her mouth made her vocalizations sound like a whimper.

Carl spoke directly to her husband. "Of course, your girls are safe for now. In fact, I'm going to ask you one simple question, then I'm going into the front room to check if you've told me the truth or not. If you have, then you and your family will be returned home unharmed. If you have not told me the truth, I'm coming back down the hall, except I'm going into the other room." Carl paused and allowed both of them to feel the fear. "Do you understand me clearly?"

The man nodded. He was maybe fifty or so. He had a full head of gray hair and was a little soft in the body, but that was expected of a man perhaps ten years past active field duty. Carl saw understanding and acceptance in the man's eyes. He had no power, nothing to barter or negotiate with. He had no choice but to comply.

Carl removed the tape from the man's mouth, and Heinmann flexed his jaw a bit.

"You're going to kill us anyway, aren't you?"

Carl smiled and said, "The answer to that question has no real relevance. All that matters is what I'm going to do to your girls if you do not comply with my instructions."

Heinmann nodded, but Carl decided to put him at ease a bit. He wanted the man's full cooperation.

"Surely, however, you know my—What is the term you use?—MO, my modus operandi. I'm in the pharmaceuticals business, not the killing business, although I do occasionally diversify into the kidnapping arena if it advances my business agenda. I never kill unless it is an absolutely necessary demonstration of retribution. If I kill you, my own government might bow to pressure from *your* government and place uncomfortable restrictions on my business enterprises. We can't have that, now can we?"

Carl shrugged and continued, "However, that does not mean I won't do unspeakable things to your family and make you watch." Carl nodded. "Not me personally, of course, for I find such barbarism distasteful. But there are men in the other room," Carl said, glancing over his shoulder, "that are very attracted to your young girls and your plump wife. I fear I would not be able to control them."

The FBI agent opened his mouth to speak, but Carl held up his hand. He knew firsthand the cop's power trick. He who asks the questions has the power.

"You will answer my question now. You will say nothing other than that. Do you understand this?"

Heinmann nodded.

Right on cue, Garcia knocked on the door and opened it a few inches. "Señor Reyes?"

"*Si?*" Carl answered. That was pretty much the extent of his Spanish vocabulary.

Garcia spoke rapidly in Spanish. Carl knew what he said only because he planned Garcia's interruption before he entered the room. The young man was telling Carl the computer system was set up, and they were ready for the next step.

Head fake.

He figured a career field agent would be somewhat fluent in the dominant cultural language used by a large percentage of the local population, as was the case of Spanish in New Mexico. Heinmann would likely understand a good portion of what Garcia was saying.

"Very well." He turned his attention back to Heinmann. "We need access to the FBI database and that of the Department of Homeland Security. What is your password?"

He took out a pen and pad from his shirt pocket and wrote down the fourteen-character complex password as Heinmann dictated it. Then he stood.

"Thank you for your cooperation. I'll be right back."

He went into the living room and handed the notepad to Erickson, the computer whiz, who sat at the fold-up camp table that served as his desk. His open laptop rested on the table. It had a seventeen-inch screen, and several overlapping windows were open on the monitor. A tiny USB modem stuck out the right side of the laptop and connected Erickson to the local cell phone network.

The man fidgeted like a teen gamer getting ready for a tough competition, except he was in his mid-thirties. He had a thin, hawklike face with a prominent nose that bisected his face unevenly, maybe as a result of a broken nose way back. He was dressed in denim pants and a cheap knit pullover sweater, and his hair and mustache were unkempt masses of brown hair. He smelled like sweat, but Carl assumed that was normal for the kind of guy Garcia referred to as a "tweaker."

Hygiene aside, the man had performed admirably so far. Yesterday, he'd found Special Agent Heinmann, Carl's first target, in two minutes flat. When Erickson was given the notepad with the password on it, he poised his fingers over his keyboard for a few seconds like a pianist ready to launch into a performance. Then the man went to work. He entered the password at the login prompt on the FBI website, and when he hit Enter, a search page popped up with a query box along with a warning in large, red capital letters that all the information in the system was for official government use only.

"Pull up the personnel roster for Albuquerque, New Mexico. Women only. This particular agent has tied-back, shoulder-length blonde hair and brown eyes. She's about five-eight and weighs maybe a buck-forty or -fifty. I want her home address, cell phone number, next of kin, parents, kids, brothers, sisters, significant other. I want everything you can find on her."

Erickson pulled up a roster with almost three hundred names on it. "They don't have a search parameter by gender."

"Can you sort into a grid of pictures only?"

"Dude, this is the FBI, not a dating site."

"Shit!"

Carl felt the itch of a memory, a faint tug at the edge of his consciousness. He closed his eyes and tried to tease the memory into focus. He drifted back a month in time when the FBI woman had cold-cocked him upside the head with her elbow and then slammed his head into the table. The memory came to him slowly. Just before he was sedated,

Agent Klipser was speaking to the FBI woman, and she lied to him about speaking to Carl. Then Klipser called her by name.

The memory flashed into focus in his mind. Klipser had said her name like it was a curse word, and Carl remembered his visual image of the man with the smoky voice speaking like he might have been poking her in the chest with each word.

Special. Agent. Cummings.

Carl said, "Her name is Cummings. Special Agent Cummings."

Erickson typed in her name, and up popped her personnel file, including her address, unlisted cell, and all her family information. Carl wrote it all down on his notepad. He handed the page to Garcia and smiled. Cummings was a single mother—no surprise there, being that she was a kick-ass field agent—and she lived in a multi-generational home with her mother and daughter.

To Garcia, he said, "Have your men do whatever is necessary to secure the daughter after Cummings goes to work tomorrow. Subdue her mom any way necessary, but don't kill her unless it's absolutely necessary. I need this agent free to do my bidding for now. If the FBI discovers a dead body in her house, they may assume it's related to the Heinmann kidnapping, and they'll take her off the case. Please make sure your mercenaries understand what is expected of them.

"Tomorrow's Monday, a school day, so the daughter," Carl glanced at the note pad, "Lisette, will either take the bus to school or the grandmother will drive her. Intercept Lisette before they leave and take her to our operations house."

Garcia said, "Roger that. Capture and avoid killing, if at all possible."

"There will come a time very soon where that restriction will be removed. Right now, though, we're not on the FBI's radar. If we start leaving dead bodies around town before I'm ready, then the FBI won't react the way I want them to." He paused with a distant look in his eyes. "I want to keep them guessing and not yet fully mobilized. The first time I hit them, I want to catch them off guard, give them a real bloody nose that they'll have to step back and really think about."

Garcia nodded.

To Erickson, Carl said, "Now look for the names Klipser and McGrath. They won't be in the FBI database. They'll be in the

Department of Homeland Security, or CIA, or NSA, or somewhere else in highly classified files."

"That's gonna take some time. Can I get a fix first?"

Garcia said, "You can have your fix after you find those names." To Carl, he said, "What shall I do with the FBI agent and his family?"

"Remove their blindfolds and put the kids in the same room with the parents so they can hug and all that. Then take them back home, but not before the workday starts tomorrow morning." Carl grinned. "He still has an important role to play for us. Once they're at home, leave them all bound. I figure it'll take him less than five minutes to get loose, report in, and change his password."

To Erickson, he said, "After he reports the hack, how long will it take them to trace it back to this location?"

"I've disguised my internet connection through half a dozen servers, but they should be able to back-trace us in an hour, two tops. But once they know we were in there with his login, it won't take them any time at all to figure out what information we accessed."

Garcia had a thoughtful look on his face as he worked the numbers in his head.

"So, if we take him back at eight o'clock, they'll locate the house by nine at the earliest, perhaps ten, and have us under surveillance shortly thereafter. They'll have a tactical team ready to raid us by eleven or twelve."

"Perfect." Carl nodded. "Leave the blindfolds off the family on the way home. I want Heinmann to be able to visually verify this location when the back-trace locates this house. I don't want the FBI wasting time with their raid. But make sure your mercenaries are covered up. I don't want Heinmann to ID them. And I have no doubt Special Agent Cummings will be running point on the raid. She knows our Homeland boys, so she'll call them as soon as word gets out that Heinmann was held by a man she thinks is Alfonso Reyes."

Carl wondered how McGrath would react when his FBI lapdog told him that Reyes was searching the FBI database for their names. Would he be surprised his target actually knew of them, or would he even care? He hated not knowing who these men were—McGrath and Klipser—but when he asked Cummings about her Homeland friends, he'd also quiz her on the man who pulled the trigger on Mark.

He paused as feelings of satisfaction and confidence swept through him. Everything was going according to plan so far.

"And that means," he continued, "Agent Klipser will be on a plane to Albuquerque by noon tomorrow. Mr. Erickson, can you set up a program on this machine to make it look like you're still in here doing internet work?"

"Sure. I can control it remotely if you like."

Carl shook his head. "No, when the FBI agents get here, I don't want any external connection, wireless or otherwise, that might lead them to our other operations house. Leave the computer here and keep it operational so they'll think we're in here working. They've got computer analysis folks whose only job is to sit around all day and all night and try to trace our computer. They'll analyze every piece of data and every signal emanating from this house, and they'll be very thorough. The only trail I want them to follow is to the second house."

Garcia said, "Which is a dead end. Another head fake, right?"

Carl nodded. "I want the FBI preoccupied with the dead end until Klipser gets here. If they bite at the second house, that'll keep them off our backs for a few hours."

Erickson nodded. "So we don't actually plan to be here when the FBI arrives, right?" He shrugged at the obvious. "I'm just sayin'…"

Carl shook his head. "Absolutely not, but I want to leave a clue for them—a reward for their efficient investigative work."

CHAPTER 31

THE FBI'S SWAT PEOPLE—ERICKSON CALLED them crisis response personnel—arrived at the house for their raid at fourteen minutes before noon on Monday. Carl felt a measure of safety, or even isolation, from the event because his operations house was twelve miles away in the far Northeast Heights of Albuquerque. Garcia stood beside him, and they watched the raid unfold on a fifty-five-inch, high-definition monitor in the living room.

One of the four mercenaries Garcia had hired through his father's Mexican connections lay on the roof of the second house they had rented. It was a two-story home a half mile from the first house, which was now the target of the FBI raid. Carl remembered seeing the camera Garcia had bought through which he now watched the event. It had a long telephoto lens attached to a video camera. It was several inches wide at the front and very narrow at the back end where the camera was attached. In fact, the lens itself was so cumbersome that it sat in a cradle atop a tripod, and the camera hung off the narrow end like a forgotten appendage.

A thin wire connected the camera output via a micro-USB connector to the merc's smartphone so Carl and Garcia could watch the unfolding scene. Carl felt a shiver tingle up and down his spine as he watched the precision of the two assault teams as they converged on the property. His sense of safety diminished a bit, and he found himself looking around the living room. Garcia was tense also, but the remaining three mercs were focused only on the monitor. Erickson was hard at work on his new laptop.

Carl knew he was playing a dangerous game with combat-trained professionals, and he could tell the FBI troops were trained every bit as well as military special ops soldiers. For all he knew, these troops may have been recruited from the military ranks because of their assault expertise. Regardless, the FBI cops he was watching on the monitor enabled his mission.

Find McGrath and make him pay.

The target house sat almost forty feet off the road in the middle of a one-acre plot of land. It was deep in the South Valley, three miles south of Rio Bravo and a tad east of Coors Boulevard. It was one of several homesteads on a dirt road edged by acres of irrigated farmland.

The front and back yards of the homestead were merely dirt, except for a few tufts of wild grass, and were devoid of even minimal xeriscaping. It was the gravel landscape typical of many New Mexico homes, although most local folks pronounced it *"zero-scape."* Most of New Mexico was high-desert country and under perpetual water conservation, so grass yards that were popular in past decades were gradually being replaced by xeriscape yards.

The target house was a cheap structure with years of deferred maintenance, and it looked like it could have been an old mobile home that had been resurfaced decades ago with vinyl siding. Its roof was sloped at a very shallow angle and was covered with rolled asphalt sheeting instead of shingles.

The two assault teams lined up in front of the house next door. A sniper's head, the barrel of his rifle, and the binoculars and head of his spotter could be seen just over the ridgeline of the pitched roof of the neighboring house to the west.

Each of the two assault teams had four men. One man from each team carried an elongated pole that Erickson said was for forcing their way through locked or barricaded doors. Those guys were the breachers. Those two men, one in the front and one in the rear, would facilitate entry for the assaulters, the guys with the shotguns and automatic rifles. Once they forced the doors open, the breachers would drop their poles and follow the group through for containment and mop-up since they only carried handguns for weapons.

Carl saw Special Agent Cummings bringing up the rear of one of the assault teams, so he figured she was the agent in charge for the assault. He'd already watched her and another agent clear the house next door to make sure no one was home.

Carl noticed that Cummings was in full black tactical gear this time. She looked just as badass as the rest of her men. Her black Kevlar helmet hid her blonde hair, and he noticed that she wore clear goggles to keep shrapnel and spent shell casings out of her eyes. There was still enough of her face showing that he could see her cream-colored skin shining like a beacon among all that blackness.

At the front of the pack, one of the men peeked around the edge of the house and scanned the target house with a small handheld device. It looked like an oversized flashlight with a small screen attached to it. Erickson said it was a thermal scanner. He said the agent was looking for heat signatures inside the house to determine the number of potential hostiles inside.

Garcia's mercenaries had predicted that particular maneuver, as they had plenty of experience taking down enemy terrorist strongholds. It was agreed the FBI would arrive prepared to deal with all the windows being covered with blackout curtains. The thermal scanner would verify the actual presence and locations of targets in the house and also locate any lookouts peeking through tiny holes in the curtains waiting to ambush them.

All four *hostiles* were gathered in the kitchen, but they were actually nothing more than mannequins wrapped in electric heat blankets with the temperature regulators set to about ninety-five degrees. One was even seated in a rocking chair with a small, motorized piston to keep the chair in motion. Carl considered that deception to be the masterstroke of genius of his plan, and it had taken Garcia some serious effort to locate the proper equipment for the thermal dummies.

Erickson and the mercs had promised the handheld scanner was not sensitive enough to distinguish between the dummies and real human bodies. After all, the FBI agents were looking for life-sized heat signa-tures. They wouldn't be looking for *fake* heat signatures.

At least, not the first time.

The assault teams paused while the FBI tactical agent continued scanning. Carl knew this was where his plan succeeded or failed.

Garcia voiced his thoughts. "Do you think they'll fall for it?"

"We'll soon see."

Carl realized he was holding his breath, and when the observer moved back into the pack and put his scanner device away, he let out his breath with an audible sigh. Cummings gave a hand signal, and the assault teams converged on the house. Then she and the other agent in charge waited by the house next door.

Merc One panned his camera around the neighborhood. Police had converged around the rural area as close as they could without being seen by the target house. Dozens of local PD and FBI vehicles lined the streets out of sight from the target. It was an impressive sight, Carl thought. That was the reception he'd get if they ever found him.

Merc One settled the camera view back on the house. One group of four assault agents ran straight to the front of the house, and the second group ran around the back. The stocks of their assault rifles were pressed against their shoulders, and the agents sighted along the barrels as if the weapons were extensions of their bodies.

On the front porch of the target house, the breacher gripped the door-knob, and Carl knew he was gently testing to see if the door was locked. It was not, nor was the back door. Carl had wanted to make the raid as easy as possible for them.

The breacher carefully laid his pole aside, pulled his sidearm, and took his position at the rear of the team as they waited, presumably to make sure the rear entry team was in position. Then the group charged through the door.

There was no sound with the picture, but Carl could imagine the assault teams screaming at the top of their lungs like they had when they had attacked him a month ago at the downtown Starbucks. He figured maybe two of each team would head toward the kitchen, where the thermal signatures of the hostiles were located, while the rest would methodically clear the other rooms. Carl figured it would take five seconds at most for the units to reach the kitchen and realize they'd been had. He nodded to Garcia.

"Do it."

CHAPTER 32

1157 MST, MONDAY

ALBUQUERQUE, NM

G ARCIA SPOKE INTO HIS CELL and uttered a command to Merc One, whose real name was Trevor Flosk.

"Roger that," came the reply over the speaker mounted on the wall under the TV.

Garcia had introduced Carl to all the mercenaries as "Mr. Smith," and he immediately told them he thought of them only as operational assets. They were illegal combat soldiers, he said, and their function was solely to engage Carl's enemies with extreme prejudice, a task for which they were being paid extremely well.

Now, Carl studied the three mercenaries who had remained at the operations house with him, Garcia, and Erickson. He referred to them as Mercs Two through Four. Like Merc One, the other mercs were dangerous-looking people in their late thirties or early forties. The two men Carl referred to as Merc Two and Three were named Rich Brewster and Trent Englebaum. They looked very much like older versions of the man he knew as Agent Klipser. They both had the same deadly eyes with empty deadpan expressions and constantly roving gazes. They both seemed completely aware of everything around them.

Merc Four was a woman introduced as Cassiopeia Englebaum. About thirty-five, she looked like a female version of the others. Slender and fairly tall at five-ten, she looked just as capable and deadly as the men. At first, Carl thought the female merc was constantly smiling with a sneer, which only enhanced her deadly look. As he looked closer, though, he could see what could only be a knife scar angling upward from the left corner of her mouth. She and Merc Three on her right stood close together, in each other's personal space, as he would expect of any married couple. This particular couple carried automatic weapons instead of grocery bags.

He didn't know any details about the group, and he hadn't asked where they were from or if they had any kids. All he knew about them was what Garcia had reported. They all had been dismissed from various special operations outfits, either Rangers or Delta or SEAL units. They all had problems with authority, had abused their skills, or enjoyed killing too much. They were all fit and in shape.

They were each receiving two thousand a day, and a five-day advance had been deposited into their bank accounts. The remainder of what Carl told them would be a two-week employment would be paid upon completion of the mission. Mercs Two, Three, and Four stood to the right and slightly in front of Carl and Garcia, and they watched the raid unfold. Every now and then, they would whisper among themselves as if studying the opposition's tactics.

The detonation on the high-def monitor was spectacular. The mercs added their comments of admiration.

"Whoa! That's gonna leave a scar!"

"Booyah!"

"Man down!"

Inside the target house, Carl knew there had been no red blinking lights as the explosive detonators were armed—no beeping tone or flashing LEDs counting down to let the FBI assault teams realize they were about to die. Instead, the eruption of fire and the concussive blast were so massive and so sudden that none of the tactical team could possibly have had any awareness of their demise.

On the monitor, Carl watched fire wash out of every window and door in the house. The roof lifted and splintered, then collapsed. The front face of the house blasted outward, and the right and left walls collapsed inward after a few seconds.

Carl said, "Shift the view to Agent Cummings."

Mr. Garcia relayed the order through his cell channel, and the monitor showed the front of the house next door. The east wall had significant blast damage, and in the front yard, Cummings and her partner were getting shakily to their feet, gazing at the destroyed target house.

Carl pulled his cell phone from his pocket and quickly tapped his way to the text menu. He had already typed out a text message, attached a picture, and saved it in the draft folder, so he simply opened the message and hit Send.

A few seconds later, he saw Cummings on the monitor as she reached into her pocket for her cell. To her credit, she was cool and did not visibly react when she read the message.

I have Lisette. Comply or she dies. -Reyes

The picture she was looking at on her cell was that of her eleven-year-old daughter bound and gagged.

Carl handed his cell phone to Garcia because the agent would undoubtedly remember Carl's voice from a month ago. She'd know instantly he wasn't really Reyes. "Call her. Give her proper English and a very slight Spanish accent, then relay the instructions we discussed."

Cummings's cell number was the only number in the contact list. Garcia hit Send and put the cell on speakerphone.

She answered immediately. "What the hell did you do?"

"In this business, threats and warnings are useless and would have gone unheeded. You and I both know this, so I gave you a demonstration."

He paused, and Carl listened intently to the speakers on the monitor. He could hear Cummings breathing heavily. Her voice sounded shaky. Eight of her men had just died. She was the field agent in charge, and her commanders would be looking to her for an explanation.

"Your instructions are simple. I want Agent Klipser here in Albuquerque before nightfall. If he is not here, I will carve your daughter into pieces before I kill her. I will call you before midnight with the coordinates of a destination in north-central Mexico, where we shall meet to discuss the return of a particular American girl. Do not attempt to contact me or trace this number. Believe me, I will know."

"Mexico? We can't conduct operations across the border."

"I am not interested in what you cannot do, Special Agent Cummings. I am more interested in what you *can* do. The US government secretly invades countries all over the world. You can do whatever task you set your collective minds to. Deviate from these instructions at the peril of your daughter."

He terminated the call and handed the phone back to Carl. "You realize the first thing the FBI is going to do is trace this phone, right?"

"Doesn't matter," Carl said. "You weren't on long enough for them to identify the cell towers the signal went through."

Erickson had said they'd need upward of thirty seconds to trace a call. Carl pulled the battery from the device, laid the cell on the floor, and stomped on it. "I'll be needing a replacement now."

Garcia stepped to the side of the room and retrieved a phone from one of the power strips plugged into the wall. There were ten power strips connected to extension cords along the wall, and each strip was filled to capacity with charging disposable cells. They had almost a hundred more cells to use one time each. Garcia programmed his own cell number into the new cell and handed it to Carl.

"Thank you, Mr. Garcia. I know I said this before, but just as a reminder, I want to make sure you use your personal cell only to contact me. If you need to make other calls, use a different cell and destroy each cell after every use. Don't give the FBI any electronic trails. I heard that the NSA has a facility somewhere up in Colorado dedicated solely to eavesdropping on cell phones."

Carl paused and glanced at the monitor again at the bombed-out house. Garcia dismantled the cell he'd been using to communicate with Merc One.

"Call Merc One in," Carl said.

Garcia retrieved a new cell to make that call, then dismantled that one too.

Carl turned sideways and made eye contact with the other three mercs. He almost addressed them as "Gentlemen and Lady," but the looks in their eyes told him that would not be appropriate. These people were killers for hire, nothing more. He sensed they expected to be addressed as such.

"People, we've broken many laws up to this point." Carl nodded at the burning house on the monitor. "As of this moment, we are America's most wanted."

He paused for a moment. Carl had seen in the mercs' eyes that they hadn't previously considered him a serious player. After all, he was just a civilian. They didn't care about his agenda or his mission. If the operation folded for some reason, as one of them had said, they'd simply take their advance money and disappear, leaving Carl, Garcia, and Erickson holding the bag.

He expected nothing less from the mercenaries, but now he saw a grudging respect in their eyes. They had all been soldiers, and even as mercenaries, they were accustomed to taking orders. They'd planted the explosives in the house because they were paid for that task, but it was clear that until that very moment, none of them thought he had the backbone to give the command to kill. Now they had witnessed his conviction.

He said, "The FBI is not even our true enemy." He paused long enough to let the statement sink into their minds. "My target is an unknown covert agency, and you can be sure they will now take a very intense interest in our operation. These agents tortured me and killed my son. They have proven to me they will do anything to anyone, even innocent civilians, to accomplish their mission. If you get captured," Carl said with a glance at Garcia, "you can expect them to find your family members too—all of them, everywhere in the world—and they will use them against you. They operate with impunity. They are not accountable to anyone, and no one will prosecute them for any crimes they commit in their attempts to find and capture us. They will not negotiate. Instead, they will bend or break any law."

Carl took a breath and looked at the monitor again before he continued, "Finding them is my sole mission, and I have no doubt that as of this moment, we are now their mission as well. When this operation is concluded, it is my intention that these covert government agents and their FBI lapdog will all be dead. Like them, I also will do anything to anyone to make that happen. I will not surrender, and I will not compromise. Either they die or we die. Are we all clear on that?"

None of the three mercenaries said anything, so he continued, "I intend to take prisoners, and I intend to treat those prisoners as harshly as these covert government agents treated me, as harshly as they will treat any of us if we are captured." He paused and evaluated the soldiers again. "Our prisoners will include their family members, if I can find them." He nodded toward the bedroom where Lisette Cummings was tied. "Does anyone have any mental reservations about the mission or any questions about the consequences if we are caught?"

Merc Two raised his hand halfway, and Carl nodded at him.

"Our rules of engagement, sir?"

"I think I just covered that," Carl answered. "There are no rules other than kill or be killed. Anything else?"

Carl looked at each mercenary, and each shook his or her head. "Very well, then." He looked at his young assistant. "Mr. Garcia, we are officially in the fan business."

Garcia's voice trembled a bit. "They're coming for us, aren't they?"

When Carl answered, his voice sounded foreign to him, reminding him of Agent Klipser's gravelly voice. He gave Garcia a grunt that sounded more like a growl. "Actually, for the next few hours, they're going to be looking for a man named Alfonso Reyes. So now it's time to give them another head fake."

CHAPTER 33

A ARON MCGRATH WATCHED THE UNEXPECTED terror event on the center monitor in silence. The perspective was from a camera he knew was mounted on the nose of a police helicopter. His second, Nancy Palmer, stood next to him in the ops center.

Palmer shook her head slightly, then brought both her hands up and finger-combed her short hair back. She'd been asleep upstairs until two hours ago when he hit the "All hands on deck!" button on the wall next to the management workstation. Now, he was standing close enough to catch a hint of her mild shower fragrance.

"This makes no sense, Aaron," she said. "He deliberately murdered eight field agents, and for what? We paid his ransom. What does he gain by this action?"

"He did this specifically to get Cummings to tell us to send Pete out there, presumably to negotiate Melissa's release."

After a month, the search for America's darling daughter had stalled, and the TER team had downsized. Only two analysts remained—Joey, the big bald young man, and Jimmy, the one with the big Afro. Jimmy was on duty now.

It was presumed Melissa had been transported out of the country. No one knew if she was alive or dead because she had not been returned after the ransom was paid. Still, the operation proceeded on the premise that she still lived. Now, it seemed she was alive, and Reyes was willing to conclude his terror event.

Mexico had topped the list of possible locations of the girl, only because Alfonso Reyes lived and conducted most of his business in that country. The call from Special Agent Cummings in Albuquerque was the first new intel on the whereabouts of the kidnapper in several weeks.

The room was eerily quiet after the explosion. All conversation had ceased. McGrath realized he could easily hear the fans of the computer stations on the floor. It was midday, but the blackout curtains shielded against any outside light. When he looked up at the ceiling to contemplate the enormity of the ambush he'd just witnessed, he noticed the bright bulbs of all six of the halogen floor lamps were angled straight up, and they all made similar rings of light and shadow.

The two workstations on the right side of the ops room were abandoned. The management workstation sat directly behind those two. Jimmy occupied the workstation third from the right, while the fourth analyst had been sent back upstairs for rack time. He'd need to be fresh for his next shift, McGrath had said, because now that Reyes had surfaced again, the team would likely shift into overdrive. And they had been...until the kidnapper detonated the house with the FBI officers inside.

Palmer continued, "Cummings is not even the senior agent of the Albuquerque field office. That assault team should have been commanded by any of two or three more senior agents, yet Reyes specifically took her daughter hostage."

McGrath nodded. "Because he knew once we knew he was in-country, the operation would fall under our jurisdiction, and we would assign Cummings to lead the assault. Which means Reyes knows her connection to us."

"And our agency identity."

"And Pete's identity." McGrath paused and reached for his mug of now cold coffee on the desk next to their workstation.

"Pete's after-action report of the hit on Mark Johnson indicated that Reyes saw him and Cummings standing near Johnson at the shooting. Maybe he used facial recognition to ID Pete."

McGrath nodded. "Yet, he not only queried Pete's name in the FBI database, but he queried mine also."

She had significant doubt in her voice. "He'd have to have very high-level military connections either here or in Mexico to access intel resources that could find Pete's file. He and his team are as deep black as we have." She paused. "As are you and I. Still, that doesn't explain how he could know your identity or your affiliation with Pete."

"You're suggesting we have a leak." There, he'd said aloud the thought that had been nagging him all morning.

"Possibly," she said. "But our team is small. Just the two analysts we have here and the two who were reassigned last week, and you and me. And the president and a limited number of her senior staff."

McGrath nodded. "We're operating at Special Access Level Three, and I report only to the president. So unless she has a high-level leak in her cabinet, I think we can assume the intel is coming through Mexican military channels." He paused for a moment, then continued, "Pete has a five-year special ops history before joining us. It's at least conceivable that a foreign intelligence agency has a file on him." McGrath made that statement like he knew it was not really possible. Still, it was something he had to say just to be thorough.

Palmer added, "We've suspected that Reyes is connected to high-ranking officers in the Mexican military. That's presumably how he obtained transportation and the sophisticated weaponry used for the original snatch."

"If we uncover clear evidence that there's a foreign military component to Melissa's kidnapping, things are going to get a lot more complicated."

"I agree," Palmer said. "This incident in Albuquerque, especially if connected to Melissa's kidnapping, could start a war, or at the very least provoke a significant international event."

McGrath shook his head. "None of this explains why Reyes has resurfaced again like this"—he pointed at the monitor—"or why he started a bloodbath in Albuquerque. If he wanted to negotiate the girl's release, he could have made contact the same way he sent the ransom demand. That would have given him more credibility than murdering FBI agents.

Or he could have just killed Heinmann and his family and left a note with them. He doesn't need a face-to-face meet with Pete."

"Unless he has some other agenda or some personal interest in Pete." She paused. "And you."

There was a subtle change in her tone, a slight inflection or maybe a tiny pause at the end of her statement that froze the blood in McGrath's veins. He glanced sideways at Nancy Palmer, and his gaze lingered on her sky blue eyes for a moment. Then he took a deep breath as an impossible scenario suddenly stood foremost in his mind. He turned fully to face his deputy. "What are you thinking?"

"I'm thinking this isn't Alfonso Reyes's work. I'm thinking this is Carl Johnson."

"Carl Johnson is dead. He committed suicide."

"It certainly appeared that way," Palmer said. "But the motivation for this ambush fits more with Johnson than Reyes." She paused, and McGrath got the feeling she was still working through the scenario in her mind. "He knows we're looking for Reyes and a 'particular American girl.'" She did the quote-unquote thing with her fingers as she mentioned the phrase given to Agent Cummings. "We've put Lenore in charge of that op before. He might assume we'd do so again."

McGrath shook his head. "He specifically said he wanted to negotiate Melissa's release, but she's been missing over a month, and we've kept this out of the media. There's no way Johnson could possibly know she's still missing. Besides," he added, "there's absolutely nothing in his records, either during or after his military service, that suggests he has the training or the skills to conduct an ambush like this, nor that he has the disposition or the capacity to murder people or to take that kind of revenge. He's a law-abiding citizen!"

"That was before he was interrogated and before his son died." Palmer paused. "He was a professional project manager and planner. Given adequate resources and a mental imbalance caused by emotional distress, I'd say he might be able to pull this off."

McGrath shook his head. "It's still too far-fetched to believe an off-the-street model citizen could turn terrorist in four weeks." He stood silently, considering all the facts. He continued to glare at the wall monitor like it might reveal previously undiscovered information. Then he said, "What do you recommend?"

Palmer turned to the management workstation. "I'll take another look at Johnson's suicide and the house fire to see if I can positively verify his remains."

He nodded. "If this is Johnson, we've got to put him down ASAP. We can't have him interfering with our primary mission."

Palmer nodded. "He'd need help. A blast like that," she said with a nod at the monitor, "would take military-grade explosives, and that'd be very expensive. He'd need money, and he'd need someone with military experience to set the detonators. And to do the kind of computer hacking the FBI is reporting, he'd need a specialist with prior high-level intel service."

"Okay, follow up on those angles," McGrath said. "But his mention of a rendezvous location was too detailed, too intentional. We have to proceed with the dual possibility that this still might be Alfonso Reyes with a new agenda. If so, he's getting bold or greedy, or maybe he really is willing to negotiate for the girl's release."

McGrath turned to the analyst. "Jimmy, one of Alfonso Reyes's estates is in north-central Mexico, isn't it?"

The young man did some fast keyboard work and nodded. His big Afro wobbled with the gesture. "Yes, sir. It's one of several he maintains throughout the country. But that specific estate he mentioned is a fortified compound a couple hundred miles south of the border, east of a place called Nuevo Casas Grande. The compound is pretty isolated too. It would be a good place to hide a hostage if he had one."

"Coordinate with Customs and Border Protection to get a surveillance drone in the air over that compound. I want to know what's happening down there." He turned back to Palmer. "I'm going to send Pete out to Albuquerque heavy."

Heavy meant Pete was going out with a six-man tactical assault force fully armed and ready for any contingency. If the enemy was Carl Johnson, Pete would be licensed to kill. If the enemy was Reyes, he was fully authorized to conduct any negotiation necessary to secure Melissa's release.

If negotiation proved ineffective, then he was authorized to perform any on-site experimental interrogation necessary to determine the girl's location. If successful in that objective, he was further authorized to conduct full-envelope covert intrusion, even across the border, into whatever property—public, private, or government—and in any country, to retrieve the girl. In short, he had full authority to act without accountability.

The analyst cleared his throat and said, "I have Special Agent in Charge Figueroa on video link from Albuquerque."

McGrath nodded, and the monitor showed the director's small conference room. The eight chairs were filled with the director's senior staff, and half a dozen other agents stood against the walls.

McGrath said, "My condolences on the loss of your people."

Figueroa nodded.

McGrath continued, "I assume you're at a heightened security readiness?"

The local FBI commander looked haggard, and McGrath could only imagine how a lawman would feel after suffering the worst attack of his career. His suit jacket hung from the back of his seat, and the sleeves of his white shirt were rolled up. His black tie was loosened, and his top shirt button was undone. He stood at the head of his conference table and leaned forward, braced by his fist knuckles on the surface. His holstered sidearm was visible on his right hip. The man looked very no-nonsense.

"We are," he said. "The building is locked down, and all field agents and personnel accounts with access to classified information are being sequestered, along with their families. Also, all computer access codes have been changed, so no one outside the building can access our servers now. Cummings will be debriefed as well when she returns."

"That won't be necessary."

"Director McGrath, police have responded to a call at Special Agent Cummings's residence. Armed men broke into her house, assaulted her mother, and kidnapped her daughter. I believe this action is connected with the ambush of her team. With her daughter hostage, she is part of the case, and I have specific protocol requirements."

"A foreign national has performed an act of terrorism on American soil," McGrath said. "Since the individual responsible is currently under investigation in connection with another terror event, this case falls under the jurisdiction of the Terror Event Response agency. My office has already taken the lead in all operations regarding this event going forward. We'll need your cooperation and resources, but as of this moment, Special Agent Cummings is reassigned to my office as liaison to your office. There will be no debriefing, clear?"

Figueroa paused, clearly not happy. "Understood."

"Special Agent Cummings, are you still on the line?" She had been patched into the briefing on her cell.

"I'm here."

"How are you holding up?" McGrath asked.

She paused, and he heard her take a deep breath. "My daughter has been kidnapped, sir. How do you think I'm holding up?"

He glanced at Palmer, and she nodded, obviously making the same assessment that he had. Cummings's voice was shaky, which was expected after her ordeal, but she had a good mix of anger and anxiety. She was still in the game.

"Your security clearance has been raised to Special Access Level Three. You report directly to Agent Klipser. He will brief you when he arrives, clear?"

"Yes, sir."

"Very well," McGrath said. "We're going to put a trace on your cell." He glanced sideways at the tech analyst.

"On it," Jimmy said. "Thirty seconds."

"If Reyes contacts you again, tell him that Klipser is en route. And don't worry. We'll get your daughter back."

The monitor went blank as both sides terminated the briefing, and McGrath told the analyst to put Klipser on the speakerphone. He briefly summarized the new information regarding the possibility that the Albuquerque ambush was conducted by still-alive Carl Johnson, not Alfonso Reyes.

"I'm flagging Johnson as a Tier-One terror suspect, Pete."

"Understood," Klipser said over the speaker.

Palmer tented her eyebrows. "You're basically putting out an assassination order on Carl Johnson, and yet Reyes is only a Tier-Three suspect?"

"That's because we need Reyes alive regardless of what he's done or what he does going forward. Right now, he's our only link to finding Melissa. However, if the perpetrator of today's ambush is really Carl Johnson, then he just murdered eight federal agents and left American wives and children without their husbands and fathers. He's Tier One."

Palmer started to say something, but McGrath interrupted her, saying, "Look, if this is Johnson, and I'm still not convinced that it is, then he deserves what he gets. He put himself in the game, and now, he's got to play by the rules."

Palmer nodded. "But after having seen this," she said, pointing at the center monitor displaying the burning ambush house, "I'd be very careful about escalating this if we're dealing with Johnson. We haven't yet profiled him, and we don't know his state of mind. Personally, I'm seeing a man who has nothing to lose. He's not afraid to play large."

"Pete can handle escalation just fine."

Palmer put her hands on her hips and faced him. "And what of his hostage, Lenore's daughter?"

"Collateral damage."

"What? The president would never approve of this."

"The president is not running this op, Agent Palmer. I am."

"Haven't we done enough to this man? Hell, he looks so much like Reyes, maybe we should recruit him. We should figure out how to use him to get Melissa back."

"I've made the call, Nancy, so get on board with it." McGrath turned away from her and spoke at the monitor, even though Klipser was only on audio. "Are you clear on your instructions, Pete?"

"Perfectly."

McGrath turned to Jimmy. "See to Johnson's Tier-One status."

The analyst nodded. "I'll have to coordinate with the FBI executive assistant director for national security, sir, because their Counterterrorism Division deals with terrorism threats inside the US."

"I'm aware of that," McGrath said. "Just get it done."

Klipser said, "How shall I handle Agent Cummings?"

McGrath glanced at Agent Palmer, but she just stood there with her hands on her hips, glaring at him.

"Think real hard about this, Aaron. You're too close to this, and you're headed down a very slippery slope."

"All I care about is getting Melissa back, and I'll do whatever I have to." He took a deep breath and spoke to Klipser. "Pete, keep Cummings close in case she is contacted again, but consider both mother and daughter compromised and expendable."

"Understood. My team and I will be wheels-up by three, and we'll be in Albuquerque just before sundown. Have the FBI agent meet us at the airport."

The commlink went dead, and Palmer looked like she was going to continue the debate, but the young analyst gasped.

"Agent Figueroa's office just found Alfonso Reyes's Albuquerque base of operations!"

CHAPTER 34

1232 MST, MONDAY
ALBUQUERQUE, NM

I T HAD BEEN A SHOT in the dark, a Hail Mary pass, a Plan B. He didn't know who the girl was or what had happened to her, or if she was even still missing. That wasn't why he'd kidnapped the agent's daughter, but he was still going to use her against her mother. The ruse had simply been an easy way to get Klipser to Albuquerque. If they—whoever *they* were—hadn't fallen for it, he'd have to figure out some other way to find those agents.

He'd hit pay dirt, though. They thought he was Reyes. They thought he had their girl. And they were coming for her. In a deep corner of his mind, he started planning a scenario where he might find out who she was and how he could find her and use her against the government. Maybe Cummings knew who she was. Maybe she'd trade information in exchange for her daughter's life.

The ops center was practically empty. A foldout table from Walmart served as Erickson's computer desk. The only piece of equipment on the desk was the man's high-end laptop. It was connected by cable to the high-def wall monitor. The only other equipment in the ops center was the bank of power strips charging the disposable cells. That was it—no tables, couches, chairs, or lamps.

Garcia continued to give Erickson instructions according to the plan Carl had outlined. The mercenaries stood in the middle of the ops room, watching the data cascade across the wall monitor and listening, Carl was convinced, to every word spoken by Garcia, Erickson, and himself. All four mercs wore black cargo pants and black turtlenecks. All were armed with knives and guns, but they'd left the heavy weaponry and body armor in the garage.

Carl addressed his team. "To be clear, the people who are coming for me are probably CIA black-ops guys."

The female, Merc Four, jutted her chin forward and said, "What exactly is our mission?"

Carl gave her and the others a sly grin. He wasn't sure where he got his new confidence, but it felt good. "Kill everyone except these two." He pointed at the wall monitor.

A badge photo of Special Agent Cummings from her personnel file filled the right half of the screen. She was dressed in her typical FBI dark suit with a light blue blouse. Intense brown eyes stared at the camera. Her blonde hair was pulled severely back. Minimal makeup adorned her oval face.

On the left half of the screen was an artist's conception of Agent Klipser. During his hacking foray into the FBI's computers before the lockdown, Erickson had found no surveillance photos of the man or team who had retrieved Carl from the FBI building a month ago, so he concluded that the building's security videos had been erased. He downloaded a software program and used it to produce a likeness of Klipser as described by Carl. It was a good likeness, Carl thought—slender face, square jaw with its perpetual scruffy five-o'clock shadow, thin lips, narrow nose, closely spaced hawklike black eyes that seemed to bore through their target, close-cropped military buzz cut that was very short on the sides of his head, but a little longer on top. It was an intense face he would never forget.

"I'm fairly sure this woman, Special Agent Cummings, knows the identity of a man named McGrath, who gives them their marching orders, but I'm absolutely certain that Agent Klipser knows him. I want them both alive if possible, but if I can't have both, then I'll settle for only the woman. Because we have her daughter, she is more likely to respond favorably to my requests for information. This man, Klipser, will be too hard to break."

"If we can't break him, why capture him?"

Carl looked at Merc Two. "Retribution and demonstration." He swept his gaze over the other mercenaries. "Mr. Erickson has identified an unscheduled government Gulfstream flight out of Andrews Air Force Base bound for Albuquerque. A last-minute flight plan was filed right before takeoff." He paused. "That's our boy and whatever team members he's bringing with him, so they'll be here before dark. Once they land, I figure they'll take a helicopter north to the FBI building."

"No," Merc One said. "That'll be like sending up a flare, like, come and shoot me down. After what you did to the FBI assault team this morning, they won't take the chance that you don't have a heat-seeker missile or an RPG capable of bringing down an aircraft."

Carl said, "Which we do have, by the way."

Merc Four nodded and added, "They'll assume that. They'd likely need a military chopper to carry their entire team or at least a couple of police choppers. That'll be a mighty tempting target. They'll be safe over the airport and the base, but over the city, they'll be vulnerable, and they know you could launch from pretty much anywhere, especially when they're on approach to the FBI building. They'd know they can't adequately secure the airspace over the entire city."

Merc Two agreed. "I'd expect two tactical teams, a primary team, and a backup, both with a minimum of four men each with supplies and weapons, or they might send a single six-man unit. Typically, a modified covert Gulfstream owned by the government would be used for this kind of transport operation, and it wouldn't be able to hold much more than six or eight guys fully equipped."

Merc One said, "It'll be safer and more flexible to move them with ground transport. All you need is a couple of big SUVs. Armored, of course. They'll use random surface streets through Albuquerque, so we'll have to hit them at the airport or at the FBI building. They'll avoid the interstate because there are too many overpasses we could hit them from."

Merc Four said, "This airport is fairly unique since the civilian part of the airport shares facilities with Kirtland Air Force Base. They'll want to avoid driving through the base fully armed because they'd have to coordinate with base personnel, which potentially compromises their operational security. Is there a way for them to get off the airport quietly, maybe a fuel supply gate?"

Erickson put a map of the base and airport up on the wall monitor and highlighted the gates that fit Merc Four's request. "There's the east-side gate that exits onto Eubank Boulevard. They'd have to go through the science compounds of what's known as the Sandia part of the base. There's also a gate on the south side where they get fuel supplies delivered, but that's kind of out in the middle of nowhere. They might think that exit is too risky because the landscape is too open and vulnerable to attack."

The computer nerd looked at the mercs, and Carl got the feeling he was looking for validation on that point. The mercs just looked at him with four sets of deadpan eyes.

"What else?" Carl said.

"Well, there's the gate on the southwest side of the runways near the cargo hangars. It's primarily used for cargo delivery and pickups."

Carl had forgotten about that one. "I used to make pickups back there in one of my previous businesses, so I know they can avoid a lot of civilian traffic by using that route. They'll likely park their aircraft at one of the cargo hangars and disembark there. And it's pretty much a straight shot from that gate to the interstate, or to surface streets past the rental car compound."

"That's likely where the FBI will pick them up then," the female merc said. "And we'll be waiting for them after they get off base. We'll have surprise on our side, but if they have more than two or three vehicles, we'll be outgunned. If we can't take them all out in the first ten to fifteen seconds, they'll hand us our collective asses on a platter."

The others nodded in agreement and looked at Carl.

He said, "All right, if you can't pull off an ambush without a firefight, bag the op, and we'll figure out another way to get those two." Carl pointed at the images of Cummings and Klipser on the monitor again.

Merc Three said, "Is it too late to ask for a pay raise? We're going to have to leave the country and never come back after this op."

The others chuckled.

Carl answered quietly. He wanted to come across as sincere as possible. "Actually, this would be a good time to quit if you're of a mind to do that. Any other questions?"

"Yeah," Merc Two said. "We got any food up in this joint? I'm starving."

CHAPTER 35

1738 MST, MONDAY
ALBUQUERQUE, NM

C ARL WATCHED THE SECOND AMBUSH of the day unfold from
his headquarters house. Two big, black SUVs with darkly tinted
windows blasted past a flower truck that was stalled on the shoulder of the airport's cargo road.

"Only two vehicles," Garcia said. He held the smartphone close to
his mouth. "So that means the first go/no-go decision point has passed,
and the op is still on."

"Copy that," returned Merc One's voice from the cell speaker. He'd
been elected as the team leader by the group, although it was clear to
Carl that all of the four soldiers were equally qualified.

Two small video cameras were mounted on the top rear driver's side
corner of the flower truck's fourteen-foot cargo cabin. One faced west,
and the other faced east. On the west camera, Carl identified Special
Agent Cummings as the driver of the first SUV. He had predicted that
since she was McGrath's go-to agent, she'd be the one dispatched to
pick up Klipser and his combat team. Chances were good that she would
be driving at least one of the vehicles.

The SUVs came forward on the west camera view and retreated on
the east view. A portion of the rental car complex could be seen on the
left edge of the image of the back of the SUVs. It looked to be about
half a mile from the cargo access road. From an overhead map they'd

all studied earlier, Carl knew that road curved south a bit, then east, and ended a mile later at the cargo gate.

A tow truck with a bright yellow cabin and black lettering sat in front of the flower truck. A light bar flashed with yellow and white caution lights on the roof of the truck cabin. The tow truck driver, Merc One in disguise, fiddled with some chains like he was going to haul the front of the flower truck up onto its heavy-duty tow bar. Merc Four trotted across the road with her load after the SUVs disappeared around the bend. She lay down in the depression that dipped off to the side of the asphalt.

The depression was typical of paved roads in the southwest, and it aided rainwater drainage off both sides of the roads. Laying in the depression, she'd be virtually invisible to the returning SUVs until they were within a hundred feet of her position. At that distance, it wouldn't make any difference if the drivers saw her or not.

From the mission plan, Carl knew that Merc Four's equipment consisted of a military-grade MP5 assault rifle, extra mags in the pockets of her desert camo field jacket, and two RPGs. One was armor-piercing, and the other was not. Her specific part in the operation was, first and foremost, to keep the government agents from exiting their vehicles and setting up defensive positions. Also, she was the backup RPG shooter. If Mercs One and Two missed their targets, then she was to destroy the second SUV with the armor-piercing RPG. She would also try to stop Cummings's SUV by shooting a "normal" RPG into its engine compartment.

For Carl, RPGs were the stuff of action movies and thriller books he used to read. Now, he had actually stolen money and bought a crate full of the damn things, and the only way he knew how to distinguish the two types was to call the least deadly model "normal."

The only reason he believed the current attack had a prayer of a chance of success was because Henry Erickson had been monitoring police radio bands, and he had confirmed that police and FBI teams were still in the middle of a stakeout and raid of the second decoy house. He and Garcia had left just enough breadcrumbs to let the feds think that Alfonso Reyes owned that house. It had taken several hours because the bomb squad was called in to clear the structure before the investigators moved in. According to Erickson, that exercise was just now beginning to wrap up.

Carl's gut told him McGrath's people had to have seen through his deception by now. The only real advantage he had remaining was that McGrath might have doubts about whether he was engaging Carl or Reyes. Hopefully, that doubt would allow Carl to find and kill him. He just needed a day or two more. His mission would either be complete by then, or it would be impossible to complete.

A month ago, he was a normal guy, a real estate agent blissfully unaware of the shadow world of terrorists that government agencies like the FBI battled every day of every week of every year. Fast-forward a month, and he was living in that shadow world. He was one of the terrorists.

Carl concentrated on the tingle of excitement he felt about the pending operation, even though he wasn't on the front line. He was the McGrath of his little team, with limited resources doing battle with the *real* McGrath, who had a much larger team with unlimited personnel and resources. It was a true David and Goliath story. He'd won the first round, no doubt demonstrating his resolve to McGrath.

He thought about the slain FBI men. Who were they? Were they married? Did they have kids? Sometime in the next few hours, an FBI agent in a dark suit with a somber expression on his or her face would show up at the home of the families to deliver the terrible news. Then those families would face days, weeks, and months of grieving for a loved one they would never see again.

He thought about his nemesis, the government man who got his son killed. He tried to picture McGrath in his mind, but all he could conjure was a generic outline of a man's head, grayed out like an online dating profile shadow with no photo. He mentally placed a bull's-eye over the gray outline.

He felt someone close by speaking to him in a hushed whisper.

Young Garcia said, "You okay, boss?"

Carl realized he'd been cursing at McGrath under his breath. He took a deep inhale and unclenched his fists. He had no time for anger, grieving, or self-doubt. The mission was everything.

Find McGrath and make him pay.

The young man added, "Are you having second thoughts?"

"Negative," Carl said. "Not in the slightest. What's our status?"

"We've got eyes on the jet. They disembarked at the cargo terminal. Looks like a six-man team plus the commander who fits the description of Agent Klipser." Garcia paused, and they listened to the chatter from the cell phone speaker. It occurred to Carl that he and Garcia should be using hands-free Bluetooth earpieces or headsets to be more efficient.

Garcia continued, "All six team members are in the rear SUV, and one of them is driving. Klipser, Cummings, and the other FBI driver are in the front SUV." He paused, and his eyebrows went up. "And get this! All the heavy weapons are in the rear SUV!"

Carl smiled. "Cocky bastards," he said. "And predictable."

"Excuse me?"

He looked sideways at the young man. "If you know what your enemy wants, give it to him. Then beat him over the head with it." He returned his attention to the monitor. "McGrath and Klipser want Alfonso Reyes and that missing girl. That makes them predictable."

"Who is the girl, Boss?"

"I don't know," he said. "But *they* do." He pointed at the two black SUVs approaching the ambush point.

The east view showed long shadows on the road as the sun began its descent to the horizon. That was an added advantage for Carl's mercs. The feds were driving with the sun in their eyes.

The opening salvo of the battle was quick and decisive. An RPG exploded against the lead SUV, and at first, the battle looked like it was going to be a short-lived slam dunk for David and a devastating defeat for Goliath. Then, in the blink of an eye, the plan went to shit.

He didn't remember what famous military commander once made the statement, but it certainly applied to the current battle.

"The best-laid plan falls apart as soon as the bullets start flying."

CHAPTER 36

1745 MST, MONDAY
ALBUQUERQUE, NM

Special Agent Lenore Cummings drove the lead SUV. The armored truck was protected by steel plating all around, including the roof, undercarriage, and engine compartment. The windows were composed of a thick multilayer glass and Lexan laminate that could stop most close-range subsonic bullets. The big twelve-cylinder engine roared as she quickly got the heavy vehicle up to fifty miles an hour.

But for Director McGrath's intervention, Cummings knew she would have been removed from the investigation. Her daughter was a hostage. She was compromised, and she knew it. Still, she fought against giving in to the anger and the fear that gripped her. She had a job to do. Two jobs. Find the kidnapper. Find her daughter.

Bureau protocol clearly called for the removal of a compromised agent from a case. Such an agent could not be trusted to remain objective. McGrath had kept her because she was essential to his mission. She had a rare opportunity to accomplish her first priority—save her daughter—and accomplish McGrath's mission to find the kidnapper. She certainly couldn't leave her daughter's fate up to professional killers who had no interest in saving Lisette. She had to do that herself.

She gripped the steering wheel tightly as she drove, but that was the only outward discomfort she allowed herself to show. With every minute that passed, she understood that seeing her daughter again was becoming less and less likely. On the other hand, she knew something about the case she didn't think McGrath and his team knew.

"I know my daughter is not your mission, but I don't think this is Alfonso Reyes," she said. "From what I've learned in Director McGrath's debriefings, it's not his MO. An ambush like this morning would be bad for his business and bad for his reputation south of the border."

Agent Klipser sat in the passenger seat like a caged lion, wary and watching. He was hunched forward a bit. His dark eyes constantly scanned his surroundings. He sat without his seat belt fastened, as though he thought he might need to jump out of the moving vehicle at a moment's notice. She knew she should not show any weakness in front of him or his men.

Klipser looked at her but said nothing, so she continued, "I think it's Carl Johnson with a vendetta. I think he staged his suicide, and now, he's coming after us because his son was killed in your operation. I think I'm his only link to finding you, so he grabbed my daughter to force me to contact you. My assumption is that Reyes has other ways of making contact. He wouldn't need me."

She glanced at Klipser again, but the man's eyes were totally devoid of emotion. They also held no surprise, and that was confirmation enough for her to assume McGrath had already proceeded down the same path of reasoning.

"This isn't news to you, is it?" she said.

Klipser turned his gaze back onto the road ahead and was silent for a brief moment, as if he was trying to decide whether or not to share with her what he knew.

"No, it is not." He paused. "We've considered this possibility."

Cummings nodded. "Look, I don't care what you intend to do with this man when you find him."

"If it is Carl Johnson we're dealing with, I intend to kill him."

"If it's Johnson, give me a few minutes with him first so I can find my daughter. It won't interfere with your mission."

Klipser looked at her again and nodded with a single down-up motion of his head. "I can do that."

He looked like he was going to say something else when his eyes suddenly widened. Cummings had been squinting at the setting sun moving through her field of view as the truck followed the curve in the two-lane road. A puff of smoke seemed to appear right out of the ball of fire. Panic gripped her gut as she yanked the wheel to the left and then to the right, but the tiny missile compensated in a millisecond and slammed into the SUV's armored front grill.

The force of the explosion stopped the SUV on a dime and jammed the front end into the asphalt. The SUV's forward momentum carried the back end upward and forward. Cummings knew in an instant they were going to flip ass over front, so she gripped the steering wheel as her harness dug into her waist and shoulder.

For a brief moment, a ball of fire obscured everything in front of the truck. The armored windshield cracked but did not shatter. Then the fire cleared, and the road tilted upward and rotated to the left. Cummings was now looking *down* and saw the well-armed woman in desert camouflage right *below* her. The woman lay in the depression beside the road. The woman's eyes widened as she and the ground raced upward toward the windshield.

Cummings was vaguely aware of the crunching of metal. Then something struck her hard against the right temple. As darkness settled in, she realized she was hanging upside down.

CHAPTER 37

1747 MST, MONDAY
ALBUQUERQUE, NM

CARL SAW THE TRAIL OF smoke and fire flash from the right bottom corner of the wall monitor. Erickson had expanded the east-facing camera view so it filled the monitor. The lead SUV swerved first to the left and then to the right. The missile course-corrected instantly and slammed into the front of that vehicle.

According to the plan, the mercs had identified Cummings and Klipser in the lead SUV, and the truck was hit by the non-armor-piercing RPG. The tiny warhead exploded in a spectacular ball of fire. The force of the explosion squashed the front of the heavy vehicle down into the asphalt, and the back end lifted skyward.

The front left wheel was blasted away and ripped right through the space where Merc One stood behind the tow truck rig, ready to fire his armor-piercing RPG at the second SUV. He was instantly decapitated, but he pressed his trigger anyway, the final instinctive action of his dead and falling body. His missile blasted harmlessly skyward.

The second SUV skidded to a stop crossways to the road, and armed men in full tactical gear scrambled out on the far side. At the same time, the lead SUV completed its cartwheel, landing upside down in the depression beside the road.

Right on top of Merc Four.

The operation died in that single instant of time. As Carl watched the monitor, the feds deployed behind their armored SUV and concentrated their fire at the flower truck and the tow truck. The camera feed jittered violently as hundreds of rounds impacted the cargo box of the truck.

It didn't appear to Carl that Klipser's agents engaged in any kind of verbal or signal communications at all. For the moment, the six agents remained sheltered behind their armor-plated SUV, firing at the flower truck, but Carl knew it was inevitable that they would press their advantage in numbers and surround or kill his mercs.

"Shit!" Carl said. "Get them out of there now!"

Garcia listened intently to the chaotic noise coming from his speakerphone, but Carl couldn't make sense of the panicked shouts that were mostly drowned out by the clattering of automatic weapons fire.

"Three is down," the young man said. "But Two is still in the fight. He says he's almost out of ammunition."

Carl saw two dark round objects roll across the ground toward the feds' SUV. The first grenade stopped midway and exploded harmlessly. The second bounced against the front wheel of the SUV, but its blast did little more than rock the heavy, armored truck.

Garcia lowered the cell and turned to face Carl. "Two says they can't get to the Pathfinder, and even if they could, they'd get nuked before they got a hundred yards away. He's requesting instructions."

"Fuck!" Carl reached for the phone. "Two, I want you to throw out your weapons and surrender. I'll do what I can for you on this end, but this isn't your mission to die for. You've done all you can for us. Cooperate with them and stay alive."

"Copy that."

The surprise ambush had turned into exactly what Carl didn't want—an extended firefight against highly trained and well-armed federal agents.

"All right, Mr. Erickson, close up shop. We're leaving right now." Carl looked at Garcia. "We're going to need replacement mercenaries to continue the mission. And a new operations house ASAP."

He was just about to say more when he was distracted by movement on the monitor. A flash of flame and smoke erupted from *beneath* the front portion of Cummings's upside-down SUV and streaked toward the second fed truck. The armored vehicle exploded in a massive spew of fire and ripped metal as engine parts, tires, doors, weapons, and human parts flew everywhere. Klipser's men had absolutely no chance for survival as fragments from the blasted SUV sliced right through their body armor and literally shredded the men.

Carl gasped and involuntarily took a step back from the monitor as bloody pieces of the agents were tossed dozens of feet from the destroyed vehicle. Whatever excitement and thrill he had previously felt evaporated immediately at the sight of the strewn body parts. He saw heads, arms, legs, boots, and wads of bloody guts flop onto the asphalt, and then the war zone was completely still.

Carl shivered and leaned over to brace his palms against his kneecaps. Nausea gripped him, and he found himself unable to control the trembling in his arms and legs. This was the real war he had become involved in. This was the mission.

He breathed through his open mouth and tried to prevent his stomach from bringing up his lunch. Erickson raced from his laptop and threw up in the trash can.

Next to Carl, Garcia echoed his astonishment. "Fuck *me!*" He paused. "Did you see that shit?"

With great effort, Carl squashed his nausea and stood up. "Get our people the hell out of there! The feds have had plenty of time to call for help, and the cops will be all over their asses within five minutes."

On the TV screen, Merc Four slithered out from under the first SUV. Her partner, Merc Three, joined her in front of the upside-down truck. He had his exterior Kevlar vest unstrapped, and his desert camo combat shirt was ripped open. He massaged the center of his chest. Carl listened to the exchange through the cell phone headsets that each merc wore.

"You okay, babe?" Merc Four said.

"Got hit in the chest, but the vest saved me. You?"

"Goddamn thing landed right on top of me," Merc Four said. "Pinned me in the space between the windshield and the engine hood."

The two mercs moved to the driver's door, but it was locked.

Four said, "She's conscious, but she won't open the door, and we don't have time to wait her out. She just got off the phone, so I'm thinking she's got help coming."

Carl pulled out his cell and selected Cummings's number. When she answered, he said, "This is Carl Johnson. Open the door, or I'll strap your daughter to a table and do to her what Agent Klipser did to me. I'll put it on YouTube and show the world how an FBI agent let her daughter get tortured." He disconnected the call.

"Okay, she's opening the door."

A few seconds later, they dragged Cummings into the dirt. When they stood her up, Merc Four punched her hard in the gut with one hell of a windup that she launched from the center of the earth, and her partner dragged the agent over to the Pathfinder.

Carl said, "Drug her up and strip her naked, undies and all, in case she has any kind of transmitter or beacon on her clothes."

Merc Four said over the net, "And don't have too much fun doing it either."

Erickson regained his seat and hit some keys on his keyboard, and the wall monitor split into the east and west views again. On the west view, Merc Three dropped Cummings to the asphalt behind the Pathfinder. He injected her in the neck with the contents of a syringe prepared specifically to render captives unconscious and keep them that way for several hours. It was the same type of concoction used on Carl. That was, in fact, the experience that gave him the idea.

Merc Three grabbed a wicked-looking knife from a leg sheath and expertly sliced the back of Cummings's black jacket and both her pants legs. Then he sliced her shirt and underwear. He rolled her onto her back and pulled all her clothes off with one yank. Then he pulled off her combat boots and socks. He wadded up the garments and carried them back to the SUV while Merc Two dumped the agent unceremoniously into the back of the Pathfinder.

Carl studied the naked agent sprawled facedown in the back of the escape truck. She looked about like he'd expected. Her legs, butt, and back were white while her arms were slightly tanned. She appeared fit and muscular—not petite, but not chunky either. She looked maybe thirty-five or forty.

He started formulating a plan to take advantage of his captive, but the female merc interrupted his thoughts.

"Looks like Agent Klipser is still alive too, but unconscious. Dumbass wasn't wearing his seatbelt."

"Drug him up and strip him too," Carl said. As an afterthought, he added, "Can you get to the other FBI agent?"

"He's dead for sure," Merc Four said. "Head's damn near severed from his shoulders."

She dragged Klipser from the vehicle and hauled him around to the front. She pulled a syringe from a Velcro pocket and jammed the needle into his thigh. She squeezed the plunger down to its limit. Her partner came over to help get the agent across the street, out of his gear and clothing, and into the back of the Pathfinder.

"All right," Carl said. "Evac as fast as you can."

Merc Three said, "You want us to bring back Trevor's body?"

Trevor Flosk was Merc One.

The voice of Merc Two answered, "Which part?"

Four said, "Leave him. It's not like we can bury him or anything."

Carl said, "He did his job, and now he's gone. The FBI will take care of him."

Three said, "They're going to ID him."

"That won't help them. Return to base. Take Cummings and Klipser to the warehouse Mr. Garcia set up. I'll meet you there."

"Roger that."

"And nuke that SUV with an incendiary grenade. I want the FBI to have to do some serious CSI work before they figure out I have their agents. That'll give me a few hours to get personal with them."

He was one step closer to McGrath.

"Mr. Garcia, they're going to try to back-trace Cummings's cell, so dispose of all our used cell phones, tell the mercs to toss theirs, and go to backups. And see if you can get us moved in two hours. Get Erickson set up with new equipment too and dispose of his old stuff." He glanced at the fidgeting computer geek. "You can have your fix now and some downtime to enjoy it." He patted the man on the shoulder. "You've done good, Mr. Erickson. Real good."

"Mr. Garcia," Carl continued, "have the team get off the interstate ASAP." They'd be headed north on I-25 back into the city. "If Cummings reached her people with a distress call, the FBI and local police are already on the way, and they probably already have a police chopper in the air from their other op. Have our guys cross the median and go south to

Rio Bravo, then go west and hit Second Street northbound to the parking garage, where we've stashed our backup vehicles. Have them switch vehicles twice at the other garages before proceeding to the warehouse."

Carl considered that the operation ended well, despite the near disaster. The final mission objective was now in play. He wanted information—the identity and location of McGrath—and now he had two people in custody who possessed that information.

And they knew about the missing girl too. He wanted that girl.

CHAPTER 38

0004 EST, TUESDAY
ARLINGTON HEIGHTS, VA

A FTER REVIEWING THE AFTER-ACTION REPORT from SAC Figueroa's office, Aaron McGrath had zero doubts about who they were dealing with. He was certain Nancy Palmer needed no further convincing either.

"Mercenaries, I can understand," McGrath mused aloud. "I can even see how he could come across cash and guns. But high-explosive, armor-piercing, rocket-propelled grenades? Where the hell does a *citizen*, a goddamn real estate broker, acquire that kind of weaponry?"

Palmer nodded her agreement. "My guess is he hired the mercenaries first and tasked them with weapons acquisitions. That's what I'd do if I was in his situation."

McGrath was troubled that he had not considered Carl Johnson more of a threat. He was clearly more than simply an ordinary civilian. He was steps ahead of the TER at every turn, and he'd predicted their actions and reactions. McGrath had helped him by severely underestimating the man.

That the lead SUV had been gutted by fire caused by an incendiary grenade only compounded the mystery until the field investigator reported there appeared to be only a single occupant inside that vehicle. The corpse was burned beyond recognition, but McGrath knew what it meant.

"So he has Agents Klipser and Cummings. By deliberately burning the SUV, he delayed discovery that they were missing and earned himself a few hours to advance his agenda."

Palmer nodded and said, "And it's curious that they left their dead soldier behind. Johnson would know we'd identify him."

"Even if they took the body away, the FBI's crime scene investigators could ID him through a DNA analysis of his blood, though it would take longer. Johnson is smart enough to know that."

"So Carl is not the insane, out-of-control lunatic bent on revenge that he'd like us to believe," Palmer said. "He's pragmatic. He knows the FBI would dispose of the body in their normal course of doing business. That means identifying Trevor Flosk is no threat to his plans."

McGrath glanced sideways at Palmer. They were standing in front of the monitor wall behind Joey, the big bald analyst, so he gave her a head-nod to follow him into the hallway.

"You're on a first-name basis with this guy now?"

"I'm in his head, Aaron," Palmer said. "And you better get there too. Carl Johnson is not the mission. He doesn't have Melissa." She paused. "We lost that battle, Aaron. Let's get back to the main objective."

"He's an amateur, so he's unpredictable. But he has an agenda, and he's a professional planner with a shrewd command presence for someone with no formal military combat training. And he's learning to adapt extremely fast." McGrath paused. "And he's after us."

"And he'll continue to adapt and escalate as long as we keep playing his game."

McGrath looked down at the floor for a moment. "You're suggesting we close the book on Johnson and abandon his hostages."

"Let the FBI deal with him. Pete Klipser won't talk, and Lenore Cummings can't give him anything."

McGrath didn't like that the terrorist had no formal knowledge of covert ops and couldn't be expected to follow wartime rules of engagement. He wouldn't likely do what was expected, even of a run-of-the-mill terrorist, because those individuals also received training in their craft at established training camps. Standard terrorist training was also well understood.

Johnson was likely making up his own rules of engagement as his plan progressed, which made it almost impossible for McGrath's team to plan counterstrikes against him. Even FBI criminal profiling depended on the systematic collection of data to establish a pattern of criminal behavior, and Johnson was moving too fast and too unpredictably. Eventually, they'd profile him, but not in time to help the hostages he held.

McGrath also didn't like that his second-in-command was right about their course of action. He had a personal interest in the operation.

He nodded. "Very well. Let's get the local FBI on comm."

They went back into the ops center and waited while the analyst secured the video link. Figueroa looked as tired as McGrath felt. The SAC's white shirt was crumpled, and his sleeves were rolled up to his elbows. The man had dark shadows under his eyes.

McGrath said, "We no longer believe Alfonso Reyes is the key suspect in today's events. The most likely suspect is Carl Johnson. He strongly resembles Alfonso Reyes, and we brought him in for questioning a month ago. His son was collateral damage in the investigation, and Johnson blames the FBI for his death." McGrath paused. "And he blames me and my people."

Figueroa leaned back in his chair and considered this new information.

"Okay, so he's got a vendetta, and he's clearly got skills and resources. How much damage can we expect from this man? What is he, a former Delta operator or a SEAL? Is he one of yours, or maybe a rogue CIA specialist?"

"No," McGrath said with a sigh. "He's a pissed-off father with absolutely nothing to lose and no reason to continue living except to kill us."

CHAPTER 39

0230 MST, TUESDAY
ALBUQUERQUE, NM

He watched Special Agent Lenore Cummings drift slowly out of her drug-induced sleep. She moaned a bit, and her eyelids fluttered.

He whispered in her ear, "Hey, sweetie. Time to wake up."

She smiled and purred, then frowned as she must have realized she was restrained. Suddenly, she was fully awake and saw Carl's face near hers. A slew of language that would make a sailor blush exploded from her mouth. Carl just chuckled and stood up straight. She struggled against her bindings, then raised her head—her only body part not strapped down—and examined her surroundings.

"You're not so tough strapped to a table, are you?" He paused. "Special. Agent. Cummings. In a moment, we'll discuss the time when you felt empowered to beat the shit out of me—when you had me chained to a chair. I'm sure you realize that was illegal for so many reasons. But I've found that's typical of you and McGrath's people. You all think you can do any damn thing you want to anybody you choose, don't you?"

Cummings didn't answer, but he didn't expect her to.

She was strapped to a hospital gurney with her legs spread wide apart and her arms extended over her head. Her wrists were duct-taped to the metal edge of the bed. Years ago, Carl had read in a psychology book that specific positions create ultimate fear in people. For men, that position was being restrained naked on their knees, their head forced to the floor, and their butt sticking up in the air, available for abuse. The book said that sometimes even the strongest men could be broken in minutes just by forcing them into that position, so great was the fear of assault on their manhood.

For women, the position of ultimate fear was being restrained naked, spread-eagled. It was in that position of helplessness and vulnerability that Cummings now found herself, and Carl enjoyed her discomfort immensely.

He had no doubt the FBI gave its agents intensive training in resisting interrogation and psychological torture, but he doubted their training included resisting physical torture. One thing Carl now knew from personal experience was no amount of training could prepare any man or woman for the real thing. When it happened, the only thing one could do was suffer through it. Either you were tough enough, or you weren't. Either you would break or you would not.

Having survived severe torture—if one could call going berserk and declaring war on the US government *survival*—Carl now knew that every human being had a breaking point. It was only a matter of finding that point. In most cases, it was more a matter of discovering what a person was afraid of and exploiting that fear.

He didn't know how tough the FBI woman was, and unfortunately, he didn't have access to the government's torture table, its electroshock device, or its collection of pain-inducing chemicals. Cummings was probably tough enough to withstand rape, fingernail pulling, bone-breaking, or other kinds of physical beating or disfigurement. She might even resist waterboarding, though probably not the method he'd endured, having a funnel tube shoved down her throat.

If he was completely honest, Carl thought as he looked at the naked woman lying before him, a part of him—a *huge* part—wanted to do all those things to her just to hear her scream and beg for mercy like he'd been forced to do. Unlike McGrath's doctor, who seemed to enjoy eliciting Carl's pain, Carl didn't want to torture the woman for enjoyment. He was going to do it to extract specific information, and he knew physical torture would not produce the information as quickly as he needed.

He had to get the information within a few hours. He had to instill fear in the FBI woman very quickly and break her will in mere minutes. Fortunately, he knew exactly what she was afraid of. She was, after all, a mother.

He watched Cummings scan her surroundings. She had no idea where she was. The extent of her world was the fifteen-foot square space enclosed by the thick white canvas sheets hanging around her. Tightly stretched canvas also formed a ceiling over the space. It was cold, despite an electric heater trying in vain to heat the room from the far corner. The drone from a gas-powered generator drowned out all sound from outside the cubicle.

A high-definition camera was mounted on a tripod in the corner near the space heater, and floodlights in each corner of the room were angled upward at the walls and ceiling of the cubicle to provide indirect lighting off the sheets. Carl wore a wireless microphone on the collar of the white bunny suit he wore. The one-piece suit covered his entire body up to his chin. The suit zipped up in the front, and only his head and hands were uncovered by the material.

He wore latex gloves and a white face mask like the kind dentists wore. He had the mask pulled down under his chin. A massive amount of blood stained the front of his bunny suit, and he could tell by the look on her face that she was wondering whose blood it was.

"Turns out, our friend Agent Klipser was pretty goddamn tough. He wouldn't break, but then I think it was pretty clear to him that I was going to kill him, whether he broke or not. He had my son killed, after all, so I think he just decided to tough it out. By the way, I hold you responsible also, so I'm going to kill you after you tell me what I want to know. I just want you to know upfront what's going to happen, in case you want to be tough like your friend over there." Carl thumbed over his shoulder. "And by the way, feel free to scream as loud as you want, especially when we get to the good part, the really painful part. Trust me. You won't wake up the neighbors." Carl paused and chuckled, though there was no humor in his eyes. "And you can believe me when I say that this is going to be very painful. It's going to hurt a lot."

Carl stepped toward the foot of Cummings's table and pulled a white sheet from a second gurney. Cummings still had her head cranked up, so when he stepped aside, she gasped when she saw what was left of

Klipser's body. The skin of his midsection had been cut and pinned back and his intestines—still connected to the inside of his body—lay in a messy pile over his hips and thighs.

"I read in a book somewhere," Carl said, "that in some third-world country—I forget which one—the women would capture enemy soldiers when they wandered too far away from their camp in the night. They'd stake the soldier to the ground spread-eagled, slitting his torso from collar bone to hip bone and left to right across his belly button. Then they'd peel back the skin, tack the flaps down, pull out his intestines, and leave him that way. They say the procedure was fairly painless. They say a man can live for fifteen or sixteen hours in that condition before infection and dehydration kill him. The women would actually hold lotteries to see who could correctly guess how long the soldier could hold out."

He paused and grabbed Klipser by his hair, then raised the man's already severed head from the table. Cummings gasped again. The man's eyes and mouth were wide open like he'd been screaming in pain in his last moment of life, even though the man had remained silent to the end.

"Of course, Agent Klipser was far too dangerous to let live that long," Carl bobbled the head around, then slammed it back down on the gurney so the dead face peered at the FBI agent.

"Now, I'm wondering how long an eleven-year-old girl can survive with her intestines laying in a pile outside her belly. Just for full disclosure, I think I already mentioned that I'm going to kill you for your part in the death of my son." He paused and stepped back up to the head of Cummings's gurney. "So, the only relevant decision you'll need to make is whether you're going to tell me what I want to know *first,* or will you watch me mutilate your daughter."

Carl stepped over to another gurney and pulled a white sheet from it. Lisette Cummings was strapped to the table, naked just like her mother, except her hands were strapped at her sides. The girl had gray duct tape on her mouth. She had been silent and motionless, but with the sheet pulled back, she began to cry and whimper and struggle, no doubt frightened by the sight of a bloodied man leaning over her.

"So let's begin, shall we?"

CHAPTER 40

1302 EST, TUESDAY
ARLINGTON HEIGHTS, VA

NANCY PALMER WAS WORKING AT the management workstation when Joey's terminal beeped. When she looked over her shoulder, she saw the young man had his right arm extended toward her, his index finger pointing loosely at her monitor. At the same time, he drained the last drops from a Red Bull can and then tossed the can in the bin beside his desk.

Palmer turned back to her monitor as a dialog box opened on the right side of her screen. She skimmed the report and lightly tapped the "All hands on deck!" button on the wall to wake everyone up. A couple minutes later, McGrath and Jimmy came downstairs.

"Figueroa's people report that a text message was sent to Cummings's cell, which was left outside the burned-out SUV and collected by the evidence team." Palmer said, "Joey, put it up on the left monitor."

Dead bodies at the old train warehouses. -Johnson

"The warehouses?" Joey said, stifling a yawn. He rubbed a massive hand over his bald head and finger-combed his long beard. "Isn't that where they filmed those *Transformers* movies?"

"And one of the *Terminator* movie," Jimmy agreed. "And *The Avengers* too, I think."

Palmer wasn't in the mood for trivia. "What's your point?"

"Those abandoned warehouses are great for big-budget movie

scenes, but someone might also use them to hide hostages for…you know."

Palmer nodded. *For interrogation.*

No one would hear the screams.

Joey said, "The FBI is already en route."

An hour later, the analyst's computer chimed.

"Aw, damn! They found a make-shift torture room in one of the south warehouses. Agent Klipser is dead, but Special Agent Cummings is alive. She's been taken to the Presbyterian Hospital emergency room. The on-scene investigator is reporting a video camera in the room. The memory card is still in the device, so he took the video cam back to the field office, and now he's uploading a copy to me." Joey paused. "Um, I'm seeing a report that the agent's daughter was there too."

Palmer said, "Johnson's note said 'dead bodies.' "

"Yeah." McGrath sighed. "That means the daughter is dead."

Joey's computer beeped. "Got the video file."

Palmer said, "Put it up on the center monitor." The analyst did so. "And Jimmy, next time you're in the kitchen, grab me one of those Red Bull things. I have a feeling it's going to be a long day, folks."

McGrath stifled a yawn. "I'll have one too."

Jimmy had just returned from the kitchen, so he simply turned around and went back. A moment later, he returned with two more Red Bulls. He popped the tops and distributed them.

The high-definition video captured the entirety of Pete Klipser's torture. The operator was taped naked to a hospital gurney. There was no interrogation involved. Carl Johnson didn't even ask him any questions. The procedure reminded Palmer of the report she'd read of Carl Johnson's first interrogation session, and she knew the similarity was intended. On the monitor, Johnson just went to work on the man, talking to him calmly all the while, explaining what he was doing and why.

"Jesus," was all McGrath said, and Palmer was certain that single word escaped unintentionally.

"Look how he's dressed," Palmer said. "He planned his whole operation down to the smallest detail. Look at his tools. He knew he'd need every specific item he has with him right now. Nothing extra, nothing wasted."

McGrath nodded. "Like leaving Cummings's cell phone *outside* the SUV so that it wouldn't get burned. He knew he'd need a way to contact us." He paused. "He had the logistics of this interrogation planned and implemented *before* he even captured them."

Johnson was dressed in a white coverall like the kind one might see in a microchip manufacturer's clean room. With a scalpel, he made two perpendicular incisions, one from Klipser's chest down to his pubic bone, and the other side to side across his belly. He tacked the flaps of skin to the sides with long stainless steel medical pins, then carefully reached into the man's intestinal cavity with his gloved hands, pulled out its contents, and laid the mess across the agent's hips and thighs.

During the procedure, Johnson had to stop twice to raise his face shield out of the way and vomit. He even apologized to the camera, explaining this was his first time torturing someone, and he wasn't as tough as the doctor who had worked on him. Then he promised to get stronger and tougher for his next torture. He added with a shrug, like a footnote to a story, that though he had already killed the doctor in his failed attempt to get Klipser to kill him, he was nonetheless upset he didn't get to torture that man.

Then he continued talking to Klipser. "They say a man can live the better part of a day in your condition. Of course, I'd be a fool to let you live that long. Be just my luck they'd find you, stuff all this shit back inside you, and sew you up. Next day, you'd come looking for me." Johnson paused and looked at the camera and said, "And I certainly don't want that."

Palmer got the feeling Johnson was taunting McGrath. Torturing a federal agent was exactly the activity that would amplify the government's effort to find the man, but Johnson seemed not to care. He simply leaned down and pulled a thin tree branch saw from under the gurney. He laid the tool on Klipser's chest.

To the agent, Carl said, "I just wanted you to spend your last moments of life feeling how I felt when I was strapped to your table—completely helpless and vulnerable, unable to do or say *anything* to make the torture stop. Of course, you're a lot tougher than I am, and I know you're not going to break. But then, that's not what this is about. Is it, Agent Klipser?

"It's really about control and power. It's about using that power to bend others to your will, whether or not they're actually guilty of a crime. It's about doing whatever is necessary to accomplish the mission because for men like you and your boss, it's always about the mission, right? It's *only* about the *fucking* mission."

Johnson nodded to himself. "This is about ordering the FBI to arrest someone and beat the shit out of him just because you can. It's about torturing someone because you're the US *fucking* government, and you know no one can do a goddamn thing to stop you. It's about being above the law. It's about killing someone's son and considering him an acceptable loss simply because you can operate with impunity and without accountability."

Johnson picked up a helmet that looked like a cross between a bee-keeper's hood and a welder's headgear. It was white, like the bunny suit he wore, and it had a large acrylic window in the front. He put on the helmet and smoothed the flaps of fabric over his shoulders, then picked up the two-foot-long saw.

Johnson looked into the camera with a sinister smirk on his face that McGrath could easily see through the acrylic splatter shield.

"But guess what?" Carl paused. "Today, you people start paying. You're going to be held accountable for your crimes and for the lives you've stolen."

Johnson stepped over to another gurney and pulled a white sheet from the unconscious and naked Special Agent Cummings. Palmer gasped, even though she knew she was going to see the agent at some point. Next to her, McGrath cursed softly.

Johnson continued, "But this particular exercise was never about breaking a tough guy like Klipser. This is all about breaking *her*." He stepped back over to Klipser's gurney, hefted the saw from Klipser's chest, and said, "Okay, Agent Klipser, this is the part where you can scream as loud as you want." Then he went to work on the agent.

Palmer stood stunned, not only by the viciousness of the act she was witnessing, but it was also by the fact that it was happening to Pete Klipser. Carl Johnson was unworthy of such a conquest.

Blood erupted from the operator's neck and splattered everywhere as Johnson pulled and pushed on the saw. He put all his strength into it, and she could hear him grunting and gasping with the effort. It took him a dozen strokes to accomplish the deed. Then he stepped back, removed the hood, and dropped the saw to the floor. His bunny suit was drenched in blood.

Johnson, still breathing hard from the exertion, exclaimed, "Damn, that's a lot of blood!"

Still looking down, the man shifted his gaze to the camera. The effect of the indirect lighting off the wall sheets and the diffuse shadows cast across his face gave him an ugly, sinister look. Without looking directly at the dead agent's head, he grabbed it and set it on the corpse's chest facing the camera a short distance beyond the man's feet.

"He isn't such a badass now, is he, Director McGrath? In fact, if you have some more badass mu'fuckers you want to send after me, be my guest. What's the score now?" Johnson paused thoughtfully and mimicked like he was counting on his fingers. "Sixteen to one? The *one* being my son, of course."

Then he turned his attention to Cummings, who was stirring on the other gurney.

"Make it seventeen to one in a moment."

CHAPTER 41

1322 EST, TUESDAY
ARLINGTON HEIGHTS, VA

McGRATH WATCHED AS JOHNSON STRIPPED off his bloody latex gloves and pulled a clean pair from a box on a medical tray table next to Cummings's bed. As he worked his hands into the new gloves, he again spoke to the camera.

"Mr. McGrath, I've had ample time to reflect on my stay with your people out there in Virginia, and I've often wondered how you felt as you watched the videos of my interrogation. Funny how perspective changes things, isn't it? I suspect you're experiencing a far different set of emotions now, as you watch your own people tortured and killed as opposed to, say, an innocent civilian and his son."

Johnson seemed genuinely pensive for a moment. "I have to admit, though, I didn't think I really could do what I just did, and I'm still feeling a bit queasy." He shrugged. "It's my first time murdering a man with my own hands. Sure, I killed your doctor, but that was more of an unplanned event. This…" Johnson said, waving a hand at Klipser's dead body. "This premeditated murder was really hard, and we all know the first time is always the hardest. The second time…" Johnson said, glancing over at Cummings. "Yeah, it probably won't be so hard. But I also have to confess to feeling a rush of exhilaration. It's a kind of power that makes me acknowledge that maybe I *can* be like you people."

Johnson stared at the monitor for a moment, and McGrath got the eerie feeling the man was staring right at him. "You know, Mr. McGrath,

I figure the FBI or the cops are watching this also. You think maybe they'll forgive me for what I've done, for the agents I've killed? You think maybe they'll give me amnesty once they realize I'm just doing the same thing that you did to me and my son?

"You think maybe they'll grow a fucking conscience, hunt you down, and prosecute you for what *you've* done? Or will they take the easy way out and simply agree you're authorized to use *harsh interrogation* techniques on an innocent man and kill my son in the name of the US *fucking* government? Maybe they'll just say you can do it, but I can't, and so that makes me a criminal and a murderer, but it just makes you a hero, a loyal *fucking* government servant.

"You know, as I was gutting your agent, I found myself wondering how it was for you twenty or thirty or forty years ago, on your first kill or your first torture. Were you like Klipser, hard as nails? Hell, maybe you still are, but I guess that remains to be seen.

"And then I wondered… When you killed my son and then realized that I was not, in fact, the kidnapper you thought I was, did you feel any remorse? Did you send flowers to my son's funeral or maybe send an anonymous letter of apology to his grieving mother? Did you turn to your staff out there and admit that you just killed an innocent young man and fucked up another man's life?

"Did any of your staffers out there ever even raise their hand at *any* time during this whole clusterfuck and say maybe they thought you had the wrong man? Or did everyone just go along for the ride because you're all untouchable? Maybe I'll ask them if they're still in the building when I come for you."

Johnson walked over to Cummings's naked form. "And who is this *fucking* girl that my son had to die for? Maybe I'll find her first and ask her if she's worth my son's life. Maybe Special Agent Cummings knows who she is."

As Cummings awoke, Johnson began speaking to her the same way he had spoken to Pete Klipser. Then he said, "So let's begin, shall we?"

Carl grabbed a scalpel from the medical tray and stepped over to Lisette's gurney. Lenore Cummings—the mother, not the special agent— broke in mere seconds. The torture setup was really nothing more than a psychological ploy, a brief one-sided explanation that Johnson would not hesitate to mutilate her daughter because of what Cummings had helped McGrath do to his son.

He placed the tip of the scalpel against the girl's chest right between her nonexistent breasts and pressed the sharp tip a fraction of a millimeter into her skin. With duct tape across her mouth, the girl whimpered through her nose, and her slender body trembled. Cummings cried out in anguish and begged and pleaded, so Johnson stopped. The woman cried and sobbed, helpless to protect her child. She agreed to tell him whatever he wanted to know.

He looked over at the FBI agent. "Where can I find this mu'fucker named Alfonso Reyes? What's his address so I can go saw his fucking head off?"

"We don't know where he lives. He moves around Mexico and South America a lot. He has several estates, so we never know for sure where he is."

"Yeah, I suppose that figures. If you knew where he was, you wouldn't have grabbed me. So who is this missing girl they kept asking me about?"

"I don't know anything about the girl. They didn't tell me who she is."

"Reyes kidnapped some billionaire's daughter. Agent Klipser kept asking me about her."

"I swear I don't know," Cummings cried. "They never briefed me about who she is."

"Come on, Lenore. Some little rich bitch gets taken, and you're telling me the FBI doesn't know about it?"

McGrath watched as Johnson kept asking questions. Cummings cooperated. She had no choice. She clearly believed, as did McGrath, that Johnson was angry enough to torture her child to get what he wanted.

To Palmer, he whispered, "I had Agent Cummings over to the house when she interviewed with us earlier this year. She knows where I live."

"I'll get more security over there. Johnson is an amateur, but he's resourceful. If it's humanly possible, he'll find a way to get there."

Suddenly, McGrath gasped and grabbed her arm. "Christ!"

"What is it?"

"She met my daughter when she was here."

Palmer turned to Joey. "Get a protection detail over to Anita's house in Santa Fe. FBI, local off-duty cops, private security firm, whoever you can get. Pay any fee necessary." Palmer turned back to McGrath. "He captured Pete and Lenore at dusk yesterday, and it's almost noon out there now, so he's got at least a nineteen-hour head start on us."

McGrath studied the ugly visage of the man on the video. Johnson's eyes were dark and angry. His mouth held a tight-lipped frown as if the man was struggling every second with his anger, and he had dark bags of fatigue under his eyes.

Carl Johnson was extremely dangerous, but it wasn't because he was a trained killer. The man wanted justice for his son's death, and he was absolutely convinced his vendetta was morally justified. He was committed and was now a threat to McGrath's entire family and staff. He was the worst kind of enemy because he didn't care what happened to himself, and he didn't care who he hurt or killed on his quest for vengeance.

The worst part for McGrath was the realization he had forged Johnson into the raging vigilante that he was. In a very real sense, what had happened to him and what he had become was McGrath's fault.

To Palmer, McGrath whispered. "If he discovers my relationship to Melissa, and if he somehow finds her before we do…" He left the remainder of his thought unspoken.

McGrath watched the monitor and listened as Cummings told Johnson the FBI had been ordered to classify him as a Tier-One terrorist earlier that morning. Then she explained what that meant. His photo and his crimes had been aired on every network across the country, and he was being called the "American Terrorist."

Then she told him everything she knew about McGrath and his Terror Event Response agency.

"One last question," Johnson said.

He leaned on Cummings's gurney, his face near hers in an almost sensually intimate posture. He seemed to study her as if weighing his next actions. He glanced over at the woman's daughter, then looked back at the FBI agent.

She seemed to understand what he was thinking. She shook her head slightly, and her eyes watered again. Her lips trembled. "Please don't."

"How does it feel?" he said.

"Please." She shook her head. "Please don't hurt my baby," she sobbed. "Kill me. I'm responsible."

Johnson looked over at the girl. "I wish I could have traded my life for my son's. I wished I could have taken those bullets for him, but your boss, McGrath, didn't give me that opportunity." He shook his head and looked at Cummings again. "And you don't get that opportunity, either. I want you to wake up every morning and feel what I feel for the rest of your miserable *fucking* life."

"Please," Cummings cried. Tears streamed from her eyes. "She's innocent."

"Yes, she is." Johnson nodded. "As was my son."

He stepped over to the girl's gurney and flipped the scalpel in his grip until he held it like a stake in his fist. His hand was poised a foot over the girl's chest, and he gazed down into the girl's frightened brown eyes. Then he plunged the blade downward.

CHAPTER 42

1329 EST, TUESDAY
ARLINGTON HEIGHTS, VA

MCGRATH, PALMER, JIMMY, AND JOEY collectively gasped at the scene on the TV monitor as Johnson plunged the scalpel blade toward Lisette's bare chest. The girl gave a muffled scream, and her mother let out a long mournful wail. She begged for mercy with renewed fervor when the tip of the blade suddenly stopped a fraction of an inch from the girl's chest.

Johnson looked down at Lisette Cummings in silence for half a minute, the tip of the scalpel a tiny distance from piercing the girl's chest. Lisette Cummings trembled, sobbed, and looked at Johnson, then she turned her head and tried to communicate with her mother. Lenore Cummings, also sobbing, muttered words of comfort to her daughter. She told Johnson she'd do anything he wanted if he spared her daughter's life.

McGrath could see Johnson's fist that was wrapped around the scalpel was trembling. He could tell the man really wanted to kill the girl to punish Cummings. Johnson seemed to be fighting a battle—maybe conscience versus consequence—in his mind. Finally, he pulled the blade away from the girl.

Johnson stepped back over to Cummings's gurney and leaned down, resting his elbows on the mattress. "Anything?" he said.

She nodded.

"Well, then tell me, Lenore," he cooed at her. His lips were almost touching hers. "Do you know where Aaron McGrath lives or where he works? Do you know his address?"

She told him.

"Mm-hmm. Does he have any children?"

The woman whispered, "Don't do this."

Johnson whispered back at her. "I'll trade your daughter's life for the life of just one of his kids. Maybe he's got a bunch, and he can afford to give up one. Maybe I'll let him choose which child dies. Or maybe he's like me and only has one child." Johnson paused and said, "*Had. One. Child.* Answer my question, and I'll leave you and your daughter here. Alive. Lie to me, and I'll just come back, and we'll have this conversation again, except, you know, without the conversation."

Cummings closed her eyes and whispered. "Anita Chapman."

"The kick-ass news reporter?"

"Her maiden name is Anita McGrath."

"Well, maybe she'll consent to an interview before I kill her on national TV."

Johnson injected Cummings and her daughter with a clear liquid that he said was a sedative, then stood and stripped out of his bloody bunny suit. He looked at the video camera for a few seconds, and McGrath could feel the man's hatred emanating from the monitor. The man's jaw muscles worked like he wanted to say something, or like he was trying hard *not* to say something.

Johnson's head was lowered a bit so that it seemed he was glaring at the camera from under heavy brows. The man looked both evil and insane. He spoke to the camera, his voice almost an inhuman growl. In fact, the man's voice reminded McGrath of Pete Klipser's voice, with that intense gravelly sound no enemy wanted to hear whispered in his ear. He felt a chill of fear worm its way up his spine, and he shivered involuntarily.

"Aaron McGrath, I'm coming for you."

McGrath grunted at the monitor. "Not if I find you first, you bastard."

Joey's computer beeped again, alerting him to a keyword on one of a myriad data sources.

"Um, Boss, I found Carl Johnson."

McGrath and Palmer turned to face him.

"He's on network TV." The young man paused. "He's with your daughter."

CHAPTER 43

1206 MST, TUESDAY
ALBUQUERQUE, NM

CARL FACED ANITA MCGRATH CHAPMAN from his seat ten feet away. The canvas material of her director's chair squeaked as it rubbed against the wood under her constant nervous motion. The three camera lights captured all the fear and terror on Anita's face as she stared at Carl Johnson. Enjoying her discomfort, Carl continued to tell her and the American people about his capture, torture, and the events of the last thirty days.

"So I welcome you to Downtown Albuquerque, Ms. Chapman," Carl said. "I know this isn't quite what you expected when you agreed to do this interview, to actually become part of the drama." Carl nodded. "And I know that some of the media—maybe even you—have tried to sensationalize this whole *terror* thing. Maybe you saw an opportunity to try and uncover a new angle here. Maybe let me have a chance to proclaim my innocence or explain the unfortunate misunderstanding that got me into this mess. But let me assure you and your audience, I haven't been framed or unjustly accused. I am exactly who they say I am. I've done exactly what they say I've done, and I will not hesitate to kill again to get what I want. Understood?" He looked at the two cameramen. "You two, get the hell out of here."

The men exchanged glances, but neither moved, so Carl reached inside his windbreaker and pulled a gun from his shoulder holster. With a two-inch tubular suppressor attached, the black handgun looked very sinister. "Go now before I change my mind."

As the two men hurried toward the door, Anita Chapman sat clenching the arms of her chair with a white-knuckled grip. As Carl followed the men, he reached up and pulled down the backdrop curtain. He didn't want to leave any visual barrier for the men to hide behind momentarily. He didn't want either of them to try to be a hero.

Chapman had arrived dressed in her typical professional manner. She wore an expensive, two-piece, dark gray skirt suit. The blazer was a well-tailored, one-button piece over a muted maroon blouse. Only the first button of her blouse was undone. There was no cleavage showing. Carl knew from seeing her television interviews that kind of thing was not her image.

She was an ample woman, he thought, but she didn't seem overweight. Her expensive clothes were tailored to conceal what needed to be concealed and to accentuate what she wanted noticed. She appeared forty or so, and though she didn't possess the physique of his idea of the typical anchor newswoman—slender, beautifully styled hair, lots of makeup, and pretty eyes—Carl got the impression Anita Chapman was the kind of woman who succeeded on skill and accomplishment rather than on opportunism. Still, she was not unattractive, either.

Chapman had a round face that was probably oval fifteen years and four kids ago. She had intense green eyes, high cheekbones, a narrow nose, thin lips, and a prominent chin. She wore minimal makeup and no earrings. Her hair sat in a style he had never seen on any other woman in her line of work. It was short, almost mannish, and was either dark brown with blonde streaks feathered in, or blonde with dark brown streaks, depending on one's perspective. It was a style that only a well-established professional woman could get away with in an industry where striking good looks and bold style—for women *and* men—contributed as much to success as skill.

"Now, Ms. Chapman, let's continue with the interview. What the world wants to know is how this story will get tidied up into a conclusion they can wrap their brains around. They want the underdog—me—to somehow become the good guy. They want me to become the champion for all the folks out there trying to fight back against 'the man.' They want to know how I'm going to rise above the hatred and the killing and become a hero of the people. They want me to have my say in front of the national court of public opinion—the media—and then release my hostages, walk out of here, and surrender like in the movies.

"But that's not *this* story. This is personal between me and your father. You see, your father is, by definition, the good guy in this war because he works for the US government. I understand that. He says I'm a terrorist, and so everyone believes it. I understand that too." Carl shrugged. "But I didn't ask for this. Your father sent assassins armed with grenades, sniper rifles, machine guns, and knives to kill me, so my bodyguards killed them instead. His people tortured me, so I tortured his people. He killed my son, and for that, he's a goddamn loyal soldier in the war on terror, and I am a Tier-One terrorist. But you know what?"

Carl Johnson paused for a few moments so Anita Chapman and the rest of her audience could digest what he had told them. Chapman's face was composed, as though finally coming to grips with being a hostage.

"They can't threaten me or hurt me anymore. I've got nothing left to lose, and I don't care if they burst in here and kill me. But I will take you with me, and they know it. All this was because the government thought I was someone I wasn't. It was a case of mistaken identity, and they simply covered it up because they had the power to make it all disappear. Because they don't have to own up to their mistakes. Instead of doing the right thing, they did the easy thing and put out a legal assassination order on me. And the world believes it simply because your father says it is so. So your audience wants to know why I'm a terrorist? It's because I killed the men your father sent to kill me. It's because I sawed off the head of the man who tortured me."

Carl stood and walked over to the window facing Gold Avenue. Mr. Garcia's men had hung dark thermal blankets over the windows and the walls so that when the hostage rescue teams mobilized, they would be blind about what was going on inside. Carl carefully parted a seam in the thermal blanket with the fingers of his left hand and peeked through the tiny gap. Gold Avenue was deserted, though it was the middle of the workday.

He looked east and west, but he could see no movement on a street normally bustling with noon pedestrian traffic from all the downtown offices. The HRT—Hostage Rescue Team—would likely be staging on the next street south, probably just behind the big bank building. Maybe they'd prep for their raid on Third Street, just east of the jewelry store, or maybe in the alley behind the store. He couldn't see them, but he knew they were there.

Yes, they're just about ready to raid the place.

He picked up a large ax leaning in the corner by the door. Then he turned and walked back into view of the camera placed behind Anita's shoulder. He faced the reporter.

"I know I don't have the means to get close to a man like Aaron McGrath. He's too well protected." He stepped over behind his chair and hefted the ax to his shoulder. "But you can only truly understand someone's pain of losing a child when you've watched your own child die." He looked as menacingly as he could at the camera. "Of course, I'm not a total savage. I won't make the world watch while I carve you into pieces."

He heaved the ax high over his head and swung the blade down to the floor, severing the cables that sent the camera feed to the transmitter truck outside.

CHAPTER 44

1418 EST, TUESDAY
ARLINGTON HEIGHTS, VA

McGRATH WATCHED AS THE INTERVIEW feed went black. His gut twisted in a knot.

Christ, he's going to do it! He's going to kill my baby girl!

The monitor on the left showed the front view of the abandoned jewelry store from a SWAT camera mounted on the third level of the parking structure south of Gold Avenue. The monitor on the right showed a view of the alley behind the store from another SWAT camera.

Dread settled in the pit of McGrath's belly, and he let the chatter of the rescue team's comm channel force its way through the palpable fear gripping him. He heard the on-scene commander give the order to breach.

Good. Get the hell in there and kill that insane bastard.

In a moment of painful acceptance, a gruesome potential image settled in his mind of Johnson hacking his daughter to pieces. He imagined that when he finally read the autopsy, he'd discover his daughter lived through the terror until Johnson finally decided to put her out of her misery.

He heard Palmer's voice next to him, whispering, and he realized he'd closed his eyes. He refocused on the wall-mounted TV monitors.

"It has only been a few seconds," Palmer said. "They can still save her. They're going in now."

The business just west of the jewelry store was a two-story office building that had been evacuated. Sharing the right wall was the old bank building on the corner of Gold Avenue and Third Street. McGrath recognized the structure from a distant memory of time spent in Italy.

He'd read that the Occidental Life Building was a historic building, a unique example of US Venetian Gothic Revival architecture. Modeled after Doge's Palace in Venice, the building had street facades on the south and east sides, each faced with white terracotta tile and decorated with elaborate floral patterns. A row of pointed arches ran along each facade below a row of quatrefoil windows that somewhat resembled four-leaf clovers. The old bank dated back to the 1920s, maybe earlier.

The TV van sat parked directly in front of the vacant jewelry store, where Johnson held Anita Chapman and her family. A spiral antenna mounted to a vertical pole extended from the top of the van to transmit television signals back to the main studio. Thick cables led from the back of the van through the bent lower corner of the metal frame of the store's glass front door.

McGrath watched as black-clad figures moved quickly toward the front of the jewelry store. Four men moved in from the left, and four more moved in from the right. He could tell they weren't going for the door, as that entrance was likely wired with explosives. The front man of each group held a tool that looked much like a sledgehammer, and they were going to use it to break out enough of the window wall to storm the store.

Hurry up, goddammit! He's been in there too long with my daughter!

Fifteen seconds. That was time enough for a deranged man to sever two limbs, even if he had to chase down a panicked fleeing victim.

A single-file line of four more HRT members headed straight for the front door using the television van as a shield. They lined up behind the van, and all the teams halted, no doubt while the commander verified the rear assault teams in the alley were also in position to breach the back of the jewelry store.

In an instant of clarity, McGrath realized they were all playing right into Carl Johnson's game plan. He had shown he wasn't the kind of planner who would leave this particular milestone to chance. He'd know the HRT would breach as soon as he severed the camera feed. He'd know he would have mere seconds to complete his task, and he would have planned for exactly that eventuality.

"Nancy, have the HRT pull back. Quickly!"

She relayed the instructions, and almost immediately, the teams on the monitor withdrew.

"What are you thinking, Aaron?"

Aaron McGrath's heart sank as he realized his daughter was already dead. If not, she would be very soon, along with her family and the FBI men and women prepared to breach.

"It's a trap," McGrath said. "Johnson's no longer in there."

CHAPTER 45

1419 EST, TUESDAY
ARLINGTON HEIGHTS, VA

McGRATH HAD JUST UTTERED THE words when the store blew. He knew it was going to happen, and he knew his daughter was still inside, but it still kicked him in the gut.

"No!" He turned and upended a vacant analyst's desk. The keyboard and monitor tumbled to the floor. "*No!*"

The explosion was nothing short of spectacular. It was clear the terrorist had wired not only the front and back of the store but also the ceiling and both walls. The concussive blast shattered the windows of the jewelry store, the adjacent office building, and the historic bank building. The men of the assault teams had begun to pull back, but they were still inside the concussive blast zone. They were tossed into the street like tiny toy soldiers.

The blast slammed the TV van over on its side and then onto its top. The HRT members sheltered behind it had just begun to withdraw, so they were spared a crushing death, but McGrath could see they were all injured. Had he not given the order to withdraw, the terrorist would have claimed nearly twenty more lives.

Christ! What does it take to stop this man?

He turned back to the monitor and watched a huge fireball billowing outward and upward, an angry boiling rush of orange and red flames, and thick black smoke. A similar ball of fire erupted from the rear of the jewelry store. If there was any doubt as to the fate of the hostages, it vanished completely with the collapse of the store ceiling. The shared right wall and part of the ceiling of the historic bank also collapsed, and the second floor of the office building to the left simply folded over into what had been the jewelry store only seconds before.

McGrath's encrypted cell began to ring, but he didn't answer. He simply unhitched the cell from his belt and threw the device against the far wall, where it shattered. He knew who was calling. The president had ordered the team to keep her updated on the Albuquerque situation, and she had been patched into the HRT video feed.

McGrath and his team had predicted a number of possible outcomes to the hostage interview, but never in a million years would he have predicted that particular outcome. An hour ago, as he'd watched the terrorist's interrogation video, the subsequent interview with his daughter hadn't made any sense. Now it did.

Johnson had baited them with the video. He'd planned every aspect of the interrogation down to the smallest detail. It had been an act, a splendid performance. It was yet another misdirection.

He'd been several moves ahead of the TER every step along the way in his quest for revenge. He had asked Agent Cummings for his address because he wanted McGrath to think he was coming for him. But that wasn't his endgame at all. His true objective was to make him watch his daughter and her family die. McGrath had fallen for the ploy, and now Anita was dead.

But the terrorist was not.

McGrath felt an anger unlike any he'd ever felt before. He clenched his fists to keep from trembling as he stepped past Palmer and growled at the young bald analyst. "Get HQ on the line," he said with a hoarse whisper. "I want three code-black teams deployed to Albuquerque by midnight. I'm going to put an end to this threat."

"Aaron." She drew his name out slowly, like she wanted to object. "What are you doing?"

Nancy stepped to his side and laid a gentle hand on his shoulder, but he brushed her hand away roughly.

"I'm doing what I should have done yesterday. I'm going to kill that sick bastard."

CHAPTER 46

1422 EST, TUESDAY
ARLINGTON HEIGHTS, VA

PALMER NARROWED HER EYES AT the look on her commander's face. He was in shock, and he was angry, and she could see he was on the verge of losing his self-control.

"Johnson is not the mission, Aaron. You need to think this through."

Palmer faced McGrath's right side as he faced the wall monitors. Joey, the analyst on duty, sat in front of them. His desk faced the monitors, but he swiveled sideways in his chair. He looked expectantly at Palmer, knowing McGrath's instructions violated protocol.

Palmer shook her head at the analyst. "As you were." To McGrath, she said, "Focus on the mission, Aaron. The more you escalate this conflict, the more Johnson will escalate in return. Surely, you can see that trend in his behavior." McGrath looked like he was going to object, so she shouted at him. "The mission is to find Melissa!"

"I'm the director of this agency *and* the event commander, and *I* establish the mission!"

McGrath reached out to grab the analyst by the shoulders, presumably to turn him back to his workstation, but Palmer reacted instinctively. She swept his hands aside, shoved him away from the analyst, and stepped in between them.

"Security!" She hollered for the guard in the front foyer. "Get in here!"

The cell phone on her belt began to ring even as the burly guard rushed into the operations room. As soon as McGrath refused to answer his cell, she knew the president would call her because she was the deputy commander.

"Ma'am?" the guard said.

He was a big Black man with biceps the size of her thighs. The guard glanced from her to Joey, and finally to McGrath, who stood several paces away. The director had a wild, angry look in his eyes, and he breathed in shallow gasps.

"Remove Director McGrath from this room and confine him upstairs until I tell you otherwise. Sit on him if you have to, but do not let him out of that room. Understood?"

McGrath countered. "You don't have the authority—"

"Aaron, you're a threat to the mission, and the mission is only to find Melissa, not to send assassins after a civilian. Johnson will have contingencies for that action. We know this now. The more this escalates, the more collateral damage we'll have." She paused and said, "Now, we'll do this my way."

The guard stepped to McGrath's side and said, "Sir, will you please come with me?"

Palmer looked at her commander, and for a moment, she thought he was going to charge her. The fire she'd seen in his eyes calmed quickly, though, and he nodded. The guard escorted him out of the room, and Palmer realized she was holding her breath. She started breathing again and patted Joey on the shoulder as she retrieved her ringing cell.

"Palmer."

"What the hell is going on over there?"

"Madam President," Palmer said. She paused, then said, "I had to relieve Aaron from duty."

The president was silent for a moment. "I understand. I saw the live feed. Anita and her family were in that store when it blew."

"No, they weren't," Palmer said. "Johnson is becoming a master of deception, and as you can see, he's interfering with our primary mission. We have to take him out of the game, and for that, I'm going to need your help."

"I'm listening."

"There's only one way to neutralize Carl Johnson now. We have to give him what he wants."

Palmer outlined her plan.

"How will you find him?"

"I won't have to," Palmer said.

She glanced at the center monitor again. Numerous fire trucks were spraying streams of water into the burning rubble of the store and its two neighboring buildings. She couldn't see the fire trucks on Third Street, but she could see their streams of water arching in from the right.

"Madam President, there's no way Johnson would consider his mission complete as long as Aaron and Alfonso Reyes are alive. I think he had an exit strategy, and I think he's coming here to Virginia. I think he's going to walk right up to Aaron's front door."

CHAPTER 47

0639 EST, WEDNESDAY
MCLEAN, VA

CARL JOHNSON'S TAXI DRIVER LET him out where Dolley Madison Boulevard and Old Dominion Drive intersected. He skirted the west edge of a huge park his cell phone GPS map labeled McLean Central Park. Three blocks later, he stood in the morning chill facing the house of his nemesis. The security gate at the end of the gravel driveway stood wide open.

He's expecting me.

It had been many years since he'd taken a one-year project management job on the east coast, and he'd forgotten how bitterly cold the winter weather could be. Thirty degrees in Virginia felt a lot colder than the same temperature in New Mexico. It was the wind that made the difference. And the humidity. It soaked through the clothing and into the bones.

As he examined the government agent's house, he reveled in the thought that McGrath's demise was imminent. Then he would turn his attention to Alfonso Reyes.

Carl had pulled Anita McGrath Chapman into the basement of the jewelry store, and they made their way under the historic bank by way of an access hole jack-hammered in the connecting stem wall. Then Carl detonated the C4 explosive planted by the mercs, destroying the aboveground part of the jewelry store.

He had planned to force Chapman into an old safe that measured about ten feet wide, six feet deep, and eight feet high. He figured the safe was left over from the bank's early days nearly a century past, but it was clearly too massive to move without destroying walls.

Garcia had his guys modify the door lock. It now featured a twenty-four-digit cipher lock. A large warning sign on the door of the safe proclaimed a half pound of C4 explosive was attached inside the safe, along with trip wires and vibration sensors, which could only be deactivated by the cipher lock. When he opened the safe to shove her inside, she discovered her family was not in the safe, so she went berserk and attacked him.

He shuddered at the uncomfortable memory. Because of Anita McGrath Chapman, the mission had suddenly and unexpectedly changed.

Movement in his peripheral view drew his attention to his right.

A woman stepped from behind a thick tree beside the driveway. "Do you have any weapons on you?"

The woman was tall and slender, a couple inches taller than he was. She had a narrow face with a cute little upturned nose and sinister, sky blue eyes. She looked extremely fit and…lethal. She looked like a younger Merc Four, like a female version of Agent Klipser.

Carl growled at her. "You're one of them, aren't you? The ones who got my son killed."

The woman wore black tactical pants, with Velcro pocket flaps everywhere, and assault boots. She also wore a thick, black turtleneck shirt under her black field jacket, which no doubt hid a weapon or two. Most of her blonde hair was hidden under a black knit cap.

"Yes." She nodded. After a long pause, she added, "My name is Nancy Palmer. The operation wasn't supposed to go down like that."

He tried to muster up some anger or hatred for the woman, but her honesty had somehow defused his emotional turmoil.

She repeated her question. "Do you have any weapons?"

"I don't need weapons," Carl replied. "I have his family."

She searched him anyway. "We found the safe."

Carl nodded. "Then you know she probably has less than six hours of air left."

"But her family is not in the safe?"

"Correct." There wasn't enough room or air in there for everyone.

"I figured you held them off-site to control her."

He narrowed his eyes, wondering where she was going with that line of questioning. What did she hope to discover about him? Maybe she was trying to profile him. Maybe she was trained in finding his weaknesses by watching his body language. "Correct again."

"You had a SWAT uniform with you, didn't you? That's how you got out of the building."

Carl cocked his head a bit. He thought he detected a hint of grudging respect in her words, but he wasn't sure. She was fishing for something. Maybe she was assessing his resolve.

"I had fireman's gear hidden in the basement," Carl said. "I couldn't assume your boss would figure it was another ambush, so there was a strong possibility all the HRT folks would be dead or injured."

"In which case, you'd be easily identified if you walked out of there in black." She paused for a moment, then said, "We had State Police and National Guard on all the roads. How did you get out of New Mexico?"

"There are many unmarked jeep trails in and around the mountains. I got up into Colorado, then across and down into Oklahoma, then onto a flight in disguise."

"Yes, we picked you up at Reagan National Airport on facial recognition. You planned that too, didn't you?"

He'd discarded his dreadlock disguise as soon as he landed.

"I wanted McGrath to know I was coming."

Palmer regarded him silently for a long while, but her expression was unreadable. Finally, the agent said, "You should go inside."

Carl pivoted and looked around. McLean was definitely not a town for normal folks. Though the lots on which the houses of McLean were built were fairly small, all maybe a quarter-acre, the houses themselves were totally upscale. Every house had a privacy wall of some sort with secure driveway gates. Most of the homes were of Victorian design, two and sometimes three stories high.

Well-tended front yards, fancy light fixtures, and lamp posts decorated the homes. Some of the properties had crushed coral driveways, and some had cobblestone. There were no ordinary concrete or asphalt driveways, not in this high-end neighborhood.

Some of the homes had open shutters—either real or fake—and Carl guessed that the wood-clad, oversized windows that decorated the fronts of the homes were triple-pane, energy-efficient fixtures he knew trended toward very expensive, especially when you had twenty or thirty of the huge windows in a single house. That alone would set an owner back a hundred grand, he thought. Most of the front doors he had seen along his ride were extra-tall, extra-wide, expensive hardwood doors with fancy knobs and intricate, inlaid windows.

He turned back toward McGrath's house, which he guessed was worth upward of one and a half million. The lights were on throughout the house. The sun was just dawning, and the morning had a cozy feel as the sun began to break through the high clouds.

As Carl gazed at the front of McGrath's house, he thought about Anita Chapman again. In all his years, he'd never hit a woman. Ever. And now, he had beaten a woman senseless. With his fists. With his elbows. With the hard plastic butt of his gun. Because she wouldn't get in the safe. Because she was the daughter of the man who got his son killed. Because he lost control and took out his frustrations on her instead of him.

He could hear her screams and curses echoing in his head. He could see her bloody face as she kept coming at him. She wouldn't quit. She wouldn't stay down. Finally, he kicked her so hard, she tumbled to the back of the safe, and he swung the heavy door closed. Then, right before the door slammed shut, Anita Chapman screamed and charged again, and for a moment, Carl thought she was going to get smashed in the doorway. There was no way he could stop it because the door weighed several hundred pounds.

And he had seen her bloody face up close the instant before the door closed. She looked like he felt inside.

It was one thing to order mercenaries to do his dirty work. It was quite another to actually get his own hands dirty and bloody. Torturing and beheading Klipser and breaking Cummings had been things Carl considered victories, rites of passage, but beating Chapman filled him with a deep sense of shame that haunted his very soul.

He paused halfway up the drive and stood there for a moment, wondering what kind of man he had become. He could justify, or at least get mentally past, killing federal agents or cops whose crime was that they took orders from a rogue government agency, but seeing Anita Chapman's bloody face every time he closed his eyes tortured him. And what he almost did to Cummings's daughter shook his conviction. He remembered seeing her big brown eyes, wide with fear, staring at him.

In a moment of clarity, he knew exactly what kind of man he'd become and was not happy with his conclusion. He was Klipser and McGrath wrapped up in one shell.

The mission has to change.

Carl continued up the long cobblestone drive. He heard the crunch of Palmer's combat boots as she followed. He turned onto the pave-stone footpath that led off the drive, across the grass, and up to the front door. The extra-wide door was already open a few inches, so he pushed it open and stepped in without knocking.

He'd spent the entire trip eastward trying to form a mental picture of what his nemesis would look like. He pictured a balding man of medium height with dark beady eyes, maybe sixty years old, with the physique of a former special ops soldier—bulky and muscular with maybe a bit of a gut from good eating and drinking in his advanced years. He imagined McGrath as a man who now fought his covert wars from behind a desk, doling out death and destroying lives from the comfort of a leather chair behind a huge mahogany desk. Maybe the man wore large bifocal glasses with metal rims.

Carl stepped into the foyer and followed the aroma of his favorite coffee—toasted almond crème. It occurred to him that McGrath must have checked all his financial records and found that every month, he ordered that particular flavor of coffee online. He thought it was pretty gutsy of the man—waving the power of government resources in his face. Or perhaps he was trying to offer some kind of truce.

He left the front door open because he knew Agent Palmer was right behind him. As he walked leisurely up the hall, he had a bizarre memory of his mother from forty-five years ago that almost made him smile.

Close the door, Carl! I'm not paying to heat the outdoors!

He turned to his left, into the living room, to confront the man who had used his son as bait, but the man looked nothing like he expected. He looked like...

A woman!

He saw her in profile as she dropped two sugar cubes and a dollop of cream in a black coffee mug.

Then she turned toward Carl and held out the mug. "I hope you like cream and sugar," she said.

Carl's jaw dropped to the shiny honey oak wood floor.

"Madam President?"

CHAPTER 48

0653 EST, WEDNESDAY
MCLEAN, VA

C ARL HAD SPENT FIFTEEN HOURS and two thousand miles contemplating what kind of reception he would receive when he found Aaron McGrath—everything from arrest and more torture to witnessing a distraught man falling to his knees, begging for the life of his child. Being served his favorite coffee by the president of the United States, though, didn't even crack his list of the top one thousand possibilities.

There were three comfortable-looking couches of tan leather arranged in a square U, facing a huge stone fireplace opposite the arched entry into the living room. President Shirley Mallory stood inside that U, and behind her, an impressive fire roared in the fireplace. Next to her was a massive granite coffee table, on which sat a steel coffee thermos and a porcelain tray with the sugar and cream bowls. Two spoons and another black mug completed the set.

Carl stepped into the room and walked cautiously toward the president. The room was comfortably warm, but as he got closer to the fireplace, he realized the raging fire was putting out a tremendous amount of heat. He peeled off his gloves and pocketed them, then shrugged out of his overcoat. He laid the coat across the back of the nearest sofa, then swiped off his black head glove and set it on top of his overcoat. Then he stepped through the space between the two couches on the right and faced Mallory.

"Mr. Johnson, they tell me you're insane, that I shouldn't be alone in a room with you."

Carl grunted at her. "Obsessed, perhaps. And since Agent Palmer allowed me to enter, I assume she's not in the camp that thinks I'm insane."

"She thinks I should reach out to you. She thinks that might defuse the path of escalation that you and Director McGrath were on."

He looked at her for a moment. "I'm going to decline the coffee, but thank you for the thought."

Mallory nodded and took a slurping sip from the mug. At least, now he knew there was no poison in it.

"You know," she said, "there's sort of an old custom from back in the Old West days about sharing coffee over a frontier fire."

Carl nodded. He knew that custom well. He'd written about it in one of his historical westerns, which she had clearly read, likely in the few hours since Anita Chapman's broadcast.

Get to know your enemy and all that.

Still, his respect for the president just ratcheted up a good amount.

"It was a frontier man's way of sharing a drink when there was no saloon nearby."

"Frontier women too." Mallory reached out with the cup to him again. "A way for adversaries to have a truce while seeking common ground."

"Adversaries," Carl said. "Now that's an interesting word choice coming from you, Madam President."

He took the proffered cup and sipped. She picked up the other cup and sipped also.

"Mmm." He closed his eyes and savored the flavor. The coffee had a smooth, creamy texture with a strong, nutty after-flavor. "Perfectly brewed too." He cupped the mug with both palms and turned to face the raging fire. He said, "A Black military officer, turned engineer, turned historical western novelist, turned real estate agent, turned terrorist. Now that's got to be some kind of world record for career changes."

He paused for a moment and looked at the woman beside him. For some reason he couldn't identify, he felt comfortable standing beside her, but he also felt a strange anxiety. He gripped the cup tighter to prevent his hands from shaking. He was actually standing in the presence of the president of the United States.

"Why are you my adversary, and why are you here?" he said softly, turning his gaze back to the fire. "In Aaron McGrath's house. In this room with a terrorist." He paused. "What is your involvement in…"

Mark's murder.

He couldn't even say the words without the tears threatening to cloud his eyes. Couldn't think the thought without seeing his dead son. He closed his eyes and bit his lip to keep it from trembling.

Finally, he regained his composure and sipped again. As he stared into the fire and waited for the president to respond, he found it was easy to become mesmerized by the dancing flames. Smoke billowed from the top of the pile of burning wood and was sucked up into the chimney. Occasionally, a pocket of sap popped with a burst of sparks, so he knew there was some soft pine mixed in with the hot-burning hardwood.

"Aaron's daughter and her family are important to me. We're…very close."

The simple statement hit him like a brick, and he nearly gasped. He was at war with the president's boyfriend, the head of a covert agency that had his son killed, and she was upset because Carl threatened to kill the man's daughter.

"I'm sure they are important to him also," Carl said. "And he has a few hours remaining to save them."

"What is it you want, Mr. Johnson? Revenge? Money? Power?"

"I want that mu'fucker to—" Carl stopped, took a deep breath, held it, then let it out slowly. He set the coffee mug down on the coffee table. It made a loud clinking sound, the echo of porcelain on stone. He turned his gaze on the president. "I want my son back, Madam President. Barring that, I want Aaron McGrath to feel my pain. Or die."

President Mallory had a reputation of being old-school, a country girl, whenever she wasn't in Washington. She stood an inch taller than Carl, and at the age of sixty-two, she was a stately figure. She was neither slender nor frumpy, but she did look her age. He assumed the stress of her job contributed to that. She was attractive in a matronly sort of way.

Today, she was dressed in denim pants, and the white collar of her blouse was visible at the top of a thick pullover knit sweater patterned with deep blue-green colors. Her short silver hair accented her light blue eyes, giving her an air of provocative wisdom. Dress her in an expensive suit, and she'd certainly look the role of CEO of any company—or any country.

"I won't allow that."

"Your influence in the outcome of the matter is limited solely to a conversation between you and him. I came here today to see him dead, or he sees his daughter and her family dead. It's a simple choice for a father to make."

He could feel the anger boiling inside him again and decided it was time for him to leave before he did something that caused hidden Secret Service agents to rush the room. He'd lost track of Agent Palmer after she followed him up the driveway, but he figured she was inside the door or in the foyer.

He stepped back away from President Mallory and walked around to the back of the couch on which he'd laid his gear. As he put on his overcoat and thin head glove, it occurred to him that now that the president had lost her appeal to his humanity, Agent Palmer likely wouldn't allow him to leave the house. He retrieved his gloves from his coat pocket.

Hell, maybe they'd strap him to the table again. What more could they do? He had no more kids for them to kill, and he was pretty sure he could hold out under torture longer than Anita Chapman could hold her breath.

"Thank you for the coffee," Carl said as he turned to leave.

It was at that moment the president dropped the bomb on him, and he froze in mid-step.

"The girl who was kidnapped is Melissa, my daughter. We've told the country that she's ill, bedridden. Alfonso Reyes is holding her for ransom. She's still alive."

He turned slowly and faced Mallory. Suddenly, everything was clear to him.

Then she said, "I know I'm responsible for your son's death. I wish I could…undo things."

Carl felt a jolt of electricity shoot up his spine. After a few seconds, he stepped back over close to her. He cocked his head a bit to the right and stared at her as if seeking the real truth. His gaze danced between her eyes, but her gaze didn't falter.

Mallory spoke softly, almost in a whisper. "We thought you were him." She paused and took a step toward him. "I authorized Aaron to use any means necessary to save my daughter."

"Did you authorize him to use my son as bait?"

"He thought…*we* thought Mark could be useful as leverage against you—against Reyes—in exchange for Melissa."

"Leverage," he mumbled.

Her gaze faltered for the first time. "Because of my daughter's kidnapping, I'm personally involved in this entire affair. In all the…mistakes. I have already decided not to seek a second term. I'll go on record with a personal and public apology to you, Mr. Johnson. I promise you that."

"Your apology won't bring my son back." Carl paused, and Mallory remained silent. "You all were so convinced I was Alfonso Reyes and that I didn't break on that table after eleven days of torture." He grunted at her. "Did you see the videos of my interrogation? Did you see what they did to me?"

She said nothing, but he could see in her eyes she had.

"Hell, they broke me on the first day. They broke me *in the first goddamn minute!*" A sap bubble popped in the fireplace, and he looked over her left shoulder into the dancing flames. "They never considered the possibility that they had the wrong man and that my son and I were never involved at all." He closed his eyes for a moment as a shudder shook his body. "I just wish some of those bullets had taken me too." He took a deep breath to recover his composure. "Your boyfriend fucked it up, Shirley."

"I know," she said softly. "And he knows."

"That's why he's going to die. Or his daughter will. His choice." Carl started to turn away but hesitated. "Tell me, Madam President. Who is the real terrorist here? The drug lord who kidnapped your daughter, or Aaron McGrath who tortured me, or me for avenging my son's murder?" He shook his head sadly. "I wouldn't stop now, even if I wanted to. Not after what that man has taken from me." He looked President Mallory in the eye. "I'm committed to seeing this through. You folks are welcome to do whatever you feel you need to do to me after he or his daughter die. I don't give a damn."

"Mr. Johnson. Carl. I'm sorry about your son." He saw genuine regret in her eyes. They were the eyes of a mother, not a politician. "You've paid a terrible price for my mistake, and I'm so sorry." She reached out to touch his shoulder.

"Don't…you…even…think about it."

Her hand froze inches from his shoulder for a moment before she withdrew it. Carl took a step back and realized his fists were clenched, and he was trembling. Finally, he forced himself to relax and shook his head.

"It wasn't your mistake. No mother would ever use a child as bait, not even an adult child. That just isn't human nature. Only a man would do something like that. Only a man could be that despicable."

"Are you that kind of man, Mr. Johnson?"

"A month ago, I wasn't. Now, I am."

"Will you murder an innocent family?"

"Madam President, the question you should be asking is whether or not Aaron McGrath is the kind of man—the kind of father—who would die for his family. Only he can save them now." He pivoted and started for the entry hallway.

She said, "Mr. Johnson, I understand how you feel, but—"

"No, Madam President, you don't." He stopped and looked back at her. "You have no idea how I feel." He paused. "Not yet, anyway." He saw a momentary flash of rage in President Mallory's eyes. "But when that piece of shit druggie kills your daughter, and you know he will, then you will understand exactly how I feel. And—" His voice caught in his throat. "And you'll have to wake up every morning and feel your heart ripped open again and again when you realize your child is gone forever."

Mallory stepped forward. "Tell me what I can do to make this right. Please!"

"I think I've made my position perfectly clear." Carl Johnson turned to leave. "I want Aaron McGrath's head."

CHAPTER 49

0715 EST, WEDNESDAY

MCLEAN, VA

CARL JOHNSON WALKED PAST AGENT Palmer in the foyer without making eye contact, but he could feel her gaze on the side of his head. Strangely, she took no action against him. He turned the doorknob and pulled the door open, then she called to him softly.

"Help us get Melissa back."

He stopped and looked at her. "Excuse me?" She didn't immediately respond, so Carl said, "After what you've done to me, after what you've taken from me, you want me to help you? You must be *fucking* kidding me."

"She's only sixteen," Palmer said.

"You know where she is, don't you?" It was a question to which he also wanted the answer.

"You look like him. You look exactly like him."

"So what do you want me to do, pretend like I'm him? Become a commando at age fifty-three and sneak in there? Maybe go all Rambo on them or something? Hell, I haven't even fired a gun in almost thirty years."

"You could do recon for us. Get eyes on the package so we can retrieve her."

"Don't you have Army Rangers or Delta or SEAL Team Six for ops like this? Aren't they the baddest of the badasses?"

"We can't send a military unit in unless we're absolutely certain it's her because we'll only get one opportunity. If we tip them off or if she's not there, she's dead. Or we'll start a war with our closest ally."

Neither of them said anything for a long while.

Finally, Palmer said, "Why didn't you kill Lisette Cummings?"

He looked away for a moment, then turned slightly toward her. "I didn't need to," he said. "Special Agent Cummings felt it. When she thought I was going to kill her girl, she felt my pain."

There was more to that event, he knew. He broke that woman fast and hard. He destroyed her future. Of that, he had no doubt. He could have killed her daughter, but the damage he sought was already done. He could see it in the agent's eyes. She'd never be the same, and looking back on the event, he wasn't happy with what he'd done.

And then there was Anita McGrath Chapman. A part of him had been hoping that McGrath wouldn't yield so Carl actually *could* kill her. He wanted to feel the satisfaction of revenge. He envisioned witnessing the man's capitulation and savoring his agony when his child died. He wanted the man to hurt forever.

And what he almost did to that little girl, Lisette, was unspeakable. He was going to cut that girl open to punish her mother. He could still see her slender body trembling as he almost plunged the blade into her chest. What if that little girl was emotionally scarred for life? What if she couldn't find a way to deal with what had happened to her? What if she got hooked on drugs or committed suicide?

Oh, Mark. What have I done?

As he reviewed his conversation with the president, he felt a bitter disappointment in leaving McGrath's house not having met his nemesis. He wanted, *needed*, to see the man's face and feel his fear and revel in his desperation, vulnerability, and pain. Now he realized he would never get that satisfaction, not with the president running interference.

Suddenly, an overwhelming feeling of frustration and despair overcame him. Up to that moment, he'd had a purpose, a mission of revenge that prevented him from accepting that he'd have to live forever without his son. Now the floodgate to those raw emotions threatened to blast wide open. He knew those emotions could cripple him without a new mission on which to focus his energy.

Find the girl and bring her home. Find a way to atone for the lives I've wrecked.

Agent Palmer stepped close and hesitantly reached out her hand to his shoulder, and Carl surprised himself by not objecting. Her touch was oddly comforting, and her eyes were suddenly not devoid of emotion, as they'd seemed out front. He sensed her loss even before she spoke.

"My sister," she said. "Five years ago."

She gave no further details, and they looked at each other until it became awkward.

Finally, she said, "You just have to live with the pain until you learn how to put it away in a safe place you can get to when you're ready."

Carl grabbed her hand, and he fought against his sudden impulse to pull it away. So he just held her hand for a moment. His voice cracked, and all he could manage was a hoarse whisper. "I don't know how to do that."

"I know." She pulled her hand back. "It's hard." She paused. "But killing is not the answer. At least, it wasn't for me."

"It depends on who we're killing."

Clearly, the child of his enemy was not the right target. He pulled out his disposable cell and dialed Garcia's number from memory. For the first time, he wondered what the young man's real name was.

Garcia answered immediately. "Are we getting out of the fan business?"

"Soon. Call the FBI and give them the code to the safe so they can get that woman out of there. Be sure to tell them there isn't really any C4 inside." He paused and made eye contact with Agent Palmer. "And tell them to take paramedics with them. She's…injured." He paused for a moment. "And have the mercs release her family."

Garcia hesitated. "Does this mean you found McGrath? You killed him?"

"No. He's untouchable…for now."

"You realize that holding his daughter is the only thing keeping him from bringing the full weight of the government down on you. May I ask what has changed?"

"She's not my enemy."

Garcia sighed. "To be truthful, Boss, I was never happy with that part of your plan, not after what we saw on the video. I mean what almost happened with Cummings's kid. I'm glad you've changed your mind."

"I'll call you back shortly."

Carl looked at Agent Palmer for a moment.

She smiled slightly. It was a cute, girlie smile, and her nose crinkled up a bit with the effort. "Thank you."

He grunted at her. "Doesn't make us best friends or anything." They looked at each other again. "So, where is the girl?"

"Um, we received some intel. We're pretty sure Melissa is being held at one of Reyes's fortified compounds in Mexico."

"You trust this intel?"

She hesitated a moment, then looked away briefly, almost like she was embarrassed. Carl found that reaction curious.

"We're trying to verify she is at the location…that you gave us."

"Wait. What? *I* gave you?"

"When you told Special Agent Cummings you wanted to arrange a meeting with Agent Klipser in northern Mexico, we assumed you meant Reyes's compound in the north-central part of the country near a place called El Chappa."

"Are you telling me that line of bullshit I gave Cummings to lure Klipser into my ambush actually led you to her location?"

She nodded. "We launched a drone to observe the compound, and we think we saw her there, but it was before the drone was within optimal visual range. We saw *a girl*, but we haven't verified it's Melissa. We think she's still there."

"And Reyes is there too?"

"We think so, but that is unconfirmed as well."

He nodded and closed the front door, then walked past her and turned into the living room. President Mallory had taken a seat in front of the roaring fire. She half-turned when Carl reentered the room. He removed his overcoat and skullcap and took a seat beside her on the couch facing the fire. He leaned forward for a moment with his elbows resting on his knees.

They both were silent for a long time. They sipped toasted almond crème coffee and gazed into the fire. He wondered what she, the most powerful person on the planet, was thinking.

Carl remembered the firestorm of controversy Shirley Mallory ignited four years ago when it became clear she was the front-runner to be the next president. He remembered her speech to the nation as she addressed the issue.

"Yes, I had sex," she'd said, "and I wasn't married. Yes, I had a baby in my mid-forties. What of it? It just means I'm like millions of other single mothers with careers who are trying to make this country a better place for our children."

And *blam!* Just like that, all the conservatives were silenced, and she surfed that wave of popularity right into the White House. She was the role model for every girl in the country and the symbol of empowerment for every woman on the planet.

Carl said, "You know, parents nowadays say the internet is corrupting kids. All they do is download games on their phones and walk around texting or Facebooking all the time. But back in our generation, before the internet, they said the same thing about TV. But you know what? I think TV was a good influence on kids sometimes." He fell silent for a moment. "When Mark was about seven, he was visiting me for the summer, and we were watching a show where the commander of this space station was a Black man. That was a first back in those days—and he was a single father with a son about Mark's age. Well, Mark was never a hugging kinda kid, but when he saw that brown-skin space kid hugging his dad, all of a sudden, it became cool to hug Pops."

Carl fell silent for a moment as his mind drifted back almost twenty-five years in time.

"We've been hugging ever since. We'd walk down the street, you know, two grown men with our arms parked around each other's shoulders, and we'd sit in theaters without a seat between us and not feel weird." He glanced over at the president. "I'm gonna miss that closeness. My son was…" He felt his bottom lip trembling, and he had to take a moment to recover. "He was everything to me. *Everything.* I can't even begin to describe how it feels to know I'm going to have to live the rest of my life without him. To be honest, I don't think I want to try. I can't tell you how much it hurts. Every day."

Carl was silent for a while. Then he looked sideways at Mallory. "You can't prepare for that kind of pain." He paused. "So I'll go get your kid, Shirley, so you won't have to feel what I feel. But it's going to cost you." He glared at her. "It's going to cost you a lot."

CHAPTER 50

0732 EST, WEDNESDAY
MCLEAN, VA

PRESIDENTIAL PARDONS FOR HIS MERCS, his CIA tech wizard, Garcia, and himself. Forgiveness for everything they'd done and everything they were about to do. Tech support for the operation. Weapons too. And a lot of money. That was the cost, and the president didn't even blink.

"You run your side of the op, Agent Palmer," Carl said. "I don't think you want me talking to your boss."

"He's been relieved. My boss is sitting next to you."

She gave no further details. He looked at Agent Palmer and then at the president.

"I don't believe the end always justifies the means. One of these days, we all are going to have to answer for what we've done." He stared into the fire. "But that day is not today. You want the girl back, and I want Alfonso Reyes dead, so our missions are aligned. We're allies until this is over."

Palmer said, "We should get back to my office, then, and start planning the op."

"Nah, Sista," he said quietly. "That's not how the game is played. I've seen enough of your fucked-up government missions to last me a lifetime. You go getting all covert on this guy, and he'll see that shit coming from a mile away. Then the girl dies, and he goes into hiding."

He looked at her. "I'll plan the op with *my* people, and *you* will assist *us*."

Palmer nodded, and Carl pressed redial on his cell. He enabled the speaker so the women could listen and placed the device on the stone table.

"Go 'head," Garcia said.

"Get ready to dictate our account number because we have a client."

Palmer angled her head so he could see a tiny flesh-colored comm device stuck in her ear.

"Ready," Garcia said.

"Go."

Garcia spoke the account number, and Palmer nodded. Carl assumed that her team on the other end of her comm device had received it. No one said anything as they waited for the transfer to go through.

Carl looked over at the president. "You have any more coffee left?"

She nodded and poured the remaining coffee from the flask into his mug. It filled it up only halfway. He added cream and sugar, then sipped. As he gazed into the fire, he sensed that both women were staring at him.

He looked to his right first and locked gazes with Agent Palmer. Her face was completely unreadable. He sensed that her brief show of emotion by the door had been a side of her that people rarely saw. She'd allowed him to take what he needed from that encounter so he could stay strong.

Still, he could tell she was a government agent to her core. He sensed that if she didn't get what she wanted from their alliance, she would be every bit as dangerous as Agents Klipser and McGrath.

When Carl turned his attention to the president, he sensed conflicting qualities in her. She was both vulnerable as a threatened mother and strong as a world leader. But she was also a politician. He knew she had unequaled capacity for betrayal if it was necessary for the good of the country. In the back of his mind, he began to formulate some contingencies.

"Dayum!" Garcia said a few seconds later. "Is this a mistake? What the hell kind of client is worth *$250 million*?"

"The president's daughter," Carl said. "That's who Alfonso Reyes kidnapped."

"The president of what? The United States?"

"Our mission is to go down there and rescue a girl and kill a man. Call your people in-country and tell them I want a meeting with Reyes. Tell him I tricked the government into paying his ransom to me. He's seen me and knows I look like him, so he'll understand how I could have pulled it off. Tell him if he wants his money, he has to give me the girl and guarantee me safe passage back across the border. Tell him if he agrees, he can have $200 million, and I keep fifty. Then I'll sell the girl back to the president for another hundred. Tell him that's the price he and the US government have to pay for killing my son. If he doesn't agree, tell him he can keep the girl, I'll keep all the money, and then I'll hunt him down at some later date when he'll never see me coming. Remind him of our exploits against the feds this week, so we'll have credibility."

"Okay," Garcia said. "I'm on it, but I've found out a few more things about Alfonso Reyes. Apparently, he's well-connected on both sides of the law. It's rumored he's cozy with a phantom military man called *El Patron*."

Carl glanced at Palmer, and she nodded. That was not new information to her.

"El Patron?" Carl said hesitantly. "What does that mean?"

Garcia said, "Literally, El Patron means 'the landlord' or 'the boss.' In this case, 'boss' is probably more appropriate. The man is a very powerful crime lord, but he's in the military. Anyone associated with him is going to be well protected."

"Very well. I'm going to give your number to Agent Palmer, and she's going to coordinate with you from her office here in Virginia. She'll be sending you a blanket pardon signed by the president for you, me, and the rest of the team, and she'll send along some intel, some surveillance drone comm channel access codes, and she'll arrange some special military hardware for the mercs."

"Um, don't take this the wrong way, Boss, but do you really trust these people?"

"I trust them to look out for their interests, and right now, their interests coincide with mine. What they really need is a team that is effective, expendable, and not related to the government. If this op goes sideways, I'm sure the TER will blame it on the 'American Terrorist.' Either way, now this is a business transaction between two rival terrorists, not a power play between a terrorist and a US president."

Palmer agreed. "Reyes gains nothing by killing her before he gets his money, so as long as we control the meeting site, Melissa stays alive. We have a recovery unit standing by near the border, but we can't intervene across the border if you get in a bind." She paused. "Unless we're absolutely certain we can recover Melissa by that action."

"Understood."

Palmer spoke the thought Carl knew she and the president were thinking. "What's to stop you from simply disappearing with the ransom money?"

"The problem with that scenario, Agent Palmer, is that it leaves Alfonso Reyes's head attached to his shoulders." He paused for a moment and reached for his coffee mug. He took another sip, then looked to his left. "Madam President, there is one more thing you can help out with."

Mallory raised an eyebrow.

"If I get the girl, and it looks like Reyes is going to get away, I'll need a backup plan."

"Agent Palmer will get you anything you need to get my daughter back."

"Anything?"

CHAPTER 51

0018 MST, THURSDAY
NORTHERN MEXICO

TWO HUNDRED AND FIFTY MILLION dollars. That was the latest ransom demand for Melissa Mallory, and that was how much the president and her people paid...to Carl Johnson. That amount of money was so mindboggling that he had no real concept of its value. The money was in Carl's accounts, so if Reyes wanted his money, he'd have to negotiate for it like a businessman rather than make political extortion demands of a head of state.

By Carl's way of thinking, there were many better candidates one could kidnap for ransom that would not result in Reyes becoming a covert ops target for the rest of his life. So his objective, in addition to the money, must be to realize some kind of power play at the expense of the president.

Agent Palmer acknowledged McGrath's team had already considered that was Reyes's agenda, but she seemed genuinely surprised when Carl suggested the drug man would kill Melissa anyway, most likely after the second ransom was paid.

"He gains nothing by killing her," Palmer had said, "other than becoming a target of US forces."

Carl had said, "He's already a target, isn't he? Whether he gives the girl back or not, right? He's not stupid, so you can expect him to know that. He wanted to get on the map with the boost in status he would have earned by giving the US a bloody nose. Except now that I have robbed him of that status by stealing his ransom money, we have to keep him in damage control mode. If he messes this up, he'll lose his status *and* his money."

So the president green-lighted the mission.

Carl considered his entry into Mexico as the easiest part of the mission, even though the operation hadn't really started yet. Garcia had put out the word through his in-country contacts that Carl was coming for a face-to-face meeting Thursday afternoon, so there was no need for him to sneak illegally across the border. In truth, though, Carl and his team were making their move before sunrise.

Carl drove down to the crossing at Columbus, New Mexico. The mercs, all with valid passports, had done the same in a different SUV while Carl was flying from Virginia back to Albuquerque.

I-25 from Albuquerque International Airport, or the Sunport as it was known, was almost a straight shot to the El Paso crossing, but everyone agreed it was better to avoid that congested port of entry. The TER team wanted to keep the kidnapping and the rescue secret, and that would not be possible if they brought Melissa back through El Paso.

So, at Las Cruces, Carl turned west and merged onto I-10. He passed the signs indicating a turnoff to the Santa Teresa Port of Entry and kept driving toward Deming. He then turned south to Columbus, a tiny town he passed through in two minutes flat. He dimmed his headlights and slowed as he approached the port of entry gate three miles south of town.

Both sides of the crossing were well-lit and modern, and Carl got the feeling the facility had been recently remodeled. There was a rest stop advertising refreshments, snacks, and maps. The port of entry crossing looked modern and inviting. The building encompassing the border gate seemed new also, though only one lane on each side of the building led to the opposite country.

The crossing looked more like the entrance to a nice metro parking lot with a modern, curved roof covering the guard office and the transition point. It wasn't like the monster crossing he'd seen at El Paso, where there were many lanes entering and exiting the country, as well as dozens of buildings and miles of traffic jams on both sides, with people waiting for hours at all times of the day or night.

Carl approached the border crossing in his White-man disguise.

There were only two guards on evening duty on each side of the border, and none of them showed the slightest bit of interest in him. Garcia had already taken care of the documents needed to take his car across—temporary Mexican insurance and the required deposit intended to make sure drivers didn't leave cars south of the border—so he simply presented the papers at the crossing and was allowed to drive right on through after only a cursory inspection.

He drove into the darkness, following the dim green map on the GPS screen of the tiny device stuck to the old SUV's dash. The map rotated every time he made a turn or when the road changed directions, but the arrow representing his car always pointed *up*. He was many miles from his destination, so he turned off the female voice that offered turn-by-turn directions.

"In one hundred five miles, turn left on…"

He'd never been to Mexico before. In fact, the darkness enveloping the border town of Puerto Palomas after midnight was so complete that Carl was hard-pressed to even see there was a town outside his SUV. Every couple of minutes, he saw a few estates with well-lit fences a mile or two away from the highway. He glimpsed other structures along the road, but they were mere shadows in the night.

Almost half an hour later, he turned west onto a road without a number. Then he hit Highway 10, which reached south into the empty desert lands of north-central Mexico. The uneventful trip gave him plenty of time to reflect on the unexpected turn of events that day.

Driving across Mexico on a mission of mercy, he found himself in league with the very people he despised. He had blamed these people for his son's death, so he had wanted them to be the bad guys. He needed the president and her minions to be evil. Now, he just couldn't see them that way anymore.

After Agent Palmer's briefing on his capture and interrogation, he had grudgingly admitted to himself that had he been a part of that decision-making group, he would have come to the same conclusions they had arrived at. The TER had adequate checks and balances and multiple decision points throughout their mission. They'd gone outside their small circle for an independent assessment. They had not acted rashly. They had not targeted his son for assassination.

Despite all that, Mark was still dead, and Carl couldn't get past that. He struggled to find reasons to continue to blame those people for trying to save the president's daughter. He tried in vain to find a difference between them and the *new* Carl Johnson. He was a killer of their magnitude, if not of their experience.

It quickly became clear to Carl why he despised Aaron McGrath so much—why he still wanted the man to die. It was because McGrath needed no absolution for what he had done to Carl and Mark. That man lived and breathed in the abyss. He was in the business of death. He was not remorseful, and Carl hated that.

Carl had also stepped into the abyss, and there was only one manner of absolution available to him. That was why he had agreed to an errand of mercy to save a sixteen-year-old girl he didn't even know and would ordinarily never meet in a million years. When all the emotions, blame, guilt, and past evil deeds were set aside, only one fact remained. Melissa Mallory was going to die unless he saved her. No one else could do it— not SEAL teams or CIA covert operators or hostage rescue teams.

Still, it was beyond any stretch of the imagination that a drug lord, who was now a kidnapper, could defeat the US Secret Service. Carl figured even a small contingent of the well-trained agents should have been able to hold off a bunch of drug-dealing thugs.

Carl thought the snatch had to have been an inside job, or at least executed with inside help. He hadn't shared his thoughts with Agent Palmer on the issue, and he hadn't been briefed on the actual kidnapping. That event didn't impact his current mission.

He shook his head in the darkness at the irony. An innocent child had become a pawn in a terrorist plot against America, and Carl Johnson—a real estate broker who was now a terrorist—was the only man on the planet who could rescue her. After all the people he'd killed in his berserk rage, he was a *fucking hero*.

About to be, anyway, unless he screwed it up.

He'd had several hours to contemplate all the events of the past week, but it always came down to *too much time* to think. He kept seeing the same faces over and over again. He saw his son's face, peaceful in death. He saw Lisette's terror-filled face and her mother's desperate face as she begged for her daughter's life. He saw Anita Chapman's battered and bloody face. He even saw the struggle for emotional control on President Mallory's face. She was, after all, a mother facing the very real possibility that her daughter would die within a couple of days.

On his drive into Mexico, Carl tried to tell himself that in a year, he'd be okay without his son, that he'd be able to get on with his life, and that the month from hell he'd just experienced would simply turn into a dim and distant memory. It would merely be an anomaly in the fabric of time—a speed bump along the path of life.

He'd lost a child, and he would learn to live with the loss, just like thousands of other parents did every year. Meanwhile, in the here and now, he had to *feel* it, like Palmer said. He had to look into the eyes of the faces in his memory, and they were not forgiving faces.

He grazed on snacks and water almost continuously until he reached his destination. The well-lit fuel stop just north of a place his GPS labeled Nuevo Casas Grandes first peeked out of the darkness as a blur of light some five miles ahead. Slowly, as the miles passed, it materialized into a modern convenience rest stop with half a dozen pumps.

Funny, Carl thought as he pulled in, he hadn't expected to see *modern* in Mexico. He'd never traveled to the country, but he'd always viewed it in his mind as a third-world country, though he had no logical basis to do so. The rest stop was as modern as any found on long stretches of interstate highways in the US. It had modern electronic pumps with ATM card readers under a well-lit roof that kept the elements off the people refueling their vehicles. The small complex featured a modern convenience store with signs advertising Cokes, juices, coffee, donuts, and snacks. Separated from the store by a covered walkway were men's and women's restrooms and two water fountains, one high and one low.

He bypassed the pumps and parked in front of the convenience store. He got out and stretched every muscle in his body for a few moments, then proceeded up the hallway toward the restroom signs. He looked for surveillance cameras but saw none. That was good because after he relieved himself, he continued out behind the convenience store instead of going back to his SUV.

He followed a walking trail beyond the restrooms, where families could walk their dogs, and passed a couple of poop disposal stations. He walked past several park benches and then went along a short driveway leading to a utility service stand that provided fresh water and sewage removal for RVs. He approached a nondescript Volkswagen bus with tinted windows waiting at one of the utility pumps.

Then he saw a flurry of dark shadows moving around the vehicle. Backlit by dim utility lights, two men jumped toward him. The shadows were armed with machine pistols, and Carl heard the metallic sounds of slide mechanisms being racked back.

CHAPTER 52

0230 EST, THURSDAY
ANDREWS AIR FORCE BASE, MD

SHIRLEY MALLORY AND AARON MCGRATH sat in the president's private stateroom on *Air Force One* as the big aircraft sped down the runway at Andrews Air Force Base. They sat next to each other on a black leather couch, seat belts fastened. The president held McGrath's right hand with both her hands. She looked sideways at him and clenched his hand tighter as the front of the plane tilted skyward, and they left the ground. She heard the drone of the engines through the well-insulated fuselage, and she felt herself pushed back into the cushions of the couch.

Aaron had been her pillar of strength for two decades, and he'd been a friend even longer. Their relationship was one of the best-kept secrets in Washington, mostly due to his covert occupation, and only a few of her closest confidants even knew of his existence.

There was something ominously symbolic about this particular take-off.

She was flying to New Mexico to be reunited with her daughter, but the man she had to rely on was wounded, spiritually and emotionally. He was untrained, untested, and unpredictable. Aaron had made his position clear about relying on Johnson. Only Agent Palmer was convinced the terrorist could succeed, but she hadn't explained why.

Not that they had any choice. There were simply no other nonmilitary options. In the end, either Johnson would succeed, or Mallory had to be prepared to beg a foreign government for a very costly favor.

"He's my last hope. If he can't bring her back…"

"We can still send in the Delta unit from Fort Bliss. They've been on standby since we identified Alfonso Reyes as the man responsible for Melissa's kidnapping."

"I know." She paused for a long time. "But I can't start a war by invading an ally, not even for my daughter. We'll have to try a diplomatic solution if Johnson can't locate her and bring her back quietly."

"*Quietly* is not one of Johnson's strong points."

"Madam President. Aaron." Agent Palmer's voice came through their earbuds since the wall monitor was muted. She waited until they both looked up at her image on the monitor. "I have an update on Anita's condition in Albuquerque. She's out of emergency surgery and is stable. Her family is with her."

The president glanced to her left. She knew Aaron's moods, and she knew what was going through his mind even as she felt him tense. It was difficult for him to work with Johnson after seeing what the man had done to his daughter. That Palmer had removed Aaron from command turned out to be the best possible scenario. Otherwise, Mallory knew she would have had to.

She loved Aaron, and their relationship was strong, but she had to think of the best way to get her daughter back. They'd had several heated discussions in private, but she agreed with what she'd read in Palmer's report. Aaron had crossed the line by trying to send more covert units after Johnson. He was compromised.

The mission was probably equally difficult for Johnson, though she was surprised she felt empathy for the man. They needed him, but so many things could go wrong with the operation or with him.

"This has all been one big mess," she said. Aaron remained silent, so she addressed the monitor. "Agent Palmer, what's our operational status?"

"The surveillance camera at Columbus Port of Entry showed Mr. Johnson crossing over a little more than an hour ago. His team picked up transportation, weapons, and tech from our CIA contact earlier this afternoon and are at the rendezvous coordinates. Also, the *Marine One* contingent will land at Holloman Air Force Base within the hour and will be deployed by the time *Air Force One* lands."

"Good. I want to be at the border when he brings my daughter back."

"*If* he brings her back," McGrath said. "We should have a backup plan in place."

"You mean other than the diplomatic channel? In case he is unsuccessful?"

"No, Shirley. I mean in case he *is* successful. In case he decides to renege on his agreement."

"You think he might betray me…us."

"I know he will," McGrath said. "As soon as he has Melissa, he'll think about revenge again. He knows your role in all this, Shirley. When his pain fades, he'll want to hurt you along with me. And if Reyes is dead, he'll have Melissa. That will be his endgame."

Palmer interrupted, "I disagree. He's not going down there to get Melissa to use against us."

McGrath said, "You saw what he did to Anita. He damn near killed her."

Palmer was silent for a moment. "His moral compass is fractured, and he doesn't know how to fix it. Saving Melissa can help him."

The president said, "Explain."

"What I saw in his eyes at Aaron's house was a controlled viciousness. We brought it out of him, and we honed him. He has his own rules of engagement, but he's not sure whether revenge or mercy will heal him. Right now, though, he's on our side, so let's use him."

McGrath shook his head. "I've seen many men like Johnson. After he gets what he wants, he'll—"

Palmer shook her head. "He's smart, and he'll be prepared for a takedown, I guarantee you. We've seen how quickly and easily he is willing to escalate, and that's the last thing we want."

The president nodded at the monitor. "I agreed in writing to his terms." Mallory looked out the starboard portal at the city lights as the big plane banked. "So what if he returns without Melissa?"

CHAPTER 53

0220 MST, THURSDAY

NORTHERN MEXICO

T HE FIRST THING THAT WENT through Carl Johnson's mind was the fact that he was unarmed. He couldn't risk bringing weapons across the border, though the guards hadn't even searched his car. Now he stood in the middle of a no-man's-zone, too close to the van to escape getting shot and too far away to even attempt to go down fighting.

Then he recognized the two men pointing silenced weapons at him. It was Merc Two and Merc Three.

"Yo, what the hell?" Carl said.

"Boss, is that you? Dammit! I almost killed you."

Both men quickly lowered their weapons away and glanced around to see if they'd been spotted. The area was not well-lit, but it wasn't completely dark either.

Merc Three said, "See what happens when we work with the government? They didn't tell us you'd be in disguise."

They all bumped fists and got in the van.

"Am I free of surveillance?"

Merc Two nodded and started the van. Merc Three sat in the passenger front seat, and his wife, Merc Four, sat on the bench seat behind the driver. Carl pulled the rickety door closed behind him but had to slam it twice before it caught and stayed closed. Two revved the engine a couple times, then started the van into motion with a grinding of gears. They followed the road to the south, and at a sign proclaiming Fierro Grande, the bus turned east.

Merc Four said, "Here. Put this in your ear." She handed him a small tan earpiece smaller than his index fingernail. It looked exactly like the one he'd seen in Palmer's ear. He stuck the device in his left ear, pushing it in deep to spread out a cushioned barb that held it tightly in place.

She said, "It's a two-way encrypted intranet plus voice comm."

Carl nodded as he pulled his wig from his head. He rubbed his scalp with his fingers to get rid of the itchy sensation caused by the synthetic hair fibers. Merc Four handed him some alcohol wipes, which he used to scrub the color from his face and neck.

"Radio check," he said. "Mr. Garcia, you with me?"

"I'm here, Boss."

"Good," Carl said. "If this thing goes sideways and Reyes escapes, plan on him learning as much about your people as you know about his. If we're compromised on this end, close up shop, no questions asked."

"Roger that."

"Agent Palmer, you promised me a Predator surveillance drone."

"It is orbiting overhead as we speak, and it will stay with you for the next thirty-one hours. By the way, I apologize for not mentioning your disguise. That was my oversight."

"Well, they didn't shoot me," Carl replied.

Merc Four said, "If we're in-country for thirty-plus hours, I think we can count that as a mission failure. Operational success should occur in ten hours or less."

Palmer said, "The one you call Merc Four has a tablet for you. I've already gone over the layout of the estate with her and the others, but let's review it once more."

Carl took the tablet offered by the female mercenary and listened while Palmer described the latest intel on the estate. Map locations and terrain features became highlighted on the tablet as Palmer spoke, and Carl got the impression she was manipulating the highlights on her own display in Virginia and transmitting to his tablet in real time. It was remarkable high-tech gadgetry, and it reminded him again how over-matched he was in his war against the government. It was only a matter of time until they would have found him and killed him with all that tech. Of that, he was now certain.

Carl tried to get a sense of their current location in relation to the border that Mexico shared with Texas and New Mexico. The New Mexico border was minuscule, while the border of Texas stretched in a twelve-hundred-mile wavering line from northwest to southeast. A mere two-hour drive due east would put him back on US soil, assuming there was a border crossing in that area.

A blinking red triangle indicating the location of the Volkswagen bus popped onto the western edge of the terrain map. He actually felt the van swaying into curves as the blinking triangle followed the curved outline of the road. The topographical lines indicated hills outside the windows, but it was too dark to see them.

Merc Two pulled the van to the side of the road about a mile from the estate. Carl could see on the tablet map that Reyes's mansion sat nestled in a shallow valley at the end of a narrow road that branched off the road they were now on. Agent Palmer reported that earlier Wednesday evening, Alfonso Reyes was seen getting into a Hummer, which then drove away from the estate and proceeded farther east on the same road they were parked alongside. After sundown, another vehicle left the compound with two occupants showing on thermal imagery, but it was unclear who those people were.

The critical part of the deception was getting Carl into the compound without arousing suspicion. Agent Palmer's plan was to make him seem drunk, since Reyes was known to be a sophisticated but wild partier. Once Carl was escorted inside the house and left alone, he could begin his search for Melissa. Carl made no comment on the simplicity of the plan, but he had expected something more...*military*.

Palmer's voice answered. "I admit it's not a perfect plan, but it's the best we could come up with on short notice."

Three grunted from the front seat. "There's *best,* and there's *good enough*. This plan ain't either."

The dome light in the center of the van provided little light, and the two mercs in the front seats sat mostly in shadow. Carl could see both men were dressed casually in slacks and short-sleeve shirts. Neither were what Carl would consider big men, though both were taller than his five-nine height. They both outweighed him by a good twenty pounds, but neither topped the two-hundred-pound mark.

Carl recalled that Two had blue eyes, and Three had gray, but in the shadows of the van, their eyes seemed almost black. Three had let his stubble grow into a respectable half-inch beard over the last three days, but Two was still clean-shaven. They didn't look like killers, as they did when he had first met them. They looked like any ordinary men he'd encounter at Starbucks. He marveled at their ability to jump in and out of combat mode.

Carl turned his attention to Merc Four on the bench next to him. She was also dressed casually, and she'd separated her hair into two loosely braided ponytails. He hadn't noticed how long her hair was before, but now her shoulder-length ponytails made her look innocent.

"Well," he said to Four. Then he looked back at the other two mercs. "We'll do the best we can with what we have." The three mercs nodded. "We get the girl, kill the man, and high-tail it back to the US border."

He pointed his index finger at his chest with that comment, then pointed three fingers at the mercs and jabbed his thumb over his shoulder. They nodded their understanding. He would deliver the girl to safety while the mercs disappeared and made their own way to safety. He felt an innate trust of Agent Palmer, though he could not explain why, but after Mallory got her daughter, Carl knew she'd transition from vulnerable mother back to being president. Mallory, or even McGrath, might change the rules of the game, and Agent Palmer would have no choice but to follow orders.

Carl turned his attention back to the tablet and studied the floor plan of Reyes's house. The house was a huge mansion, and Carl tried to memorize the floor plan as he studied the tablet. He rotated the three-dimensional schematic and studied it from every angle.

The mansion was a U-shaped structure. The pool and atrium sat in the middle of the U. Several bedrooms lay on the third floor, and the office and home theater occupied the second. The kitchen and entertaining areas comprised all of the first floor. The three-thousand-square-foot separate garage east of the main house was nearly as big as his foothills home.

He handed the tablet back to Four and began changing into clothes provided by the CIA asset, clothes he was told resembled those seen in a recent picture of Reyes. The interior of the van was cramped with the mercs, their supplies, and weapons. Legroom was limited, and overhead room was nonexistent, so the dressing activity turned into a gymnastic contortion workout.

When finished, he wore a light pastel maroon playboy shirt under a beige sports coat. He had the shirt buttoned up because, as Agent Palmer pointed out, they had no intel on whether or not Reyes had any tattoos or scars or even chest hair. The single button of the sports coat was also buttoned to conceal his shoulder holster. He wore a fedora hat and dark-framed glasses with nonprescription lenses. He wore beige chinos and dark shoes. The sports coat was crumpled and looked like he slept in it in the van.

Merc Two said, "If the same guards are on duty now as when he left, they'll know these aren't the same clothes he was wearing earlier."

"Negative," Palmer said. "There was a shift change of the gate guards an hour after Reyes left, and there was another shift change a couple hours ago."

Carl said, "Any of the same guards back on duty?"

"Unlikely. It's equally improbable the guards at the gate saw what he was wearing. The gate is over two hundred feet from the house and the garage, and all of his vehicles, have darkly tinted windows."

"I hope you're right."

Merc Four pulled a whiskey bottle from a bag on the floor and opened it. Then she poured the liquid into her cupped palm and doused the front of his shirt and jacket and a little on his pants. He took the bottle from her, put it to his mouth, and upended it.

"Jesus, Carl! Don't drink that shit!" Four said.

"Dammit, Boss," Two said. "We can't run this op if you really are drunk."

Carl looked at Four with bulging cheeks. He swished the liquid back and forth and muscled the van's sliding door open. It squeaked loudly on ungreased rollers. Then he leaned through the opening and spat out the whiskey.

"Christ!" Four said as she climbed over his legs to get out.

Three got out of the front passenger seat and slammed his door closed. Carl climbed over the seat back and settled onto the bench next to Merc Two, and Three and Four unloaded tactical gear and supplies. Then Two ground gears and got the van moving again. They turned south immediately.

The road approaching the gate reminded Carl of so many parts of New Mexico outside of the city of Albuquerque. It was a dark rural area with only the moon providing light. The landscape he could see was minimal, mostly scrub brush and wild grasses.

Two pulled up fifty feet shy of the entry gate, and Carl made a show of nearly falling out of the passenger door. He slammed the door closed and fell against it. Regaining his balance, he staggered forward and moved to slap the front of the van to tell the driver it was okay for him to leave. He missed, then took three steps to regain his balance.

Agent Palmer's voice teased his inner ear. "The drone's multi-spectral sensors show two guards on patrol. One is walking the perimeter of the house, and the other is patrolling inside."

Carl faked another swig and spilled a lot of the liquid down his front, then walked toward the gate guards, all the while looking like he was concentrating on maintaining his balance on a plank moving beneath his feet.

One of the guards started speaking to him in Spanish as he approached. He didn't understand what the man was saying, but he heard the uncertainty in his voice. According to Garcia's people, Alfonso Reyes was known as a brutal man with a quick temper. It was said that he was extremely unforgiving of mistakes and managed his people by playing on their fear. If true, Carl figured the guards would be unlikely to seriously challenge him and face his wrath.

"Speak English, goddammit!" He kept his voice hoarse like Palmer had told him to since there was no way he could mimic the voice of the real Alfonso Reyes. "I proclaim that today is an English day."

He stopped a few paces from the gate. One of the guards pushed open one of the wide double gates and stepped forward. Carl took another fake swig and stumbled forward. The man reached out to help stabilize him.

"Don't let him touch you!" Palmer said. "If he grabs you around the waist, he might feel your holster."

Carl turned on the man and brushed his hands away, then pushed the man back toward the gate. He stumbled after him and grabbed the man's arm for balance, then followed him through while continuing to mumble nonsense. He turned toward the carriage house that held the drug lord's Hummers and limos, then stumbled as he and the guard made their way toward the front door of the mansion.

"The outside perimeter guard is behind the house."

Carl and his escort approached the mansion's grand entrance. He'd seen pictures of mansions like this one in travel magazines and in movies, but he'd never visited one. The property was well-lit, and his realtor's eye told him the house itself, not including the land or the huge carriage house garage, was easily a ten-million-dollar structure.

The outside of the house was tiled with small granite slabs, giving the building the same look and charm as an old turn-of-the-century museum. The huge double front door was actually gilded in gold trim. Two ten-foot posts stood guard on each side of the double entryway, and atop each post sat a golden eagle. One eagle was perched, but the other golden eagle had its wings spread as if ready to take flight.

He figured the driveway he walked on was crushed coral, likely imported from Hawaii. Carl remembered walking along Maui beaches that looked like Reyes's driveway. The elegant path ended at a three-level set of curved, polished granite steps that led up to the front porch.

Carl pushed off from the guard and made a great show of stumbling up to the front door. He stood up straight and wiped at his mouth with his left sleeve. With apparent difficulty, he got his hand on the push-down thumb lever of the door handle and shoved the big door open. He stepped inside and closed it quietly behind him.

"Okay, I'm in," he whispered to Palmer. He set the whiskey bottle on the floor beside the door. He scanned the foyer. It was huge, with shiny, forty-inch granite tiles decorating the floor. He'd have to be careful, or his soles would squeak when he moved or pivoted. "Where is the interior guard?"

"Infrared scan shows the guard is moving toward you on the first floor, right wing. He's stopping frequently, probably checking doors to the patio and pool deck."

Through a wide window wall on the opposite side of the foyer, Carl could see the water of the pool shimmering in the light of the high moon. He also caught a hint of fragrance in the air and looked around the room. His gaze settled on a clear crystal vase with half a dozen scent sticks immersed in a golden liquid.

"The guard skipped the last two doors and is bearing down on your position. Move up the spiral stairs to the right of the foyer. Quickly!"

CHAPTER 54

0255 MST, THURSDAY
NORTHERN MEXICO

H IS RIGHT SOLE SQUEAKED SLIGHTLY with his very first step, and Carl knew he could not run up the stairs. Like the floor, the stair steps were inlaid with exotic granite tiles of black, gold, and silver swirls. He tried another step as carefully as he could, but he still made noise.

"Move, Carl. Move!"

He bent down and removed his shoes, then ran upward, trying not to slip in his socks.

"Continue to the third floor," Palmer said. "Recall that our best guess is that all the bedrooms are up there."

He continued up the winding stairs.

"Stop and duck, Carl. The guard is coming into view."

He didn't stop. Instead, he looked down into the foyer and saw the top of the guard's head. The man wore all black and carried an AK-47 slung over his shoulder. Then the man began to look up like he'd noticed something or heard a noise.

Carl leaped the last three steps in one bound and crouched on the landing against the wall. His heart raced, and he heard it thumping in his ear. He breathed deeply to catch his breath.

"Did he see me?" he whispered.

"Standby." Palmer paused a long time. "Remove your handgun and attach your suppressor. Quickly and quietly."

Carl unbuttoned his sports coat and pulled the Glock-17 from its holster. He reached into his left pants pocket and pulled out a thick, ominous-looking black tube, which he screwed into the barrel of the gun. He closed his eyes and mentally cursed his luck. He had just gotten in the door and was going to have a shootout. The gamble to get off the staircase was worth it. Palmer couldn't see on her sensors that the railing was open, and the guard would surely have seen him if he'd stopped as she suggested.

"Okay, you're clear. The guard is moving off toward the west end of the first floor. Thermal imagery shows that six of the bedrooms are occupied in the right wing, so those are likely the off-duty guards. Bobcat is most likely in one of the two occupied bedrooms in the left wing."

Bobcat, he knew from his brief conversation with Agent Palmer before he left Virginia, was the Secret Service designation for the president's daughter.

"Except for the guard on the first floor, the rest of the house, including the basement and wine cellar, is unoccupied."

"Copy that," he whispered. He stood and slipped his nonskid shoes back on. An elastic sock-like boot fit firmly around his ankles, so there was no need for laces, buckles, or Velcro.

"You're doing fine, Carl."

He found reassurance in her words. He got the feeling that she'd directed many such ops with newbies. He proceeded up the hall with the weapon in a two-handed grip, the business end pointed at the floor six feet in front of him.

He whispered, "Where are the heat signatures?"

"Both are in adjacent rooms at the far left end of the hallway."

"Remind me again," Carl said. "Julia and Luisa. Which one is the wife, and which is the daughter?"

"Luisa is the wife."

"Copy that."

According to the tablet schematics, the third floor housed ten huge bedrooms in each wing, each with its own private bath attached. Carl now proceeded down the left corridor. The carpet was an expensive-looking beige material with a tight weave that seemed made for heavy foot traffic. The hallway was wide, and dark wood paneling adorned the lower thirty inches of each wall, while the upper portion was covered with light-colored, expensive wall fabric. Wall light sconces and paintings decorated the walls.

As Carl cautiously made his way down the hallway, he felt increasingly irritated. He quickly realized it was the glasses he wore to look like Reyes. The thick plastic of the stylish frames was interfering with his peripheral vision, and he kept turning his head slightly to the left and right to see what might be in the blind spots. He hadn't worn glasses since his Lasik surgery, and he'd forgotten how much a part of his face the frames had been. Now the facial appliance was merely an irritant.

He stepped to his right, removed his glasses, and laid them gently in a huge empty vase made of some kind of crystal. The vase sat on a three-legged, antique, half-round wooden table. He sat his fedora on top of the vase, then continued his journey toward the end of the hall.

"Wait! We have movement!"

Carl didn't have time to even think about ducking into the closest unoccupied bedroom because the door immediately ahead of him and to his left opened suddenly. A teenage girl hurried into the hallway. Carl's movement must have registered in the girl's peripheral vision because she turned toward him. She took a breath to scream, but he jumped forward and clamped his hand over her mouth with his left hand. His momentum pushed her into a small table outside her door, and it banged loudly against the wall like a gunshot in the quiet house. The glass vase on the table crashed to the carpet and shattered.

In his ear, Palmer announced, "You have movement in the adjacent room, and the guard is moving rapidly up the stairs toward your location. Get out of the hall now!"

In the dimness between the pools of ceiling light, he could tell the girl he held was not the president's daughter. She was too slender, too short, too young, and too brown. He started to yank her back into her bedroom.

"Do you have the package?"

"Negative on Bobcat."

"The other occupant is approaching the door. Take them both in one room."

The girl was dressed in preteen girl's pajamas, and when he quickly glanced downward, he saw she was barefoot. If he pulled her toward the next bedroom, she'd slice her feet on the glass pieces. So he released his grip on her mouth and shushed her, then picked her up with an arm around her waist and carried her toward the door of the other bedroom. His shoes crunched over the glass fragments of the broken flower vase.

Just as the adjacent bedroom door started to open, he pivoted and rammed his right shoulder against the wood slab and forced his way in. He dumped the girl to the floor at the feet of a very surprised Luisa Reyes. The woman stumbled backward and started to scream, but Carl stuck the business end of the silencer right in front of her face and made a shushing sound at her.

Luisa held her scream and did that cross-eyed thing, focusing first on the black weapon and then on Carl. A fleeting look of familiarity mixed with confusion flashed across her countenance. Then he reached behind him with his left foot and kicked the door closed.

He said, "You scream, you die. Now, where is the American girl?"

Luisa spoke harshly in Spanish, knelt beside her daughter, and hugged her. Both stared up at him in confusion. The guard called from the hallway, and both ladies glanced at the door behind Carl. He lowered the gun away from them and squatted. He looked Luisa Reyes in the eye and repeated the question.

Luisa looked him up and down, no doubt noticing how similar he looked to her husband. Her gaze took in the wet whiskey stain on his shirt and pants. Then she started talking again in Spanish.

"Mr. Garcia," he said quietly. "I don't think these folks can understand me. Can you translate for me?"

The girl said, "I speak English." Carl looked at her, and she looked at her mother, who nodded. "They kept her in the cellar, but now she's not here."

"Where is she?"

Palmer said, "The guard is coming up the hall. He'll be at your door in ten seconds."

Julia said, "They took her."

"When? Where?"

The girl shook her head. "They left last night. We don't know where."

"Palmer, did you copy that?"

"Affirmative."

Carl heard the guard hollering. The doorknob moved, but the door didn't open. The door was locked from the inside. He heard the sound of a fist pounding on the massive door. Only the front gate guards knew he—as Reyes—had returned. The inside guard and the guys who had been asleep in the other wing didn't know. He was in serious trouble.

Palmer said, "We have multiple heat signatures moving in the east wing of the house. You need to get out of there fast!"

CHAPTER 55

0257 MST, THURSDAY

NORTHERN MEXICO

"GET OUT? HOW THE FUCK am I supposed to do that?" In an instant, the whole op was screwed, and Carl had no idea what to do. "C'mon, Palmer, I need instructions!"

"Stand by. We're working on it, but stay calm, Carl."

"Calm?" he whispered harshly. "These guys have AKs, and there's fucking ten of them! Send in the mercs!"

"They're too far away and won't get there in time, so take a deep breath and trust me. I'll get you out."

This was precisely why he'd initially thought getting personally involved in the rescue effort was a bad idea. He didn't have field experience. He couldn't think on his feet in a combat scenario. He didn't know how to improvise on a mission. Sitting in an op center somewhere watching it happen on a TV monitor and giving orders to mercenaries was one thing. Actually being in the shit was an altogether different scenario. The covert kids practiced for years how to do that stuff, and now Carl, with all of his thirty days of experience, felt paralyzed with indecision and fear.

What should he do? What *could* he do? He damn sure couldn't shoot his way through almost a dozen guards.

In his earpiece, he heard Palmer, her analysts, and the mercs chattering about options, but he could only see one card to play. From his position in a squat, Carl pivoted to face the door and aimed. To Julia, he said, "Tell him I'll shoot you both if he doesn't back off."

Luisa and Julia traded words, and the girl said, "My stepdad hates my mom, and he hates me too. He'll just tell them to break the door open."

They exchanged more whispered words in Spanish, then Luisa shouted something at the door, and the banging stopped. She stood up, as did the girl and Carl, then Julia started ruffling up her mother's hair. The woman had long luxurious black hair that reached to the middle of her back. The woman kept whispering instructions, and the girl grabbed hold of her mother's full-length nightgown and pulled, and Carl understood what they were doing.

Luisa rocked forward when Julia tugged, but the gown wouldn't tear. Carl stepped forward and grabbed the silky material. He yanked downward, and the gown ripped, exposing Luisa's front. For a brief second, he saw her from neck to navel, and he wondered how any man could possibly hate such a beautiful woman.

Luisa had smooth caramel brown skin. Her breasts were medium-sized and firm, with dark nipples. She was slender with a narrow waist and curvy hips. She quickly covered her body, but not before he saw the scars. She had old scars from small cuts and maybe cigarette burns, and she had new bruises over her breasts and belly. She spoke again.

Julia said, "You have to hit her so she will look bloody." The girl dropped her gaze to the floor. "He does that a lot."

Carl understood the deception and stepped in front of the woman. As he holstered his weapon, Luisa squared her shoulders in preparation. She closed her eyes, but he couldn't bring himself to do it. Maybe Klipser could. Maybe McGrath could. Maybe Palmer could do whatever it took to salvage the mission, but Carl could not. As long as he lived, he didn't think he would ever be able to hit another woman, not for any reason.

Instead, he took her face gently between his palms and kissed her. She gasped, and her eyes flashed open, but she didn't resist. Her breath was warm and sweet, and she tasted of chocolate mint. Her lips were soft, and her tongue was strong as she wrestled with his. Then he bit her bottom lip hard. She winced, and he released her, but when she fingered her lip, she came away with blood that she wiped on her gown.

Even as she smeared the blood, she held his gaze. In her eyes, he saw a mixture of surprise, gratitude, and something else. He saw lust, or maybe a wish for lust—a wish that she could be married to this new man who looked like her husband but wouldn't hit her.

Holding her ripped gown in place, Luisa reached for the doorknob. Julia grabbed Carl's arm and sat him on the side of the huge bed. She had gone into the bathroom, returned with a wet facecloth, and administered to his fictitious head wound, received from a wife who didn't want her drunken husband trying to force himself on her.

Julia sat next to him on the bed and explained their plan, saying, "The guard will believe it. That's what he does to her all the time."

Carl pulled his Glock and was prepared to shove Julia to the floor if he had to start shooting. He wasn't afraid to kill, but so far, none of the men he'd killed were shooting back.

Luisa turned and opened the door, holding the pieces of her gown together. She exchanged conversation with the guard, and Carl heard the hinges of the door squeak a bit. She was opening the door wide enough for the guard to see what had happened. The story of an aborted rape attempt wouldn't be hard to imagine because the whole room stank from his whiskey-soaked shirt. The gate guards would corroborate his un-scheduled drunk arrival, but hopefully, no one had called the *real* Reyes yet.

She closed the door, and Carl heard the crunch of glass as the guard retreated up the hallway. He heard voices in the hallway briefly, but they faded into silence. Luisa sat at the foot of the bed facing the door, while the girl and Carl sat on the side of the bed and faced the magnificent bathroom.

Luisa still held the front of her torn gown in place, but her back was revealed almost down to her butt. Her body was toned, slender, and curvy. "Little in the middle," as Carl liked to say. She truly looked mag-nificent. She turned sideways and saw him looking.

In his ear, he heard Palmer say, "That was quick thinking."

"It was the ladies, not me." He smiled at Julia. "You saved my butt, young lady."

Julia smiled and leaned against him, and for a moment, Carl was bewildered by her attachment to him, a stranger. Then he realized that while she was a stranger to him, the man he appeared to be was not a stranger to her. From her perspective, this familiar-but-new man didn't hate her, and she needed that attachment.

He said to the girl, "My assistant says you did good."

"Assistant?" Palmer said. "Seriously?"

Julia said, "You look like him. And you smell like him."

He nodded. "The girl your dad kidnapped is my president's daughter."

"He's not my dad."

"Yeah, well, she sent me down here to get Melissa because I look so much like him." Carl rubbed his left shoulder against her right shoulder affectionately. "And I'm sorry about the smell. It was all part of my disguise to get past the guards and find her." He paused and looked at the girl beside him. "How old are you?"

"I'm almost twelve."

Just like American kids, he thought. Never content with how old they were at that moment, but very intent on how old they would soon be. She was the same age as the girl he almost killed two days ago. He shuddered at the memory, then found he had reached his right hand across his body and was caressing the girl's cheek. She smiled at him.

Julia had her mother's dark brown eyes, her long, luscious hair, and her rich brown skin color. He suddenly wondered how he could ever have considered harming a girl like her or Lisette. Over the girl's shoulder, he saw Luisa watching him, and he saw something new in her eyes.

She said something that ended with *Estados Unidos*. He didn't have to speak the language to understand that she now viewed him as her ticket out of the country, or maybe just out of a bad situation she could not otherwise escape.

The girl said, "Mom thinks she knows some places where they might have taken Melissa, but she wants you to take us to the United States." The girl had a hopeful look in her eyes and added, "Please."

"Agent Palmer, what is our status?"

"The drone is detecting an increase in cell phone traffic. It's extremely likely you've been compromised."

"Understood. Melissa is not on the premises, but I may have a lead.

Mrs. Reyes may have some possible locations for Bobcat, but she wants evac to the US."

"Is it likely she truly knows?"

Carl looked at Luisa. She got up and went into her huge walk-in closet with Julia to get dressed. The woman probably thought she already had a deal.

"No doubt she's working her own angle here," Carl said. "But I'd bet good money she at least knows her husband's phone number, so perhaps I can arrange a meeting."

Palmer said, "Do whatever you need to do to locate Bobcat."

"Copy that."

He went into the bathroom and removed his whiskey-soaked shirt. He quickly washed and gargled. He sensed the girl standing beyond the doorway behind him, so he glanced back there as he dried off. Julia was now dressed in some of her mother's clothes, which fit reasonably well. She wore denim jeans, a red plaid shirt, and expensive sports shoes. She gave him a shy smile.

"Have your mom grab one of your dad's shirts for me, okay? And some pants too."

Julia smiled and nodded, and he followed her into the bedroom. Julia was a cute girl, still innocent-looking, with big friendly brown eyes.

Luisa Reyes was dressed in beige cargo pants with a light blue denim long-sleeve shirt. She wore expensive brown hiking shoes that sort of looked like sports shoes but weren't really for sports or for hiking. Carl figured they were some kind of fancy, super-expensive cross-trainer shoes.

She looked good. Her long jet-black hair hung unbraided down her back. She had a black band restraining her hair at the back of her neck, and another band held her hair together near the center of her back.

Her face was more round than oval, kind of attractive, yet kind of ordinary, and she had a scar that began on her left cheek, crossing the lower part of her left nostril and extending down across her upper lip. The scar spoiled what might have been a perfectly flawless face, but Carl thought it gave her a ruggedly sexy look, in a kick-your-ass kind of way. He guessed she was in her mid to upper thirties.

Luisa had dark eyes he could only describe as wounded. She looked like she was uncertain whether or not she was doing the right thing trusting him. She looked like someone who figured she had no other choice.

He stood there and watched Luisa watching him. He was shirtless, and he knew he was in excellent shape for a man of fifty-three. Her gaze danced over his torso, and he saw that her eyes held two distinct but clearly visible emotions. There was desire in her eyes, but there was also strong anger, hatred even, that was punishing the look-alike for all the misdeeds of her real husband.

She turned away just as Julia came out of the other walk-in closet and playfully tossed Carl some of her stepdad's clothes. He stepped back into the bathroom, quickly putting on dark corduroys and the deep blue and beige plaid flannel shirt. The man's clothes fit perfectly.

Stepping back into the bedchamber, he said to Luisa, "Do you have some car keys?"

He had plans of sneaking out the side of the mansion, into the carriage house, and stealing one of the Hummers. By the time the guards reacted and were able to chase, Carl and the girls would be beyond the first bend in the road where the mercs waited to ambush the pursuit. Then he wondered if a Hummer could slam through the sturdy front gate.

Luisa shook her head and spoke while Julia translated. "He doesn't let her drive. It's his way of controlling her."

Carl had a feeling the girl added that last part as her own opinion.

Palmer said, "You're out of time, Mr. Johnson. Two of the guards that had previously gone outside to the front gate are returning to the house. Their posture is aggressive, and they are weapons-ready. Other guards inside the house are mobilizing."

Carl stood and looked around the room as if that action might reveal a new escape route.

"Agent Palmer, can we get to the basement from this end of the house?"

"Affirmative. Proceed out the door and to your left. The door at the end of the hall enters the stairwell."

Carl looked at Julia Reyes and said, "Let's go!"

He pulled the bedroom door open and quickly glanced out. The hallway was clear for the moment. He grabbed mother and daughter by the hand and pulled them along with him. Once in the stairwell, he realized quickly that Julia couldn't run down the stairs. She looked down and carefully placed each step, and that was as fast as she could move. He picked her up again and carried her. He descended the stairs two at a time, glancing back once to find Luisa right behind him.

He realized that in his haste, he had left his gun and holster on the bed, but he knew he wasn't going to win a gunfight with a ten-shot Glock-17.

"We need to get creative here, Agent Palmer. You have that special package I requested?"

He'd asked Palmer to have a bomb strapped to the surveillance drone to use on Reyes if it looked like he was going to escape. "What kind of bomb?" she had asked. Carl knew nothing about military ordnance, so he simply said, "Make it the kind that explodes and kills the bad guys."

"Affirmative. The package is in place," Palmer said.

"Good. Get ready to drop it on the house."

"Carl, you're *in* the house."

CHAPTER 56

0302 MST, THURSDAY
NORTHERN MEXICO

BOVE THEM, A DOOR SLAMMED open. Guards were in the stairwell. The sound of multiple sets of boots echoed from above.

"Prepare to drop the bomb, Agent Palmer. The mercs can mop up anyone who survives the blast. Which way to the wine cellar?"

Julia pointed at the door at the bottom of the stairs. "Go left!"

Palmer added, "We'll target a drop site just to the west of the house. That should clear the estate of all structures and hostiles. If we drop *on* the house, the blast would likely compress the basement and cellar as well, and kill you."

"Well, we certainly don't want that."

"Indeed," she said. "We still need you to get Melissa."

Carl wasn't sure if Agent Palmer was sending her brand of humor or if she was serious. He tried to engineer a witty retort but came up empty.

She said, "We'll detonate fifteen feet above ground so the blast wave propagates laterally without significant downward effects."

Palmer's assessment of the pending bomb damage seemed oddly clinical. She sounded like someone who had conducted a good number of bombing missions and damage assessments.

The west wing of the house on the first floor housed the kitchen and dining room, and the wine cellar was directly under the kitchen. Carrying Julia, Carl led Luisa out of the stairwell and across a huge pantry. They went down a few steps to the cellar door, the top of which was just below the level of the kitchen floor. The cellar door could only be locked from the inside, and Carl locked the thick wooden door behind them just as the thunder of boots entered the pantry.

"We are secure!" he said to Palmer.

"The package has been released. Detonation in five seconds."

Carl ushered the ladies into the farthest corner of the cellar and huddled them down. Then all hell broke loose.

When the bomb exploded outside the mansion, Carl felt a deep, rumbling vibration. Luisa let out a gasp and clung tight to Julia. Then the shelves snapped like crackers. Carl ducked his head and pulled the girls' heads down. Jars, packets, and cans rained down, thumping onto their backs, smashing on the hard floor, and filling the air with flour dust and a sharp pickling smell.

When the dust settled, they went back up the stairs. He opened the cellar door and gasped. He wasn't sure what he expected to see, but he certainly didn't expect to see the night sky. There was absolutely nothing left of the mansion above ground. There were no walls or even wood or steel framing to be seen. There was not even a pile of debris. It was as if the mansion above ground had never existed.

All the lights were off, and in the moonlight, Carl could see that the guard shack at the front gate a couple of hundred feet away was also gone. Some portions of the security fence still stood, but the closest sections along with the front gate were bent over flat. Only a couple of the walls of the brick carriage house that served as the garage remained standing. Since that structure was on the far side of the mansion, away from the bomb impact site, it had partially survived the blast though it was severely damaged.

Inside what remained of the carriage house, Carl found only one Hummer not buried under the rubble. He assumed the keys were in the ignition since the entire property was—or had been—secured by the steel perimeter fence. As soon as he opened the passenger door, he saw a shiny key fob dangling from the side of the steering column. He turned back to the women, but Julia had already opened her door and climbed into the truck.

He gave Luisa a head-nod and said, "Up you go."

She didn't understand him, so he stepped behind her, gently grabbed her waist, and helped her into her seat. She glanced back at him again, and her eyes were filled with the same conflicting emotions as before.

"Seat belts, ladies," he said, then closed the doors.

He'd never driven or even ridden in a Hummer, so he took it slow toward the front gate. He and the ladies swayed gently as the luxury SUV bounced over bricks, Mediterranean-style roof tiles, and sheets of metal from the garage doors.

"Stop!"

Agent Palmer's voice in his ear was calm but firm, and Carl slammed on the brakes without questioning the urgent command. The big truck slid to a quick stop.

"Thermal scans show there is a survivor just beyond the security fence. He's several feet beyond where the guardhouse was."

Carl saw the figure rise from the road in the glare of the Hummer's bright headlamps. He expected the man to be charred after a bomb blast, much like he remembered from movies. Then he remembered Merc Two's lecture on the devastating effects of the GBU bomb.

There was no fire associated with the type of bomb they'd used. Instead, the detonation had caused a massive compression of air to blast away all structures. Anyone inside the blast zone would have their insides turned to jelly by the overpressure wave.

The guard stood shakily and wavered as he stared at the Hummer. He still held his AK-47 at his side. Most of his black pullover shirt was torn away, and his black cargo pants hung from his hips in shreds, with one pant leg completely missing. The man bled from many open wounds, and he was caked with dirt that clung to his bloody body.

Carl shuddered at the sight of the man. He guessed maybe the man had been somewhat sheltered in the guardhouse rather than caught out in the open. There were pieces of wood, glass, and tile shards sticking out of his chest, belly, face, and neck.

The guard raised his weapon unsteadily, and Carl felt a sudden rush of hatred. Maybe the guard had been in the truck with Reyes when Mark was gunned down. Maybe he was the driver or the second shooter. Carl squeezed the soft leather of the steering wheel with both hands. He heard his own voice growling.

"Motherfucker."

"Carl, back away," Palmer said. "He appears gravely injured and will not be able to aim properly."

"Back away?" Carl whispered. "I don't think so."

He jammed his foot on the gas pedal. The sound of the roaring engine filled the cabin, and Carl heard dirt and debris pinging against the undercarriage as all four wheels spun against the ground. The Hummer instantly caught traction, and Carl was pressed back against his seat. He aimed the front of the Hummer straight for the man.

Luisa gasped as the front of the big truck hit the man, then she screamed as the guard's weapon bounced against the windshield. Carl glanced at his side mirror, but he could see nothing of the man in the darkness behind the car.

"Motherfucker."

Palmer said, "Carl, that was reckless."

"Mm-hmm." He glanced over his shoulder at Julia. "You okay back there, sweetie?"

The girl was barely visible in the light from the dashboard, but he saw her nod.

"I'm okay," she said.

Carl checked the road, then glanced sideways at Luisa. She still clutched her seat with both hands. He reached over and gave her left hand a slight squeeze of reassurance and saw her nod in return. Then her eyes widened, and she gasped.

"That's okay," Carl said, nodding at the mercs in the road ahead. The trio was dressed in black combat gear. "They're friends."

Julia translated as he slowed the Hummer. The VW bus faced them at the side of the road with its headlights dimmed. Carl stopped his SUV alongside the bus. The mercs' weapons were lowered, and Carl realized he had mentally tuned out Palmer's instructions during his brief drive from the compound as she continued to choreograph the operation from Virginia.

Carl got out, walked around the truck, and helped Luisa out. Julia jumped out on her own, and he led them both to the front of the bus. Then he joined the mercs in front of the Hummer.

The mercs were back in combat mode. All three wore black, skin-tight, long-sleeve pullovers. Balaclavas covered their hair, neck, and ears, and black paint darkened their exposed faces. They wore Kevlar vests with numerous pockets, and their black cargo pants had even more pockets. Every pocket seemed filled with weapons or supplies.

Palmer said, "Mr. Johnson, what is your status?"

"Ready to continue the search for Bobcat."

"Reyes may have been suspicious of your motives for meeting him, or perhaps he may have suspected we had deduced Melissa's location."

"Yeah," Merc Two said. "Or maybe someone told him." Carl looked at the man and nodded, but he said nothing.

He'd had a similar thought when Julia Reyes said they had taken Melissa the evening before. The timing of her removal and the launch of the mission was too perfect.

"So where is the girl, Agent Palmer?" Carl said. "Where did those cars go?"

"Unknown." She paused. "I couldn't risk retasking the drone to follow one or both cars. That would have left the house, your primary target, unsecured."

"Copy that. Now we need to pull him back into the game somehow." Carl looked over at Julia. "Do you or your mom know Alfonso's cell number?" The girl spoke with her mother, and Luisa pulled out her flip-model cell phone and scrolled through a menu.

To Palmer, he said, "I think we need a more direct approach. I'll tell him I've got his wife and daughter as insurance."

Agent Palmer said, "I thought I heard the girl say he hated them."

"I have an idea to use that." He told them his plan.

"Oh, yeah," Garcia said. "That'll work, Boss."

Palmer agreed. "That's a good cultural play."

Carl looked at his mercs, and they each nodded. He said, "Besides, I'm guessing he wants his money sooner rather than later."

Garcia interrupted "What if he objects to the bearer bonds and wants an electronic transfer of payment?"

Carl shrugged, even though he knew Garcia couldn't see the gesture. "They're fake bearer bonds, right?"

Palmer said, "No, they're the real thing. It's too easy to do a field test."

Carl nodded. "Well, the only way he gets his money is by taking the bonds. I'll tell him to take it or leave it."

Carl took Luisa's open flip phone from her and hit Send to call the contact she highlighted. He stuck the device against his left ear so Garcia, Palmer, and the mercs could hear both sides of the conversation through the comm channel.

A man's voice started talking rapidly in Spanish. The voice sounded angry. It sounded sinister. A picture formed in Carl's mind of the man, of his own image, leaning out of a black SUV, killing Mark Johnson. A familiar rage filled him, and he growled into the cell.

"Shut the fuck up and pay attention."

"Who is this?"

Carl shouted at the phone. "Who the fuck do you think it is?"

He took a deep breath and saw Mercs Three and Four trading glances of concern. Merc Two held his hands out toward Carl. He patted the air like he was trying to tell Carl to calm down.

Carl nodded and said, "I'm the man who has your wife and daughter." He paused. "And $250 million in US dollars that almost belonged to you. I'd like to discuss that trade now. The money and your family for the girl you kidnapped."

"I see." Reyes's English was nearly perfect. "Your people made no mention of bringing my family into the transaction."

"I want to make sure you remain sufficiently motivated. But I'll be happy to keep your wife if you don't want her back. Except I'll be nice to her. No more scars, you know what I'm saying?"

The implication was that Carl had to have seen the man's wife naked to see her scars. Reyes would be wondering how and why Carl had gotten Luisa out of her clothes. He'd be thinking maybe Carl took advantage of Luisa before she realized he wasn't her husband. He'd be thinking maybe she liked it. He'd be feeling angry, insecure, and vulnerable. He'd want a confrontation to make things right.

"You play a dangerous game, Mr. Johnson."

Carl said, "I want the American girl."

"I see," Reyes said.

Carl couldn't hear any anger in the man's voice, but he knew curiosity was eating at his insides. It had to be.

"And I understand your fee for this transaction is fifty million dollars."

"Correct."

"And why would you take less than what you already have in your possession?"

"A presidential pardon and another hundred million will be part of my deal with the US government." Carl decided to play his vulnerability card. "Unlike you, I don't have the infrastructure in place to disappear. I don't have high-level military friends to protect me. I can have less money with a pardon and be a hero by returning the girl, or I'll have a target on my back for the rest of my life."

Reyes was silent for a few seconds. "Since my business dealings have been somewhat lucrative lately, I agree to your terms." Reyes dictated some coordinates. "I'll expect you to be at the foothills of El Chappa at dawn. That's northeast of La Laguna Chiquita."

"I will see you at sunrise." Carl flipped the phone closed, terminating the call.

CHAPTER 57

0335 MST, THURSDAY
NORTHERN MEXICO

C ARL HELD THE CLOSED CELL phone in his hand for a moment. He found himself wishing he could reach into the device and across the airwaves to wrap his fingers around Reyes's throat.

"Motherfucker," he whispered.

Palmer took charge of the op again and started outlining their plan of engagement.

"As soon as you have Bobcat, proceed immediately to the Columbus Port of Entry. If you meet resistance on your return, we'll launch the recovery team, but only if it appears we can engage without firing on Mexican military or police forces. If this goes sideways, you'll be on your own. We can't risk a shooting war with our ally."

"Plan B then?" Carl said. He looked at his mercs. "Just in case things do go sideways."

Everyone was silent for a moment.

Agent Palmer said, "Can any of you fly a small plane or a helicopter?"

Carl and his group all looked at each other, but no one spoke.

"That's a big negative," Carl said.

"Okay, I'll get a pilot down to that municipal airport you just drove past." Palmer paused, then said, "Nuevo Casas Grandes."

Carl said, "Where are you going to find a pilot after midnight?"

"It's what we do, Carl."

Merc Four added, "There's an FBI field office over in El Paso. They'll be happy to wake up at oh-dark-thirty in the morning and lend us a hand."

Three said, "There's an army base over there too. And we already know there are CIA in-country assets."

"Okay," Two said. "Plan B is we evac to the airport if we encounter resistance, steal a plane, and take our chances in the air. Plan C is we fight it out on the ground and drive to the border if we can, and Plan D is we hike and carry the girl if we have to."

Carl glanced at the Reyes girls as they conversed in Spanish.

"Agent Palmer, I don't know how high up your drone is, but is our immediate area clear? Can you see to the trade site from here?"

"We've got it hovering at twenty thousand feet now, and, yes, you are secure. There is no traffic within ten miles of your current location. Our plan is to divert the drone over the trade site shortly before your rendezvous. I want to keep the bird with you; otherwise, I can't guarantee your operational security."

"Understood."

Merc Four brought out the tablet. She placed it on the hood of the Hummer, and they all began to put together a plan to cover the trade site. As the mercs and Palmer finessed their plan, Carl found himself looking over at Julia and her mother again. The girl smiled and waved at him, but Luisa Reyes was more reserved. He went over to them.

Julia said, "Mama thinks you're going to leave us here after you find the American girl."

There were many reasons—excuses, really—he could use to explain why he was using them, but he decided to cut right to the chase. He wasn't like McGrath, and deep down in his soul, he knew he didn't want to be. Not anymore.

Carl nodded, then took the girl's cheeks between his palms and kissed her on the forehead.

"Julia, I'm sorry, but I can't take you with me. I don't have passports or visas for you or your mom." He paused for a moment. "Truth is, I didn't come down here for you. I'm only here for the American girl." He paused. "And I'm here for Alfonso Reyes. He murdered my son. As soon as Melissa is safe, I'm going to kill that man." He looked at Mrs. Reyes. "That's the best I can do for you."

Julia leaned into her mom and spoke quietly. Mrs. Reyes hugged the girl and gazed at Carl for a few seconds. Then she nodded.

Carl couldn't understand how a young girl could live in an environment surrounded by men like Reyes and still find fragile hope in the words of a stranger like himself. Then he found himself wanting to do something for Julia. He wanted to rescue her and her mother. Maybe by saving them, he could balance out the red in his ledger, make up for some of the terrible things he'd done in the name of vengeance.

Still, he had one more act of vengeance to complete. He had to kill Alfonso Reyes. For Mark. For Julia. For his own sanity. And then what about McGrath and all the others responsible for Mark's death? When would there be enough blood spilled that he could be okay with the loss of his son? He knew the answer.

Palmer's voice interrupted his thoughts. "Carl, are you with us?"

"No."

All talk on the comm circuit in his ear ceased. He could sense his mercs staring at the back of his head. Even Julia and her mother looked at him.

It was at that very instant he realized that regardless of his words to the contrary, he was still on the path of vengeance. His agreement with the president validated that path because Mallory couldn't get her daughter back without allowing his own gratification. Now, as he looked into Julia's innocent brown eyes, he realized that killing Reyes wouldn't help her. It wouldn't help her mother, and it wouldn't help Melissa Mallory.

Killing Reyes damn sure wouldn't help Mark. He knew it was just an excuse to satisfy his own thirst for revenge. It would add more blood—more red to his ledger. The only real way to balance that ledger was to help people.

He looked at Julia and said, "Thank you, sweetie. Thank you for setting me straight."

He turned back to his mercs and said, "Agent Palmer, we have to change the mission."

CHAPTER 58

0612 MST, THURSDAY
NORTHERN MEXICO

CARL DROVE THE ORANGE VOLKSWAGEN bus across the desert flats. The old engine roared and rattled. Luisa Reyes sat on the bench behind Carl while Julia leaned over the backrest on her elbows and kept her left arm in contact with Carl's right shoulder. She gazed out the front window.

He glanced over at her. She looked at him in return and smiled. She was a cute kid. In a different world, he'd hang out with her. He could see himself being a big brother or a role model, maybe helping her with science projects or library research or something.

The landscape he drove through looked quite a bit like a lot of New Mexico. He saw lots of scrub brush, wild grass, and even a few bunny-ear cactus. Even the climate was similar. It was warmer than in Albuquerque, and the early December temperature hovered around forty at night before it would rise to the mid to upper sixties during the day, according to Agent Palmer's people. The air wasn't as dry as high-desert New Mexico air because the elevation was slightly lower in Mexico, maybe three thousand feet above sea level instead of five.

Normally, driving across empty land put Carl in a thinking mood, but the closer he got to the exchange site, the more anxious he felt. He gripped the steering wheel tight with both hands and began to sweat, despite the cool air blasting in through his open window. Merc Four made him chug down a power drink, but now, he felt like a stimulant was running through his veins. Or maybe it was just adrenaline.

"Ten minutes, Carl," Agent Palmer said.

"Copy that."

He kept telling himself he had to stay in character. He had to keep his cool when he faced the man who murdered his son. He had to be like McGrath, even though he had only a fraction of that man's mission experience.

He kept affirming he was the FBI's most wanted badass. The feds had described him in their Tier-One proclamation as being "fearless and ruthless." They also said he was "calculated, demented, and bordering on suicidally insane." That was the man he had to be when he faced Mark's murderer.

"By the way, Carl. The president sends her gratitude." She paused. "I think it was a good move changing the mission parameters. I'm curious why you decided to do that."

Before Carl changed the parameters, Palmer had said he and his team needed to anticipate a *fluid* mission. That's what happened at Reyes's house, though, and Carl knew he hadn't handled that fluid situation very well. He'd just been lucky.

He'd learned his lesson. The new operation was complicated enough, fluid enough, with only one mission goal. Up to that point, they were still trying to get the girl and get Reyes. That implied both objectives were equal, and satisfaction of either objective meant a successful mission.

"It was simple, Nancy," Carl said. "I asked myself what that fucker Aaron McGrath would do."

One mission, one objective.

The man wouldn't be blinded by emotion or any desire for revenge.

He added, "We're here to get the girl. If Reyes gets away, I can live with that. I'll just hunt him down another day. If the girl gets killed, though, I wouldn't be able to consider that a successful mission outcome." He paused. "Fucking McGrath," he muttered. "That's what he'd do."

"Contact, two minutes," Palmer reported. "Mercs Three and Four are in position. Merc Two is on standby."

Like the mercenaries, Carl had changed into all-black assault gear.

Somehow, the gear looked a lot more sinister on his mercs than it *felt* on him. He wore a black head glove to keep his dome warm. The black turtleneck fit comfortably, and it was made out of a high-tech fiber like outdoor athletes used. The fabric was light and tight but breathable, so it would pass sweat away and keep him cool in active situations. At the same time, it retained his body heat during the cool night temperatures.

His armored vest had the same pockets, grenades, and knives the other mercenaries had, and he'd been told there was a first aid kit in one of the pockets, as well as two small tubular canteens and several energy bars. Merc Two replaced his lost Glock-17 with a Glock-21, which was holstered on his right hip, and he carried half a dozen forty-five caliber, thirteen-round clips in his side pockets.

The flat road curved around a knoll and passed between two of the hills. Carl listened to the report in his ear from Agent Palmer, who re-layed the scene out of sight ahead, as viewed from the drone cruising overhead. Then he saw the exchange site. He saw a white Hummer and a gray pickup about two miles up the road. Men stood outside the vehicles.

"Agent Palmer, do you have eyes on the package?"

"Negative." She paused, and he pictured her and her analysts bent in front of a computer monitor, maybe shifting between the various sensor feeds from the drone. "Slow your van to a stop fifty yards from the vehicles, and park sideways across the road."

"Copy that."

The mercs had scavenged pieces of the carriage house garage doors to build what basically was a ten-layer, somewhat bulletproof shield on the driver's side of the van's passenger compartment. Carl's sole task was to get Melissa into the van while the mercs dealt with Reyes's men.

He wasn't comfortable bringing Luisa and Julia to the trade site, but he had no other choice. Agent Palmer had plainly said he'd have to show Reyes he actually had them for the trade.

"Merc Four," Palmer said, "a tango has just ascended the low hill Carl just passed. Looks like a shooter. His distance to the trade site is 410 yards."

Three's voice answered, "We see him. He appears to be armed with only a short-range sniper rifle. Recommend we designate him as 'Tango One.'"

"Approved."

Carl slowed the VW bus and motioned Julia and her mother down, out of sight.

"I know Four is on the closest hill with an unobstructed line of sight, but can she cover me from there?"

Agent Palmer said, "She is exactly 0.92 miles from you. She won't miss."

Three added, "She'll hit the apricot from there."

"Excuse me? Apricot?"

"The apricot is the medulla oblongata. It's located at the base of the skull. It's the part of the brain that controls involuntary muscle movement. Hit the apricot, and you get an instant kill with no reflexive response or involuntary trigger-pulling."

"Seriously? From a mile away?"

Palmer said, "It's true, Carl. You needn't worry. Besides, she has a modified Barrett M-107 sniper rifle, compliments of the US government."

"That means absolutely nothing to me."

Four said, "It means I've got your back, Boss. I won't miss."

Reyes's big white Hummer was parked sideways across the road. Parked tail-to-nose directly in front of the Hummer was the other gray truck that also looked sort of like a Hummer, but not quite. He saw a man climb up on the back and pull aside a blue tarp.

"Holy shit!" Four's voice said.

Carl said, "Is that a fucking machine gun on top of that truck?"

CHAPTER 59

0625 MST, THURSDAY

NORTHERN MEXICO

A GENT PALMER GAVE HIM THE specs, but her analysis didn't make him feel any better.

"That truck is a modified Hummer with a cut-back cabin and a roof-mounted, 50-cal, belt-fed gun."

"Fuck." He slowed the van to a stop and gazed through the dust-streaked windshield.

Merc Four said, "That 50-cal will rip right through that sheet metal we put inside the bus. Recommend that gunner as my target of first priority."

"Roger that," Palmer said.

"Only if he's shooting at Bobcat," Carl said.

Three objected, saying, "But the Reyes girls will be completely unprotected in the van."

"I know," Carl said. "But Melissa Mallory is the mission. Collateral is secondary." For the first time, Carl considered the possibility that he might not survive the operation. "Mr. Garcia?"

"Here, Boss."

"If I go down, get our people safely home and paid."

"Copy that."

Carl had to smile at the young man's operational parlance. He pulled Luisa's flip phone from a vest pocket and flipped it open with one hand.

He pressed Send, and the same number he called a few hours ago was dialed again.

"Mr. Johnson," was all Reyes said.

"Where is the girl?"

Reyes ended the call, and in the distance, men moved around the two trucks, though Carl couldn't identify them.

Palmer said, "I have eyes on the package."

Three said, "Confirmed."

"I also have four tangos on-site," Palmer added. "Including Alfonso Reyes and Ricardo Guzman."

Guzman had been identified as the second gunner hanging out of the SUV right after Mark was killed. Carl closed the phone and tossed it to the passenger floor.

"Reyes and Guzman are standing at the back of the white Hummer, and Bobcat is with them. There is a driver standing near the front of the Hummer, and he appears to be armed with a machine pistol—likely an American-made Colt or an AK with the shoulder stock sawed off. The top-mounted machine gunner appears locked and loaded and is sighting on your van."

Carl inched the VW bus forward again. He hauled the steering wheel to the left, then to the right, and parked the bus perpendicular to the road with the driver's side panel of the bus facing the trade site. He got out but left the door open and the engine running. Then he strutted around front like the FBI's most wanted badass, in clear view of Reyes and his men. He eyeballed them like he dared them to shoot him.

He slid open the side door and helped the girls out. Julia rocked forward like she wanted to hug him, but he quickly grabbed her shoulders.

"No, we can't do that in front of those men." He smiled at her and added, "Be brave, sweetie. I'll be back for you in a minute." He smiled at Luisa, then pulled both ladies by their arms and led them around the front so Reyes could get a good look at them. Then he pulled them back around the side and gave Julia one last instruction.

"If they start shooting, stay behind the engine." He pointed at the back of the bus, and she nodded.

He opened the passenger door and hauled an oversized metal briefcase from the bench. It was constructed of brushed steel with reinforced corners and edges that made it look like it could withstand a grenade blast. He wobbled slightly under the heavy weight as he made his way toward Reyes. He stopped halfway and put the briefcase down, then stepped a dozen paces to the side, careful to stay out of Merc Four's line of fire. He waggled his hand—*come here*—at Alfonso Reyes, his cue to send Melissa over.

Melissa Mallory was a sorry sight to see. Carl couldn't see evidence that she'd been beaten, but her shoulder-length brown hair was a mess, and her face was drawn and filthy. She wore a man's shirt that was much too big for her and was probably white a month ago. She wore beige canvas pants. Her clothes were dirty and stained. She looked like she hadn't been allowed to bathe for weeks.

She was a big girl for sixteen, and she reminded Carl of the typical American teenage couch potato who didn't get out to play much and had no interest in school sports. She stood nearly as tall as Carl and probably weighed a buck-fifty. Her hands weren't restrained, but there was no need. She was gaunt and weak, looking like someone who understood she was a prisoner with no hope of escape. Whether or not she was tied up was irrelevant.

The girl probably didn't even realize she was about to be released. Or maybe she thought she was going to be killed. Then again, she looked like she didn't care either way.

Reyes called behind him. His driver stepped around the back of the Hummer and listened while his boss gave him his instructions. The man set his sawed-off rifle on top of the Hummer and grabbed Melissa by the arm, yanking her forward. She shuffled along on bare feet. She simply looked at the ground and let herself be dragged to whatever destiny awaited her.

When they were almost even with Carl, the gunman let her go and jogged toward the case beside Carl. Carl heard the man pop the latches on the case.

Palmer said, "As we expected, he's doing a chemical analysis of the bonds."

Melissa had stopped one step away from Carl and kept her gaze on the ground.

Carl whispered to her, "Your mom sent me for you. Just a few more minutes, and you'll be safe."

Palmer said, "Wait, Carl. Do not approach her. Remember, she's been in captivity for over a month, and she's probably afraid of everything and everyone. You have to try to bond with her, but you must do it very quickly."

Melissa fidgeted with her hands, alternately interlocking her fingers and rubbing her hands together like she was washing them.

"They call you Bobcat, don't they? The Secret Service?"

She stopped fidgeting for a moment. Her gaze came up, and her blue eyes focused for just a moment. Her bottom lip trembled, and she grabbed her left hand with her right.

"I look like him, don't I?"

She nodded.

"That's why your mom hired me. Took me a while to find you, though. I had to drive all over Mexico, but now we can all go home. Your mom's waiting for you at the border." He thumbed over his shoulder.

Melissa glanced that way for a second.

"I can keep you safe, but I need you close to me, okay? I want you to grab hold of my vest and never let go."

He got her to relax just long enough so he could step forward and take hold of her hands. She tried to pull away, but he held her close. She smelled of a mixture of bad breath and hungry breath, as if they had barely fed her and never let her brush her teeth during her captivity. She smelled like they had kept her locked in a dungeon with no toilet or shower and made her soil herself. He knew that humiliation also. At least Klipser's men had hosed him down daily. Melissa's captors had not done the same for her.

"Don't worry, Melissa. You're safe now. I won't let anything happen to you." He placed her hands on his armored tactical vest. "If you stay attached to me, I can protect you from anything. I have friends nearby."

Melissa's gaze darted toward the VW bus.

"Boss," Three said, "I don't like what I'm seeing down there." Carl recalled the man had extremely long-distance binoculars with huge lenses. "The 50-cal shooter's posture is very aggressive."

Four added, "Roger that. The sniper is sighting. I think he's going to shoot. Request permission to engage."

"Negative," Carl said. "Stick to the plan, people."

Palmer sounded hesitant. "Remember, Carl, the plan is fluid."

Carl countered, "Reyes probably thinks I have commandos in the bus. He won't start shooting until he has his family back."

Palmer said, "Begin moving toward the van."

"Copy that." He brushed filthy hair from the girl's face and tried to get eye contact. "Okay, Melissa, I want you to come with me. Let's walk over that way."

She resisted and moved her left hand to the right edge of his vest near his armpit. With her right hand, she grabbed the back of his vest at the neck. She clung tight, but she wouldn't move with him.

"Agent Palmer, this isn't working," Carl said.

"Shit!" Four said. "The sniper is locking and loading!"

Carl heard the man snap shut the briefcase again. He shouted something in Spanish.

Mr. Garcia translated, "He said the bearer bonds are real."

Alfonso Reyes smiled. "Thank you, Mr. Johnson, but you see, I'm not afraid of the US government or your president. In fact, I'd feel much more comfortable if you and my family all went straight to hell."

Carl felt surprisingly calm. When he couldn't get Melissa to walk, much less run, to safety, he realized he had his fluid situation. He had only one option open to him, and he made his decision with the analytical coolness Agent Palmer always displayed.

He pulled his sidearm and started shooting.

CHAPTER 60

0637 MST, THURSDAY
NORTHERN MEXICO

H IS FIRST AND ONLY SHOT hit the gunman at the money box square in the face. The man's head snapped back, and he folded right to the ground. Then everything happened at once, but it wasn't like the movies, where there was always an orderly destruction of bad guys.

He heard the deep ratcheting clatter from the truck-mounted machine gun. At the same time, he heard the pinging sounds of the huge shells punching holes in the van's metal side, and he heard the shattering of the windows. He also heard the controlled chaos of Agent Palmer and the mercs exchanging instructions in his ear. Somehow, they all seemed able to understand everything that was said.

He also heard the high-pitched whine of an Uzi submachine gun, yet he absorbed all those sounds before the first man he shot even hit the dirt.

Over Melissa's shoulder, Carl saw Guzman bring up his Uzi. He squeezed the trigger and swept the weapon to his left—left to right from Carl's perspective—aiming chest-high on a direct path across the space he occupied. Except the girl was standing between him and Guzman.

Carl acted instinctively, totally without thought, and did the only thing he could to save the girl. Like ballroom dancers, he stepped forward and twisted to his right. With her hands locked to his vest, Melissa instantly pivoted with him, out of the path of the bullets.

Pain exploded in his back as he took the hits. He heard himself scream in pain, and he flopped down in the dirt on top of the girl.

"Oh, God. I'm hit! I'm hit!"

All Carl could see when he fell on top of Melissa was the rise and fall of her chest. He straddled her, his left cheek resting between her breasts. He was rapidly fading. He could no longer feel anything, not even the pain, and he couldn't breathe.

Suddenly, the gunfire fell silent, and a cacophony of voices were shouting at him.

"Get up, Johnson! Get up! Reyes is going for a gun!"

Four said, "I don't have a shot. He's behind the Hummer."

"I can't move," Carl whispered. "I'm hit bad. I can't breathe. I'm dying."

Merc Three said, "You *are* moving, goddammit! If you couldn't breathe, you wouldn't be able to talk, so roll your rookie ass over and shoot that mu'fucker!"

Merc Two added, "I'm on my way. ETA is sixty seconds."

Carl heard Agent Palmer's voice in his ear also. She was calm and controlled, like it was just another day at the office. "Carl, you are not dying. You've just never been shot before. The vest protected you. Try to take a deep breath and roll over."

He opened his eyes, looked past the girl's chest, and saw his right hand in the dirt. The hand still held the Glock, and his arm was *moving!* He felt the pain in his back again, and it suddenly became very intense. He screamed again and struggled to raise his head. Then he tried and failed to roll off the girl.

"Melissa, push me over."

With her hands still locked to his vest, she helped push him off, and his body sprawled belly-up beside her. Carl saw two things. He saw his legs moving in spastic uncoordinated movements, as if his appendages were trying to claw their own way to their feet, and he saw Alfonso Reyes fiddling with an Uzi. It was the weapon Guzman had shot Carl with, and that man lay in front of Reyes with a huge, messy chunk of his chest missing, compliments of Merc Four.

Reyes looked like he was trying to clear a jammed mechanism, so Carl struggled to bring up his Glock. It wavered in front of his face, and Carl realized Melissa's arms were interfering with his sight. She had never let go of his vest, so when she rolled him off her, she rolled with him and ended up lying halfway on top of him.

Carl coughed in pain, and his eyes watered. Alfonso Reyes became a hazy shadow, a splotch of darkness against an unfocused, sand-colored landscape. He pointed his gun in the general direction of that shadow and squeezed his trigger. He wasn't sure of his aim, so he kept firing until the slide locked back. His gun was empty.

He heard Agent Palmer's calm voice in his ear. "He's down, Carl."

"Good." He laid his head against the dirt. "Is he dead?"

"Negative. He's still moving."

"Well," he said with another painful cough. "I better go fix that."

Carl holstered his Glock, then groaned with the effort required to roll to his hands and knees. He paused, breathing heavily.

He'd been beaten, tasered, electrocuted, and waterboarded to within an inch of his life, but he'd never been shot before, and it hurt like hell. Being shot in the back half a dozen times was one hell of an indoctrination.

When Carl started to feel his strength returning, he raised Melissa up with him so she was also sitting up.

"You did good, baby girl." He cupped her cheeks with his palms and kissed her forehead through her mat of dirty hair. "You never let go, just like I told you."

Carl got them both to their feet, but he had to pause for a moment to catch his breath. His back throbbed. He looked around and saw the VW bus. It looked like Swiss cheese, and daylight shone through the myriad holes in the skin of the bus. The 50-cal rounds had punched through the sides of the bus and all the layers of protective sheet metal. Every window in the vehicle was blasted out, and the tires on the side of the bus looked like tiny bombs had exploded under them.

Even as he wondered about the Reyes girls, they peeked out from behind the back of the bus. The engine block was basically a big chunk of metal, and he was relieved to see that it had withstood the 50-cal assault. He smiled and waved them over, and they cautiously walked arm-in-arm toward him.

Mercs Three and Four had saved him. Four's first long-distance kill, the headshot, had undoubtedly saved them from the hilltop sniper. Her second shot ripped right through Guzman's chest. The machine gunner had several seconds to pepper the VW bus before he lost a significant portion of his chest and back. His body had actually been launched completely out the back of the modified Hummer, and he'd landed in the space between the gray truck and Reyes's whiteHummer. Only Alfonso Reyes still lived, and Carl watched the man squirm behind his Hummer.

He eased Melissa's grip from his vest. "These are the friends I mentioned, Luisa and Julia Reyes." He nodded to Julia. "This is Melissa Mallory, the president's daughter."

Julia smiled and said, "*Hola,* Melissa."

Carl said, "Let me go see about Mr. Reyes, then we'll get you back across the border to your mom, okay?"

Melissa nodded and said, "Is my daddy going to be there too?"

"I don't know, baby girl. I don't know who he is."

"His name is Aaron."

Time seemed to stop for a few seconds, and Carl finally realized that his comm channel was utterly silent.

"Aaron McGrath is your pops?" he asked.

The girl nodded.

Four said, "Holy shit."

Three added, "Well, fuck me sideways."

"Boss," Two said, "we can change this mission *right the fuck now*. You just say the word, and we'll keep this girl and engage our in-country assets."

"That's right. We got your back."

"Boo-yah!"

The government side of the comm remained silent, as if they were all holding their breath, waiting to see what he was going to do. He felt the thrill of having power over Aaron McGrath, but the sensation faded quickly.

"Negative," he said. "Punishing the director is not the mission, not yet anyway. Let's get this girl home to her mother." To Melissa, he said, "I'm sure your pops will be there too."

Carl looked at Julia. "Will you and your mom take care of her for me for a minute?"

As the two ladies comforted Melissa, Carl loaded a fresh magazine into his weapon and walked over to Reyes. The man had a single gunshot to his left hip. He lay on his back. He looked up with an expression Carl could only describe as contempt. Carl laid his assault boot hard on the gunshot wound, and Reyes screamed.

"You killed my son." He pointed the Glock at Reyes's face.

"Wait! Wait!" The man gasped. "I have money."

"I already have money."

"I have *more*. You can have the ransom. All of it."

It was part of the psychological torture Carl had learned at the hands of Agent Klipser. Even in the presence of complete and utter hopelessness, even imminent death, it was human nature to want to stay alive as long as possible. A person would do anything to delay certain death. That instinct made a person cling to a tiny figment of fantasy that there was something you could do or say to make your enemy change his mind and let you live.

"Well, that's a start," Carl said. "Give me the account number and your password." Reyes did. "If my guy can access the money, then I'll let you live."

Garcia said in his ear, "I'm on it."

Carl glanced over at the girls. Luisa and Julia hugged Melissa, but the president's daughter seemed uncomfortable. She rocked from foot to foot and fidgeted with her hands again. She alternately clasped her fingers, then wrung her hands for a few seconds, then shook them like she was trying to get dirt off. She started scratching the inner parts of both arms at the elbows.

"I have information," Reyes said, drawing Carl's attention. "I know people. Powerful people. But you have to let me live."

"What kind of information?" Carl stomped on the man's hip wound again, and Reyes howled in pain. "What people?"

Garcia chimed in. "Got it! I just drained his account of every last penny. He had a balance of $237 million and change."

"My sources." Reyes gasped. "You don't think I could have kidnapped the president's daughter by myself, do you?" He shook his head. "I want asylum. I want immunity."

"Carl," Palmer said, "the drone is detecting radar signals—" He heard a brief squeal in his ear, followed by a couple of beeps, and suddenly his team was silent.

A shiver of panic gripped Carl's gut, and he turned away from Reyes. "Agent Palmer, are you there? Nancy, talk to me. Garcia? Anybody?"

His brain raced to understand what was happening. Radar signals? Sudden loss of comm? That meant inbound aircraft with jamming equipment.

"Fuck!" He ran over to Melissa and the Reyes girls. "Come on, we've got to get out of here, right now!"

He grabbed Melissa by the arm and turned toward the sound of a racing engine. It was the Hummer that Merc Two was driving. The vehicle was slowing and had just started to navigate around the VW van.

Even as the thought tumbled through his mind that the mission wasn't over, the Hummer exploded in a tremendous fireball.

CHAPTER 61

0642 MST, THURSDAY
NORTHERN MEXICO

ARL FELT THE HEAT FROM the explosion, even though the Hummer was nearly fifty yards away. Just before the fireball erupted, Carl's peripheral vision registered a flash of light streaking into the truck from the left. Merc Two had been hit by a missile, but before Carl could even process the thought, he saw the trail of fire from another missile streaking skyward. Its point of origin was somewhere beyond the hills immediately to the south of him. A third missile slammed into the top of the near hill and exploded exactly where the drug lord's sniper had been perched, and a fourth streaked into the distance toward Carl's mercenaries.

Carl tracked the second missile's smoke trail upward until it finally hit the orbiting drone and exploded. A few seconds later, the source of the missiles arrived in the form of two combat helicopters flying side by side over the nearby hills. One, a modern troop carrier, banked high above, while the other, a smaller escort gunship, flew to the west. That one, Carl knew, was heading off to make sure the mercenaries were dead.

The olive green combat helicopters looked as modern and deadly as anything in the US Army inventory. The troop carrier had one missile pod attached to each side of its fuselage above the open doors. A machine gun was also mounted in each doorway. The smaller chopper was similarly armed, and Carl figured it was also outfitted with sensors good enough to find and kill Merc Four and her spotter.

A puff of fire and smoke erupted on the distant hilltop as the fourth missile hit. If Three and Four weren't dead, they soon would be. A sniper team versus an armed combat chopper were not very good odds. They had heavy weapons and RPGs as backup, but Carl knew the military chopper had defensive capabilities. It would make quick work of the mercs.

Carl and the women stopped and watched as the army-green troop carrier flew one complete orbit over them, then settled into a hover. One of the machine guns was pointed at Carl's group. Finally, the aircraft settled to the ground with a whirlwind of dust a hundred yards to the south.

Half a dozen soldiers in desert camouflage uniforms that blended with the landscape jumped from the far side of the helicopter and raced away to form a partial perimeter. Half a dozen more jumped from the near side of the helicopter. A fellow who looked maybe ten years Carl's senior exited the chopper last. He was dressed in a formal army-green uniform. The man had several rows of ribbons and medals over his left breast pocket, but he wore no name tag.

Carl figured that meant the man was a general. In the US military, generals didn't wear name tags either. He never knew the official reason for this, but he figured if you're a general, everyone is supposed to know your name anyway, so you don't need a name tag. There was no such thing in the US military as an unknown general.

The officer placed a standard military beret on his head after he moved from under the rotors and away from the turbulent prop wash, then he strode confidently toward Carl.

Beside him, Luisa whispered, "El Patron."

When he glanced at her, he saw fear in her eyes, and she even took a step back behind Carl and pulled Julia with her.

Carl felt a curious mix of emotions as he watched the man approach. The fact that Luisa whispered his name spoke volumes. He got the feeling people weren't allowed to speak his name. Maybe people weren't allowed to *know* his name. No doubt Luisa knew who he was through her husband's business dealings.

Agent Palmer had mentioned that the US government believed Alfonso Reyes was connected with high-level military personnel, and

Garcia's sources had said the same. Carl got the feeling the man's sudden appearance wasn't a coincidence, and he wasn't there on official military business despite his show of force. Carl figured the man had a personal stake in the outcome of Reyes's transaction.

Instinctively, Carl felt a degree of safety. He knew there was no way the Mexican army would be complicit in the kidnapping of the daughter of the American president unless they wanted to fight a war with the US. By the same argument, a rogue army general would have the same limitations since his actions, though unsanctioned, could put his government at risk and would therefore imperil his own empire.

"Melissa, stand behind me with our friends, okay?"

The general stopped within arm's reach of Carl and looked down at him with his arms clasped behind his back. He was a bear of a man and stood a head taller than Carl. His gray hair was buzz cut on the sides below his cap.

"Mr. Johnson, would you mind holstering your weapon? I'd hate for one of my soldiers to shoot you by accident."

Carl had forgotten he still held the weapon he'd wanted to use to end Reyes's life. He nodded and very slowly put the gun away.

He concentrated on controlling his outward appearance. He couldn't afford to show even the slightest concern. Inwardly, he feared for the lives of Melissa and the Reyes women. While the general sounded polite and civilized, his eyes gave Carl the impression he would order their deaths without hesitation.

Carl dipped his head down a bit and looked up at the man from under his brows, hoping to impart a sinister look that might unnerve the military officer. He also held the barest hint of a sneer at the corner of his mouth.

The general didn't seem intimidated, though. He just stood there. He had bars and stars and something that looked like a woven ribbon all over his upper arms and shoulder epaulets, but Carl had no idea what all that meant.

The man glanced behind Carl at the three women. He examined them as a child might examine an ant before he squashed them or burned them with a magnifying glass. Carl decided to take the offensive and get control of whatever negotiation was forming in the man's mind.

"Are you here to clean up his mess?" He nodded at Reyes.

"They told me you looked exactly like him, Mr. Johnson, but I never truly believed it until this very moment." He paused a moment.

They?

"He still owes me a great deal of money," the general said. "So, it is fortunate that you did not kill him, although I'm curious why you let him live."

"We're fifty miles from nowhere. I figured I'd let him bleed out." Carl glanced over near the burning VW bus and Hummer. Black smoke billowed into the sky and drifted to the north on a light breeze.

"But if it's money you want, there's a bunch over there in that case. Untraceable US government bearer bonds." Carl shrugged. "I'm told they're real, not forged."

Carl made the statement like he knew what he was talking about, but in truth, he was only regurgitating what Agent Palmer had told him. In his previous economic strata, none of his clients ever dealt with bearer bonds. In fact, the denomination of each single bond in that case was far more than his highest annual salary had been when he worked in the defense business. He hadn't even taken the time on the op to examine the bonds to see what one actually looked like. He didn't need to. They were simply a tool to facilitate the trade for Melissa Mallory.

The general glanced at the briefcase. "They may be real, but I'm sure the US government has any number of high-tech devices they could install in the bonds, no? A nanofiber transmitter, perhaps? Or a lightly radioactive ink with a suitable half-life of, say, twenty-four to forty-eight hours. That would be long enough to track me to my stronghold or my warehouse, where they could then invade or even hit me with a bomb." He glanced over his shoulder and up into the sky, where smoke of the stricken drone was still drifting on the wind. "Well, not with a bomb from *that* drone, yes?" The man paused as he turned his attention back to Carl. "So my preference is for real *electronic* money, Mr. Johnson."

Carl found it curious that the general mentioned the drone's bomb. It was as if he knew the drone had carried one but didn't know they'd used it on Reyes's house. The general spoke to one of his soldiers, and the young man trotted over to where Reyes lay.

"My dilemma now is what to do with you," the general said.

"You should let us go. My ops center knows I have the girl. Anything happens to her now, and President Mallory is going to kick your ass and anyone close to you."

"Ah," the general said. "So you *are* in league with your president. Not quite the terrorist you led us to believe, eh?"

"She and I have a mutual mission objective." Carl head-nodded toward Reyes. "You could call her a client. I promised to get her daughter back, and she gave me a pardon and let me keep Reyes's ransom."

"You have my money?"

Carl nodded. "Not only the second ransom, but just a few minutes ago, he gave me the rest so he could live. That's almost $500 million."

"I would advise you to return the money immediately."

Carl said nothing, and after a moment of silence, the general continued, "Look around, Mr. Johnson. How is your *client* going to save you now? Your president has no idea who I am. I know that for a fact. And your closest retrieval team is half an hour away, that is, if they even dare to cross the border, now that they are uncertain you are even still alive."

The depth of the man's intel troubled Carl, but he didn't change his expression. "The way I see things, General, I don't need saving," he said. "Your problem is that *my* people, not the US government, hold all of the ransom money in my accounts. Seems to me, you might consider negotiating for its return, minus a small handling fee, that is."

The general said, "That was not his money for you to steal. It was mine."

Carl shook his head. "I'm sure we can reach terms."

The general grunted. "I grow weary with this exchange. Why don't we discuss how quickly you can return my money, and I might just let you live."

The man raised his right hand and waved two fingers. Several of his soldiers stepped forward into a rough semicircle around Carl and the girls, the business ends of their rifles pointed at Carl's group.

Carl eased his right hand to his gun. The holster was not snapped, so all he had to do was pull the weapon free. With his left hand, he reached back for Melissa's arm and pulled her up against him. She didn't have to be told what to do. She grabbed onto his vest with both hands.

Unfortunately, there was little he could do for Julia and her mother, who were also behind him. Melissa was the mission. The Reyes women weren't.

"You'll die with us, General. And if Melissa Mallory dies, the president will bomb your country back into the Stone Age. That, you can count on."

"You're playing a dangerous game with the lives of these young women."

Again, Carl remained silent.

"My investors demand a certain return on their investment. These are powerful people who would not hesitate to facilitate a war between your country and mine."

To Carl, the general's revelation was nothing less than a confession. His investors were the financiers of Reyes's operation to kidnap the First Daughter, and the ransom money was their return on investment. He and Agent Palmer had Reyes's motivation all wrong.

This was never a simple kidnapping to propel the status of a mid-level drug lord onto the global terrorist landscape. With money in the hundreds of millions, though, Carl figured there had to be some other reason for the high-risk kidnapping. Reyes was merely a pawn, a minor player, though he had tried to make the game his own. It was more important than ever now that Alfonso Reyes lived, so he could be inter-rogated. The thought of seeing him on one of McGrath's tables filled Carl with a sadistic thrill.

There was a more sinister plot unfolding at a high political level, and Carl sensed the endgame of that plot would not culminate with the release or rescue of the president's daughter.

"I understand your immediate need, General, so let me make a counter-proposal that might serve us both a little better."

The general nodded.

"Even if you take that man back with you," he nodded over at Reyes, "he won't be available to conduct business for several weeks because he'll be recuperating. Instead, let me assume his identity. Let's leave him here in the desert to suffer and die. Luisa and I can run his business. That's good for, what, ten million a year in profit straight off the top, right?"

The general nodded. "Closer to thirty million."

"Okay, so I get your money back for your investors, and you help me get settled into Reyes's life and his business and his identity, then we split the proceeds of the business. After all, I'll get my pardon, but I'll still be a terrorist. I need a new country to call home."

For some reason, lying through his teeth felt immensely gratifying. He had little choice, though. If he couldn't convince the general he could help him, Melissa and Luisa and Julia would die with him. He recalled Agent Palmer's words:

Do whatever it takes to complete the mission.

They discussed the intricacies of the exact monetary split, and after receiving slightly more than half, the general nodded.

Gunshots suddenly erupted from the burning wreckage of Merc Two's SUV. Carl and the general ducked, and Melissa clung tighter to the back of his vest. The soldiers closest to the wreckage instantly covered the area, and even the helicopter machine gunner swung his weapon over. The gunfire was short-lived, and Carl figured it was Two's ammo mags cooking off. He stood upright and glanced behind him to make sure his women were all right.

"Well, that was unexpected," El Patron said. "Anyway, you don't mind if I keep these two as my insurance policy." He nodded at the two Reyes ladies behind Carl.

"Hostages would give the appearance that this is not a business transaction and would portray me as being weak. That would not be acceptable." Carl shrugged. "You let them drive out of here, you and I shake hands, and then it looks like you and I are business partners. Besides, if I fail to perform, I'm sure you know where to find them. In business, appearances matter greatly. I'm sure you understand."

The general nodded. "Still, I would feel more comfortable if they stayed with me."

Carl glared at El Patron. "Look, General. I can guarantee you that I'm coming back down here to Mexico after I deliver the president's daughter. The only question is whether I'm coming back to do business with you or to go to war with you." The general started to object, but Carl waved him quiet. "If you fly out of here with these ladies as hostages, you're just slapping me in the face. That means war."

The general smiled and looked over his shoulder at his helicopter. "My guns are bigger than yours."

Carl shrugged. "I'm sure that's what the FBI and that covert kill squad thought before I kicked their asses and killed their assault teams with a drug-addict CIA flunky, a laptop, some cell phones, and four mercenaries." He paused. "If we go to war, General, I guarantee you'll see zero investment return, whether you win the war or not. Personally, I'd prefer to do business with you because it's more profitable. But I don't have anything to lose, so I'm okay either way."

The general smiled suddenly and let out a loud laugh to cover up his tenuous negotiating position. He needed his money back, and Carl knew it. El Patron waved his soldiers away, and they retreated back toward the troop carrier.

Then he stepped close to Carl and snarled with his smile still spread across his countenance. "Mrs. Reyes and her daughter can go," he said. "Then I will fly you and the president's daughter to the border. But if you are not back within seventy-two hours, then we most certainly will be at war, Mr. Johnson."

Carl stuck out his hand, and he and the general shook briefly.

"I do not want a war with El Patron." He cocked his head to the right and said, "Julia, tell your mom to take you home. Take your dad's Hummer."

The engine was still running.

"He's not my dad."

"Whatever. Just go, right now."

Julia grabbed her mother by the arm and practically dragged her to the Hummer, all the while translating Carl's instructions. Luisa got Julia into the front passenger side, then hurried around the front of the truck, pausing to look back at him before climbing into the driver's seat.

He gave her a quick head-nod, then looked at the general. "I'm ready when you are, General. I would be grateful if you could fly us to the Columbus Port of Entry."

The general pivoted and waved his right arm graciously toward the waiting helicopter. As the man turned to walk away, Carl knew without a doubt that El Patron was going to betray him.

CHAPTER 62

0721 MST, THURSDAY
COLUMBUS, NM BORDER CROSSING

THE HELICOPTER LIFTED OFF WITH the roar of the turbines and a tremendous dust storm. Carl felt the aircraft's vibrations through his boots and through the bench where he sat. It banked over the site of the trade. Merc Two's Hummer and the VW bus burned, releasing a thick column of black smoke into the sky. Carl caught a brief glimpse of Alfonso Reyes's body lying behind the space left by the departed white Hummer. The man was still moving, reaching out to the departing aircraft. Carl imagined Reyes screaming, begging them not to leave him behind. At least, that's what he wanted the man to do.

The Hummer, driven by Luisa Reyes, kicked up a cloud of dust as she got the big truck back onto the unpaved road and raced away to the west.

Melissa's head lolled against his shoulder.

"You feel better now? We're on our way home."

She shook her head. "I feel sick. And dizzy. And my arms hurt."

He noticed she had started wringing her hands again. After a few seconds of that, she interlocked her fingers. Then she started waving her hands like she was shooing flies. He held her through it all, but a knot of fear was growing in his gut.

"My arms hurt," she repeated. She started rubbing the inner muscle of her left arm near the elbow.

"Here, let me see." The sleeve of the shirt she wore was far too big for her, so he easily pushed it up over her elbow. What he saw made him gasp. "Jesus! What did they do to you?"

Her arm had a dozen needle marks. Some of the tracks were old, with hardened blisters and scabs where she had no doubt scratched them. Others were new, with purple bruises around them. Now her reactions made sense. They had drugged her up repeatedly for some reason, and now, she was coming down off her latest high. She was nauseous and increasingly agitated.

He willed the chopper to fly faster, but it took an interminable twenty minutes before he saw the miles-long metal of the border fence gleaming in the sun. Melissa had fallen asleep, but it was a fitful sleep. Her arms and legs jerked, and she muttered almost continuously.

Carl held the trembling girl and scanned the troop cabin. He found the general watching him, and he wondered if the man knew what Reyes's people did to her. The soldiers filled the three bench seats behind him, sitting four abreast. Everyone rocked and swayed as the helicopter encountered air turbulence.

Closer to the border, Carl heard a subdued whine and several clicks in his left ear. Then he heard Agent Palmer's voice. "Mr. Johnson, can you hear me?"

"Affirmative. I have the package. How are you communicating with me? Do you have another drone up?"

"You are within range of *Marine One's* comm system. We're using one of the president's secure channels. What's your status?"

The racket inside the aircraft was thunderous, but Carl still whispered. He leaned his head closer to Melissa's and pretended to talk to her. "We're in a helicopter approaching the Columbus border crossing."

Suddenly, Melissa woke up with a jerk that head-butted Carl on the chin. Then she started screaming and flapping her arms at the air in front of her, fighting off unseen demons.

Carl said, "I need a medic ASAP." He fought to hold the agitated girl. "And a sedative."

He felt the familiar lurching sensation in his stomach as the aircraft quickly lost altitude. The border fence drifted under the aircraft, then the red metal roof of the welcome center passed below. It occurred to him that if he was within radio range of *Marine One*, then that meant the president was also.

"Agent Palmer, is McGrath on *Marine One*?"

"I'm here." The man's voice was deep and measured. It sounded like the scripted voice of a man who chose every word very carefully.

Carl's heart raced as he realized he was finally going to meet the man who orchestrated the death of his son. "You and I need to have a private conversation. Alone and off comms."

In the vista that rotated past the open starboard door, Carl saw an armada of US Army combat choppers, all bristling with cannons and rocket launchers, hovering several hundred yards away between his approaching troop carrier and a fairly bizarre sight.

On the ground beyond the wall of airborne weaponry sat not one, but five gleaming *Marine One* helicopters. Carl knew wherever the president traveled, the helicopter—like the limo—was stuffed inside a huge cargo plane and was flown ahead of *Air Force One*. He never figured he'd see more than one of the presidential transport helicopters in any particular place.

For a moment, he wondered which one the president was on, but then he figured that must be the point of multiple helicopters. Maybe it was sort of like a presidential shell game. Keep the bad guys guessing.

The general's aircraft drifted slowly northward and hovered over the center of a wide circle of combat troops in desert camo. All had weapons pointed at the helicopter. Outside the circle, Carl saw a soldier waving hand signals at the pilot.

Finally, the man held his arms high, crossed at the wrists, and the helicopter touched down. Carl was in motion immediately. He hauled the clinging girl out of the cabin with him.

The general hollered, "Seventy-two hours, Mr. Johnson."

Carl nodded.

Melissa was so disoriented, she could barely stand on her own. They hunched down under the spinning rotors, but he practically had to drag her along. As soon as they cleared the rotors by a good distance, the helicopter's engine pitch rose to a scream that tortured their ears. He sheltered Melissa from the hurricane-force rotor winds buffeting them as the chopper rose. Then it peeled away toward the border fence.

Carl turned his attention to the cluster of helicopters on the ground. Four Secret Service agents in black suits ran across the desert toward him. Two of the agents carried a gurney between them, and the other two carried automatic weapons. A young man carrying a white bag with a red cross on it followed them.

He thought about trying to carry Melissa partway toward them, but he knew he wouldn't get very far. He squatted next to the girl and held her while she trembled. Every few seconds, she screamed and shook violently, flailing her arms and legs wildly. The first time she did that, he thought she was having a seizure until she calmed down again.

The combat troops that had encircled the helicopter closed in around Carl and Melissa. They all faced outward, maybe twenty feet away, and formed a protective shield around them. The agents arrived and unfolded the gurney onto its wheels. The young man, who looked about thirty, arrived after the agents and opened his case on the gurney. When he tried to give Melissa the sedative in a syringe, she instantly became violent.

Carl tightened his hold. "It's okay, Melissa. You're safe. They just want to help."

She twisted, screamed, writhed, and clawed at the young man and two agents who tried to restrain her legs.

"Wait! Back off! Everybody, back off and give her some space."

Immediately, Melissa calmed down and grabbed hold of Carl's vest.

He pulled out a stainless steel canteen and tossed it to the doctor. "Mix it in that." After they mixed it, Carl held it toward her. "Here, baby girl. Drink up."

She refused, twisting her face away. "They made me drink stuff. I don't want any more."

"C'mon, it's not poison. See?" Carl took a small sip from the canteen. "It actually tastes pretty good. Kinda like cherry Kool-Aid. Have some for me, okay? I know you're thirsty, aren't you?"

She nodded and grabbed the canteen with trembling hands. He helped her hold it steady, and she drank all the sedative water. She quieted rapidly. The doctor took her vitals while the agents got her strapped onto the gurney. Then they hustled her across the hundred yards of scrub grass to *Marine One*.

Carl trailed the doctor's team, then stopped when the group began to haul the gurney up the stairs. He saw a very worried President Mallory step aside so the team could get her daughter aboard. Then he saw the man she'd been standing with in the doorway of *Marine One*.

Aaron McGrath looked nothing like Carl imagined. He was tall and slender, with close-cut, stately salt-and-pepper hair, and fashionable wire-rim round glasses. He wore a black turtleneck shirt over blue jeans, and his black flight jacket was unzipped midway to his belt. Despite his advanced age, his eyes held the same intensity Carl had seen in Agent Klipser and Agent Palmer's eyes. The grayed-out profile photo in Carl's mind finally had a face.

President Mallory caught Carl's gaze for a moment before she descended the steps. She paused in front of Carl. "Mr. Johnson," she began. She wore jeans and a thick white pullover sweater. For a moment, she just stood there. Then she surprised him with a hug. "Thank you for bringing my baby back to me." She stepped back and wiped a tear from her cheek. "Thank you."

She hurried up the steps, followed by the rest of her security detachment. The big helicopter's engine began to spool up, but McGrath slowly came down the steps. A few seconds later, the rotors began to spin.

The crew chief stuck his head out the door and hollered at McGrath, "Sir! Wheels-up to the nearest hospital in thirty seconds!"

McGrath waved his hand over his head, giving the crew chief what Carl always thought of as the universal whirly-bird sign. The crew chief nodded and powered the door up until it was closed. McGrath walked cautiously toward Carl.

Carl's gaze slid down McGrath's slender frame and back up as he assessed the man. He looked fit, and Carl got the impression he still worked out rigorously for a mid-sixties man. He planted every step carefully, like he was ready for combat at any moment.

Carl also worked out every day, and today it had paid off. He'd taken his life test that morning and succeeded. He saved the girl. Still, he wondered if he could take McGrath in a one-on-one contest.

"You wanted to have a conversation with me."

They stood outside the radius of the accelerating blades and eyeballed each other. McGrath reached up and pinched his comm device out of his ear. Agent Palmer must have immediately detected that McGrath was off comm because she called out to Carl.

"Wait, Carl—"

Carl pulled out his comm unit also and slipped it into a Velcro cargo pocket.

Marine One's rotors picked up speed and sliced through the air with swishing sounds.

"I have intel for you."

"Intel?" McGrath narrowed his eyes.

Carl turned away from the blast of dirt as the armada of *Marine One* helicopters got airborne and flew off to the east. The army combat choppers escorted them. He guessed they were headed to the big hospital in Las Cruces. The combat troops that had established ground security were running toward the last troop carrier, which was powering up. He wondered if they were going to wait for McGrath.

Carl looked up at the cloudless canvas of the big blue sky. He squinted against the early morning glare of the sun and inhaled the sweet scent of sage in the cool air, kicking at the dirt beneath his boots. There were so many things he wanted to say to the man, but he knew he would receive no closure from venting his thoughts or feelings to a man such as McGrath.

"The general that flew us up here, El Patron, didn't just happen by the exchange zone. He wanted his money back. Reyes was just a tool, a pawn who got out of control. Maybe he had his own agenda. I don't know."

"El Patron was on US soil?"

"He all but confessed to funding the kidnapping through people he called his investors. He knew about the recovery team you had on stand-by. He knew exactly where they were located, what their response time was, and what their rules of engagement were. And he said he knows for a fact that the president's people don't know his identity."

Carl paused to let McGrath digest his information.

"That's why you wanted to be off comm."

Carl nodded, and McGrath pulled a smartphone from his pants pocket. He dialed a number and touched the tab for speakerphone.

"Palmer," the woman answered.

"Code alpha-six," McGrath said.

"Stand by."

The line was silent for a while, and Carl got the feeling the code was an instruction for her to clear her command center of nonessential people. While he waited, he stared at the senior covert agent. He watched the man's square jaw muscles work and wondered what he was thinking. All the death and destruction they had caused over the past few days fighting each other had now brought them to the brink of an alliance. They had both been pawns in a larger conflict choreographed by an unknown common enemy.

Palmer's voice returned. "COMSEC level alpha-six is active. This channel is restricted to the two of us. It is not being recorded on the mission records."

McGrath said, "Johnson has confirmed an executive-level leak."

Carl added, "And El Patron's investors are very highly placed in the Mexican government."

McGrath said, "You assume Agent Palmer and I are not the leak."

"If you were, you wouldn't have taken me in the first place."

McGrath nodded.

Palmer said, "Sitrep."

Carl knew she wanted to know the mission status and their personal situation. He summarized his encounter with the general.

Carl said, "I think Melissa's kidnapping wasn't about money. That was just the cover. They did something to her. Drugged her up or something. I think they intended to release her all along, but she's not the endgame. We need to know what they did to her and why." He paused. "And we need to know who they are."

"Agreed," McGrath said.

Palmer added, "Carl, what is your interest in this going forward?"

Carl took a deep breath and kicked at a tuft of grass. It was true he had almost half a *billion* US dollars and a presidential pardon. He could retire and disappear anywhere in the world now.

"These people who financed the general led us down this path." Carl paused. "They hurt that girl. And me. And a lot of other people. I'd like to see them pay."

"As would I," McGrath said. "If you can ID El Patron, I can put the full might of the US intel apparatus on finding all his known associates."

"Mm-hmm. That would certainly be the efficient government way to handle it."

"You have something else in mind?"

Carl nodded. "These people have eyes and ears in your camp at a high level. They use the same playbook that you use." He turned to face McGrath again and looked him straight in the eye. "I use a different playbook."

"We've noticed." McGrath studied him for a moment with gray, emotionless eyes. "What would you do, Mr. Johnson?"

"I'd do something a bit more...public." McGrath notched an eyebrow in question, and Carl said, "If I had a missile right now, I'd smoke that El Patron mu'fucker and see what prominent people on both sides of the border go into hiding. Then I'd go have a chat with them."

Apparently, the government man approved of his strategy because Carl listened to a lot of tactical jargon as Aaron McGrath authorized one of the fighter jets that flew the president's CAP—Combat Air Patrol—to break formation.

A moment later, an explosion of sound blasted over the desert as the fighter slammed through the sound barrier. Carl looked up. He couldn't see the plane, but he saw its white contrail far above. A few seconds later, he saw a bright flash as two more smoke trails sped away from the first.

McGrath said, "Consider El Patron smoked, along with his escort chopper. What do you need for this next phase of the mission?"

Though he was still following the twin contrails into the distance, Carl was considering the near future in terms of logistics, weapons, and manpower.

"I need Agent Palmer out here. I have a feeling the people we're going after will make Alfonso Reyes and his crew look like rookies. We better do it right this time."

"Agreed."

"Can you conference Mr. Garcia on this call?"

McGrath nodded, and Carl gave him the number.

"Go for Garcia," the young man answered.

318

Carl couldn't help but smile. The kid had his mission jargon solid. "Sitrep."

"Boss! I thought we lost you!"

"Almost did. But we lost our team."

"Negative. Three and Four called in by backup cell. They got off the hill and surrendered, and they said the attack chopper spared them. I'm bringing them home by commercial flights later today. What about Two?"

"He's gone." Carl gave Garcia a quick summary of the encounter at the trade site. "Our mission is not over yet. Have Three and Four go back to the trade site and get those bonds."

"We're going to keep them, right?"

"Negative. We earned our fee fair and square, but the bonds belong to the US government. Also, tell them to bring in Alfonso Reyes. Our client would like to ask him some questions."

McGrath notched an eyebrow. "You didn't kill him?"

"He knows some of El Patron's people," Carl said. "It might be helpful if we knew them too."

The TER director nodded. "Mr. Garcia, will you have your people deliver him and the bonds to the CIA contact they met earlier? Agent Palmer will make the arrangements."

Garcia said, "I'll take care of it."

Carl added, "Then have Three and Four stay in-country to provide security for Luisa and Julia Reyes. If El Patron contacted his network, those two ladies are in imminent danger."

"Will do."

"Set up another op center ASAP. I'll contact you when I arrive in Albuquerque tonight." He nodded to McGrath, and he cut the connection to Garcia.

McGrath regarded Carl. "I continue to wonder how an untrained civilian like yourself has been so successful in this arena."

"I *am* trained, Aaron." He gazed at his nemesis. "I was trained by the best in the business." He took a deep breath, then changed the subject. "How are Special Agent Cummings and her daughter?"

"Their injuries were…psychological." He paused. "With treatment, they should recover in time."

Carl nodded and looked away. "Anita?"

McGrath paused for a long time, and Carl knew the man was fighting the same internal emotional battle he was.

"She's alive." McGrath fell silent for a while, then he said, "You took a bullet for Melissa."

Carl nodded.

"Shirley is very grateful. As am I."

"It's what we do for our kids…when we are able."

"You brought her back even after you learned I'm her father."

"You were not the mission, Aaron." Carl gazed at the man. "The mission was to save the girl."

An eerie silence settled around the two men. The only sound Carl could hear was the low drone of the army helicopter idling in the distance.

"Proceed with the new mission when you are ready, Mr. Johnson."

Carl looked to the south. "I'm ready now."

"Good hunting."

TO BE CONTINUED…

If you enjoyed this adventure, check out Jeffrey Poston's other action adventure thrillers at JeffreyPostonBooks.com or wherever you buy books. Please let other readers know what you thought of the book by leaving a brief review at your favorite retailer. It only takes a moment and reviews are very valuable to authors.

ABOUT THE AUTHOR

Jeffrey Poston is the acclaimed author of the Jason Peares histori-cal western series, as well as the fast-paced adventure thriller series *American Terrorist* and *Call Sign: Raven*. Blending traditional and revisionist historical research, his historical westerns have been praised as "fast-moving" (Kelton) and "exciting, page-turning" (Zollinger) and "among the best writers of westerns" (Biblio.com). His thriller books are lauded as "so realistic," "powerfully intense," and "action-packed page turners." He is a self-described *Rambling Man* and writes his novels wherever he happens to be in his travels.

Find Jeffrey at http://www.jeffreypostonbooks.com/

Facebook: http://www.facebook.com/JeffreyPostonBooks

Twitter: http://www.twitter.com/BooksByJPoston

ACKNOWLEDGMENTS

As writers, we often go into our creative caves to compose a book, but when we come out, there are often dozens of people who help refine a story and turn it into a really good book. No writer can succeed without this special group of people—critical readers, cover artists, professional editors, marketing and PR specialists, and publishers.

I especially want to thank my critical reader and sounding board, Dr. Stephanie McIver. She's helped me through many of my books, offering insight and analysis that added depth and breadth to my characters and my plot.

Special thanks to Debra L. Hartmann, The Pro Book Editor, and her team for copyediting and proofreading. I also want to give a shout-out to the cover art designers of my books: Deanna Dionne.

I'm also thankful for the active imaginations (and the suspension of disbelief) of all the readers who enjoyed my Western and Thriller adventures. I'm especially grateful to the dozens of beta-readers who previewed the book and sent back invaluable advice. Your help means the world to this author!

www.ingramcontent.com/pod-product-compliance
Lightning Source LLC
Chambersburg PA
CBHW020330120726
47904CB00002B/350